Acclaim for *High Hopes*:

'It was a great pleasure to read this highly entertaining sequel to *Our Kid*. Its mixture of fact and fiction, class divisions, failures and triumphs set in the aftermath of the war recalls vividly memories of a Manchester I knew' Dan Murphy, Retired Teacher, Manchester

'I read *High Hopes* faster than many books I've read all year. I both laughed and cried throughout . . . Billy is a loveable character with an irrepressible sense of humour' Mrs Kathleen Rawcliffe, Infants Teacher, Fleetwood, Lancs

'When I received the book, I thought I'd just have a quick peek at it. I became utterly engrossed . . . I thoroughly enjoyed it right up to the last page. *High Hopes* is very readable, unpretentious and brimming with humour. It lifts the curtain on life in the '40s – as it was for students and for a young teacher in an inner-city school' Joan Kennedy, Retired Teacher, Manchester

'The pawkish humour of Billy remains and bubbles out frequently in unexpected places . . . This latest book is a wonderful sequel to the life and career of Billy the Collyhurst Kid' Dr Jennie McWilliam, GP, Staffordshire

'A little masterpiece' Dr Darragh Little, GP and writer, Limerick

'Everyone will enjoy *High Hopes*. The story is easy to read, no complicated plots to cause confusion and the events move quietly and quickly. Everyone will warm to Billy, a likeable young man, full of life with an unquenchable optimism in everything he does. The book reflects the exuberance of youth in those early days of post-war Britain. Thank you for providing such a good read and for bringing so much pleasure to all who enjoy tales of Manchester' Bernard Lawson, M.B.E., Retired Private Secretary to the Lord Mayor of Manchester

Acclaim for *Our Kid*:

'The book is like a best friend – no one likes to see the friendship come to an end – and that's just how I felt when I reached [the last] page' *Visiter*

'Reading *Our Kid* was a very moving experience! I was born in Salford and so you can understand my deep emotion at reading your wonderfully written, deeply touching, extremely heart-warming memoirs. Congratulations!' John Sherlock, Hollywood producer

'I half-read my mother's copy of *Our Kid* when the team was playing in Italy. Enjoyed it so much I thought I'd better order my own copy, [and] also one for a friend' Brian Kidd, Football Manager

'I read *Our Kid* on the train and I laughed so much I was getting funny looks off my fellow passengers' John Kennedy, *Catholic Pictorial*

Billy Hopkins, who is better known to his family as Wilfred Hopkins, was born in Collyhurst in 1928 and attended schools in Manchester. Before going into higher education, he worked as a copy boy for the *Manchester Guardian*. He later studied at the Universities of London, Manchester and Leeds and has been involved in school-teaching and teacher-training in Liverpool, Manchester, Salford and Glasgow. He also worked in African universities in Kenya, Zimbabwe and Malawi. He is the author of five novels – for a full list see page ii.

Billy Hopkins is married with six grown-up children and now lives in retirement with his wife in Southport.

Our Kid, Billy Hopkins' first novel, was first published under the pseudonym Tim Lally.

First published in 2000
by HEADLINE BOOK PUBLISHING

First published in paperback in 2001
by HEADLINE BOOK PUBLISHING

This edition published in 2008
by HEADLINE PUBLISHING GROUP

2

ISBN 978 0 7553 4319 5

Typeset in Times by Avon DataSet Ltd,
Bidford-on-Avon, Warwickshire

Printed and bound by CPI Group (UK) Ltd,
Croydon, CR0 4YY

Headline's policy is to use papers that are natural, renewable and
recyclable products and made from wood grown in sustainable
forests. The logging and manufacturing processes are expected to
conform to the environmental regulations of the country of origin.

HEADLINE PUBLISHING GROUP
An Hachette Livre UK Company
338 Euston Road
London NW1 3BH

www.headline.co.uk

High Hopes

Billy Hopkins

headline

Also by Billy Hopkins

Our Kid
Kate's Story
Going Places
Anything Goes
Whatever Next!

For my daughter Catherine

I find that the further back I go, the better I remember things, whether they happened or not.

Mark Twain

Preface

1945

There are certain dates in history which are indelibly imprinted on our minds: 1066, 1492, 1815, and 1914 to give but a few examples. To this list we must add the year 1945 for it witnessed the end not of one major war but of two: Germany capitulated in May, Japan in August. In human terms, the cost of the wars was estimated at 55 million dead. The year itself reads like the last episode of a great epic novel. It's all there: the final dénouement and the triumph of justice, the death of some of the main protagonists, and the events run the whole gamut of emotions from euphoria to horror.

Horror in February when we learned that Allied bombers had devastated Dresden, incinerating 130,000 people; horror again when we heard of the Nazi death camps with their gas ovens, the mounds of skeletal corpses, and the emaciated survivors; and yet a third time when, in early August, atomic bombs vaporised the Japanese cities of Hiroshima and Nagasaki, killing and maiming countless numbers of citizens.

Sadly, President Roosevelt died in April at the age of sixty-three on the eve of victory in Europe and was replaced

1

by Harry Truman. Later in that month, Mussolini and his mistress were shot by Italian partisans, and strung up by their heels. Shortly after that Adolf Hitler and his new wife Eva Braun took their own lives in their underground bunker whilst Russian troops were virtually hammering on the Chancellery doors above.

The revered British war leader, Winston Churchill, survived in good health all right but received the shock of his life in July when the British electorate rejected him at the polls and gave the Labour party under the leadership of Clem Attlee a landslide victory.

It was also a year of great rejoicing. On 7 May, when it was announced that the war in Europe was officially over, thousands of people took to the streets around Whitehall to celebrate and to listen to the voice of Churchill who ended his speech by singing and conducting the crowd in 'Land of Hope and Glory'. And on 15 July when the lights of Britain were switched on once again after more than two thousand nights of blackout, euphoria knew no bounds. Families flung open their curtains and switched on every light in the house and it was this action more than anything else that brought home the fact that the war really had ended.

There was yet more joy to come when the defeat of Japan was proclaimed at midnight in London on 14 August. The government declared a two-day holiday which triggered off a wave of hysteria with a blatant cacophony of ships' sirens and railway train whistles, a relay of bonfires blazing across the country, and triumphant street parties in every town and village. In London's Piccadilly, the festivities continued well into the night with American GIs sporting carnival hats, waving the Stars and Stripes, leading im- promptu processions, beating drums, blowing whistles, and throwing fireworks.

But for many families, the jubilation was tempered by the pain of knowing that their loved ones would never be coming home. As for the survivors, the demobilisation scheme, with its provisions for staggered release, meant an agonising wait before they could be allowed to return to Civvy Street.

The war had left Britain almost bankrupt. With peace came an austerity greater than the country had ever known. Nearly everything was rationed: meat, fats, eggs, cheese, sugar, sweets, clothing, petrol. Towards the end of the year, the screw was turned even tighter when severe food cuts were announced – the fat ration (inclusive of butter, margarine and lard) was reduced from eight to seven ounces a week. Coal and other fuels were as scarce as they had ever been during the war. Bread with its greatly reduced wheat content was next to be rationed, whilst the importation of rice was halted altogether. Cigarettes – informally rationed by shopkeepers – were obtainable only for long-term, regular customers and were always kept 'under the counter'. The only things that were plentiful were job vacancies – there were five jobs chasing every worker, with the result that it proved well nigh impossible to fill the more menial tasks.

For many, the one bright note in that autumn of 1945 was the resumption of professional football and such was the enthusiasm that on one Tuesday afternoon in November, 85,000 fans turned up to watch Chelsea draw with Moscow Dynamo at Stamford Bridge.

It was against this backdrop that Billy Hopkins in Manchester was persuaded by his best friend, Robin Gabrielson, to quit his job as junior clerk in the Inland Revenue and go to London to train as a teacher, along with their other close school chums. It was to be an exciting new start and his joy knew no bounds. Then tragedy struck one week before he was due to take up his place at the college. All Billy's hopes and dreams collapsed like a pack of cards.

Chapter One

Decisions, Decisions

Billy Hopkins sat alone in the church. The funeral was over and now all was quiet save for the muffled roar of traffic on Plymouth Grove.

He stared at the space where the coffin had rested less than half an hour before. He couldn't take it in – Robin Gabrielson, his closest friend in the world, dead. His mind was filled with disbelief. Surely, there'd been some mix-up or other, a case of mistaken identity that you read about in the paper sometimes. He couldn't be dead, surely to God. Taken so brutally and without warning.

The tears that would not come during the Requiem Mass now flowed freely.

He was so wracked with sobbing he failed to notice the old priest who had approached.

'Can I be of any help, my son?' he asked gently.

'I don't think so, Father,' said Billy. 'No one can help me. I've lost the best friend I ever had. I can't understand why God let it happen.'

'You mean the young man who fell so tragically to his death on the Derbyshire Hills last week?'

Billy nodded.

'Indeed, that was a terrible thing but you can't blame God for every human disaster.'

'Why not? He's supposed to be in charge. Where was He when He was needed? He could have prevented it so easily. Why didn't He do so?'

'Who knows? Perhaps your friend had completed his journey and was here on earth to kindle a light in the darkness. Your personal darkness. To show you the way you should go.'

'If that's true, why am I so confused? I can't get over the idea that it was Robin who persuaded me to apply for college. Now the war is over, this year was to mark a new beginning for us. We'd got it all mapped out. The way we'd study together, what we'd do, the places we'd visit, the things we'd see, the people we'd meet. And now – nothing. Our future plans gone for a Burton.'

'Someone once said, "The way to make God smile is to talk of future plans". You may have your plans but God has His and the two are not always the same. Robbie Burns said it best: The best laid schemes o' mice an' men/Gang aft a-gley.'

'But my friend was so young, Father. He was seventeen years old and his death seems such a waste.'

'Depends on how you view death. If we see it as an enemy, death causes anxiety and fear. But if we see it as a friend, our attitude is different. It's simply a transition from earthly life to life eternal.'

Billy and the old priest talked in the deserted church for over an hour, and when Billy finally left, he had much to think about. He had to make a decision – yes or no.

* * *

He caught the 53 bus home because it took the scenic route past Bradford Road Gasworks and Philips Park Cemetery – a long rambling route across the Manchester suburbs which would give him time to think things over. At Smedley Road he got off and began the long walk past the bomb sites, the dilapidated public air-raid shelters and the numerous blocks of tenement flats which had been thrown up pre-war by the authorities in a wave of optimistic slum clearance – Jasmine Crescent, Heather Close, Hyacinth House – until he reached his own building, Gardenia Court. Wearily he climbed the graffiti-decorated, malodorous stairwell, and arrived finally at his own front door. Before he could turn the key in the lock, his mam opened the door and looked up anxiously into his face.

'You've been crying, Billy,' she said.

'I wasn't the only one, Mam. The whole school was there and I don't think there was a dry eye in the church. It was so sad to see his mam and dad – so heartbroken. I don't think they've taken it in yet.'

'And what about you, Billy? Have you taken it in?'

'Not really. I'm still in a state of shock. I feel numb and can't grasp the fact that he's gone, never to be seen again. Titch Smalley feels the same way. I had to take over one of the readings when he broke down in the middle.'

'Titch Smalley? The lad who was with him when he fell on the rocks?'

'That's right. He's one that'll never get over it. Neither will I.'

'The family feels for you, Billy, and we're so sorry for your loss. But you know, you're going to have to put this behind you and move on.'

'Easier said than done. This death has changed things

7

so much for me. After the funeral, I had a long talk with a priest in the church. All the way home on the bus, I've been weighing things up and I've finally made up my mind.'

'And that is?'

'I'm not going to college. That's definite.'

She looked thunderstruck. 'Not going . . . but what will you do? I mean, what about your big plans of going to London and all that?'

'I can't see the point in any of that now. The big idea was that we'd go together, study and enjoy London life together. He was always painting a picture of the places we'd visit – the cinemas, the theatres, the West End, and . . .' There was a catch in Billy's voice and he was unable to finish the sentence.

'You can still do those things, Billy,' Mam said disconsolately.

'No, Mam. All that's changed. I don't want to go to London without him. I'll stay on at the Inland Revenue job and take my chances there. If I work hard, I could become a fully qualified tax officer in a few years' time.'

Dad, who had been pretending to read his newspaper all this time, looked up and, addressing the unseen companion he seemed to carry on his shoulder, said: 'At last the lad's come to his senses. Instead of taking money out of the house, he'll be bringing it in. Tax officer's not as good as a proper trade but it's better than going off to some lah-de-dah college where he'd learn all kinds of daft, useless things. And as for London, I've heard some right bad stories about it – he'd pick up a lot of bad ways from the toffs down there.'

'You've never been to London in your life and neither

have I,' Mam protested. 'So how do you know what it's like and what he'd be learning?'

'I've read about their goings-on in the *Evening News* and I hear it on the wireless.'

'Anyway,' said Billy. 'My mind's made up. I didn't get much sleep last night thinking about the funeral and all that. So I think I'll try to get forty winks after tea.'

It was turning dark when Billy was awakened by the sound of talking in the room next door. It looked as if Mam had organised one of her family 'conflagrations' for he recognised the voices of his two sisters Polly and Flo and their husbands, Steve and Barry.

Must be important, he thought, if they've gone to the trouble of arranging baby-sitters for all their kids. May as well go and face the music, he said to himself.

He went to the bathroom to freshen up before joining them in the living room.

He found them sitting round the white-scrubbed kitchen table, like a board meeting in session. Mam sat at the head, Polly and Flo to her left, Steve and Barry, to her right. The subject appeared to be Billy and the London college.

Steve was the first to speak.

'Billy, we're so sorry for this terrible tragedy. Today must have been hell for you.'

'I feel as if my whole world has come to an end,' Billy replied. 'The worst day of my life.'

'If you make the wrong decision,' said Mam, 'it *will* be the worst day of your life. Now your father's gone to the boozer, it's time to get down to brass tacks without him putting his spoke in.'

'But I think Dad's right in a way,' Billy said. 'Going to

college will cost a fortune not only in kitting me out and that but in keeping me supplied with spends. I've got too used to earning a wage and being independent.'

'Independent on thirty shillings a week!' exclaimed Mam. 'Listen, Billy. All of us here are prepared to make sacrifices to see you through. When I think back on what we've done so far – like pawning Grandma's teapot to send you to Damian College, all that you went through on evacuation to Blackpool . . . it'd be such a waste if you gave up now. In so many ways all my hopes have been pinned on you.'

'Sorry, Mam,' Billy said, 'I don't understand. Why on me?'

'Look, our Billy,' she said. 'The one thing that's kept me going all these years has been the thought that at least one of us'll get somewhere in this rotten old world. You're the youngest in the family with a chance that none of the others had. If you throw it away, you'll be letting all of us down. Don't be such a fool. If you decide not to go, I don't know what I'll do. . . . If you can't understand that, I can't . . .' Mam broke down and began to weep.

Billy was dumbstruck. He could only watch helplessly. Mam crying was something he couldn't handle.

'I had no idea that my going to college meant so much to you,' he faltered.

'Of course it does, you great loon,' said Flo. 'Your success is our success. Don't you see that?'

'You've got this offer on a silver platter,' added Polly, 'and you're thinking of turning it down. You must be mad. Have you forgotten the letter Steve had to write to the college to ask them to reconsider when they turned you down the first time? What was all that for?'

'And think of your friend Robin,' said Barry. 'In a way

you'd be letting him down as well.'

'Not only that,' said Steve. 'Look at the job you'll be going into when you finally qualify. Teaching! One of the noblest professions. Imagine it! I can see you now in the classroom. Eager faces looking up to you, children hanging on to your every word. What a contrast to the stiff-backed, crusty old strap-wielding teachers we had to put up with as kids. I can see you refereeing football matches in the winter, umpiring cricket in the summer, taking your class on hikes at the weekends, a life out in the fresh air. Compare that with your present job sorting out taxes on the clerical treadmill in a smoke-filled office for the rest of your life.'

When Steve had finished extolling the teaching profession, Billy's mind was in turmoil. For over three months, he had carried around in his head Robin's vision of life in London until it had become part of reality. Now with Robin's death, the imagery had changed and he couldn't adjust to the new scene. London without Robin was too painful to contemplate and now here was Steve appealing afresh to his imagination, creating new scenes for him to envisage. Fine, Billy thought, but he could also see ahead a two-year stint of being permanently broke, of penny-pinching and trying to make ends meet. There was also another thought, one that he was reluctant to admit to himself. Was he capable of a course in higher education? His School Certificate results were nothing to write home about and going back to the tax office was a way out which let him forget the little snags gnawing at him. Then he thought – tax office, a way out? More like a cop-out.

'Hey, hey! Hold on!' Billy said at last. 'I'm taking a beating here. Outvoted! There are too many of you to argue with. If you want the real truth, I'm not sure I'm cut out to be a teacher. Not even sure I have the brains for higher education.'

'Nonsense!' said Steve. 'Of course you've got the brains. Think positively and banish negative thoughts like "I can't". Stop talking defeat. Think "I can and I will".'

'These are great ideas,' Billy replied, 'but have you worked out how much they're going to cost?'

'Leave that to us,' said Steve. 'First we'll have a family whip-round. Sam's due to be demobbed from the navy soon, and I hear he's got marriage on his mind. But I'm sure he'll put in a few bob to help his kid brother. I think the same will go for Les even though it'll be a couple of years before the army releases him. Barry and I are ready to do our share.'

'How am I supposed to pay you back?' Billy asked.

'It'll be up to you to look after us when we're old and decrepit,' Polly laughed.

'Why use the future tense?' Billy answered in the same vein. 'But I didn't know teacher's pay was that good.'

'Don't forget the big pension you'll get at the end,' said Mam, thinking of the pittance she was due to receive in a few years' time.

'And look at the holidays you'll get,' Polly added. 'Three weeks at Christmas, three at Easter, six in the summer, and that's not counting the odd bank holidays and half-term breaks.'

'When I think of the time I'll spend not doing it,' said Billy, 'I think maybe teaching is the only job for a layabout like me. But suppose I do decide to go, what'll Dad say? He won't like it.'

'You leave your father to me,' said Mam darkly. 'I know how to keep him quiet.'

12

'One last thing,' said Polly. 'If and when you get to that college of yours, for God's sake, see if you can put some weight on. I hope the food is good down there because you're looking more like Frank Sinatra every day. No wonder they call him the "skeleton".'

'So I should look like Sinatra! So I should worry if I had his voice or his money,' Billy said, in the manner of their Yiddish neighbours.

It was the first attempt at a joke since he'd heard about the death.

'You're all very persuasive,' Billy continued. 'You've made so many thoughts whirl around my brain, I don't know whether I'm coming or going. The best thing is to sleep on it and then make up my mind.'

On that note, the family 'conflagration' broke up, with Billy promising to let them know the next day.

Before he went to sleep that night, he lay on his bed alone with his thoughts. His mind went back to that joyous day when he'd learned that he'd been accepted by the London college. He could hear Robin's voice in his head when he'd told him the glad tidings.

'Hoppy,' he'd said, using the gang's nickname for him, 'it's the best news I've heard this year. And what a year it's going to be! Nineteen forty-five! Just think about it! You and me and the gang together in Chelsea. A dream come true. And I'm so happy you're getting out of that terrible humdrum office job. We were getting worried about you. You were beginning to look like a dried-up, miserable civil servant. This offer of a place is a golden opportunity – don't mess it up, no matter what. Remember our motto: *carpe diem*! Seize the day! Opportunity knocks only once at every man's door. So make sure you open it when she calls.'

Exhausted by the day's events and the heated family debate, Billy fell into a deep sleep.

Next morning, he awoke with a fresh mind but Robin's voice was still echoing in his head: 'A golden opportunity – don't mess it up, no matter what.'

He went into breakfast.

'Well, Mam, I've slept on it and I've decided to go,' he said.

'Thank God, you've come to your senses,' she said. 'But that was a sudden change of mind, wasn't it? What happened? Was it what we said last night? You heard the voice of reason?'

'No,' he said. 'More like a voice from the grave. Or maybe it was that talk about the long holidays. I'll go to this college and at least give it a try. But if I don't like it, I'll be back before Christmas.'

Sunday afternoon – the day Billy was due to depart – he left the tenement with self-doubt still gnawing at his heart, not only about leaving behind the familiar and going into the unknown but wondering if he had what it took to make the grade and become a teacher. Was he making the right decision? Though he still wasn't a hundred per cent sure, it was good to have reached some kind of conclusion. And it would be good, he thought, to join his old school friends on this new adventure.

Dad shook his hand. 'All the best, son,' he said. 'Don't forget us and where you come from. Remember your home's always here if you change your mind. I know you think I've tried to hold you back but I only wanted what was best for you. And to show I'm behind you, here is a little present from me.' He handed Billy a Rolex Tudor wristlet watch. 'Take care of this, son,' he said. 'You'll need a watch when you get to that there college of yours. I bought it from a pal in the Hare and Hounds but I won't say how much I paid for it,' he added, tapping his nose. 'Ask no questions and you'll hear no lies.'

'Thanks, Dad. You couldn't have got me a better present.'

Mam wanted to accompany him to the station but he wouldn't let her. Her eyes were wet as she helped him lift his bulging suitcase into the taxi.

'Now, are you sure you've got everything?' she asked. 'Your money, your ration book and your identity card?'

'Don't worry, Mam. I've got them all here safe in my inside pocket.'

'You go off, Billy, and make something of yourself,' she said. 'I know you'll make us proud.' She kissed him on the cheek. 'Ta-ra, son.'

'Ta-ra, Mam. I'll do my best.'

As the cab drove off, she watched it till it had turned the corner of Gardenia Court and was lost from view.

Half an hour later, the taxi pulled in at the Central Station approach. Billy got out with his luggage, paid the driver, and, watched by several porters leaning against the wall, struggled his way across the station concourse. He consulted the large railway timetable board.

'Platform six,' he said aloud to himself.

He handed his ticket to the collector at the barrier.

'Better get a move on, mate,' said the man. 'That train's due out in a few seconds.'

He hurried as best as he could with his suitcase along the platform, looking for a particular compartment.

And there they were! His friends, their heads sticking out of the windows as if it were a cattle truck – the Damian College Smokers' Club.

'Trust you to be late, Hoppy!' called Oscar.

'Come on, Hoppy!' shouted Titch. 'Get a move on! Or you're going to miss the train.'

Chapter Two

To travel hopefully is a better thing
than to arrive . . .

Robert Louis Stevenson

Billy hoisted his suitcase onto the luggage rack; the train lurched forward and they were on their way.

He looked happily round the compartment at the adolescent gang that was such an important part of his existence. They sprawled on the seats and puffed on their Park Drives, full of *joie de vivre*, the arrogance of youth and confident hope in the future. He'd spent his life with them since the age of eleven when they'd 'passed the scholarship' and been accepted into Damian College. He'd shared so many experiences with them, happy and sad, that he'd developed a deep understanding of and affection for them all. He had come to know every nuance of their moods; knew precisely what each one was going to say even before he knew it himself; knew who'd tell which story, who'd laugh and for how long over a particular type of joke; knew their foibles inside out – who claimed to be what and why. To the outsider, however, they were a motley-looking crew.

Each of them had his own particular nickname. Billy himself had been awarded the sobriquet Hoppy after subduing the class bully in a boxing match.

Tony Wilde had been nicknamed Oscar because of his name and his disposition and because of his efforts to emulate the great aesthete with his epigrams and his venomous wit. Billy, along with the rest of them, was wary of him and a little afraid of his vitriolic tongue. It was a moot point, though, whether Oscar's character was the result of his nickname or whether his nickname was the result of his character. One thing was sure, his physique in no way resembled the original Oscar, for he was tall, thin, and lanky – a regular beanpole.

Sitting at the window seat was Titch Smalley, born Dick Smalley, a name which had caused him a certain amount of inconvenience at school. He was the antithesis of Oscar. Small and down-to-earth. Happiest when miserable and believed things were going to get worse before they got worse. Titch came from a poor background and Billy was especially fond of him. Perhaps because they had one important thing in common – they were both stony-broke.

The third man in the compartment was Oliver Hardy – Ollie to them – a bit of a know-all who fancied himself as a walking encyclopaedia. At school he'd made it his life's work to compile the definitive dictionary of dirty words and phrases. He'd reached the letter 's' and was finding it a rich source of synonyms for sexual intercourse with such words as screw, shag, stuff, and the Yiddish *schtup*; his favourite phrase was *score between the posts*, an extraction from Australian folklore. He was a mine of useless information and could be relied on to chip in with the facts when nobody wanted them.

18

Fourth fellow traveller – Nobby Nodder, the lady's man and obsessed with sex. Claimed he'd had it off almost every night when he was going round with a nymphomaniac called Ronnie. 'She was so hot,' he claimed, 'she made the Kama Sutra seem like Hans Andersen.' But when he said 'almost every night', Billy was sure that 'almost' was the operative word. Almost on Monday, almost on Tuesday . . . They had to admit, though, he was a well-read student. He'd read the sex manuals and was an expert on perversions.

Finally, there was Rodney Potts or Pottsy as he was known, son of a well-to-do Manchester businessman; none too bright but he'd managed to scrape enough qualifications to get into college – even this college. The smokers' club hadn't accepted him into their clique at first but he finally made it when he told a blue joke – one about an elephant: 'There was this primitive early man wandering naked through the forest when he met an elephant. The elephant looked down at his thing, studied it for a while and said, "You'll not get much food with that, my lad".' Not bad, they'd said, and his joke was accepted as an entrance fee. Pottsy was a likeable, handsome lad, fair-haired, fair-complexioned, pale of eyelash, and uncomplicated. He'd turned down the chance to join his father's retail business and had opted instead for the training college, not because of any burning vocation to teach but for the companionship of his school cronies. As he had nothing but three older sisters at home, it was understandable. Billy felt a certain sympathy for him.

'For a while, Hoppy,' said Oscar when they'd settled down, 'we thought you'd changed your mind about coming.'

'I nearly did,' said Billy, 'but my family told me about the holidays teachers get and that clinched it.'

'Of course, you've been working in an income tax office for the last year,' remarked Titch. 'You must have found it hard to leave a good job like that.'

'Good job!' echoed Billy. 'You must be joking. As soon as they found I'd been to a grammar school and knew how to write, they set me the task of copying out the names and addresses of the entire British population from great ledgers onto things called con-cards – part of the new Pay As You Earn system.'

'What about those secretaries who work there?' said Nobby, lecherous as ever. 'I've heard they're hot stuff. The really randy ones wear an anklet chain as a sign they're up for it.'

'Dead right,' said Billy. 'Some of them were hot stuff. I tell you, it wasn't safe walking through the typing pool. A man was likely to lose his trousers. And the work was so monotonous we spent our time thinking about how we'd get off when we got off at five o'clock. But Nobby, how come you knew that stuff about the anklet chain? It's supposed to be a state secret.' Our secretaries were shrivelled up old maids, thought Billy, specially picked for their ability to curb lustful thoughts in the randy young male clerks.

'With so many glamorous girls around,' Billy continued, 'it was very hard to concentrate on the main task in hand, namely the transcribing – in our best copperplate hand of course – of a whole lot of dull details from stuffy old tomes.'

'Sounds Dickensian. I suppose you used quill pens and high desks,' said Ollie.

'Right,' said Billy. 'Only worse. I was bored out of my skull and I had resigned myself to a life on the treadmill. I was going quietly mad when Robin rode in like the US

20

cavalry with news of this college. He wrote to me to ask if I'd be interested in joining you lot. What a question! Like asking a wretch being tortured on the rack if he was interested in a holiday in the South of France. As soon as I heard I was accepted, it took me around ten seconds to think it over and I handed in my notice on the spot. Then tragedy struck. End of our dreams.'

'It's going to be hard for us to come to terms with his death,' Oscar remarked. 'Especially you, Hoppy, as you were so close.'

'That's putting it mildly,' replied Billy. 'When Robin died, our big ideas took a nose dive.'

Titch said nothing. He seemed to have become suddenly engrossed in the book on his knee.

'Talking of London and college,' said Pottsy, who up to this point had been silently watching the receding country-side, 'has anyone here been to London before?'

No one had.

'I suppose you're going to tell us that you and your family have stayed at the Ritz,' said Ollie.

'Not quite,' replied Pottsy. 'But my dad once came down here on business and he brought me and my three sisters on a visit. We stayed at the Strand Palace.'

'Typical Pottsy! Staying in a palace,' Nobby exclaimed. 'So what's London really like?'

'Big and expensive,' Pottsy replied. 'And you've never seen such traffic – you take your life in your hands when you try to cross the road. When we went down two months ago, the place was in ruins. Bombed-out buildings every-where.'

'Still the same,' said Billy. 'But thank God the Germans never got the atomic bomb,' said Billy 'or there wouldn't be any London at all.'

21

'I suppose we'll be OK,' said Titch nervously. 'We were used to being away from home during the war when we were evacuated to Blackpool.'

'Nothing to worry about,' said Oscar, 'as long as we Mancunians stick together. We'll be in the mire together and we're used to that. We're bound to meet some awkward types with funny accents but we'll get by. At least *we* speak the King's English, which is more than we can say for some of these other provincials – yokels from Geordieland or Yorkshire. Why, I've heard that people from Cornwall speak a foreign language. But London! Think of it! It may be in ruins after the battering from the Luftwaffe but it's still the most exciting city in the world.'

'Don't tell me,' said Billy. 'I've heard it before – the bright lights, the cinemas, the theatres, the pubs, the restaurants, the West End! I can hardly wait to get there!'

'Don't get carried away,' Titch added, looking up from his book. 'I hate to be the fly in the ointment but there's still the little matter of money. Can we afford those marvellous things you're going on about?'

'No problem,' said Billy. 'You're talking to Rockefeller. I've got over five pounds in my pocket. So what's the worry? And my mam's promised to send me ten shillings a week as well. I've never been so rich.'

'Me too,' said Titch. 'I've got five pounds to last me the term and my mam and dad said they'd try to send me a few bob a week or whatever they could afford.'

'I've no money worries,' said Potts. 'My dad's opened a bank account for me and I can draw on that as long as I don't overdo it.'

'So we can borrow off you, Pottsy,' said Ollie.

'My dad warned me about that before I left,' said Pottsy.

'He said that in business and friendship neither a borrower nor a lender be 'cos you'll lose both your friend and your money.'

At that moment, the train pulled into Crewe station.

'Time for sandwiches,' said Billy, unwrapping his packed lunch. His mam had made up his favourite, cheese and pickle. Good old Mam, he thought. She must have used up a whole week's cheese ration on these sandwiches. He had a momentary vision of her as she'd waved to him from the veranda as he'd got into the taxi – she had looked proud but sad and anxious. He pushed the thought quickly from his mind. It wouldn't do to let the others see that he was feeling homesick already.

From their hand luggage, the rest of them produced a miscellaneous collection of provisions, making the compartment smell like a delicatessen.

'God knows when we'll get to eat again,' said Billy, munching away. 'We've been travelling for three hours. I thought this was supposed to be a non-stop express. So much for the LMS Railway. I'm sure we've been going backwards.'

'With the fuel shortages they keep telling us about,' said Oscar, 'we're lucky there's any train at all. Anyway, doesn't LMS stand for Laborious and Murderously Slow?'

'I suppose we'll get to the college some time today,' said Titch.

'Talking of the college,' said Nobby, 'it's happened so quickly, we've not had time to find out much about the place. I know it's in Chelsea but how did it get this weird name – Marjons?'

'Now he asks!' said Billy. 'I suppose you've been too busy weighing up the nightspots and where the birds'll be to think about the college. Anyway, it's in the King's Road.

Used to be two Anglican colleges – St Mark's of Chelsea and St John's of Battersea. When they joined together, they became the College of St Mark and St John. Marjons for short. We were lucky to get in, though, a bunch of Papists like us.'

'That's because the college had little choice,' said Oscar. 'After we were all turned down by St Mary's College at Strawberry Hill, I thought that was the end of our hopes of ever becoming teachers. Then I read somewhere that the new Labour government had ordered all training colleges to speed things up and start training teachers as fast as they could because there's such a desperate shortage everywhere.'

'I think it's this college that must be desperate if they took us lot in,' Titch said. 'We're not exactly out of the top drawer, are we?'

'Speak for yourself,' said Pottsy. 'Anyway, what's it mean when it says training college? Does it mean military exercises, drilling and long route marches? Or maybe circus training involving whips and chairs or leaping out of pools to catch raw fish.'

'Nothing as extreme as that,' said Ollie, always ready with information. 'To train is to instruct so as to make obedient to orders, like training an animal to perform simple tricks, for example teaching a dog to jump through hoops.'

'I'd never have come if I'd known I had to jump through hoops,' said Pottsy.

'I've heard that the college was used as a mortuary during the London Blitz,' said Billy. 'The cellars were used to store the corpses before burial.'

'I definitely don't like the sound of that,' wailed Titch. 'What sort of place are we going to? Dead bodies and jumping through hoops!'

'I presume,' said Billy, 'that the dead bodies have been removed by now.'

The conversation might have continued along these lines but they discovered, much to their surprise, that the train was pulling into Euston station. The two hundred-mile journey had taken six hours.

London at last! They had finally made it. Now they wondered how they were to get to Chelsea. No one had given it much thought. They got their luggage down from the racks and made their way along the seemingly endless platform.

As they lugged their heavy suitcases across the crowded concourse, the station porters, seeing there was no tip to be had, watched them indifferently like a row of owls perched on a wall.

Chapter Three

Will your Grace command me any service
to the world's end?

Shakespeare, Much Ado About Nothing

Outside the station, they got their first view of London. Their impression was of a grey city, much of it still in ruins and relieved only by the innumerable bright red buses which seemed to be everywhere. They found a friendly London bobby who advised them to catch a Number 73 to Victoria and then a Number 11 which would take them on to Chelsea and right up to the gates of the college.

They found the bus easily enough but the conductor wasn't keen on taking them with their luggage.

'You lot should hire a taxi,' he said.

'You must be joking, mate,' replied Titch. 'We're not made of money. We're students. Can only just about afford the bus fare.'

'All right, all right!' said the conductor. 'Pile in. Put your bags under the apples.'

'Apples?' queried Titch.

'Apples! Apples and pears! Stairs! 'Ere, what's up wiv you? Don't you unnerstand King's English? You must be from up North.'

They boarded the bus, put their cases under the stairs and dashed up to the top deck for a smoke. Billy opted to stay on the lower deck to keep an eye on the luggage. He knew about these Londoners. Hadn't his dad given him dire warnings about the London thieves and spivs who were waiting their chance to pick his pockets and make off with his stuff? 'And keep your eye on that new watch I've given you,' he'd said, 'or they'll have it off you soon as look at you. Can't trust them there Southerners.' He should know – he read the *Manchester Evening News* every night.

'Which college are you lot goin' to then?' the conductor asked Billy as he clipped his ticket in the little machine that was slung round his neck.

'College of St Mark and St John's in Chelsea. Marjons for short.'

'Marjons! Sounds more like that Chinese tile game the old ladies play. What kind of students are you then?'

'Going to be teachers.'

'Cor blimey!' the conductor said. 'The Chalk and Duster Brigade. Gawd help poor England!'

What strange expressions and what a funny accent, Billy thought. Like visiting a foreign country.

It was in Tottenham Court Road, however, that he became aware that he had truly left his roots back in Lancashire. They passed a signpost which bore the legend TO THE NORTH, which sounded like an ominous warning to all passers-by that up there in the North, the land of Blake's 'dark Satanic mills', there lived savages who still painted themselves in blue woad. But when Billy saw that sign and realised its significance for him, he felt a sharp pang of nostalgia for the people and places he'd left behind, as if they were so far away in a distant world that he'd lost them forever. All their hopes are resting on my shoulders, he thought. They've made so many sacrifices for me, I can't let them down – I must succeed.

The bus wound its way through the centre of the city – shells of bombed-out buildings everywhere. Billy gazed in awe at the passing scene – the unremitting roar of the traffic, the honking of the taxis, the endless lines of buses, trucks, and cars, the thousands of jostling pedestrians, many of them still in uniform, who thronged the streets, all combining to produce the chaotic sights, sounds and smells of the great metropolis that was London. There were the theatres and the huge hoardings that loomed up on every available space crying out their blatant slogans: FOR YOUR THROAT'S SAKE SMOKE CRAVEN A: 10 FOR 1/2d; VALET FOR LONG LASTING BLADES: 3d EACH; PHYLLIS DIXEY IN *PEEK-A-BOO* WITH HER VARGA MODELS AT THE WHITEHALL THEATRE; WESTMINSTER THEATRE: ROBERT DONAT IN *THE CURE FOR LOVE*.

One particular billboard which grabbed his attention pictured a voluptuous Jane Russell stretched out in the hay. The poster read: *THE OUTLAW*. A SCORCHER OF A FILM. ODEON LEICESTER SQUARE.

Like a magic carpet, the bus transported him through London's famous landmarks whose names he'd seen only on a Monopoly board: Strand, Northumberland Avenue, Trafalgar Square, Whitehall. And places he'd only heard about on wireless programmes like *In Town Tonight* when a man with a sergeant-major voice would bring London's traffic to a standstill with his ringing command, 'HALT! Once again, we bring you the personalities that are *IN*

TOWN TONIGHT.' Billy half expected to hear Eric Coates's rousing Knightsbridge March that always followed the introduction.

As the bus crossed the great city, he was treated to a flow of tourist guide commentary by the conductor in a Max Miller, cheeky-chappie voice.

'Charing Cross. Books, books, books. Poetry books, scientific books, saucy books. Foyle's the place for you lads.' He little knew how prophetic his words were. 'Trafalgar Square. See the lions over there? Made from cannons captured at Trafalgar. Nelson's Column, one hundred and sixty-seven feet high. Statue at the top, seventeen feet high. You got nothing like that up North, I'll bet.'

'We've got Blackpool Tower,' said Billy. 'The biggest phallic symbol in Britain – five hundred and twenty feet.'

'Gercha,' the conductor said.

They reached Victoria station.

'This is where you get off,' he called to the gang upstairs. 'Catch a Number Eleven. All the best, boys. But for Gawd's sake, don't come learnin' my kids that funny Northern accent. I want 'em to speak proper like the rest of us in Bethnal Green.'

'Thanks, mate. And thanks for the conducted tour,' Titch said as he stepped off the platform. 'Cheeky bugger,' he added as the bus moved off.

'Any time,' the conductor shouted back. 'Chalk and Duster Brigade! Cor blimey, that's a laugh!'

They caught the Number 11 bus close behind.

If the first conductor was Max Miller, the next was Buster Keaton, po-faced and gloomy, as if he carried the world's problems on his shoulders. He said nothing and betrayed no kind of emotion about them or their luggage.

The Charon of London Transport, Billy thought.

The bus drove on for a while. Suddenly their ferryman announced in a robotic, speak-your-weight voice, 'World's End.'

'I knew it! I knew it! My God! Has it come to this?' declaimed Oscar. 'Is this where we end our days? The World's End?'

'World's End,' the conductor repeated triumphantly. 'Next stop the Brewery, the Power Station.' Then with a feeble attempt at sarcasm added, 'Marjon's Holiday Camp.'

'Thank you, my good man,' said Oscar. 'And do try to contain your schoolgirl giggling.' ·

'I liked that man,' said Titch. 'In some ways he reminded me of my father.'

The Damian College Smokers' Club had arrived – at last. Up to this moment, the idea of living and working in the capital had been a mere dream. A life of bliss in London! They had thought and talked of nothing else for six months as they puffed on their Park Drives in the alley behind the school. Now they were here, they were feeling distinctly apprehensive. What had they let themselves in for? What did fate have in store?

They stood together on the pavement, a forlorn group nervously taking stock of the surroundings and soaking up the atmosphere. Behind them, silhouetted against a leaden London sky, rose the massive Battersea Power Station, its great finger-like chimneys pointing and belching thick black smoke into the heavens. Ahead, over the bridge, was the Nell Gwynn pub, conveniently placed for supplies as it stood next door to Watney's Brewery, which at that moment was emitting hissing jets of steam along with a powerful aroma of fermenting hops.

'The pub's handy,' remarked Billy. 'But at one and a

penny a pint, who can afford it? Anyroad, who needs the pub? We can simply stick our heads out of a window and sniff the air.'

It was the building across the road, however, which commanded their attention – the building on which they had pinned their hopes and their dreams and where they were to spend the next two years. The first impression was not favourable. The place had fallen into disrepair during the war. It was a dirty, depressing, tumbledown affair and clearly had not seen a lick of paint in a long time. The rambling, dilapidated edifices were surrounded by a crumbling high wall and approached by a large iron gate and a porter's lodge. Like the front of Strangeways.

'Do you know that this is the oldest training college in Britain?' asked Ollie.

'Who'd have guessed?' said Oscar.

'That conductor was right,' Billy said. 'This is the world's end.'

'Two years,' intoned Titch lugubriously.

'You make it sound like a prison sentence,' remarked Nobby.

'How long is two years?' asked Potts, blowing little bubbles from the end of his tongue, a revolting habit he indulged in whenever he was puzzled or lost in thought.

'An interesting question,' replied Ollie, ready with the answer. 'It depends. According to a wise philosopher – probably Einstein – time is relative. If you're enjoying yourself, time flies but if you're miserable, time drags.'

'How do you make that out? Time is always the same no matter what, surely?' protested Potts.

'Let's put it like this,' said Nobby. 'If you're on the job with a beautiful girl, a minute is nothing. But if you're sitting on a red-hot stove, a minute is forever.'

'Then this next two years will be forever,' Titch groaned happily.

They crossed the road and entered the gates. Their new lives had begun.

Chapter Four

Day One

The first day was devoted to finding their way around. The small band of second-year students – twelve in number – who had been in residence since 1944 acted as guides and advisers. Before they set off, their particular second-year mentor introduced himself.

'My name is Bullock. I come from Taunton, Somerset,' he said. 'My friends call me Bovril. But you may call me Mister Bullock.'

'Why thank you, Mr Bovril,' replied Oscar. 'Your dialect proves my theory that the way we speak reflects our environment. Your intonation is that of a bull in a field.'

'Watch it,' Bullock snorted.

He took them on a tour of the facilities – the administration block, the library, the tiered lecture theatre, seminar rooms, the gymnasium, woodwork shop, art studio, and the science lab.

'As far as I'm concerned,' drawled Oscar, adopting his aristocratic pose, 'a science lab is a chamber of horrors consisting of foul smells and dripping taps. Hardly the place for a gentleman.'

'And this,' announced their courier proudly, 'is the college dining room.'

'The most important room in the college,' said Titch. 'When do we eat?'

'Your table's Number Six, of which I'm the head,' said Bullock, pointing to their allotted place and ignoring Titch's inquiry.

Any doubts they'd entertained about the age of the college were now dispelled by the decor of the oak dining room which was dominated by a large polished table on a raised platform. Around this were twenty smaller refectory tables complete with monks' benches. The oil portraits of previous principals looked down disapprovingly from the wood-panelled walls.

'I suppose we have to listen to plainchant whilst we eat,' remarked Oscar.

'And homilies in Latin,' added Billy.

Finally Bullock conducted them to South Block, the oldest part of the college. They climbed the stone stairs to the top floor where they came to a long, draughty corridor with thirty or forty rooms branching off.

'These are your study-bedrooms,' Bullock announced. 'Number Eighty-nine is for Robin Gabrielson.'

'He won't be coming,' said Billy quickly.

'Why not?'

'He died a fortnight ago in a climbing accident,' Billy replied.

'I'm so sorry to hear that,' Bullock said.

Titch had gone very quiet as he always did at the mention of Robin Gabrielson's name.

'Anyway, the room next door – Room Ninety. Hopkins,' Bullock continued.

The six students peeked into the room. One look and

their hearts sank. Dark and dingy were the words that sprang to mind. The room was a small, cramped box containing a narrow iron bed, a bookcase with a fold-down flap that served as a writing desk, and a small wardrobe. A prison cell.

'Are all the rooms like this or is this the one reserved for solitary confinement?' asked Billy. 'Have I unknowingly committed some crime?'

'They're nearly all the same,' answered Bullock. 'This is one of the better ones.'

'When I saw your dining room a few moments ago, I had my suspicions,' said Oscar. 'Now I've two questions for you, Bovril. First, when do we get our tonsures and second, where are the self-flagellation whips? I'd no idea we were joining a strict ascetic religious order.'

'I can see you fancy yourself as a comedian,' said Bullock. 'You'll soon get used to it.' Narrowing his eyes, he added in a Gestapo-like voice, 'And if you're looking for methods of punishment, Wilde, you'll find out soon enough how our system works. We have ways of dealing with jokers like you.'

Billy looked out of his window. 'At least I have a first-class view and smell of Watney's,' he called to the others as they were allocated their rooms along the corridor.

'I'm looking straight at Battersea Power Station,' Titch called. 'Just my luck.'

Next they were shown the bathroom which consisted of a curious arrangement of a large bath across which was stretched a wooden board with holes to accommodate three enamel basins – an ingenious device thought up by some enterprising carpenter to speed up student 'throughput' in the mornings. The kind of ingenuity that would have earned an Iron Cross in a Nazi concentration camp.

35

'Because of the national fuel shortage,' said Bullock, 'there may or may not be hot water but if you run the hot tap for five minutes, you'll soon find out. If there's a loud knocking sound in the pipes, you're in luck.'

'No doubt designed by Heath Robinson or one of his brothers,' said Billy.

'Thank you for your conducted tour of this five-star hotel, my man,' said Titch. 'But I repeat my earlier question – when do we eat around here?'

'Dinner's at seven thirty. That's in two hours' time,' replied Bullock, looking at his watch.

'Two hours! I'll never last that long,' moaned Titch.

'And what's this dinner-in-the-evening stuff?' protested Nobby. 'What kind of rum place is this?'

'In better class homes,' said Pottsy haughtily, 'dinner is always in the evening. At home we always dined at eight. At weekends, we even dressed for dinner.'

'And I suppose the rest of the week,' said Oscar languidly, 'you ate your meals in the buff.'

'No. In the dining room,' replied Pottsy, blowing his little bubbles.

'Obviously,' said Billy, 'we've joined the toffs. I don't know what my dad would say if he knew. Anyroad, a student, like the army, marches on its stomach. Let's hope that the college gets better marks for its food than its accommodation. I have strict orders from home to put on some weight.'

At seven thirty they trooped into the dining hall for their first college meal. They found their table easily enough, with Bullock sitting at the head. At the lower end was a rough-looking character around thirty-five years of age.

'Let me introduce the deputy head of the table,' Bullock

announced. 'Corporal Jack Elder of the Durham Light Infantry. Like you he is a first-year but, unlike you, he is a war hero.'

The Mancunian sextet could only stare dumbfounded. Billy was the first to move.

'Pleased to meet you,' he said and stuck out his hand in friendship.

'Likewise,' growled Jack Elder, grasping Billy's hand. Smiling maliciously, he gazed into Billy's eyes as he tightened his vice-like grip until Billy winced with pain. 'Sorry about that,' said Jack, grinning. 'Can't resist doing that. Like to see how hard I can squeeze a bloke's hand when I first meet him. Test his bottle, like.'

Billy grimaced as he wrung his injured hand. 'Very funny,' he managed to say. 'I like a firm handshake though, not the flabby kind. But what's a war hero like you doing in a college like this?'

'Always wanted to be a teacher ever since I got knocked about at school,' he replied. 'Thought I'd like to do the knocking about for a change. After I was wounded in Normandy, the gover'ment couldn't do enough for me. They gave me the Military Medal and a special grant. So 'ere I am.'

'You said wounded, Jack. What happened?' Billy asked.

'Hit in the stomach with flying shrapnel from a moaning Minnie. That stopped me in my tracks all right, I can tell you.'

Jack's little speech was interrupted by the entry of the academic staff who, in their flowing black gowns, processed formally through the dining room and up to the top table. The whole college rose to its feet. The principal rapped three times with his gavel and then intoned a blessing on the meal.

37

'*Benedictus benedicat per Jesum Christum dominum nostrum.*'

'Amen,' everyone answered and sat down.

Billy and his friends could hardly wait for the meal as it was seven hours since they had last eaten. There was an appetising smell of soup coming from the kitchen.

'I hope the soup's as good as it smells,' Billy remarked. 'It's certainly got the gastric juices flowing.'

'You bloody lot don't know what hardship is,' Elder sneered. 'I joined the army seventeen years ago and we had it rough. What were you lot doing seventeen years ago?'

'I was in bed with a woman,' replied Nobby. 'Breast-feeding.'

'Things haven't changed much then,' said Billy.

The kitchen servers wheeled out the trolleys with the tureens of steaming soup – one to a table.

'Good-o,' said Titch. 'Food at last.'

That was before he tasted the soup.

Bullock ladled out the glutinous liquid onto their plates. The concoction was so tasteless and watery that the only solution was to joke about it.

'Goes to show,' Titch said. 'Don't believe everything you smell.'

'What kind of soup is this?' asked Ollie.

'Don't ask!' replied Billy in his best Yiddish inflection. 'But if we can't eat the soup, at least we can eat the bread. Perhaps the next course will be better.'

The main course was worse. The potatoes were black and under-cooked, the beans stringy, and the meat – what little there was – turned out to be tough and gristly.

'I've seen tastier food on the floor of Belle Vue elephant house,' said Oscar.

'Too true. Only an imbecile would eat stuff like this,'

agreed Titch, tucking in. 'But I'm hungry enough to eat nails.'

'You should have tried bully beef in the army, son,' said Jack who was cleaning his plate with his bread.

'I'm still hungry,' whined Titch when the dishes had been cleared away.

'You could try Dirty Dick's café round the corner,' said Bullock. 'He's usually open till ten o'clock.'

'I'll bet he does a roaring trade from this college,' said Billy.

Grace after meals followed. 'We thank thee O Lord for your blessings and for your beneficence.'

After the meal, the gang repaired to Dirty Dick's and satisfied their hunger with cheese rolls and mugs of tea.

Later that evening when the group had dispersed and retired to their rooms, when the goodnights were said, when the joking and the bantering were over and the hollow laughter had subsided, Billy lay on his bed, hands behind his head, staring at the ceiling. The lights from the passing traffic on the King's Road cast flickering shapes on the walls around him. He could feel depression creeping over him like a mantle.

It's been a long day, he thought. A rough day. What have I let myself in for? What would Robin have thought about all this? Probably the same as I do at this moment. He should really be in the empty room next door and I'm sure he'd have been as dejected. What a dump we've come to! No wonder we got into this college so easily. That food tonight was straight out of Dickens's Dotheboys Hall. For Mam's sake, I'll stick it out for another fortnight and then I'll think about going back to dear old Manchester. Things could have been a lot worse there. I could probably get my old job back in the tax office and I could take up dancing again. Maybe I'll write to my old girlfriend Adele and see if she's free.

He lay awake into the small hours, thinking. He heard the distant hooting of an owl somewhere in the college grounds. Now his imagination ran riot and he began to fill the hush of the night with strange noises. He thought he heard the sound of quiet weeping somewhere. Was it the soft sighing of the wind round the building? Was it his imagination or the subdued sobbing of Titch – or someone – in one of the adjoining rooms?

He became aware that he was developing a stye on his eye – a sure sign of tension. Which made him even more downcast.

With these thoughts whirling round his head, Billy's brain shut down for the night.

Chapter Five

He that wants money, means, and content is
without three good friends

Shakespeare, As You Like It

On Monday, after a frugal breakfast of lumpy porridge, they started their first week with registration. They were signed up, documented, stamped, recorded and their existence formally and officially recognised. Two days of choosing courses followed. The college had not yet acquired a mathematics lecturer and as the Mancunians hadn't a single scientist among them – a reflection of the education they had received – they ended up opting for the same subjects: English, History, French. Familiar territory, they thought, but there was a snag – these particular arts courses had enormous reading lists. In addition to academic subjects, there were also professional courses like Education, Physical Education, Health Education, each with a different set of demands.

'How can we buy the books they're insisting on?' moaned Titch as they emerged from a history lecture. 'And how can we read that lot? There won't be time to go to the toilet.'

41

'Then forgo visits to the toilet,' said Oscar. 'According to you, every silver lining has a cloud. Stop building dungeons in the air, Titch. We'll get by somehow.'

In the final days of the orientation week, they had to choose a personal development course from Art, Music, Woodwork. As Billy was clueless in all three, he took what he thought was the easy way out and selected woodwork.

He turned up to the woodwork shop, along with other conscripts, for initial briefing. He started off badly.

'I know what this is,' he said, picking up a plane. 'It works like this . . .' and he ran it across a bench top. It was wonderfully satisfying to see thin shavings of wood come curling from under the plane.

There was a yell of anger from across the room.

'You bloody great idiot!' the voice bellowed. 'I've spent hours smoothing that desktop to an eggshell finish and you've bloody well ruined it in ten seconds.'

It was Jack Elder.

'Sorry, Jack,' Billy stammered. 'It was a genuine mistake. I'd no idea that you'd done so much work on it.'

'Sorry doesn't make it right,' he snarled. 'I've half a mind to kick you in the balls, Hopkins. You must be as blind as a bloody bat.'

'Look, Jack, I've said I'm sorry. What else do you want me to do?'

The apology was not accepted and Billy knew that from that moment, he had made an enemy of Elder.

He decided that discretion was the better part of valour and dropped woodwork, opting instead for art, about which he knew even less and in which he was even more clumsy. By such accidents are life's choices made.

* * *

On Friday morning, the new intake of 150 students took their seats in the steeply tiered lecture theatre and Michael Roberts, the principal, came onto the rostrum and addressed them.

'Gentlemen,' he began (this appellation was enough to make Billy's chest swell with pride. Gentleman – him?). 'Gentlemen,' he repeated in case they had missed it the first time. 'I welcome you to the college. You have been selected from the many applications we have received. It's a proud day for us because the college has been virtually closed since the outbreak of hostilities in nineteen thirty-nine. Peace has descended upon the world again after six years of a war which has devastated civilisation on a scale never seen before. Recovery will take many a year but the carnage has ceased and nations are free to turn to the tasks of reconstruction. You gentlemen are part of that reconstruction and we must begin the long, patient work of rebuilding our nation and our culture. You have been privileged to take up the task, the vocation of teaching and educating the next generation. It is a fearsome responsibility and the minds and morals of our young people – we might even say the future of civilisation itself – will be in your hands.'

Billy hadn't fully appreciated the solemnity of the task he'd taken on. The upholding of Western civilisation? Was he up to it? he wondered.

The principal went on to warn them about some of the great pitfalls in teaching.

'You must avoid at all costs,' he thundered, 'what Alfred North Whitehead has called "inert ideas" – that is, ideas which were significant once but have now been superseded. You must teach your children to think for themselves and you must avoid rote learning of incomprehensible concepts

43

like "The terrestrial core is of an igneous nature" and the arithmetic of the eighteen sixties with its gills, bushels, chains, and poles.

'To cram a lad's mind,' he went on, 'with infinite names of things which he never handled, places he never saw or will see, statements of facts which he cannot possibly understand and must remain merely words to him – this, in my opinion, is like loading his stomach with marbles.'

Billy was so inspired by this rhetoric he was beginning to forget about train timetables back to Manchester. Not now he knew he was a gentleman and that the future of Western civilisation was in his hands.

Michael Roberts turned to a contemplation of reality and an examination of Cartesian philosophy. Billy sat bewildered. Was he really there? the principal asked. Was anybody there? Did anything exist? How did they know? What irrefutable proof did they have? Billy didn't understand a word. He'd never before questioned his own existence. Of course he was there. They were all there. He could see them, couldn't he? Hear them, touch them. Definitely smell them! What nonsense! Of course they were there! They agreed wholeheartedly with Monsieur Desmond Cartes. 'I think, therefore I am.' The only trouble was Pottsy – he didn't think and therefore he wasn't.

Roberts left the rostrum and there followed a descent from the elevated to the commonplace when the domestic bursar, a sad little man, appeared like Moses with his tablets of stone.

'We are a civilised community,' he sighed, 'and therefore we have certain rules which we must abide by if we are to live in harmony together. First: female guests are not allowed in your study-bedrooms. They must be entertained in the Junior Common Room.'

'Well, that's a relief anyway,' whispered Oscar.

'OK for you, Oscar, but for me it's a tragedy,' murmured Nobby, flicking a comb through his locks. 'That's taken away my whole reason for being here.'

'Second,' the bursar continued, 'you must be in college by ten p.m. on weekdays and eleven p.m. on Saturdays. If you wish to stay out beyond these hours for special reasons – say a visit from your parents – you must get prior permission from your tutor who will issue an *exeat*. Late-returning students without *exeats* will be gated, that is, not allowed out the following weekend. This is checked by a signing-in procedure at the porter's lodge.'

'Prisoners on probation,' whispered Nobby. 'How am I supposed to pursue my love life with such restrictive hours? I'll have to climb over the walls to get back in.'

'Now for some basic rules. You must clean the bath and toilet after use. You must make your bed in the mornings as there is a great scarcity of domestic staff. You may have heard that the Minister of Fuel, Emanuel Shinwell, has imposed deep fuel cuts on institutions like our own and as a result you may find that more often than not the central heating and the hot water system are not working.'

'Shiver with Shinwell!' someone called out.

Billy didn't usually ask questions in public but he felt someone had to say something. He took a deep breath and asked, 'How are we supposed to study if we're shaking with cold?'

'You must wear extra clothing or get under the blankets.'

'May we run an electric fire if we can get one?' asked Pottsy, the letter to his father already written in his head.

'There are no electric points in your rooms. Only the electric light socket and you must not under any circumstances run anything from that other than the light. Otherwise you may fuse the lights of the whole college.'

'What if we need to iron clothes – shirts and that kind of thing?' asked a Geordie student.

'We have a weekly laundry service for which there is a small charge and so there should be no need for ironing. One last point,' the bursar went on. 'Whilst we shall endeavour to supply adequate nourishing food, the cuts in rations imposed by the Minister of Food, John Strachey, have made things very difficult but we shall do our best.'

'Starve with Strachey!' the same heckler called.

Billy looked at Titch in dismay as the commandments were promulgated. Oscar raised his eyes to heaven. But the real blow was yet to come.

'Finally, I regret to inform you that it will be necessary to levy Caution Money, that is, a contingency fee of two pounds per student to cover any damage to property that may result during your time here.'

There was a general murmur of disapproval which really did sound like *rhubarb, rhubarb.*

'Why didn't you damned well tell us before this?' protested a lad with a Yorkshire accent.

'No need for bad language. This is an Anglican college, remember. As you know, the decision to open the college was made at the last moment and in our haste we overlooked the matter in the letter giving your joining instructions. The sum, less charges, if any, will of course be returned at the end of the college course.' With that, the bursar turned on his heel and left the rostrum.

Billy quietly absorbed the news. This last announcement was a blow that spelled disaster. Goodnight Vienna. No money. No course. QED.

46

'That's it,' he said with finality. 'The last straw. That lets me out. I'm left with three pounds, and from that I have to buy books. Can't be done. Unless I starve for the next three months. I can't ask my folks for any more money. They've already spent a fortune on me. Manchester, here I come.'

'I'm left with only two pounds to last the term,' groaned Titch. 'I knew that bad news was round the corner. Nothing but grey skies frowning on me.'

The rest were in similar straits.

'What in God's name are we to do?' asked Titch. 'I can't simply give up and go home. My parents wouldn't have it.'

'Well, we can't live on air,' said Billy. 'I need five fags a day. They cost one and four for ten and that's for Woodbines, the cheapest, when I can get them.' He did a quick mental calculation. 'That's almost half my weekly spends gone for a start.'

'You could always try giving up, I suppose,' said Titch sententiously.

'Easier said than done,' Billy replied. 'Anyway, I never smoke before noon.'

'Why's that?' Titch asked.

'I don't stop coughing till half past eleven,' Billy laughed.

'Do you always make jokes in the face of disaster?' Titch asked.

'Always,' Billy replied. 'It's a thing I learned during the war.'

'Look on the positive side, you two,' said Ollie. 'It's well known that initial demands by tutors are excessive. I think we can cut their lists right down and, anyway, we don't need all the books straightaway. The demand will be staggered, surely.'

47

'And we can share books if we can come to some agreement as to who buys what,' added Nobby.

'Not entirely true,' said Billy. 'Certain books in history need to be acquired rightaway. For example, *A History of the Common People* by Cole and Postgate. We have to have that for the first lecture. Cost – fifteen bob.'

'Here's another,' said Titch. 'Grant and Temperley, *A History of Europe*. Cost, seventeen and six. That's my money practically gone on two books. We're snookered. Don't see how we can carry on.'

'We could take up the twenty pound loan offered to us by Manchester Education Committee,' said Ollie, always ready with a solution.

'I don't fancy that one bit,' replied Titch. 'If for any reason we decided to pack up the course, we'd have to pay it back and that would mean trying to sell the books which would then be second-hand.'

'I agree,' said Billy. 'Over the two-year course, we'd then owe the MEC forty quid. Fancy starting your career with a massive debt hanging over you. It's just not on.'

Some Friday night! Instead of thinking about going out to enjoy themselves, Titch and Billy were sitting in the latter's study bemoaning their financial situation when the corridor outside became Petticoat Lane market. Students facing ruin began patrolling the corridor shouting out their wares like medieval town criers.

'I have a waistcoat watch and chain here for sale,' called Ollie. 'Going at a bargain price. A sacrifice at four pounds. Any takers? A family heirloom.'

There was an opening and slamming of doors as willing buyers traded with willing sellers.

Nobby's voice was heard next. 'I'm prepared to sell

The Joy of Sex by Havelock Ellis for a reasonable price. An indispensable How To Do It manual.'

Then a Geordie voice: 'New shoes, size eight, a give-away at a coupla quid.'

'A Waterman fountain pen – one pound! One only. A sacrifice. Hurry, hurry, hurry.'

Titch and Billy were about to join the mêlée – Billy had a spare pair of socks and the watch his dad had given him, Titch had a shirt – when their attention was drawn to another piece of merchandise.

'I have a dozen new copies of Cobbett's *Rural Rides* going at half price,' sang the voice in a Southern twang which they recognised as that of Rodney Brighouse (naturally nicknamed Bigarse as that was how it sounded to their Northern ears) from Basildon, Essex.

Titch and Billy were out in a flash. *Rural Rides* was a set book and at half price! They bought one each.

'How did you manage to get hold of twelve new copies?' they asked.

'Easy,' Brighouse answered. 'A trip to Foyle's Bookstore on Charing Cross Road – helped myself to a satchelful. The old geyser on the counter was half asleep. Piece of cake. Meet me there on Saturday and I'll show you the ropes. Easy as falling off a log.'

Back in Billy's room, they thought this was the answer to their prayers. But not a satchelful – that was greedy and asking for trouble. No, just a single copy of Cole and Postgate's *History* and a copy of Grant and Temperley.

They drew lots and Billy got the Cole and Postgate, Titch, the G & T – all 750 pages of it.

'Trust me to get the big heavy tome. I'm bound to get caught and that's the end of my short college career. But what choice have I got? It's like stealing a loaf of bread in the early nineteenth century but at least I won't get Botany Bay.'

Next morning was Saturday, the busiest time at Foyle's. The two would-be shoplifters, wearing their raincoats with the big pockets, met Brighouse outside the store at 119 Charing Cross Road.

'It's best to buy at least one book,' Brighouse advised, 'as a distraction. Then you can simply walk out with the big prizes. One last thing though, the chances of getting nabbed are absolutely so remote they're not worth talking about but if one of us did get nicked, we must promise not to squeal on the others.'

'Agreed,' the two apprentices said readily.

Billy and Titch decided to buy one book each – Billy, *Hamlet*, and Titch, *Much Ado* – to divert attention from the theft.

The three of them entered the shop and dispersed to different parts of the five-storey building.

Finding the Shakespeares was no problem as all the Warwick editions were shelved together in the literature section on the second floor. Locating the history books, however, was not so easy. They walked along miles and miles of shelves, searching for their booty, but no luck.

A young male assistant dressed like a tailor's dummy saw their difficulty and came forward.

'Can I be of any assistance to you gentlemen?' he asked obsequiously.

Both students turned a bright red.

'Er . . . we're looking for the history section,' Billy stammered. Titch looked down at the floor and shuffled his feet.

'That's on the third floor,' the assistant answered readily.

'Any book in particular? Perhaps I can help you locate it.'

'Er, as a matter of fact, we're looking for *A History of Europe* by Grant and Temperley and *A History of the Common People* by G.D.H. Cole and Margaret Postgate.' Billy wondered if he'd said too much and tipped the man off as to their felonious plans.

Evidently not, for the assistant replied, 'Ah, yes. You'll find both books on the corridor immediately above us. You see, our books are classified not according to authors as you find in other bookshops but according to publishers. It's a little eccentricity of our proprietor, Christina Foyle. Grant and Temperley is published by Longmans, and Cole and Postgate by Methuen.'

'Thanks for your help,' Billy mumbled. 'Perhaps we'll go up there and take a look.'

The young salesman strolled away, looking for other customers in need of help.

'I'll go first,' Billy hissed. 'You wander away from me and I'll help myself to Cole and Postgate.'

One look at Titch by any discerning shop assistant, Billy thought, would have picked him out immediately. He looked furtive and shifty-eyed as he went off browsing amongst the bookshelves along the corridor. He was whistling softly and tunelessly – a sure giveaway.

Billy selected a Warwick edition of *Hamlet* and then climbed the stairs to the history section. A quick look round and the deed was done. Cole and Postgate were stowed in his capacious pocket. Shaking like a leaf, sure that everyone in the shop was aware of the bulky protuberance in his raincoat, Billy joined the small queue at the first sales desk. He waited his turn. What was it that Ollie had said about time? Suffering slowed time down, that was it. This waiting to be served was eternity . . .

At last he reached the desk. The assistant about to serve him was no other than the helpful young man now obviously doing a stint behind the sales desk. Heart racing, his mouth dry, Billy presented his *Hamlet*, conscious all the time of the great heavy lump in his pocket.

The man made out a bill for the book.

'Will that be all, sir?' he asked.

'Er . . . yes . . . just the Shakespeare,' Billy lied.

The assistant eyed him closely. 'Did you manage to find the history books you were looking for?' he asked.

'Er . . . no . . . er . . I changed my mind,' Billy stuttered. 'I'll just take the *Hamlet* for the time being.'

'Certainly, sir. No problem,' the man said brightly. 'Here's your bill. Take it across to the cashier on the next desk and pay him.'

My God, will this queuing and waiting never end?

'How much?' he asked hoarsely at the cash desk.

The second assistant was so harassed, he gave Billy hardly a second glance.

'Seven and six,' he replied brusquely.

Billy had to go into his trouser pocket for the money which made the bulge in his coat even more prominent.

ANY TIME NOW, HE'LL CALL FOR THE POLICE, his mind screamed.

'Thank you, sir,' the man said as he stamped Billy's invoice with the word PAID. 'Now, if you'll just take the invoice and the book across to the packing counter, my colleague will wrap it for you.'

'No need for that, thank you,' Billy stuttered.

'It's Foyle's policy to wrap the books,' the man said sharply. 'It's your visible proof that you've paid for the book.'

Billy joined the third line. My God, he thought, this is

becoming unbearable. Why is buying a book so bloody complicated?

The old man at the packing counter was in no hurry. Slowly and carefully, he made a brown paper parcel tied up with string. He obviously took pride in his work for each package had to have a fancy reef knot.

Billy was sure that his left cheek had acquired a twitch and that the whole store was looking in his direction. ANY MOMENT HE'LL CALL FOR THE OWNER AND THAT'S ME FINISHED.

At last his turn came. The elderly chap tried to engage Billy in friendly conversation while he created a masterpiece in paper and string.

'You'll enjoy this play, sir. I think *Hamlet* is probably Shakespeare's finest work.'

'Yes, yes,' Billy replied, 'I'm sure I shall.' I wish the old codger would get a bloody move on. He must think I've got all day to stand here talking about *Hamlet*.

'Yes, sir,' the man was saying, 'It was first performed in sixteen hundred and one. There's the story that Shakespeare himself played the ghost in one of the early productions.'

'Yes, yes, yes,' Billy mumbled. 'Very interesting.' Give me the bloody book, you old windbag!

At last the assistant handed over the book wrapped and tied in a neat parcel. 'There you are, sir,' he said. 'I've left you a little loop to carry it with.'

Billy took the parcel quickly and strode decisively towards the door for a quick getaway.

'Wait a minute,' the cashier called after him. 'Can you come back here, please?'

OK. It's a fair cop, guv, you've got me bang to rights, he was ready to say, wrists held out for the cuffs.

53

He returned to the check-out desk.

'You've forgotten your receipt,' the man said cheerfully. 'You'll need that in case you're stopped.'

'Thanks,' Billy muttered and slunk off. Out of the corner of his eye, he saw a jittery, suspicious-looking Titch about to join the first queue. Not far behind was Brighouse, his satchel bulging with books.

Outside, sweet relief flooded Billy's veins. He'd made it! Safe! Oh, what joy to breathe the free air! The beautiful, polluted, fume-laden London air! He was out – with a fifteen bob book! He could appreciate the thrill and the adrenaline-flow experienced by inveterate shoplifters after a successful job. But never again! He'd never make a thief. Too neurotic. He scurried along Charing Cross Road, and near Shaftesbury Avenue went into an amusement arcade. Now, it was only a matter of waiting for Titch.

He whiled away the time feeding a one-armed bandit with a few pennies but his heart wasn't in it.

What if they catch Titch with that heavy volume? He was too naïve to hide his guilt. Anyone with a modicum of sense would see that he'd swiped something. Poor Titch. This college course meant so much to him. And to himself, too, for that matter. Otherwise why was he risking everything on this crazy venture? What a stupid thing to do for a couple of books! He could imagine Titch with a nervous tic when he came to pay for his *Much Ado*. They'd see through him rightaway. The police would be called and that would be IT! In some ways, Titch would be glad to be found guilty. It would confirm his philosophy of life, namely, 'Best not to be born but, failing that, to die early.'

Billy had put his last coin in the machine when suddenly Titch was there – crimson-faced and breathless, glancing nervously over his shoulder to check he hadn't been followed – an obvious filcher.

'Got it!' he panted. 'I've got it! Grant and Temperley! Look!'

'For God's sake,' Billy said, 'put it away! Wait till we get back to college.'

There was no sign of Brighouse but that was no problem. He knew the ropes and how to look after himself. No doubt for him it would be yet another successful mission and he'd be selling his spoils on the South Block corridor that very night.

As they stood at the stop in Trafalgar Square waiting for a Number 11 bus, their hearts were filled with joy on their deliverance and they congratulated each other on their lucky escape.

Their euphoria was brought to an abrupt and shocking end when, in a police car which drove close by them, they caught a glimpse of Brighouse sitting between two uniformed policemen in the back. He looked pale and distraught, nothing like the arrogant, brash individual who'd been selling set books at half price. They hoped to God he'd keep his word and not grass on them.

Billy and Titch didn't steal again. They'd learned their lesson. Two nervous wrecks not cut out for a life of larceny. Besides, they reasoned later, they were supposed to be teachers in training, supposed to set an example to the young. How could they base their careers on theft? No, they'd manage somehow by sharing their resources with the gang, selling one or two personal items and, if it came to the pinch, taking up that £20 loan from the Manchester Education Committee.

'We'll get by somehow,' Billy said to a doubtful Titch.

Later that night, the story went round the college like a

forest fire. Brighouse had been caught outside Foyle's with his satchel crammed with copies of Aristotle's *Ethics*. He was expelled forthwith, putting paid to any teaching ambitions he might have had.

There but for the grace of God, they thought.

Chapter Six

A little learning is a dangerous thing

Alexander Pope

In the second week the students were thrown in at the deep end and it was down to business with a vengeance. Every day was filled with a round of lectures. In history, they set off on the long journey that would take them from the founding of Constantinople in AD 330 to 1914. Billy did not understand why their study of European history stopped at the outbreak of the First World War, and he never discovered the reason; Halsall, the young lecturer, said there was no time for questions or other distractions as they had so much to get through in two years.

In French, they were introduced to Pierre Loti's *Pêcheur d'Islande* and Molière's *Le Malade imaginaire* as well as poetry, composition and syntax.

English literature kicked off with *Hamlet*, Cobbett's *Rural Rides*, and Browning's dramatic monologues, with the promise of an endless stream of books and plays to follow.

Billy didn't know what had hit him.

Towards the end of the week, they were introduced to a

strange subject entitled Education. What was it? they wondered. They never did find out. The lectures were taken by a Robert Owen Travers, a short, excitable Welshman with ill-fitting dentures and unfortunate acronymic initials. He was, inevitably, nicknamed 'Taffy'.

The six of them made it to Taffy's first lecture by the skin of their teeth. They had tried to get to the toilet between sessions but in that crowded timetable, there was insufficient time to fit in such extravagances.

They scrambled into the stratified lecture theatre and found all the seats seemed to have been taken. They looked round bewildered but Jack Elder came to their rescue, pointing to vacant places in the front row.

'Thanks, Jack,' Billy called, though he was a trifle puzzled by this helpfulness. Maybe I've misjudged him, he thought.

'It's like Sunday church service where no one wants to sit in the front benches,' remarked Pottsy as he took his seat and spread his notebook, pen at the ready.

'Perhaps they know something we don't,' Titch said ominously.

Taffy bounced into the room all businesslike, spraying spit in every direction. After a severe bout of hawking, he began.

'Good morning,' he said breezily.

Everyone wrote it down.

'I am going to introduce this field of study with a few special samples to shed light on the nature of learning.'

With every sibilant, saliva rained down upon them. Billy looked down at his notebook. It was covered in flecks of spittle. He looked at his companions' books – they were the same.

'I want to begin,' said Taffy, 'by telling you a little story.

58

There were once two French peasants, a father and a son, who decided to give their goat its name. The baptismal ceremony took place in the village square and began with the father beating the animal across its backside whilst the son held it by its collar. The old man struck the beast over and over again, as if beating a carpet. With each blow he shouted "Napoleon" into the animal's ear. After some considerable time, he stopped and said, *"Eh bien!* That's enough! Now he'll remember his name." In order to make sure, the son walked across to the other side of the square and held out a large carrot, calling out to the beast, "Napoleon!" The goat trotted across to him immediately. "Yes," said the son. "He's got it. He knows his name now!" '

Travers now became excited and paced up and down the front of the room. He picked up a chair and walked about with it.

The students watched mesmerised, wondering what he was going to do with the chair. His output of mucus now became prodigious and they were compelled to cover their books from the splodges which rained down upon them.

'What does this story teach us?' Taffy hissed.

Pottsy raised his hand. His friends cringed.

'It teaches us,' Pottsy declaimed confidently, 'that the French are cruel to their farm animals.'

Taffy became apoplectic. 'Yes, yes,' he snorted. 'And what else?'

A student, Claude Evans – a Travers compatriot – offered an answer.

'It teaches us,' he announced in ringing Laurence Olivier tones, 'that the best way to teach animals and children is by the use of the carrot and the stick.'

'Nearly right,' sputtered Taffy. 'Perhaps it will become clearer if we take some other examples from the animal world. Pavlov, a Russian physiologist, found that a hungry dog salivated at the smell of food. He taught it to salivate by associating the food with the sound of a bell.'

'I always thought Pavlov was a Russian dancer,' whispered Pottsy.

'And obviously Taffy has no need of a bell to start salivating,' commented Billy.

'Can any student suggest the significance of all this?' Taffy sounded as if he himself wasn't too sure.

Ollie raised his hand. 'It teaches us,' he volunteered, 'that the best time to teach children so that they remember well is before lunch when they are hungry and the bell goes.'

'How do you make that out?' spat Taffy impatiently.

'I wouldn't let the kids go in to dinner until they'd memorised what I'd taught them.'

'No, no, no,' Taffy objected. 'The Pavlov experiment demonstrates how an animal can become conditioned to a stimulus such as a bell. We have another example from a psychologist called Edward Thorndike who trained a cat to escape from a cage. Whenever the cat pressed a bar, the door of the cage opened, allowing it to escape. He called this Learning by Association.'

'There is an alternative view,' said Billy, raising his hand. 'We could also say that the cat conditioned the experimenter.'

'How so?' Taffy exploded wetly.

'Perhaps the cat thinks, "I've really got this psychologist conditioned. Every time I press this bar, he opens up the cage."'

Travers gave up and switched from animals to children.

Ah, this is more like it, they thought. This is what we came to college for. Child psychology.

Taffy went on to describe an experiment where the psychologist placed a rubber ring on a young baby's head. He called this Stimulus 1 (S1). They jotted this down in their books. The baby cried, shook its head and the ring fell off. This was Response 1 (R1). The rubber ring was replaced (S2) and the baby cried even louder and shook it off again (R2). This was repeated to S5 and R5. They now had impressive-looking scientific diagrams representing all this – Billy's mam and dad would have been proud. In this way, the baby learned quickly how to deal with a rubber ring that a child psychologist had placed on its head.

Billy tried to imagine Miss Eager at St Chad's elementary school teaching her wards by this method. 'Rubber rings – on the heads – place! Shaking of heads – begin!'

They left the theatre baffled and made their way to the dining room.

'If that's psychology,' said Nobby, 'you can stick it.'

'A lecturer,' said Billy, 'is someone who talks during *someone else's* sleep.'

'And a lecture,' added Oscar, not to be outdone, 'is the means whereby the notes of the lecturer are transferred to the notebooks of the student without the subject matter passing through the minds of either.'

'Talking of matter,' said Titch, 'the next time we have Taffy, I'm going to wear oilskins and carry a large umbrella.'

Billy nodded. 'He was like a revolving garden sprinkler of pancreatic juices.'

'He'd be useful if ever there was a fire,' added Nobby. 'He could put it out by lecturing to it.'

On the way out, Elder met them.

'Hope you enjoyed the bath,' he sneered. 'Didn't you dumbheads hear about Travers' excess saliva problem? All of us at the back admired the way you entered and sat in the splash zone.'

'Thanks to your useful directions,' said Billy.

They went into lunch.

Chapter Seven

Manners maketh man

William of Wykeham

In civilised society, a meal is an enjoyable activity, something to look forward to, a means of allaying one's hunger and of enjoying not only food but good conversation. At Billy's table, however, there was no hope of any of these pleasures.

The standard of the food, it must be said, was consistent. That is to say, execrable. Undercooked meat, black potatoes, stale bread, cold soup continued to be the order of the day. The aftermath of war, they said. Shortage of food, shortage of staff to cook it and serve it. Sometimes, the sight of the nauseating mess served up was enough to make their stomachs heave. Their table expressed its revulsion by sending the stuff back with little notes stuck in it: 'This is disgusting' or 'Feed this to the pigs and see if they'll eat it', 'Excrement par excellence', 'Garbage', 'Slops', 'Revolting Vomit', 'We want our ration books back!'

They vied with each other to produce phrases best describing the sickly hash that was dished up. Oscar's was voted favourite. 'This soup,' he announced one day, 'is a concoction of old fags and cabbage stumps stewed in the juice of boiled boots.'

'The soup tastes different today,' remarked Titch one bright Monday morning.

'That's because they washed the plates,' replied Billy.

The students were constantly hungry; not only were they served culinary disasters, there was insufficient bulk. On one occasion before dinner, Billy followed the usual '*Benedictus benedicat*' by treating the table to his own version of grace:

> 'Heavenly Father bless us,
> and keep us all alive,
> there's eight of us to dinner,
> and not enough for five.'

Fresh fruit and vegetables were still rarities, and eggs were almost unknown. Not that it mattered to Titch because for some crazy faddish reason, he couldn't eat eggs. One unforgettable Saturday night, poached eggs were on the menu. The Damian table spotted them at once as soon as the serving trolleys emerged from the kitchen. The whole table turned as one to Titch.

'Who's having your egg, Titch?' they choroused.

There was no need to ask.

Ollie gave the game away. He wore a Cheshire cat smirk, and with lowered head stroked his knife on the table in a circular sawing motion. It was revolting and the whole table responded by imitating this loathsome behaviour. Seven knives stroked the table with seven similar smirks. Ollie turned the colour of carmine with embarrassment and was never allowed to forget the incident. Time and again, it was re-enacted. In a moment of boredom, one of them had only to ask, 'Who's having your egg, Titch?' in order to spark off the required response.

Elder didn't suffer the pangs of hunger like the rest as he had a generous War Office pension which enabled him to keep well supplied with provisions. He usually had a jar of peanut butter to supplement the meagre diet. He had the despicable habit of extracting a large quantity on his knife, watched enviously by his fellow diners like dogs observing their master, and spreading it thickly on a large crust of bread. When all was ready, he shovelled it into his mouth, belching loudly. He never offered any to his companions. They hated him for it. Little did he know that when he went to the Nell Gwynn for his nightly pint, his table companions would sneak into his room and help themselves to a slice of his currant cake, a few of his biscuits, and one or two of his Gold Flake cigarettes. He never suspected a thing. They never touched his jar of peanut butter; Jack kept a careful check on its contents and it was impossible to swipe any without detection.

One evening, to everyone's surprise, Pottsy became a source of information and a guide to correct behaviour.

'My mother always used to say,' he announced, 'that you can always tell a gentleman by the way he eats his peas.'

'And how do you make that out?' Titch asked.

'Well, you, Titch, turn your fork over and scoop them up. That's never done in the best circles. It's my mother's way of sifting the U from the non-U.'

'Your family's a bunch of snobs,' said Billy. 'How are we supposed to eat them?'

'Not snobbery but correct etiquette. You should try to spear a couple of peas and push a few more onto the back of the fork or take some other vegetable onto the fork and then add peas. Never eat them with your knife as you do, Jack.'

Elder looked angry for a moment, then as he stuffed his mouth with a peanut butter wad, he said, 'Yeah, I suppose you're right but we used to leave that namby-pamby way of eating to the officers.'

'Does any of this matter?' Billy said. 'I mean, the way we eat?'

'It matters a great deal,' said Oscar, anxious to get his two cents in. 'In Victorian and Edwardian times, there was strict adherence to formal behaviour, and elegance and refined manners reached a high point. If we ever attend such a dinner, we should know which implement to take up and which glass to use.'

'Some hopes of us attending such a dinner,' said Titch. 'Anyway, there's nothing wrong with our manners.'

Pottsy continued his instructions. 'I notice, Titch, that you drop bits of bread in your soup and you drink it drawing the spoon towards you. You're supposed to break your bread with your hands and eat it separately.'

'Have you done,' said Titch peevishly, 'or is there more?'

'Pottsy's right,' Oscar said, looking pointedly at Nobby. 'You're not supposed to drink soup noisily or belch when you've finished. I can't imagine Oscar Wilde making butties at a dinner party.'

'Then he didn't know what he was missing,' replied Nobby, munching away happily.

'What about fish bones or orange pips?' Billy challenged.

'You may spit them into the cupped hand or spoon but unobtrusively. If you choke over a bone, leave the table at once.'

'Yeah,' said Elder, 'you'll probably be carried off

unconscious. That should cause a cheer all round.'

Ollie said, 'I think I'm the only one here that eats properly. Is that right, Pottsy?'

'Almost, Ollie, except for your habit of picking your teeth with your penknife.'

'That's telling him,' said Billy.

'And you, Hoppy,' Pottsy went on, 'always put your knife and fork down wrongly when you have finished. I find it annoying when you slip your knife in between the prongs of the fork.'

'I'll try to do better,' said Billy sarcastically.

Billy had always considered himself smart and 'with it' but Pottsy had unknowingly exposed a yawning gap in his social behaviour. Secretly he promised himself that he'd buy or borrow a book on etiquette at the first opportunity.

He tried to change the subject. 'Correct dinner table behaviour is all very well,' he said, 'but what is the accepted way of sending disgusting food back to the kitchen?'

Food was a sore point; Billy was still hungry at the end of every meal. His greatest pleasure in life was to go for a meal of Vienna steak and chips at the Blue Star Café on the Fulham Road but since the meal cost two shillings, it was only on Friday night – allowance day – that he could afford it. During the week, he and Titch made do with a cup of tea and a cheese roll at Dirty Dick's. On Saturdays during the football season, Dirty Dick was run off his feet when the crowds descended on Stamford Bridge and swamped his establishment. On other days, things were quiet and they could get a little service. Money and their lack of it was the problem. Twopence for a cuppa and fourpence for a roll. On Thursdays, they couldn't afford even that as they were usually out of funds until their weekly allowance arrived on Friday.

On one of these Thursday afternoons when they had run out of money, Titch and Billy called at Pottsy's room to try and negotiate a loan.

'Sorry,' he said. 'I don't give loans – it's against my principles, remember. Neither a borrower nor a lender be, and all that stuff.'

'Come on, Pottsy, there's a pal,' Titch pleaded. 'Just fourpence until we get our allowance on Friday. Hoppy and I want to go for a cuppa.'

'Nothing doing. If I do it for one, I'll have to do it for everyone. You'll just have to go without.'

'You're a mean bugger, Pottsy,' Billy said. Then he added, 'Did I ever tell you how revolting I find your habit of blowing bubbles? It's said that many male fishes blow bubbles when they want to copulate. Did you know that?'

'I, too, can play the insulting game, Hoppy,' he replied. 'What about that spot on your face? You look hideous.'

'Look, Potts,' retorted Billy. 'Talk to us when you start to shave – why, your face is as smooth as a baby's bottom.'

With that, Billy and Titch turned on their heel and stalked out of his room. They descended three flights of stairs, crossed the quadrangle, and went through the porter's lodge. They hadn't got far along the King's Road when back at the college a window was thrown open on the top floor and Pottsy's face appeared.

'Hoppy! I say, Hoppy!' he bawled, waving and shaking his fist.

Several passers-by stopped and gazed up.

'Don't forget your Valderma ointment for your spots!' Pottsy always had to have the last word.

One Monday afternoon, Billy and Titch were lingering over their cups of tea as usual. Jack Elder was sitting alone

on the other side of the café. The phone rang in the inner
office and Dick went to answer it. In his absence, Elder
whipped over to the counter, put his arm round the glass
cabinet and swiped a cheese roll. Before Dick was back, he
had, like Francis Bacon's books, tasted, chewed, swallowed
and digested it. His two companions were disgusted by this
pilfering of food from a poor man like Dirty Dick who
could ill afford to lose even one cheese roll. And they told
Elder what they thought of him. Besides, he hadn't given
them any. The greedy bastard.

Every week, the students waited desperately for their
allowance from home – in Billy's case, a ten shilling postal
order. After the last lecture on Friday morning, there was a
mad scramble to the hall where the post rack was located.
The crowd round it was always six deep and it was a fight to
reach the pigeon holes. Billy could see his letter in the slot
marked 'G to H'. When he'd finally got his hands on it, he
tore it open eagerly, read the brief note that his mam had so
painstakingly penned.

Dear Billy,
I hope this letter finds you in good health and you are
enjoying life down there and working hard to pass out
as a teacher. We're not so bad though your dad still
slips out to the pub for a quick half. More like half a
gallon, if you ask me. Anyroad, your dad says you
mussn't mix with them there Lunndon toffs or you'll
pick up bad ways. Here's your ten shillings P.O. to
help you through the week. The family give two
shillings each.
    Keep smiling,
        Your loving Mam & Dad.

'Good old Mam,' Billy murmured to himself. 'She never lets me down.'

He noticed Titch examining the few envelopes that remained in the S to T slot.

'Everything OK, Titch?' he asked. 'Vienna steak in the Blue Star as usual tonight?'

Titch looked ashen. 'Afraid not,' he mumbled. 'Nothing's arrived. No postal order. S'funny, they usually send me seven and six every Friday.'

'I shouldn't worry, Titch,' Billy said. 'I'm sure there'll be something in tomorrow's post. Delayed, that's all. But no problem, I'll stake you a steak tonight. I'm flush. Got ten shillings.' They had their usual Friday night feast.

The following week, Titch got his letter plus a postal order for a reduced amount. His dad, who had been a bus driver with Manchester Corporation, had been sacked for turning up to the evening shift smelling of drink. From that time on, Titch was on his uppers and only survived through the generosity of his cronies who each agreed to give him one shilling a week from their own resources. Pottsy was even more magnanimous and gave him one and six.

When Billy paid for Titch's Vienna steak, he left himself short that week and had to cut down his smoking from five to three a day. He could hardly afford to smoke even those. His dad, his brother Les and his old friend Cliff Fern at the Inland Revenue sent him an occasional packet to keep him going. But Billy was annoyed with himself at his weakness and every Sunday night he emulated Mark Twain and resolved to give up, to start a fresh week without nicotine. He got through the day on Monday reasonably well, though with a struggle; Tuesday he became intolerable, his nerves on edge. On Wednesday he turned vicious and, for the sake of his friends, gave up the unequal struggle and lit up again. What ecstasy to draw on that first fag! One Sunday, though, he was particularly disgusted with the wretched habit, and he took the three fags reserved for his Monday ration and flung them out of the window into the rain.

'That's it! I'm done with smoking forever. It's a dirty, filthy habit and I feel better already.'

Next morning, Billy could be seen in the bushes below searching for his three fags.

When Pottsy had given them lessons in etiquette, he had suggested that polite dinner table topics were important. Topics like illness, religion, sex and politics were strictly taboo, he had said. But Billy's table never ran short of subjects for discussion and there were no taboos.

It is said that when caged chickens are being taken to market, they begin to peck at each other's eyes. The same is true of companions in misfortune. At Table Six, mealtimes became battlegrounds, especially in the interminable delays between courses, when the diners used the time to find each other's weaknesses and expose them to the world at large. As they had no secrets from each other, this was not difficult and even things told in confidence were put on public display. Humiliation was the name of the game and Jack Elder proved to be a master. Perhaps in some previous age, Billy mused, he had been a torturer in a medieval dungeon. Be that as it may, he revealed a hidden talent for rooting out those vulnerable spots which hurt most. And Billy was his favourite target. Sometimes Billy dreaded going down for meals. The only defence was to be ready with a counter-attacking insult. He and Titch spent much time building up a quiver of suitable vitriolic arrows ready for use whenever the need arose – which was often.

Still at the head of their table sat Bullock, their second-year mentor who was there not only to keep order but to indoctrinate them with the culture of the college, such as it was. At the lower end, Elder retained his position as overseer, with the Mancunians ranged along the monks' benches on either side of the table as befitted their inferior station.

One day when they were suffering a particularly long interval between the watery soup and the slop which constituted the main course, Oscar addressed the table.

'Are you aware that man is the only animal that blushes?'

'That's because he is the only one that needs to,' answered Ollie.

'Bloody right,' Elder said, and turned to a stranger at the next table. He tapped him lightly on the shoulder and, pointing to Billy, said, 'Have you seen this arsehole blush? Here, Hopkins, do us a favour and give us a blush.'

Billy felt a hot red tide rush into his face.

'There you are,' Elder leered. 'What did I tell you? Thanks, Hophead, for obliging us.'

'You great big oaf, Elder,' spluttered Billy. 'How dare you embarrass me like that. You tooth-sucking tosspot. May you dig up your father and make soup of his bones.' Billy had put considerable time and effort into thinking that one up.

Elder scowled menacingly. 'Don't push your luck, Hopkins, or I'll be coming for you one of these nights.'

'Is that so?' Billy said. 'One thing, Jack. We'd never stoop so low as to steal cheese rolls from a poor honest shopkeeper like Dirty Dick as soon as his back's turned. We've got higher morals than that.'

'Ah,' said Oscar languidly. 'Maybe so but he FOYLED the shopkeeper.'

Titch and Billy blushed with embarrassment, which gave

Elder yet another opportunity to draw attention to their predicament.

'Yeah, we all heard about that book-swiping expedition on Charing Cross,' the corporal hissed. 'I've half a mind to report both of you to the college authorities for theft. That'd bloody well put paid to your careers and no mistake.'

'Now, now,' said Ollie. 'This is becoming nasty. Let's keep things on a friendly basis.'

Which remark prompted the whole table to act out the 'Who's having your egg, Titch?' routine.

'Looking at you lot,' said Nobby, 'it's no wonder I prefer the company of women – they are more civilised and more polite.'

This was the signal for the whole table to switch from knife-stroking to combing their hair and wetting their eyebrows.

'Your brain, Nobby,' said Oscar, 'is between your legs. You trail about the world wondering who or what you can stick it into. You have the body of a man and the brain of a sexually perverted newt.'

So the entertainment continued until the execrable pudding brought the verbal jousting to a conclusion.

They retired to the common room for their post-prandial cigarette, whilst the lucky ones with money repaired to Dirty Dick's to supplement the meal.

On one or two occasions, they turned their malice exclusively onto Jack Elder. A dangerous thing to do.

'Is it true, Jack,' asked Billy mischievously one day, 'that your family have an estate in Durham?'

'What's it got to do with you?'

'You're not by any chance related to the rich farmers who invented elderberries?'

The suppressed laughter of Billy's mindless companions infuriated Jack.

'Here, watch it, Hopkins. Or I'll be comin' to blackarse you one of these nights.'

When Oscar saw that mud was being thrown about indiscriminately, he chose that moment to join the fray by venting his spleen on Bullock.

'In the first place,' Oscar drawled, 'God made idiots; this was for practice. Then he really got into his stride and made the second-years, producing a prize bunch of illiterate, inarticulate louts.'

'Right, that's it, Wilde,' said Bovril. 'You're for it. Tonight, we're a-comin' for you. You're due to have your arse blacked.'

'I'll join you in that arse-blackin' party tonight,' said Elder. 'Hopkins here has been asking for it.'

True to their word, half a dozen second-years plus the aggrieved Elder appeared that night on the corridor of South Block.

'Right, Hopkins first,' bellowed Elder.

Several study doors were flung open as the occupants came out to witness the arse-blacking.

'What's the matter with you lot?' Titch called out. 'Don't stand around. Do something. You're like prisoners in a concentration camp. No resistance. Come on, fight back!'

To no avail; the South Block residents were not willing to put their arses on the line.

The door of Billy's room was flung open and the seven assailants barged in and pinned their victim to the bed. Billy tried to fight back but was overpowered. His pants were unceremoniously removed and the seven attackers went to work with their Cherry Blossom, leaving Billy with an ink-black posterior. There was not the physical suffering of a caning but the pain of the indignity was worse.

'Next,' yelled Bullock, 'that bastard Wilde. He's too big for his boots. We'll see how he feels with a buffed backside.'

Oscar was ready for them and took the wind out of their sails with his languid reception.

'Come in, gentlemen,' he called. 'Let us get this tedious business over and done with. With the minimum of fuss, if you please.'

Unconcerned and trouserless, with *derrière* already exposed, he lay face down on his bed reading a book, like a recumbent statue in a Norman church. Armed with tins of polish, the septet went to work on his backside and soon had a shine that would have been a credit to Billy and Titch back in their shoe-polishing days at the American Red Cross.

'Finished, gentlemen?' Oscar asked, looking up from his book. 'Then I'll bid you good evening. Please close the door as you leave.' He returned to his reading.

Their work successfully completed, the aggressors rushed off noisily down the corridor, no doubt to dispense their rough injustice in another block.

Billy lay on his bed recovering from the shock of the assault whilst Titch, who had witnessed both arse-blackings, berated the onlookers still standing around.

'You spineless lot, you gutless lot of worms. You're the kind who'd stand and gape if the Ku Klux Klan came barging down the corridor.'

'Well, what did you expect?' Potts shouted back. 'Did you expect us to take on the British Army?'

'No,' Titch yelled. 'But we didn't have to take it lying down.'

'Oh, I don't know about that,' they heard Oscar call. 'I enjoyed it.'

When the hubbub had died down, Titch and Billy met in the latter's study.

'That's it,' said Billy. 'I've had enough of this bloody college. I've just about hit the buffers. It's been a disaster ever since I came here – one thing after another. First, no money, then we came close to being arrested for shoplifting, boring lectures about kids with rubber rings on their heads, lousy food, bickering at the table, and now assault and battery. Elder has got it in for me.'

'I agree with everything you say, Hoppy,' said Titch. 'You know me, I believe life is divided into the horrendous and the woeful, but this once I think we should give the place a little longer, say until Christmas.'

'But you always say things get worse before they get worse.'

'That's right, my double worse theory. Now it's time for my double better theory. We live in the best of all possible worlds, I'm sad to say, and it's always darkest before the dawn and all that stuff.'

'You are a mixed-up kid, Titch – but very well. Until Christmas! And if things haven't improved, I'm out of here and back to Manchester and civilisation.'

'And I'll be with you,' said Titch.

Chapter Eight

Frailty, thy name is woman!

Shakespeare, Hamlet

When Oscar spoke facetiously of the ascetic life, he was not far from the truth, especially where Billy was concerned. The others had managed to get the occasional date with girls from Whitelands training college, but during the first few weeks, Billy had been completely without the company of the opposite sex. Nobby as usual claimed he was having it off every weekend with a girl called Freda. They didn't believe him but they were entertained by his stories of conquest, of how the girls couldn't resist him and how they were always dragging him off to their beds.

'You seem to be able to attract the girls easily,' said Billy one evening at dinner. 'So what's your secret?'

'Piece of cake,' he boasted. 'First, you must remember that women are different from men.'

'*Vive la différence!*' said Billy.

'Seriously,' Nobby said. 'A woman has a completely different nature. She likes to be wooed with flowers and sweet talk. More than anything, every woman wants to get

77

a man but her nature stops her from coming out into the open about it.'

'Why is that?' asked Pottsy, emerging from one of his daydreams with a prodigious output of tongue bubbles. 'What makes them so reserved if they're so keen on hooking a man?'

'From the beginning of time, man has been the hunter, woman the hunted. She knows the rules of the game. She lets the man do the chasing while she pretends to be coy but in reality she enjoys being chased. Best of all she likes being caught though she can't admit it.'

'When it comes to women,' said Pottsy, 'I'm the one who should know about 'em. I've got three sisters at home. The one thing I can't stand about 'em is the way they always leave the lavatory seat down.'

'Well said, Pottsy,' laughed Billy. Then turning to Nobby, he said, 'But you're the one who seems to have a great knowledge of what makes women tick and to have mastered the art of catching 'em. So come on, let us in on this esoteric knowledge of yours. How do you do it?'

'Well, I'll tell you,' Nobby began but Jack Elder barged into the discussion.

'What do you young pipsqueaks know about women? I was going out with skirts before any of you were born. Pin your ears back and learn from the master. Now, most women have an inferiority complex about themselves. They think there's something wrong with them. They're too thin, too fat, too tall, too short. They're not happy about the shape of their nose, their mouth, their eyes, their ears. Even the glamour pants don't have a high opinion of themselves – they think they're not very bright or not very interesting.'

'It's probably the men who've sold them that idea,' said Oscar, 'with the advertisements telling them what they must do and what they must buy to make themselves more attractive to men.'

'Dead right,' answered Elder. 'So the best way to get round a piece of fluff is to make use of her inferiority complex by appealing to her vanity.'

'I'm not sure I like the sound of this approach,' Billy protested. 'But go on, how do we do that?'

'First, show you're interested in her. Hang on to her every word as if it's the most intelligent thing you've ever heard. Listen to her problems, let her talk about herself, show understanding and sympathy. Let her see what a nice bloke you are by being kind and good-mannered, and all that. Best of all, tell her a few jokes, get her laughing and you've as good as got her between the sheets. I tell ya, they're like trained seals – throw 'em a fish in the form of a compliment and watch 'em slap their fins together.'

'Jack, you're a cynical bastard,' Billy said angrily. 'Machiavellian. Don Juan hiding behind Sir Galahad.'

Elder narrowed his eyes and gave Billy a poisonous stare. 'Watch it, Hopkins. Don't push it. Remember what happened last time,' he said menacingly.

'So the idea is to flatter her?' Nobby said in an attempt to defuse things.

'Now you're getting it,' Elder chuckled. 'Tell her what she wants to hear, how lovely she is, praise her taste in clothes, lay it on thick. Compliment her on her hair and her dress though it's her pants and how to get into 'em that's on your mind. Make out you're interested in her intellect though it's her body you have designs on. Never fails.'

'Come off it,' Billy protested vehemently. 'That approach might work with the dumb blonde type but it wouldn't work with a beautiful, intelligent girl. She'd see through you right away.'

'That's another thing,' added Elder, ignoring the comment. 'For God's sake, don't pick the most beautiful girl in the room – she'll probably have a boyfriend already, and you may find she's vain and stand-offish. No, better to pick the fat one with acne sitting in the corner. She'll be so grateful for the attention, she'll soon be offering you crumpet for tea. And as for that flowers and chocolates shit, when it comes to the crunch, give it to her good and proper. "Wham-bam-thank-you, ma'am" as the GIs in Normandy used to say.'

Billy flared up. 'I've never heard such cold-hearted crap. You sound as if you've just fallen down from the trees. You're a nasty piece of work, Elder, to treat the fair sex with such contempt. One day, you'll meet your opposite number and you'll get your come-uppance. I only hope I'm around to see it.'

Chapter Nine

Dancing Lessons

During the week, a combination of college work, the early curfew and lack of funds ensured that they led a quiet life, and on most weekday nights they were in bed by 11 p.m. A visit to Dirty Dick's and the occasional treat at the Blue Star Café were all they could manage. Weekends were different and the Damian group managed either a walk to Putney or a visit to the pictures. For Titch and Billy, the flicks became an essential escape from the academic routine.

'Right, Titch,' said Billy one night. 'What do you say to ducking Travers' education lecture and going to see Celia Johnson and Trevor Howard in *Brief Encounter*?'

'A difficult choice,' replied Titch. 'Duck out of the lecture or take a ducking in the lecture. Johnson and Howard get my vote.'

This skipping of lectures became a habit and it's a moot point whether they learned more at films like *The Lost Weekend, The Way to the Stars, Les enfants du paradis* than they did in dry-wet talks on Watsonian behaviourism.

The film that made the greatest impact was undoubtedly *The Jolson Story* which the Damian lot saw several times.

The bathrooms of South Block rang out for many weeks with amateurish imitations of the great minstrel singer. Even Oscar the aesthete was infected with the craze.

'It's no use,' he proclaimed one night after a particularly puerile attempt to emulate the crooner. 'There is a certain silky texture to his voice which makes it inimitable.'

Most of the time at college, they were homesick for Manchester and Mancunian culture, which the Southerners declared was a contradiction in terms (an oxymoronic statement, they said). Billy often thought about his former girlfriend Adele and in his nostalgia for all things connected with home, he sometimes saw her in a more glamorous light than was actually the case. His relationship had come to an abrupt end when she had tried to lay down the law about what religious beliefs and practices she would and would not tolerate 'in our little home after we are married', as she'd put it. As for their first clumsy adolescent attempt at sex, it was perhaps best forgotten, but in the silence of his room, Billy could not prevent himself from playing the scene over again in his mind's eye.

Adele had been his dancing partner and together they'd had a few successes in local competitions. Their romance had also been making progress and they'd had one or two hot necking sessions on the settee in her front room. He'd enjoyed these all right but she'd got him so excited that he always went home feeling frustrated. Then she'd promised – reluctantly, he had to admit – to let him go all the way, to give him, as she put it, 'the full thing'.

He wouldn't forget that Saturday, not if he lived till a hundred. Most of his sex education had been acquired at school through his peers in the smoking club and he wasn't sure that they always had it right. They certainly had some weird ideas on how to stimulate a female – like fondling her left breast rather than the right, as if the left had special aphrodisiac properties. So he'd spent the afternoon in the Central Library reading sex manuals in an effort to fill the gaps in his knowledge. There was lots of stuff about contraception, sexually transmitted diseases, about things that could go wrong and the like, but he could find nothing about the best way to do it. He could leave that to nature, he supposed.

She'd pressed her parents into going out for the evening. From a distance, he'd watched them set off and when he'd judged the coast was clear, he'd knocked on the front door.

'Come in,' she'd said. 'Do you still want to go through with this?'

'Does a bird want to fly, does a duck want to swim?' he'd answered.

'Oh, very well,' she'd sighed. 'Let's get this thing over with.'

She stretched out on her back as stiff as a board and, closing her eyes, announced, 'Right, you can do it now.'

Just like that.

Hardly the most romantic invitation in the world but beggars couldn't be choosers.

She'd given him no help whatsoever and the evening had been a disaster. What had made it worse was that she had accused him of 'botching it up'. Not at all good for his macho self-image.

He shivered involuntarily at the memory of the fiasco.

Before setting off for Chelsea, Billy had made contact once more with her and they were regular correspondents. Now that Billy was at an Anglican establishment, she hoped that he'd drop that Catholic nonsense and become a normal apathetic type like the rest of her family. Her mother, though, felt that since he was studying to be a teacher – a respectable profession with a steady income, and a good pension at the end – he had become a 'good catch', Catholic or not. Besides, knowing her daughter and her ability to get her own way, she felt sure that in time Adele would bring Billy round to the family's agnostic way of thinking.

Their correspondence continued in the same vein as their former protestations of love and took the form of declaring the eternal nature of their adoration in such phrases as 'Yours till hell freezes over; till the wells run dry; till the deserts bloom'.

Billy had run out of improbable eventualities when he discovered a rich seam of unlikelihoods in the poetry of W. H. Auden and the songs of Vera Lynn. These enabled him to enrich his letters with further phrases like: 'Yours till the stars lose their glory' and 'Till China and Africa meet, and the river jumps over the mountain and the salmon sing in the street'.

Pottsy spent much time writing letters to his Rowena in Manchester and was forever singing her praises and drooling over her photograph. They would gather in a little group in his room to make toast, to keep warm by his electric fire and listen to Denny Dennis singing love songs on his record player – all plugged into an adaptor connected to his electric light socket. Inexplicably, the college fuses remained intact.

Pottsy and Billy developed the curious habit of standing in the bathroom together, their hands immersed in bowls of very hot water. Pottsy blew his little tongue bubbles, whilst Billy sang in his best Sinatra/Haymes crooning voice the romantic love songs of the day: 'Love Letters (straight from your heart)'; 'A Little Lonely on the Lonely Side Tonight'. But it was the sentimental ballad 'Saturday Night Is the Loneliest Night of the Week' that triggered a profusion of bubbles like a Monday morning washday.

The songs Billy chose always contained the word 'lonely' somewhere in the refrain – a sure indication that he was not so much lovesick as homesick. It was painful to be away from home but since it was more manly and grown-up to confess love for a girl than one's mother and her apple pie, they converted the pain into what they thought was love.

Not long after the black-arsing ordeal, when Billy was feeling particularly blue, he thought back to those happy days in Manchester when, with Adele as his partner, he had won third place in the North-West Tango Competition held at the luxurious Ritz Ballroom. He remembered that Frank Rogers, his ballroom dancing tutor in Manchester, had recommended an exclusive studio run by Alex and Carol Gibson, both ex-world champions, on Kensington High Street. For the first few weeks at college he had hesitated about turning up there for several reasons: he had been too busy settling in and, conscious of his dad's dire warnings about Londoners' so-called evil ways, he was nervous about introducing himself to such distinguished people. One evening, Billy plucked up courage and presented himself there. 'Nothing ventured, nothing gained,' he said to himself, quoting one of his mam's many aphorisms.

'I remember Frank Rogers well,' said Alex Gibson. 'A first-class teacher. I hope he told you that we do not cater for beginners and we accept only members who have reached Silver Medal level. We should have to appraise your performance before we issue you with a membership card, you understand.'

'Why so exclusive?' Billy asked.

'As you can see, the studio is only big enough to

accommodate about eighteen people and so we have to restrict our numbers. Our advanced class meets every Saturday night and we encourage the highest performance standards. On this initial visit, perhaps you would demonstrate what you can do by dancing with my wife Carol.'

Carol came forward, smiling in welcome. 'Nice to meet you, Billy,' she said. 'You've certainly got the slim build of a dancer.'

Alex switched on the strict tempo music of Victor Sylvester playing 'Fascination'.

Billy took up his hold and Carol and he moved effortlessly and gracefully across the polished floor of the little studio. He tried one or two simple variations like the 'feather' and the 'hesitation pause'. Carol was an obvious professional as she responded skilfully and sensitively. He tried a few more advanced steps and found she was equal to everything he tried.

'Where did you learn to dance like that?' she said. 'You're obviously gold standard.'

Alex watched them flow around the room with grace and poise.

'No need to go on, Billy,' he said. 'Welcome to the club. You must be one of Frank Rogers's star pupils. I'm sure he was proud of you.'

'Thank you,' said Billy. 'That's praise indeed coming from two world champions. I should be honoured to become a member.'

'Fine,' said Alex. 'We meet every Saturday night at seven thirty and I'll introduce you to the others if you'd like to come. If you are interested in joining our Formation Team, you'd be most welcome.'

'I shall be here on Saturday,' said Billy, 'but I'm not sure about the Formation Team as college keeps me fairly busy.'

'We can look at that another time,' Alex said. 'Till Saturday, and welcome once again.'

'Goodbye and thank you,' added Carol.

Billy left the studio as light as a feather. After his unfortunate experiences at college, his visit to the studio was like a shot in the arm. I think I could survive London and the college if I could take up dancing again, he thought. It'll be like an oasis in a desert.

Come Saturday afternoon, Billy's companions took themselves off to Stamford Bridge to watch Chelsea Football Club being beaten yet again by some Northern team. Provided there was a supply of hot water, he spent the time soaking in a long hot bath, with the muffled roar of the football crowd undulating in the background. At six o'clock, he signed out for dinner, took a snack of a cheese cob and a mug of tea at Dirty Dick's and caught the tube to Kensington High Street.

At the studio, Billy found an elegant crowd already assembled there. Smiling broadly, Alex and Carol came forward and shook his hand warmly.

'So glad you could make it,' said Carol. 'Let me introduce you to one or two people.'

She conducted Billy around the company, presenting various people, but his attention was drawn to a pretty, slim, dark-haired young lady who was at that moment sitting alone in a corner of the room. Billy judged her age to be about twenty-four or -five.

'Let me introduce Doris Hartley,' Carol said, taking him over to her. 'You two should make a good partnership.'

Billy spent that first Saturday night dancing only with Doris. Every dance they tried – the waltz, the foxtrot, quickstep, tango – they seemed to glide across the floor as if they had danced together for years. Her movements were natural and elegant.

'I can see you've danced before,' she said.

'The same goes for you,' replied Billy. 'Are you a professional dancer?'

'No,' she laughed. 'I thought about it once but decided it was too risky. No, I work as a secretary at the Ministry of Education in Whitehall.'

'Ah, then you can advance my career for me. I'm hoping to be a teacher one day.'

'Afraid not. I'm a lowly stenographer without influence.'

Their conversation flowed as smoothly as their dancing, even at the interval when they continued talking over a cup of tea and a chocolate biscuit. Too soon, the evening came to an end and Billy had to excuse himself in order to get back to beat the college curfew.

Any romantic notions Billy might have entertained about Doris were soon dispelled when she told him she was married.

'My husband, Harry, is in the RAF and waiting to be demobbed,' she told him. 'At present he's stationed in Malta and we can both hardly wait for him to get home.'

'Doesn't he mind you going off dancing on Saturday nights?' Billy asked

'Not one bit. In fact he encourages it. Dancing was never his scene and he knows how much I love it. We have a very happy marriage and we get along fine. We both like the theatre, especially opera, and when he's home we're regular visitors to Covent Garden. You'd like him, Billy, and I hope you can meet him one day.'

'Hope so too,' Billy said, and he meant it. 'Thanks anyway for a wonderful evening, Doris. I can't remember when I last danced with someone as accomplished as you.'

'Thank you for the compliment,' she said. 'The same goes for me. See you next Saturday.'

Billy left the studio happy and contented. So there was a life outside the college walls after all.

Every Saturday night, Billy blew half his weekly allowance on the tube fare and the entrance fee to Alex Gibson's salon. Doris became his regular partner. They danced to the silky strains of Victor Sylvester and Josephine Bradley until they moved together as one. He learned that Doris and her husband had their home in Chiswick, and that they were both five years older than he was – not that any of that mattered. They danced, they talked, they had a cup of tea at the interval, they enjoyed each other's company and they parted at 10.30 as Billy rushed to catch his tube. They were both happy with the arrangement and for Billy a new dimension was added to his life, making it more tolerable.

Around this time, the college authorities, feeling that it was unhealthy, even dangerous, to deprive so many men of female company decided to demonstrate its liberal attitudes by organising a hop in the college hall. Women students, strictly chaperoned, from Whitelands College were invited across to cheer them up. The women sat on one side of the hall and the men on the other. There was little beauty or sexual promise and nothing to tempt the men across the gap. Most of their visitors were quintessential schoolmarm types, lisle stockings, flat sensible shoes, cheap perfume, and steel-framed spectacles.

Billy stood quietly on the sidelines observing the pathetic attempts of his fellow students to dance. Bullock, their mentor, was making a reasonable attempt to waltz but it was obvious that he possessed no more than rudimentary skill and knew only the most basic of steps. As for the rest,

89

they moved like men trying out artificial legs for the first time. The affair was a minor disaster. Billy was gratified to note that Jack Elder, his tormentor, was one of the most inept. Some time into the dance, however, watched admiringly by his junior table companions, the corporal succeeded in luring a plump, blonde girl – a bespectacled Boadicea – up to his room.

'I pity that poor girl,' Billy said to Titch, 'when he employs his subtle hanky-panky love techniques on her.'

'Oh, I dunno,' Titch replied. 'She's a big girl and looks like the kind who can look after herself.'

At breakfast next morning Bullock commented on the pathetic dancing skills displayed by his fellow students. 'A disgrace,' he said. 'I don't know what Whitelands College must think about us. Our students danced like a bunch of clod-hoppers. I think we should organise dancing lessons for the lot of them.'

A little later that morning, Jack Elder came down to breakfast. He was wearing dark glasses but they failed to hide the fact that beneath them he was sporting two black eyes, a bruised cheek and a swollen ear. When Billy mischievously asked for a report on his amorous activities, he snarled viciously like a mad dog. It was some time before they learned that he'd got nowhere with his quarry, claiming that he'd been turned off when she sat on his knee. The girl weighed sixteen stone, was trained in jujitsu and had objected to his tender advances by giving him a practical demonstration of the art of self-defence. So much for Elder's theories about the opposite sex. It made Billy's day when he got the story.

A couple of days later, the following announcement appeared on the main noticeboard:

IF YOU WANT TO GET A GIRL,
LEARN HOW TO DANCE!
The recent 'hop' demonstrated an urgent need
for dancing lessons amongst our student brethren.
It is proposed therefore to hold dancing classes for
those wishing to acquire or improve their dancing
skills. Those interested should meet me in the
gym next Friday at 7.30.
YOU MAY BRING A DANCING PARTNER –
PREFERABLY FEMALE – BUT A NUMBER
OF WHITELANDS STUDENTS HAVE
EXPRESSED AN INTEREST. SO WHAT ARE
YOU WAITING FOR?
SIGN YOUR NAME BELOW
Terry Bullock, Second Year

The Damian crowd, including Billy, signed up for the class.

'If it helps me to attract even more girls, I'm for it,' remarked Nobby.

'I shall attend for the company only,' said Oscar. 'I'm not sure about the attracting girls bit. If there's a shortage of girls, I may have to have a male partner.'

Around three dozen students, including partners, turned up for the first Friday night session. Pottsy had agreed the loan of his record player and a few records of strict tempo music had been found.

Bullock opened the proceedings by announcing that students should partner off so that he could get a rough idea of individual standards.

'I noticed at the recent hop,' he began, 'that there are big differences in dancing skills. So in order to know where to begin, I suggest dividing you into different classes according to ability. Group one for absolute beginners and

91

group two for reasonably proficient. Let's start with the simplest dance – the waltz. Could you start the ball rolling, Titch?' Bullock switched on the music of Victor Sylvester's 'Anniversary Waltz'.

Titch, who had chosen a partner of the same height, danced a few wooden-legged steps.

'Group one – beginners!' Bullock called out decisively. 'Next, Nobby. Let's see if you're any better.'

Nobby made a brave attempt with his beanpole partner but was little better than Titch.

Billy watched the proceedings quietly.

'Group one again!' Bullock announced. 'You're supposed to be dancing, Nobby, not pushing a wheelbarrow. I don't suppose you lot from the North have any acquaintance with the refinements and etiquette of the dancing salon. Jack, with your experience in the Durham Light Infantry, you should be light on your feet. Maybe you can show 'em how it's done.'

Jack Elder had obviously made peace with his pugilistic Boadicea for he appeared with her as his partner. Her actual name was Bertha and he proceeded to dance with her in a style more reminiscent of a regimental march than a light fantastic.

'It's supposed to be a waltz, Jack,' called Oscar, 'not a military two-step.'

'Watch your mouth, Wilde,' Jack grunted, 'or we'll be coming for you again.'

'Any time,' countered Oscar. 'Say the word and I'll be waiting.'

Whilst this exchange was taking place, Billy's partner for the evening arrived.

'Sorry I'm late, Billy,' she said. 'I was held up at work – a rush typing job.'

92

'That's OK, Doris,' replied Billy. 'I'm so grateful that you agreed to come.'

'Glad to be of help. I'm just glad to be busy until Harry gets home.'

'Great,' Billy said warmly. 'As you will see, Doris, it's going to be like missionary work taking culture to the uneducated masses.'

'Sorry, Jack. Group one,' Bullock proclaimed, 'but I think you show definite promise. Let's try one of our other clod-hopping brethren from Manchester. Right, Hoppy, hop to it! Another for group one, I'm sure. Have you peasants from Manchester ever heard of ballroom dancing?'

'My partner and I have done a little dancing together before though we're a little rusty and need more practice.'

'More for the beginners' group, I've no doubt.'

Billy and Doris took up their stance and moved with grace and poise in perfect time to Sylvester's flowing music. A hush fell over the assembled body and the watching students gazed open-mouthed as the couple danced smoothly round the room.

'If that's rusty,' gasped Titch, 'I'd like to see them when they reach top form!'

That was the night that Billy's fortunes took a turn for the better. Even Bullock had to defer and he handed over the organisation of the dancing classes to Billy. Doris agreed to give up some of her spare time to help with the ladies. Billy decided to arrange dancing lessons for the whole college and, to this end, recruited three or four students (Bullock included) who had demonstrated a modicum of skill. Regular classes were held for the rest of the term and in the evenings the gymnasium became a ballroom and passers-by could hear strict tempo music and the voices of the instructors: 'Forward left foot, side right foot and close . . .'

Some of the students reported later that it was the most useful thing they had learnt in their time at college.

As the weeks went by, Jack Elder became not only more enthusiastic but more friendly towards Billy, even defending him one day at the dining table.

'Hey there, Hopkins,' a bespectacled student at the adjoining table called. 'Give us another one of your blushes, there's a good fellow.' He smirked at his fellow diners and waited for the result. It was not quite what he expected.

Elder stood up and towered over the Billy Bunter type. 'Watch your mouth, four-eyes,' he snarled, clenching his fist. 'Hopkins here happens to be a particular friend of mine. Insult him and you insult me. Got it?'

The bewildered student turned his attention to his soup which appeared to have acquired a sudden fascination for him.

Things didn't stop there and whilst it would be an exaggeration to say that Billy and Jack became bosom friends, they certainly became good pals. The rest of the table was left in no doubt as to the change in the relationship because at one memorable breakfast, as the Damian crowd looked on in wonder, Jack slid his peanut butter jar across to Billy and said, 'Try some of that, Hoppy. It'll give your bread more taste than the college margarine.'

By the end of the term, Jack had become one of Billy's star pupils.

'Hoppy, I want to apologise for that attack on you,' he said at one of the sessions. 'I had you all wrong. We got off to a bad start in the woodwork class but there was more to it than that. You see, I've not had a grammar school education like you lot and, well, I thought you were all trying to take the Mickey and make me look a right Charlie.'

'No malice intended, Jack,' replied Billy. 'Let's forget it. It's in the past.'

The corporal held out a hand of friendship. Billy took it happily and while it was still a firm grip it was not of the crushing variety. Billy felt a surge of happiness flow through his veins. 'Right, Jack,' he said eagerly. 'Now let's take another crack at your feather step.'

An early return to Manchester was no longer on the agenda.

Billy was appointed chairman of the Entertainments Committee which had the responsibility of organising the end of term dance and that was to be a very different affair from the first primitive hop. A small band was hired, and the event was attended by all students – first and second years alike plus members of staff. The young ladies who came on this occasion seemed an entirely different type. Or maybe they were the same ladies better groomed and more glamorously attired. Billy invited Doris and she arrived in a most attractive cocktail dress.

'Doris,' he said, 'you look really nice tonight. Every eye in the room will be on you. Your Harry must be very proud of you.'

'Thank you, Billy, for those kind words. And good news about Harry. He's to be demobbed early next year. So you'll be able to meet him at last. I've written to him about you and he's beginning to wonder who this mysterious other man in my life is. I've told him that he has nothing to worry about.'

'Don't be too sure about that,' Billy grinned. 'With a beautiful wife like you, Harry had better keep on his toes.'

'Don't worry. Harry's not the jealous type,' she laughed. 'I'll invite you over to tea to meet him when he gets back home.'

'I'll hold you to that,' Billy laughed. 'Mention tea or food to me and I'll be there like a shot.'

The learner-dancers of Marjons seemed to have picked up the rudiments of ballroom dancing and on this occasion there was no sexual divide. Watched admiringly by students and staff, Doris and Billy glided skilfully across the floor. A happy and successful evening.

A couple of days later, Taffy Travers stopped him on his way to lectures.

'I see, Hopkins,' he said, 'that you are proficient in the art of propelling yourself across the ballroom floor. All very well in its place but don't let it interfere with the more serious business of studying psychology.'

Billy thanked him for his compliment. After he had gone, he wiped the spittle from the lapel of his jacket, and went on his way.

Apart from the arse-blacking procedure dished out to miscreants, the college had no traditions or customs to speak of. Or if it had, they had become lost during the war when a much depleted college had been evacuated to Cheltenham. One Saturday night, the second years made a brave attempt to create one. Pushed and jostled by the seniors, the whole student body assembled in the college grounds and began a slow march to Piccadilly Circus in single file, each student's hand on the shoulder of the one in front, and with one foot on the pavement and one foot in the gutter. A magnificent chorus worthy of a Welsh miners' choir arose in glorious harmony from one hundred and fifty throats – 'Lloyd George Knew My Father' to the tune of 'Onward Christian Soldiers' followed by a rendering of 'The Stars and Stripes Forever' with the words:

Be kind to our web-footed friends,
For a duck may be somebody's mother.
They live at the edge of a swamp
Where the weather is always damp.
Now you may think that this is the end.
Well, it is . . .

Somebody must have tipped off the police that a political demonstration was converging on the centre of London, for the procession was soon shadowed by a convoy of police cars.

When the march had reached Piccadilly, a huge circle was formed round Eros which, after a four-year absence during the war, had been restored to its place at the centre of the Circus. There the demonstrators chanted the college Maori-like war cry – which Billy had never heard before: 'I-zaka Zomba, Zomba, I-zaka Zomba, Zomba Zee. Yakaheema.' The chant finished with a great leap of a hundred and fifty students who shouted in one voice: 'Marjons!'

On the way back, the same curious marching style was adopted until they reached the home ground of King's Road and Cheyne Walk where a huge stone bust of some long-forgotten Roman emperor was appropriated from the garden of a deserted house and transported in a wheelbarrow back to the Junior Common Room. There, with due ceremony, the bust was painted with a red letter 'T' for Taffy and installed in a place of honour on a large marble mantelpiece.

For the first time, Billy felt truly proud to be part of such an august body of men. The idea of giving up the college course had been completely forgotten.

Billy had begun the course in September unsure about how well he would settle to study and the college routine after his year away from academic work. At the end of the term, he was relieved to find that not only had he passed his exams and the initial teaching practice but had achieved grades comfortably above average.

His cup was full.

Chapter Ten

Christmas at Home

The end of the first term came at last. For weeks, Billy had been counting the days. So many things had happened since he'd last seen his family and he'd so much to tell them – about college life, the food, the lectures, the teaching practice, the college ball, the crazy student march to Piccadilly Circus.

When he and his companions stepped off the train at Manchester's London Road station, it was indeed a joyful occasion. But after such a long absence and after so many exciting experiences, the town somehow looked strange and unfamiliar and he felt like an alien. After the hustle and bustle of London, it seemed smaller, quieter and less frenzied. The Billy Hopkins that emerged from the station was not the same Billy Hopkins that had set off for London in September.

The Damian gang parted company and Billy caught the 62 bus to St Luke's Church on Cheetham Hill Road. He struggled his way down Smedley Lane lugging his heavy suitcase, pausing every hundred yards or so to change hands. Manchester may look smaller, he thought, but this lane definitely seems longer. By the time I get to Gardenia

Court my arms will reach past my knees and I'll look like an orang-utan. Thank God it's downhill.

At the bottom of the lane, outside the Hyacinth House flats, he spotted his dad waving to him. Billy had never been so glad to see him even though he looked that little bit older.

'Hello, son,' he said, taking Billy's free hand in a firm handshake and following it with a tight bear hug. 'Good to see you again after all this time.'

'The same goes for me too,' Billy said warmly. 'It's three months since I was home.'

Dad said, 'Here, let me take that case from you.'

'It's heavy, Dad,' Billy warned.

'Heavy!' he said. 'As a market porter, I dare say I've lifted heavier things than that.' He took the case from Billy's hand. 'Bloody hell!' he exclaimed. 'It *is* heavy. What in God's name have you got in it – bricks?'

'Not bricks, Dad. Books.'

'What are you bringing a lot of bloody books home for? You're supposed to be on holiday.'

'Essays. I've got about ten essays to write. They don't let up at this college.'

They reached Gardenia Court and to Billy's eye it looked more squalid than ever. He noted the broken windows, the washing hanging at every veranda, the mongrel dogs which seemed determined to have a lump out of his ankles, and Annie Simpson, the simple-minded girl sitting on the low wall, saliva dribbling from her lips.

'Ockins! Ockins!' she babbled.

'I think she's saying welcome back,' Dad said.

They turned in at their stairwell and Billy's nostrils were assailed by the familiar malodours as they climbed the stairs: pickled herrings, steak and onions, curried fish, rancid cheese, sour cabbage.

Mam was making a brew when Dad opened the front door.

'He's here,' he called. 'The one you've been waiting for – all the way from London.'

Mam came out from the kitchen wiping her hands on her pinafore.

'Billy,' she said. 'So you're home then.' She embraced him warmly. 'It's so good to have you back after all this time. The tea's made and your food'll be ready as soon as you are.'

'Food?' said Billy. 'What's that?' He had to turn his head away so that they wouldn't see the tear glistening in his eye. It was so good to be back in the bosom of his family.

Dinner that evening consisted of chips and two eggs plus copious amounts of bread and 'best' butter, followed by apple pie and custard. After the privations at college, Billy was in heaven.

At the table, they pumped him about the college. Did he like it? Did he get on with the other students? Were they sending him enough money? Did he understand the lectures? Were they feeding him right? Would he pass out as a teacher? Was he going back?

'Yes, yes, yes,' he answered to everything. 'I love it at college and I've made lots of friends. I've been made chairman of the Entertainments Committee. I've passed my first exams and I've settled into college life.'

They gazed at him proudly and drank in every word he uttered. They were enjoying his success as their own.

'You do talk posh,' Mam said finally. 'Like the news announcers on the wireless.'

'You mean like Wilfred Pickles?' said Billy.

101

'No, you daft hap'orth,' she said. 'Like that there Alvar Liddell fella.'

'It's to be hoped he's not getting above himself,' Dad said, addressing his invisible auditor, 'and joining them stuck-up toffs down there. Or he won't want to know us in a year or two.'

'Don't talk so daft, Tommy,' Mam said. 'He's our son.'

'What's happened to that watch I gave you when you went away?' Dad asked suddenly.

Billy flushed. 'It was pinched,' he lied. 'I was in the football crowd at Stamford Bridge and some pickpocket got it off my wrist.'

'Off your wrist?' Mam echoed. 'How did they manage that without you feeling it?'

Dad answered for him. 'Them thieving swine in London are that clever. I tell you, Kate, they'd pinch the stays off your back without you knowing or feeling a thing.'

'I'd like to see 'em try,' Mam answered. 'I don't think anyone's that clever.'

'Anyroad,' Dad said. 'I'll speak to my mate in the Hare and Hounds and see if I can get you another watch. You'll have to glue it to your wrist this time.'

Billy rigged up a little study in his bedroom and for much of the holiday spent his time writing essays and doing the required reading. One day his mam came into the room and looked at him fondly.

'I'm that proud of you, Billy. You're going to pass out as a teacher and you'll have a steady, respectable job in your hands and you'll never have to worry again for the rest of your life. And you'll get a pension as well. But I think you do far too much reading. One day your eyes'll pop out of your head if you're not careful.'

'I'll be OK, Mam,' he said. 'I've got to get through the assignments they've set me.'

'Assignments! That sounds important. What's that book you're reading now? Is that an assignment?'

'It is. It's French prose I have to study.'

'That doesn't sound very nice, Billy. Reading about French pro's. Let me see what it says.'

Billy showed her the first page of Maupassant's *Boule de suif*.

'What does that mean?'

'It means Ball of Fat.'

'How do you get Ball of Fat out of that? It doesn't sound anything like it.'

'It's not supposed to, Mam. It's French.'

'I don't know how you get your head round that stuff, I don't really. I suppose it's about French cooking, is it?'

'Not, it's about a French prostitute – she's a round little thing and that's why she's called Ball of Fat. It's supposed to be the best short story ever written.'

'It might be the best story ever written but it doesn't sound respectable. I do hope they're not learning you rude things, our Billy. Don't tell your father you're learning about French prostitutes, for God's sake, or we'll never hear the last of it. What else are you studying?'

'Well, I've got to write an essay on this poem, "Epistle to Doctor Arbuthnot".'

'That doesn't sound nice either. Epistle to this doctor fella. Who wrote it? Not another Frenchman, I hope.'

'No, this was written by Alexander Pope.'

'Oh, that's all right then.'

A few days later, Mrs Mulligan (''Er next door' as Mam called her) came to borrow a cup of sugar, 'Till Paddy, my husband, gets his dole money on Thursday,' she said. 'And how's that lad of yours doing at the London college?' she asked by way of conversation to justify the loan of the sugar.

'Tommy and me are right proud of him,' Mam answered. 'Though we worry sometimes that his head might burst open like a sausage one day, he's stuffing so much into it. At the moment,' she looked round to make sure there was nobody else listening, 'I want you to keep this to yourself – he's making a study of French prostitutes.'

'Ah, Mrs Hopkins,' she said, 'that doesn't sound nice. Now, why would he want to study that class of subject?'

'If he's going to be a teacher, he has to know about such things,' Mam said. 'They know what they're doing down there in London. Anyroad, he's studying some nice poetry about a doctor written by Pope Alexander.'

'That'll be one of them religious poems I've heard so much about. I'm sure the Bishop will be in favour of learning like that. I had an uncle who was high up in the Church and studying for the priesthood at Maynooth. He used to know about such things.'

'Not only that, he's reading something by that fella Shakespeare. A Danish play called Omelette.'

'Now that'll be a useful thing,' Mrs Mulligan said. 'My Paddy could do to take up a subject like that. For sure, he couldn't poach an egg without setting fire to the kitchen.'

When Billy walked out of their flat next day, he found he had been elevated to celebrity status in the district and was the talk of the tenements. He was sensitively aware of the heads that turned when he walked by. Housewives in hairnets and husbands on the dole stood around on their verandas smoking and calling to one another. Mrs Mulligan on the top store soon spread the news from one floor to the next.

'That's the Hopkins lad,' she cried to the Pitt family below. 'Sure, he's studying to be a teacher in London, so he is. Doing hush-hush research into French prostitution, and writing poetry about the papal father. Not only that, isn't he learning all about cookery as well and knows how to make Danish omelettes.'

The neighbours looked down from their eyries in awe and even the Jewish family with the three pretty but unmarried daughters were casting looks in his direction and wondering about possibilities. Now Billy had a pensionable job in view, they were prepared to forget his plum-dropping days when as a callow youth he had released succulent Victorias like bombs from the veranda onto their unsuspecting heads. They were ready to put it behind them and forge new friendly relationships. He might be a good catch despite his Catholic religion. Though some Jewish families might have considered his faith a serious disadvantage, they knew it could soon be rectified – a quick flick of the scalpel in the Beth Shalom synagogue would make him perfectly acceptable as a husband.

Billy strutted past the tenements with his head held high and tried to look intellectual and learned as befitted a local hero.

Christmas Day was a quiet affair. Billy went to early Mass with his mam, whilst Dad remained at home reading yesterday's *Daily Dispatch*. He had given up going to church a long time ago and he preferred to celebrate the birth of Christ in the Queen's Arms. Then, for Billy, it was helping to peel the spuds and to prepare the usual magnificent turkey dinner that would have graced the table of a king. At three o'clock, they listened to King George giving his speech to the Empire, after which the old couple retired to bed for a snooze whilst Billy dozed off, half listening to Henry Hall on the Light Programme.

In the evening, Mam applied a touch of lipstick and a smidgen of face powder and, dressed up in her new velvet blouse to which she had pinned her new brooch bearing the title 'MOTHER' (a present from Flo), in case anyone was in doubt as to her social status, she accompanied Dad to the local for a celebratory sing-song. Billy lay on their bright new rag rug with a box of chocolates trying to unravel the intricacies of Dryden's *Absalom and Achitophel*.

'Are you sure you're going to be all right, Billy?' Mam asked as they prepared to leave. 'I mean, it doesn't seem right you should be studying on Christmas night. You should be out enjoying yourself.'

'I'd rather be here, Mam, than anywhere else in the world. I have chocolates, a book and there's Tommy Handley in *It's That Man Again* on the wireless. What greater happiness is there?'

'Sometimes I worry about that lad,' she said to Dad as they descended the stairs.

'Nah, he'll be OK,' he answered, 'as long as he doesn't get ideas above his station.'

Christmas may have been quiet in the Hopkins household but Boxing Day saw a gathering of the clans. It was a great opportunity to catch up on everyone's news. Les was still in the army and hoping to be demobbed within two years. Sam had meanwhile married May Breslin, a beautiful girl from Ulster, and was planning to settle down in Belfast. Flo, his big sister, and her husband Barry, had brought their two children whilst Polly and Steve were with their four –

106

Billy was godfather to their youngest daughter, Kathleen. The small flat seemed to be bursting at the seams but that didn't stop the sing-song and the drinks from flowing, especially for Dad, who was putting it away like there was no tomorrow.

'I hate this stuff,' he said as he poured down yet another pint. 'I wouldn't give you a penny a bucket for it.'

'I'm sure we believe him,' Mam said, addressing the family gathered round the table. 'I'm not joking, he'd drink a brewery dry if he had the chance. When I win Littlewood's, I'll buy him a brewery and lock him up in one of the rooms.'

'Now, Kate,' he said. 'You know very well that's not true. I'd like to say a few words to the company here 'cos it's not often that we're together like what we are today. My son Billy's home from that there college in London and I want to say how proud we are of him today. I've always encouraged him to make something of hisself.'

'You've done nowt of the sort,' Mam interjected. 'You've always been against him going to college. If it'd been left to you, he'd be a mechanic's mate in Henery Wallworks.'

'Now, now, Kate. No need to be like that. There's nowt wrong with being a mechanic's mate, it's good, honest work. I know I've worked hard all my life – worked my fingers to the bone for this family.'

'And look what you've got to show for it,' she said. 'Nowt but bony fingers.'

'I've always tried to do what's best for 'em all, I have. I want my kids to grow up nice and friendly, and able to get on with other people. Not to get above themselves and think they're better than the rest of us. I don't want our Billy there to become a snob and go over to the enemy – the toffs. He mustn't get too big for his boots, that's all I'm saying. As long as he doesn't go giving himself airs, I don't mind him going to college. But in my opinion, book-learning never got nobody nowhere. It's skill with your hands that counts.'

'The only skill with your hands you've ever had,' she said, 'has been raising a glass to your lips. The whole family could've gone to college, even the girls, but you've been too fond of the bevy. You've drunk enough beer in your life to float the Royal Navy.'

'I've allus fed my family,' he protested. 'And I've never stole a penny from nobody and I could've stole thousands in my job, I could.'

'I suppose that's true,' she conceded. 'But you've never stole 'cos you've been too frightened of getting caught and being sent to the clink.'

'You're a hard woman, Kate. But you've been a good wife, a good 'un and I knew what I was doing the day I married you. I want to say to the company here today that getting a good partner is half your life. If you pick a bad 'un, your life isn't worth a light. And lastly, I want to wish everyone all the best for Christmas and a Happy New Year.'

'You're a bit late. Christmas has gone,' she said. 'And it's not New Year till next week so you're too early.'

Despite Mam's heckling, Dad's speech earned him a round of applause which made him so pleased and excited, he had to have one of his hated buckets of beer to calm him down.

At some stage, Billy found himself in conversation with Steve Keenan, the brother-in-law who had done so much to encourage him in his career.

'We knew you'd love college, Billy, once you got used to it,' remarked Steve, now a senior executive at Metro Vicks. 'It should be downhill from here to final qualification. I can see we'll be coming to you to borrow money.'

'You were right about the college, Steve,' Billy replied. 'At first I found it strange and I didn't like it one bit but after a few weeks, I finally settled down. But I'm not so sure about its being downhill. There's still an incredible amount of work to do – our lectures are proper slave-drivers. As for me lending you money, I should live so long.'

Steve laughed at Billy's Yiddish mannerism. 'Incidentally,' he continued, 'we now live in Clifton Street and there's a certain beautiful girl called Adele who's constantly asking after you. I'd say she's pretty keen. Maybe you ought to look her up.'

'I think Mam's been talking to you. She thinks I'm working too hard and should get out more.'

'Maybe she's right.'

On New Year's Eve, Billy dressed up in his best suit – his only suit – and wandered over to Harrigan's Dance Academy for the Hogmanay Ball. He treasured many happy memories of the place and he was excited at the prospect of meeting the old crowd again.

The place was heaving when he arrived but he soon found them. Oh, it was so good to see all the old familiar faces! Adele, as glamorous as ever, and Duggie Doyle; Lucy with her fiancé, Roy; Freda Pritchard and her boyfriend, Charlie Henshaw; Lofty O'Malley, the bouncer; and old Mrs Harrigan who seemed to get smaller each time he saw her. He waved and greeted them all happily.

'Great to see you all again,' he said warmly.

'Good evenin', Billy,' Adele said. 'We thought you'd deserted us and mixed only with the higher-ups now.'

'No chance,' Billy replied. 'I can't tell you how much

I've been looking forward to tonight and meeting you all again. I've really missed you lot. And thanks, Adele, for all those letters you wrote to me. In the early days at college, they were my lifeline.'

Freda said, 'You've lost your Manchester accent and no mistake.'

'He talks like a toff with a plum in his mouth,' Duggie said. He imitated Billy's so-called posh accent. 'In my orly days at college, they were my lahfline, don'cha know.'

Billy smiled good-humouredly and joined in the laughter. 'If I've lost my accent,' he grinned, 'it must have happened when I wasn't looking. I'll try to find it again.'

'Whatever you do, don't get toffee-nosed and stuck up,' Lucy added.

'As the actress said to the bishop,' leered Duggie.

This last aside caused a fit of giggles from the group.

'Oh, you are awful, Duggie,' Freda simpered.

'Nothing like that,' Billy said in answer to Lucy's remark. 'I'm training to be a teacher not the Prince of Wales.'

'I'll bet you find living in London exciting,' remarked Adele. 'Do you get out much to enjoy the bright lights and all that?'

'Not much but I've taken up dancing in a private studio in Kensington,' Billy answered. 'The standard's quite good and it helps to get me out of college at—'

'Yeah, yeah, yeah,' sneered Duggie, yawning loudly. 'All very interesting, I'm sure. I'm surprised you're even talking to country yokels like us.'

'I'm not like that,' replied Billy evenly. 'I'm a Mancunian and proud of it.'

'Hark at him!' leered Charlie Henshaw. 'Using big words – Mancunian! We're just elementary school types and don't understand words of more than one syllable, do we, Freda?'

'Don't ask me,' said Freda. 'I'm just an ignorant skivvy in a biscuit factory.'

'What subjects are you studying then?' asked Roy who seemed more serious than the rest.

'Books, reading and all that guff – women's stuff!' Duggie announced, barging across them.

'Various subjects,' Billy replied, ignoring Duggie's jibe. I've got to tread carefully here and play it down, he thought. Must avoid giving the impression of showing off. 'English, for one,' he said modestly.

'You mean Shakespeare and all that Hey Nonny Nonny crap?' Duggie snickered. 'Romeo, Romeo, wherefore art thou, Romeo? What bloody tripe it is.'

'I don't think Shakespeare is considered tripe by most people,' Billy said quietly, 'but we're studying more modern literature as well.' He didn't like the way things were going.

'You like to keep abreast of the times like,' he heard Duggie saying. 'Like Adele there.'

'Oh, Duggie!' Adele said, laughing heartily and digging him playfully in the ribs. 'You're a real card. Don't you think so, Billy?'

'He's a card all right,' agreed Billy, trying to look enthusiastic. 'The life and soul of the party.'

'All that studying,' commented Lucy. 'You must find it hard.'

'As the bishop said to the actress,' smirked Duggie. Like lightning with his wisecracks.

Another fit of sniggering.

'Not so hard,' Billy replied naïvely. 'Once you get used to it.'

'As the actress said to the bishop,' Duggie sneered.

The girls were beside themselves with laughter. Such a wit, such a wit.

If he mentions that bloody bishop or that actress again, thought Billy, I'll ram his yellow teeth down his throat.

'What other subjects are you doing, apart from English, I mean?' Roy asked.

'History and French.'

Duggie was in quick. 'So those things you were writing to Adele were really French letters?'

The group doubled up.

'That's a new one on me,' said Charlie Henshaw. 'As the monkey said when it scratched its back.'

More sniggering.

What's happening? Billy thought. They're shoving me out – giving me the elbow.

'Come on, Adele,' Duggy announced. 'Let's dance, for God's sake – all this highbrow talk's a bit too much for me.'

The music struck up with a slow foxtrot and two of the couples got up to dance, leaving Billy with Freda and Charlie.

'Anyroad, you guys,' Billy said to them, trying his best to play down any snooty accent he might unknowingly have acquired, 'you don't know how much I've longed for this night, just to be back in—'

'See that feather step?' Freda said abruptly, cutting across him and pointing to Adele and Duggie. 'Bloody useless. No contrary body movement. Duggie bends from the waist instead of using his whole body. Hasn't a clue. And as for Adele there, look at those terrible heel turns. She moves like a soldier on parade.'

'Yeah,' said Charlie. 'She's all over the place.'

Billy remained silent, unable to contribute to those spiteful comments. He was hurting at being snubbed so brusquely. Suddenly he thought, what the hell am I doing

112

here? I'm obviously not accepted any more. What's going on? I feel utterly lost.

Around eleven o'clock, he made his excuses.

'You mean you're not staying to see the New Year in?' Adele protested. 'You can't leave us now. Stay till twelve o'clock.'

'Sorry, Adele,' he said. 'I promised the old folk I'd let the New Year in at home – me being dark-haired and all that.'

'Let him go,' Duggie said. 'Let him get back to his French letters and his Shakespeare shit.'

Billy spotted Lofty O'Malley and old Mrs Harrigan at the other end of the ballroom and as he raised his hand to wave goodbye to them, he accidentally caught Duggie a smack on the side of his head. Billy had lost none of his old boxing skills.

'Sorry, Duggie,' he said. 'Hope I didn't hurt you.' As he was leaving, he added, 'As the bishop said to the actress. Goodnight, everyone, and Happy New Year!'

Outside, he put on his overcoat and raised the collar against a cold wind. He felt depressed. What on earth is happening to me? I so looked forward to this evening and to meeting my old friends again but I couldn't win no matter how hard I tried. Adele was perhaps a little more friendly but not much.

He walked down Queen's Road, bewildered and gnawed by self-doubt. I really got the cold shoulder tonight from the gang – I felt like the odd man out. And they made it abundantly clear that I no longer belonged. But then, where *do* I belong? I seem to be trapped between two worlds, my home background and the academic world in London, and at the moment I feel as if I don't fully belong in either – like one of those stateless people you read about sometimes.

Wait a minute, though. He stopped in his tracks. Perhaps, without realising it, I *am* becoming lah-de-dah! In God's name, I hope not 'cos that's *the* cardinal sin in my family – getting too big for your britches. He quickened his pace. No, not a chance. If I *am* getting above myself, Mam will soon put me in my place and cut me down to size. So will Dad for that matter, especially Dad. But *something's* happening and I don't understand what. Harrigan's the same place and it's the same old crowd all right – none of *them* have changed. But then, maybe *I* have.

Chapter Eleven

Soap and education are not as sudden as a
massacre, but they are more deadly in the
long run.

Mark Twain, A Curious Dream

The first term of the second year was devoted exclusively to
the final teaching practice and the preparation for it. They
had a brief introduction to schools in their first year but this
had been mainly observation and not real teaching. Now all
that they'd been learning was to be put into practice in a real
school with real children.

In the run-up to the practice, they had many 'down-to-
earth' lectures and there was no shortage of advice and
warnings, all of which served to make the students even
more nervous.

'Remember,' said Taffy, 'you are a model for your
pupils; they will watch every move you make and imitate
you. In morals, in your speech, in your demeanour, in
your dress, you will be setting an example for them to
copy. Not only the conscious things you do and say but the
unconscious way you behave. If they see you smoking,
they will ape you. If you say "Damn" when you drop

something, they will emulate you.'

The student body listened spellbound.

'This means you must stop picking your nose,' Billy whispered to Titch.

'And Pottsy must stop blowing bubbles,' Titch whispered back.

'I cannot emphasise enough,' Taffy continued, 'the importance of body language. Avoid displaying weak body postures, such as slouching, or sitting on your desk swinging a leg or, worse, crossing your legs.'

'I certainly agree with the last,' whispered Nobby. 'It's been the worst feature of some of the girls I've met.'

'Imagine your first lesson,' said Taffy. 'The class haven't yet made up their minds about you. They are waiting for Jackie Green, the chief troublemaker and clown, to plumb your depths and sound you out. After the novelty of weighing you up has worn off, the test will come. It's like going into the lion's den. How will you deal with it? Will you be a lion-tamer or a Sigmund Freud? Assert your authority and control by adopting a dominant posture such as standing upright or with your arms akimbo. Fingertips touching in church steeple fashion illustrates a confident attitude.'

'I love dominant men,' murmured Oscar.

'We come now to the matter of dress,' Taffy said. 'I know schools can become grubby places but it pays to look as if you're efficient. Wear a suit. See that you haven't any buttons loose or undone, especially your flies; don't have clothes with stains on them and tone down your colour schemes.'

The student body became busy examining their dress for stains and loose buttons and they realised that something would have to be done about their grubby corduroys and faded shirts.

Taffy went on, 'Finally check your personal image. Avoid beards and moustaches. See if your breath smells – you will be leaning over children. Avoid mannerisms like chin-stroking, polishing glasses, juggling chalk and hand-rubbing.'

'We shall look like tailor's dummies,' remarked Billy as they filed out of the lecture.

Next on the agenda was role-playing teaching sessions.

'Introduce your lessons,' Jock Lenzie, the English lecturer, advised, 'by linking your subject to the children's immediate experience so that they can relate to your subject.'

Titch was first victim chosen to present a lesson.

'Very well, children,' he said, addressing his fellow students. 'What did you have for breakfast this morning?'

'Porridge,' Billy replied promptly.

'Bacon and egg,' answered Ollie.

'Bread and peanut butter,' volunteered Elder.

'Yes, yes, and what else?' urged Titch desperately.

'Tea and toast,' said Oscar brightly.

'Orange juice,' Pottsy offered.

'Milk,' said Nobby.

'OK, OK,' said Titch. 'Well, I'm going to talk about coffee, see.'

Towards the end of the term the allocation of schools for the final teaching practice was posted on the college noticeboard and there was a mad rush of students all eager to find out their fate. The college authorities had made special provision for the Catholic students and arranged places in denominational schools. Billy found he was to be with Jack Elder in a small Catholic school in Cadogan Square in the World's End district – a poor, rundown area

117

off the King's Road on the outskirts of Chelsea. It was an old-fashioned school in a ramshackle building with only three classes and all teachers were required to teach English, arithmetic, history, geography, drill, art and music.

They presented themselves at the headmaster's office on the first morning and even Elder, the D-Day hero, was nervous.

'I only hope the little buggers are well-behaved,' he said.

James Farrell, the headmaster, turned out to be a stern figure who looked and talked like Will Hay. He was, however, kindly disposed towards his two students as they were the first the school had ever received and he felt honoured that his school had been selected.

'I believe in firm discipline in my school,' he said. 'Without order and obedience, no teaching can take place. The children are not allowed to talk in class – not under any circumstances. When "Sir" is talking, they must sit still and listen.'

Billy was given a class of eight- to ten-year-olds. Mrs McBride, the class teacher, was a kindly, matronly old soul who took pity on him, a skinny eighteen-year-old, and did everything in her power to jolly him along and help him overcome his nervousness. The boys and girls were well-mannered and obedient, one might say docile, and their classroom was a homely affair with a cheerful fire warming not only his backside but also the daily crate of free milk that was deposited nearby to thaw out.

Billy prepared his lessons thoroughly and taught them all subjects.

When it came to history, he found that back at college there was a well-equipped visual aids library and so was able to enliven his lessons with colourful pictures. He taught

118

them about Perkin Warbeck and Lambert Simnel and captured their interest with stories about the Princes in the Tower. In the classroom next door, he could hear the gruff voice of Corporal Elder instructing his charges.

'Right, you little buggers, watch your step with me. You be nice to me and I'll be nice to you. You can choose the hard way or the easy way. If you want to play it rough, I can be rough as well. Now, we're going down to the school yard for drill and I'm gonna show you how we did it in the army. Now shaddup, you little bastards. I want some bloody 'ush before we move.'

The final inspection came towards the end of the practice.

Mr Farrell addressed Billy's class. 'Now we are going to have some important people visit the school and I want all of you to be on your best behaviour. You will sit still – there will be no fidgeting and no talking. As soon as the inspector comes into the room, you will stand to attention and say "Good Morning, sir." What will you say?'

'Good morning, sir,' they chorused.

'You will sit down when you are told to sit and when Mr Hopkins here asks a question, you will raise your hand and there will be no calling out. Give your best answer and don't forget to call him "sir". Woe betide anyone who is reported to me. Now fingers on lips while I talk to Mr Hopkins.'

The children placed index fingers on their lips.

'Now, Mr Hopkins,' said Mr Farrell. 'Give your best lesson for the inspector and if any of these children cause you the slightest trouble, I want to know immediately.'

'Right, Mr Farrell,' Billy replied, 'but I don't think you need worry on that score. Their behaviour is always exemplary.'

The inspection passed happily enough, with the children behaving beautifully and answering intelligently. A relieved Billy thanked the visiting examiner who complimented him on his imaginative teaching and hinted that he would be given an above-average grade.

'Well, how did it go?' asked the headmaster when the inspector had gone.

'Fine,' Billy answered. 'No problems.'

'Everyone well-behaved, I trust?' the head asked.

'Perfect,' Billy answered. 'The class answered well. One small boy was very bright when he queried one of the things I was telling them.'

'What happened?' he asked brusquely.

'It was good,' Billy said. 'I'd told them about the Princes in the Tower and how they were bricked up secretly by their wicked uncle. Then one of the boys raised his hand.'

'Raised his hand without being asked,' said Mr Farrell aghast. 'How dare he?'

'It was OK,' said Billy. 'He wanted to know how the uncle could brick them up without telling a bricklayer his secret and he might tell other people. His father's a bricklayer, you know, and that's probably why he wanted to know.'

'Give me the boy's name,' he demanded. 'I told them to speak only when asked a question. This is a breach of discipline.'

'It was nothing, Mr Farrell,' Billy protested. 'I was only too pleased that he'd asked the question. It showed he was thinking about it.'

'I must have his name,' he insisted. 'Suppose you hadn't known the answer. Why, he could have ruined your whole lesson. We can't tolerate even the slightest indiscipline. It must be nipped in the bud.'

He pressed Billy and then ordered him. Reluctantly, Billy gave the young boy's name, Martin O'Dwyer. Surely, Billy thought, Mr Farrell wouldn't punish the boy for daring to ask a question.

That afternoon Martin was called to the head's room and given a severe caning on both hands. The rest of the class looked wonderingly and accusingly at Billy and he felt like a traitor.

Young Martin's return to class was a scene straight out of *Hard Times*. The little lad came back with great tears glistening in his eyes and he looked at Billy with sadness and bewilderment that he had been punished so harshly for trying to join in the lesson.

His face haunted Billy for the rest of his time at college.

Despite that heart-wrenching event, the practice was a happy one and at the end of the Christmas term, Jack Elder and Billy went back by invitation to a joyous Christmas party with lots of cake, jelly and carol-singing. Mrs McBride gave him twenty Players, a smiling Martin O'Dwyer presented him with a pound box of Cadburys – a gift from the whole class – and Mr Farrell shoved a ten shilling note in his hand and told him to spend it on a good meal. Billy blew this small fortune on a dinner of Vienna steak and chips for Titch and himself at the Blue Star, followed by a visit to the Regal cinema to see James Mason in *Odd Man Out*.

Nineteen forty-seven came in with the worst winter of the century. The central heating system of the college was permanently out of action because of shortage of fuel and the students found it almost impossible to keep warm. There was no alternative but to get into bed and study with the blankets wrapped around them. Needless to say, Pottsy was

121

the most popular student on the block because of his illicit electric fire and his record player. There was invariably a crowd gathered around his amenities until Pottsy, patient and generous though he was, had to lock his door to keep visitors at bay. 'Look, fellas,' he would call, 'give me a break. I have my own work to do.'

Despite the severe cold, Billy and his companions fell into a comfortable routine. During the week they worked hard to keep up with the reading and the endless stream of essays they were required to write. But at weekends, it was different. They relaxed. Billy became a familiar face at the Kensington High Street dance studio. He continued to dance with Doris and on one never-to-be-forgotten occasion in February he was invited back to the Chiswick flat to meet her husband, Harry, who had been finally released from the RAF. It was a happy occasion and Billy made short work of the mountains of scones with which they plied him.

Life was so busy that time flew by. The weeks became months, and the months a year. Before they knew it, the end of the course loomed up. Billy reviewed his two years. What had he learned? he asked himself. A bric-a-brac of facts.

He knew about Hopper windows and about the goodness of milk – tuberculin tested of course – which was reckoned to be the finest food in the world; about rickets, ringworm, adiposity, and the different kinds of mental defectives.

In a memorable lecture he and his companions had learned that there were different kinds of bad body posture.

'Note the different kinds of spinal abnormalities you should look out for in your pupils,' said Taffy. 'Kyphosis is a condition in which the back is hunched and bent. Lordosis, an abnormal convex curvature of the spine; and scoliosis, a lateral spinal curvature.'

'Kyphosis perfectly describes my condition,' said Billy as they left the lecture theatre.

'I claim Lord Osis,' Pottsy said.

'Nonsense!' Ollie retorted. 'What you have is Potts' Disease. Now me, I suffer from scoliosis – the result of scanning books sideways on library shelves.'

'I claim all three,' said Titch. 'They explain my peculiar gait.'

'None of these matters a damn,' said Oscar. 'Now, what I have is truly important, namely ankylosis of the sacroiliac.'

'Trust you to have a posh-sounding abnormality,' said Nobby. 'It's just a fancy way of saying backache. As for me, I'm pleased to announce that I have none of 'em. Which explains why I'm so attractive to the opposite sex.'

In their education course they heard about Sir Cyril Norwood, a classical scholar and ex-headmaster of Harrow, and his government report on secondary education. According to Cyril and his hero, the Greek philosopher Plato, human beings were of three types – golden, silver and copper. Golden children would go to grammar schools for an academic education; silver children with a practical bent would go to technical schools; finally the copper children – the vast majority of the nation's children – would go to secondary modern schools where they would receive a more concrete type of education.

'Obviously a school suited for navvies on a building site,' remarked Oscar.

For this last type, there would be no exams and the project method, that is building models or looking after animals, would be the best thing. Selection in this tripartite system of education would no longer be dependent on purse

123

strings, pulling strings or the old school tie but would be determined by means of the new intelligence tests in an exam called the Eleven Plus.

What nonsense this snooty view of human nature is, Billy thought. None of it squares up with my real-life experience of children and schools. But although he and his companions had serious doubts about this doctrinaire guff, they had no choice but to comply if they hoped to be accepted into the teaching profession.

May 1947 was the start of a glorious summer but for the students it was a time to get down to the serious business of swotting for final exams. Titch and Billy learned prepared answers off pat and after dinner strolled round the college grounds reciting to each other parrot fashion what they had memorised.

'OK, Titch, you give me the role of William of Orange in the struggle of the Netherlands against Spain.'

Titch duly reeled it off. Then he'd say: 'Right, Hoppy, now you evaluate Garibaldi's contribution to the cause of Italian unification.'

Billy would comply and ask him the next question as they walked round the fields and puffed at their fags. Education for them meant regurgitation. How much easier the task would be, they thought, if they'd had some idea of the questions in advance.

Help was at hand.

The annual inter-college sports day came round in May, and that year was held at Borough Road College, Isleworth. Attendance at this event was always excellent by the sporting and non-sporting fraternity alike for the simple reason that it was the occasion for swapping inside information on the exam topics that were likely to come up. Students from St Mary's (Simmaries) of Strawberry

Hill had the hottest tips and they were listened to with great respect. After all, their priest/lecturers would hardly tell them fibs. Students armed with notepads and pencils wandered about like stockbrokers from group to group exchanging hints and clues, and bartering possibilities. Indeed, the whole affair had much in common with business on the stock exchange floor, for many of the transactions that day were based on hope, fear, and rumour. Scant attention was paid to the sporting competitions, though the Anglican Marjons wondered why the Catholic Simmarian high-jumpers insisted on passing a holy medal from hand to hand in the hope that angels might bear them that little higher over the bar. In the end, the event was won by the Marjon candidate who, whilst deficient in holy medals, had extraordinarily long legs.

They returned to college elated like fishermen with full nets. Pottsy, who had been gated for returning after 11p.m. at the weekend and had missed the sports meeting, sought them out eagerly.

'Have you got the questions?' he implored.

'No problem, Pottsy,' they said. 'We'll dictate them to you.'

'Oh, great,' he said, pen hovering over his notebook.

'Right. First in education,' said Titch. ' "Describe how you would organise a children's party in a deaf and dumb school. Your answer should give details of food and games required as well as the various roles to be played by members of staff." '

'Do you think we'll get that?' asked Pottsy doubtfully.

'A sure thing,' said Ollie. 'Next, "Evaluate the role of the caretaker's assistant in a secondary modern school in a deprived district." That's a definite.'

'I'm not sure I'd go for that question. It's got me stumped,' said Pottsy.

'The next one is easier,' Billy said. ' "How would you teach logarithms in the dark?" That's straight from the horse's mouth, from a Simmarian.'

'Finally,' added Oscar, 'the easiest one of them all. "How would you teach history backwards?" '

'Come off it,' Pottsy protested as the penny dropped. 'You lot never take anything seriously.'

Soon after the inter-college sports, it was time for examinations. Outside, the sun shone from a glorious blue sky, the college gardens were at their best with their superb billiard-top lawns, the air was scented by a profusion of flowers and beautiful plants, birds sang from every tree. But inside the musty halls, nothing was to be heard but the scratching of pens on paper as the students wrote their finals. Nerves and first-day anxieties were soon left behind as they poured out and regurgitated the vast amounts of knowledge they had spent two years stacking into their heads. At the end of three weeks, they emerged from the stuffy rooms punch-drunk, their heads reeling but feeling distinctly lighter having unburdened themselves of the facts and theories so painstakingly acquired over so many anguished days and nights.

From that point on, it was downhill, for there followed a wonderful last week in college. First a performance of Shakespeare's *Measure for Measure*. They loved the lines:

'What's he done?'

'A woman.'

And: 'Groping for trout in a peculiar river.'

In the chapel, a mixed choir of students gave a memorable performance of Handel's *Messiah* but the culmination of that last week came on the last but one night in Chelsea. Billy and his Entertainments Committee organised a magnificent formal college ball.

It was a black tie and evening dress affair, and a ten-piece orchestra was hired. The beautifully dressed young ladies from Whitelands graced the hall with their presence and as the dancers whirled about the maple-floored assembly hall, the scene was more reminiscent of a Viennese ballroom than a London training college. Doris appeared with her husband and Billy's heart turned over with pride when he saw her. She was dressed in a ravishing white evening gown and in her dark hair she wore a single white flower.

'I want to thank you, Billy,' said Harry, 'for looking after Doris for me whilst I was in Malta. I know how much she loves her dancing. As I think she may have told you, I'm no dancer, though from now on I hope to start learning. But tonight, she's all yours . . .' Then he added quickly, 'Just for the dancing, that is.'

Laughing, Doris and Billy thanked him and turned their attention to their dancing students and were gratified to see them gliding so easily and smoothly across the floor with their glamorous partners.

Jack Elder gave them both a smile of welcome and a thumbs-up as he danced lightly by with his Amazonian partner. From the way he moved and handled himself, he seemed to have become a different person. More of a gentleman than the man who had joined the college two years ago.

'Well, Doris, it looks as if our two years' instruction has paid off in the end,' Billy said.

'I've enjoyed every moment,' she replied.

Then, watched admiringly by students and staff, they

danced easily and gracefully across the floor to the melody of 'I'll Buy That Dream'. A truly wonderful and triumphant evening.

It was not the end of the final festivities, however. In the hope of making them forget the loathsome food they had suffered for two years, the college arranged an exquisite formal dinner with the menu printed in French which, despite their two years' study of that language, nobody fully understood though they made out that *Coupe Robert* was ice cream prepared by a chef named Robert.

Next day, there followed much hand-shaking, back-slapping, tearful farewells, and vows to stay in touch, and before they knew it they were on the train back to Manchester.

The journey back was something of an anticlimax – quiet and ruminative.

'And so – it's over,' Oscar announced to no one in particular. 'What *was* it all about?'

'We're teachers,' answered Pottsy. 'At least, I hope we are.'

'As the London bus conductor put it so beautifully,' said Billy, 'God help poor old England!'

Chapter Twelve

1947

The year 1947 was momentous in Britain's history. February saw the severest winter of the century and this, combined with serious fuel shortages and transport strikes, brought the country to its economic knees. Banks, government offices and even Buckingham Palace were candlelit. Food rations were cut to the bone and austerity was the rule of the day. In a complete bucking of the trend and in spite of clothes rationing, Christian Dior introduced his New Look with its hour-glass shape and extravagant use of material, much to the delight of the ladies (and most of the men) and to the dismay of Hugh Dalton, the Chancellor of the Exchequer. Meanwhile, under Lord Mountbatten, India was partitioned and granted independence after 163 years of British rule, and shortly afterwards Mahatma Gandhi was shot dead. The marriage of Princess Elizabeth to Mountbatten's nephew, the Greek prince Lieutenant Philip, was announced, and in that summer of brilliant sunshine, Denis Compton ended the cricket season with record-breaking runs and centuries.

It was in that same glorious summer that the Damian College crowd finished their teacher training and travelled back to their beloved Manchester, their Athens of the North as they liked to call it.

Titch and Billy began their long vacation by looking for jobs to fill in the time until their future plans were settled. Jobs were easy to come by in that era of postwar reconstruction and a bright future and great possibilities lay ahead. It was a time of great hope and happiness, and everywhere there was a buoyant, optimistic atmosphere. The war was over and the British lion was licking its wounds. The world was their oyster! What joy to be young! What joy to be alive!

In due course, they presented themselves at the Labour Exchange in the city centre. The clerk who dealt with them was the same man who had interviewed Billy in the Juvenile Employment Bureau all those years ago in 1944, now obviously promoted as here he was dealing with adults.

'So you're both looking for a temporary job?' he said.

'If possible,' Billy said. 'Two jobs – one each.'

He looked at him quizzically. 'I seem to know you from somewhere,' he murmured. 'Anyway, here's a temporary job at Sherman's.'

'You mean making tanks?' Billy replied. 'I thought the war was over.'

'Now I remember you. You were the comedian who went to work on the *Manchester Guardian*.'

'That's right,' Billy replied. 'Now my friend and I are looking for a couple of holiday jobs to fill in the time before we take up full-time occupations – probably in the army.'

'Right. Got it,' the clerk said. 'Tanks indeed. No, the Sherman's we're talking about are Sherman's Pools and they're looking for one or two salesmen to promote their coupons. Pay is five pounds per week – no commission.'

'We'll take it,' said Titch quickly before Billy could blow their chances with a witty riposte.

They walked across Manchester until they reached a rickety old building which the Luftwaffe had not quite finished off. At the top of a wooden staircase, they walked along a dusty corridor to a poky little office where they found a hump-backed, bald-headed dwarf – most like Grumpy if one had to select one of the seven. In sepulchral tones, the old fellow recited the requirements of the job.

'Your task will be to persuade the punters to stop betting with Littlewoods and Vernons and to take our coupons instead. You have to collect two shillings from each punter. One shilling is tax, one shilling for the coupon. We pay you five pounds a week and we expect you to get at least five customers a day. We pay you on Friday but you hand your takings in to us every day at this office. Here is a supply of coupons. Good morning.' And he began to usher them out of his office.

'Wait a moment, slow down,' protested Titch. 'Do I understand you to say that we must sell the idea of Sherman's to new customers? And that we collect two shillings from each one of them?'

'Yes, yes,' he answered irritably, anxious to get back to Jane and the *Daily Mirror* crossword.

'And the minimum number per day for each of us is five customers, that is ten shillings per day,' added Billy.

'That is what I said,' he barked. 'You should wash your ears out.'

'And the weekly pay is five pounds a week?' asked Titch.

'Yes, yes, yes,' he snapped. 'Do you want me to give it

to you printed in red on parchment?'

'OK, OK,' said Billy. 'We're only checking. Keep your hair on.' Not that he had much to keep on.

Grumpy snorted and closed the door behind them as if they had disturbed him by being there, bothering him with stupid questions.

It was an attractive temporary job. They could choose their own hours, they were out in the fresh air, and it meant handling money – a new experience for both of them. Billy loved the feel of it and he hoped that some day he might have some of his own. They retired to a café for tea and toast and to lay out their plans for trapping unwary victims. The important thing, they guessed, in selling Sherman's coupons was to appeal to the customer's greed and to awaken visions of the untold riches which were waiting to be won every Saturday. Why Sherman's coupons, though? What did they have over their rivals? Answer: they were smaller and promised better chances. Their punters were buying dreams and fantasies for a couple of bob. We can't miss, they thought.

They decided to try their luck in Davyhulme along Lostock Road – cold calling, the trade called it. They descended on the unsuspecting housewives with their coupons. Titch had developed, after much practice before a mirror, the ploy of raising his newly acquired trilby, revealing his rapidly thinning hair which he thought gave him a look of maturity. He followed the hat-raising trick with a bright, 'Good morning, madam. I'm here to offer you a golden opportunity to make your fortune.'

He went into his spiel and explained fully and patiently what it was about.

'The reason you're being asked to pay this two bob is because of government regulations – nothing to do with us. Now, we're not offering these coupons to everyone down this road – there's some right riffraff here, I tell you. No, you've been specially selected as worthy of this honour.'

One or two comely wenches still in their nightgowns responded warmly.

'My husband's at work, luv. Won't be back till tonight. Do you want to come in for a bit – rest your feet, like?'

'Wonder what she meant by "bit",' Titch would remark.

It didn't happen often but the two young men were having none of that.

More usually they heard: 'Oh, I daren't take football coupons without asking my hubby. Come back after six o'clock.' They met with this response over and over again.

One or two were nasty and slammed the door in their faces. 'Bugger off,' they'd bawl through the letter box, 'before I set the dog on you.'

From such warm welcomes, they beat a hasty retreat.

After six hours' work and after calling on more than a hundred households, they had barely succeeded in making the day's quota of five coupons each. Triumphantly, they reported back to Grumps, each with their ten shillings.

'Only five customers each?' he grumbled after receiving their takings and giving them a receipt. 'You're not trying hard enough. But it meets the minimum requirement.'

With wobbly legs and aching feet, they retired to a café for a cuppa.

'Not trying hard enough. I like that,' Titch said. 'I'm sure I've worn my legs down. I feel like Toulouse Lautrec.'

They sipped their tea. Then the penny dropped.

'Wait a minute, Titch,' Billy said suddenly. 'We earn

five pounds a week and therefore we've earned one pound today. Are my calculations correct?'

'Correct.'

'After walking miles round Davyhulme, we have each managed to raise the required ten shillings.'

'Correct. So?'

'But we have earned one pound for our efforts.'

Titch smiled. 'So we don't need to use up all that shoe leather. We can simply hand in five names along with ten shillings and receive a pound for our trouble.'

'Exactly. Tell me an investment that will double your money every day.'

From that point on, they began their day in the local billiard hall where they consulted the telephone directory to pick ten names at random. After organising Sherman's coupons for the whole of Marjon's staff, they gave priority to names of the clergy listed under the churches, especially Nonconformists, since they knew that many ministers subscribed to Calvinist ethics and were opposed to betting on the basis that it was wrong to get something for nothing. 'By the sweat of thy brow shalt thou eat thy bread' was the rule by which such vicars lived.

That was precisely what Billy and Titch weren't doing – unless you count writing out ten names and addresses as sweaty work. After a week of this onerous calligraphic exercise, they went into town, collected their five pound weekly wage, and after celebrating their good fortune with the customary tea and toast, went their separate ways rejoicing.

Feeling flush on Fridays, Billy took to calling in at a specialist tobacconist on Peter Street to buy a twenty-packet of Passing Cloud because he liked the taste and oval shape of the cigarettes but also because of the illustration on the pink packet – the picture of the man having hallucinations.

It was on one of these Friday nights that he ran into Adele and her mother. They were waiting for the 62 bus in Albert Square and he joined them in the queue.

Adele gave him an enthusiastic wave and her mother smiled in recognition.

'Hello, Billy,' Adele called. 'Haven't seen you in a long time. Where've you been hiding?'

Adele looked as glamorous as ever in her bright red New Look coat and matching hat, with her auburn shoulder-length hair and her round blue eyes; she resembled the girl in a *Vogue* advertisement who was always being given expensive presents or stepping into the latest Rolls *coupé de ville* with a pedigree Pekinese under her arm.

'Oh, I've been pretty busy lately, working for a living,' said Billy.

'Why haven't you been to see me?' she pouted.

'I've only been back a week and my first need was to get some cash in my pocket. But I thought you were going around with Duggie Doyle. What happened to him and your dancing partnership?'

'Oh, with Duggie it's on and off. But I'm free now,' she added, giving her shy little-girl look.

'Why don't you ask Billy to tea?' suggested her mother.

'There you are, Billy. You've got an invite. Come back home with us.'

'Invite accepted,' Billy said. 'I'll have to tell them back home first though as they're expecting me.'

The two ladies alighted at Queen's Road and Billy continued to St Luke's Church. As he walked down Smedley Lane towards the Gardenia Court tenement, he wondered if he had done the right thing. Adele and he had corresponded with each other whilst he was at college but that was no big deal. Did he want to get back with her now he was home? She was a beautiful and glamorous girl in the Hollywood mould but she was also something of a self-willed personality and liked to get her own way.

But it was only an invitation to tea. What harm was there in that? And he had nothing else planned, so what the hell!

At home, Billy explained to his mam that he'd been invited to tea with Adele.

'You be careful there, my lad,' she admonished. 'Now you're a teacher, you're a good catch for any working-class girl. I never took to that girl and the way she gave you that new name of Julian. Daft name. The stuck-up bitch.'

'I'm only going for tea,' Billy protested. 'Not to announce the wedding banns.'

'You mark my words, my lad,' she said. 'I know girls like that. She'll have you walking down the aisle before you can say Jack Rubenstein.'

Despite his mam's objections, Billy walked over to Clifton Street and to Adele's home. There he found Adele's parents – the mother he'd met and the father whom he knew only through his voice when he had knocked on the ceiling and in doom-laden tones had announced from above that the hour was late and it was time to bring proceedings to an end. Adele now made the introductions.

'Pleased to meet you, Mr Lovitt,' said Billy politely, 'though I feel I know you already.'

'Likewise, Billy. But please call me George,' he said, taking a firm grip on Billy's outstretched hand.

'And I'm Rita,' said Mrs Lovitt.

Formalities over, they turned their attention to the high

136

tea which had been laid out specially in his honour. Very different treatment from the last time I was here, Billy said to himself. What's happened in the meanwhile to change things? Though the Lovitts lived in a back-to-back terraced house, the interior was tastefully decorated and furnished. And for this occasion they'd pulled out their best crockery, cutlery, and glassware.

Just as well Pottsy taught me about etiquette and which implement to use, Billy thought.

They began with a VP sherry and followed with a delicious salad complete with a wide variety of dressings, the whole thing rounded off with an exquisite Lewis's trifle.

'That was a meal worthy of the Midland Hotel,' said Billy when they'd finished.

'Why thank you,' said Rita Lovitt. 'And do you know that Adele prepared that trifle herself? She's ever so good in the kitchen.'

I must try her sometime, Billy reflected. Mrs Lovitt seemed to have forgotten that he had seen them carrying the Lewis's food package.

'Oh, Mother,' said Adele coyly. 'You're embarrassing me with that talk about my trifle-making.'

Billy offered his Passing Clouds around, and they all puffed on them contentedly.

'You must be proud,' said Mrs Lovitt, 'to have passed your exams to be a teacher. Our Adele left school at fourteen but she was ever so clever at school. That's why she got such a good job at Kendal's on the cosmetics counter.'

'That explains your skill in putting make-up on,' said Billy, smiling at Adele who was acting all bashful. 'Maybe you should've got a job in a theatre. And you dress so elegantly as well. How do you manage it on the paltry clothing ration we have to put up with?'

'She uses our clothing coupons as well as her own,' said Rita Lovitt, answering for her. 'Also her granny's. It's so important for a young girl to keep up with the latest fashions and so we don't mind giving up our share. She's our only child, Billy,' she added proudly. 'We've always done our best for her and tried to give her everything she wanted. Always made sure she's never gone without. Sometimes we think she's a bit spoilt.'

For me, spoilt meant having an extra roast potato at Sunday dinner, Billy thought. Or maybe being given the rice pudding dish to scrape when everyone had finished.

'I wish you'd shut up, Mother,' Adele said ominously. 'I'm sure Billy doesn't want to hear that rubbish about me being the apple of your eye and that.'

'Well, our Adele, you're the apple of my eye whether you like it or not,' George said, looking fondly at his daughter. 'And so, young Billy sir,' he continued, changing the subject, 'you're now a fully qualified teacher in the service of Manchester Education Committee!'

'Well, not quite,' Billy answered. 'I have to wait another fortnight before we get the final results. And before I can teach, I'll have to do a stint in the forces – probably in the army.'

'But you'll be made an officer,' Adele gushed. 'I can see you now in your smart uniform, the Sam Browne belt, the riding boots, the pips on your shoulder.'

Now Billy had joined Adele in the *Vogue* ad along with the Pekinese dog and the flash sports car.

'You'll have all the girls falling for you,' said Mrs Lovitt playfully.

'There's no need for comments like that, Mother,' Adele snapped. 'We don't want to put such ideas into Billy's

138

head. Anyroad, he belongs to me, not other girls, don't you, Billy?' she simpered.

Billy didn't like the direction this conversation was taking.

'I didn't mean anything, I'm sure,' Mrs Lovitt apologised. Then she declared brightly, 'I wonder if Billy knows that we're related to the Lovitts of Altrincham who have the big grocery chain. One day, our Adele could inherit some of that wealth, Billy. That'd help if ever you were thinking of setting up home, wouldn't it?'

'I think you're running ahead of things,' Billy mumbled. Addressing George, he said, 'As for the army, Mr Lovitt, sergeant is probably the highest rank I'll be offered.'

'Still pretty good pay and allowances if I remember from my army days,' George rejoined. 'Lance corporal is the highest rank I managed. But teaching's a good job, Billy. Long holidays and good pension, eh.' Winking at Adele, he added, 'You'll be able to look after our little princess in the way she's been accustomed to. She likes the easy life, you know.'

The discussion went on in this vein for half an hour or so until Adele suggested that they go to Harrigan's Dance Academy and take up where they'd left off so long ago.

Unsure, Billy agreed and much to his surprise had a most enjoyable evening renewing old acquaintances and recalling their days of success in the world of competitive dancing. Happily, the crowd which had got his goat at New Year were absent and he didn't have to suffer the bishop/actress repartees. Adele, still a magnificent dancer, showed she'd lost nothing of her elegant style and her ability to attract the envy of other females and the lustful looks of their male partners. In the slow foxtrot particularly she glided effortlessly with perfect timing across the polished floor of Harrigan's ballroom.

At the end of a happy evening, Billy took Adele home. They reached the door of her home and Billy kissed her on the lips and said, 'Thank you for a great night, Adele. You're still as beautiful as ever and as for your dancing, you're incomparable. But you always were. It's been great getting back with you.'

'Why thank you, kind sir,' she said, making a small curtsy. 'I share your feelings. I don't want this evening ever to come to an end. But it doesn't have to yet. Come in and have a cup of tea before you make your weary way to your lonely bed.'

'Won't your parents still be up?'

'They won't when I give 'em their marching orders,' she laughed, narrowing her eyes.

They went inside where Mrs Lovitt was listening to the wireless. She switched it off as soon as she saw them arrive.

'We're in for a last cuppa,' Adele said, signalling undisguisedly with raised eyebrows that it was time for Mother to skedaddle. 'I'm sure you'll be wanting to get to bed.'

'Don't worry, Adele, I'm off,' Mrs Lovitt said helpfully. 'The kettle's boiled and so I'll leave you two lovebirds in peace. You do make a lovely couple.'

Coupling would be a better word for it, thought Billy.

When she had gone, Adele and Billy retired with their tea to the settee in the front room.

'Remember this settee, Billy?' murmured Adele.

'How could I ever forget?'

They set their cups down, forgot about their tea, and began kissing and embracing passionately.

140

'It was here that we promised to love each other till the end of time. Do you remember?' she whispered.

'I do indeed. It was until things like the wells ran dry and the mountains disappeared. Until, that is, one of us ran out of unlikely events to love the other till. It's a case of *déjà vu* all over again,' Billy replied.

'But in my case, it was true,' she said. 'Billy, I do love you. I know we once tried to make love and it didn't work out. I want you to know that if we were to become engaged, I'm more than willing to sleep with you. But the ring must come first.'

'Adele, don't remind me of that disastrous night. We – or at least I – made a complete pig's ear of it and it's an experience I don't want ever to repeat. As for engagements, I think we're both too young. We're only nineteen and there's plenty of time. Why do we have to wait until we get engaged before we . . . ?'

'If I became pregnant,' she said, 'it'd ruin everything and you'd feel that you had to marry me.'

'We could always use something.'

'I don't trust those things,' she said.

'I suppose you're right. And anyway, I'm a Catholic and it's against our religion to use them. But engagement is out for quite some time.'

'OK, if that's the way you feel, Billy. I'll go along with anything you say. I hope, though, that when we're married, you'll drop that Catholic superstitious mumbo-jumbo. You know how I feel – I couldn't stand having them holy pictures, statues and crucifixes in my house. We'll talk about that when we get engaged. But tell me that we're together again and I'm happy.'

When they parted that night, Adele seemed happy and content, but deep in his heart Billy felt troubled and uneasy. He didn't like that talk about Catholic superstition. They'd been through all that stuff before. Whilst he was no Holy Joe, he objected to anyone making fun of his church and he reserved the right to make up his own mind. There were other things. He had noted that the Voice of Doom had not spoken through the ceiling as it usually had in the past. Furthermore, he had the uncanny sensation that he was sliding down a slippery slope and he kept hearing the words of his mam: 'You mark my words, my lad. I know girls like that. She'll have you walking down the aisle before you can say Jack Rubenstein.'

At weekends, he continued to go dancing with Adele and at times their snogging sessions threatened to get out of control. They probably would have done had it not been for Adele's insistence on a ring. Billy was not overconcerned that they didn't go all the way as the image of that first disastrous try at sex still rankled, and he didn't want a repeat performance, or non-performance as the case might be.

Adele may be a little spoiled and self-centred, he thought, but she's the only girl around in my life at the moment. Perhaps my standards are too high and my ideal doesn't exist except in storybooks. Then again, maybe I'm not Adele's superman either. So, until our fairytale hero and heroine come onto the scene, I suppose we'll have to put up with each other. Sometimes if you hold out for the ideal, you end up with nothing. But engagement and marriage are definitely out. Anyway, apart from the question of finding the wherewithal to buy a diamond ring, there's the little matter of National Service. He was looking forward to that and Adele had awakened his imagination with her talk of a smart officer's uniform.

How his own family and the relatives would like that! A
Hopkins lad from Collyhurst an officer!

It was inconceivable.

Chapter Thirteen

Sometimes a trivial thing can have dire consequences

A couple of weeks later, Billy heard that he'd obtained the Teaching Certificate of the University of London and was now a qualified teacher.

'Does this mean you know how to teach now?' Mam asked.

'Not really, Mam,' Billy replied. 'This certificate means that as far as they can tell, I won't do too much damage in the classroom if anyone appoints me.'

'That's more than can be said for some of the teachers I had at Board School,' she said.

The rest of the Damian crowd heard that they, too, had been successful. This had to be celebrated in the usual way and an alcoholic evening at the Sawyers' Arms on Deansgate followed.

The talk was about the coming spell in the forces which they would be required to do. The evening was supposed to be celebratory but in many ways it was tinged with sadness, for they sensed that fate would soon scatter them to the four winds, that they might part, go their separate ways and perhaps never meet again.

'I'd love to be in the army,' said Oscar. 'The thought of those virile soldiers taking their showers leaves me quite weak. Unfortunately, I doubt if I'll pass the medical because of my ankylosis – that's arthritis to you.'

'I'm really looking forward to it,' exclaimed Billy. 'Especially if we get commissioned. Good pay, the chance to go overseas and make new friends.'

'You know what they say,' added Ollie. 'Join the army, make new friends – and then shoot them.'

'I fancy the uniform,' said Nobby. 'Think of the birds we can pull. Why, they'll regard it as an honour to be shafted by an officer.'

'There's no guarantee that we'll get commissioned,' said Potts, 'but my dad reckons he can pull a few strings.'

'Exactly what does your father do?' sneered Oscar. 'I have the impression that he is a puppeteer in a circus.'

'I know I'll get posted to some remote outpost of the British Empire,' whined Titch. 'Far away from civilisation, and I shall spend two years wasting my sweetness on the desert air.'

So the conversation flowed, becoming progressively more ribald and noisy as the evening wore on and the alcohol began to take effect. There was an atmosphere of great anticipation and exhilaration and they thrilled at the idea that they were on the threshold of a new and exciting life. The worry and the constant studying for examinations were behind them and before them lay the prospect of new adventures, new places and new faces. As for teaching, well, that was something they could take up later. They'd cross that bridge when they came to it.

Shortly after their night out, they were ordered to report to Ardwick Green Barracks for the required army medical.

Nervous as kittens, they endeavoured to cover their anxieties with a stream of obscene and corny comments as they underwent the usual medical routine of being stripped, lined up, handled, felt, tapped, pummelled, and forced to bend down to have their innards and their anuses checked; they coughed on cue as the doctor cupped their testicles in his hand as if weighing them; they inhaled and exhaled; they read off the letters on the chart.

Throughout the procedure, they maintained a flow of what they thought were funny jokes about eye examinations and medicals in general, the 'I only came here to deliver a telegram' variety and the 'Doctor, doctor' type, like 'Doctor, doctor, how's that little boy doing, the one who swallowed the half-crown?' Answer: 'No change yet.' And 'Doctor, doctor, I keep thinking I'm a spoon.' 'Well, stand over there and don't stir.'

'I've heard them all before,' remarked the elderly GP, yawning.

Next, they were ordered to give a specimen of urine to demonstrate that they were disease-free and diabetes-free.

'You must urinate in my presence, if you please,' said the doctor.

'Piddling to order is easier said than done,' commented Titch. 'I drank a gallon of tea before I came out and now my bloody bladder refuses to co-operate. I never thought taking a slash would be so difficult.'

The six of them stood there in their birthday suits, straining to micturate into their jars. No use – none of them could make it.

Exasperated, the doctor said, 'You're like a bunch of shy virgins on their wedding night. Very well, we can't wait around here all day. Take yourself off to the toilets and come back when you've succeeded in splashing your boots.

146

And none of your tomfoolery, like swapping each other's urine around.'

Away from the tension of being under observation, the gang released awesome, Niagara-like streams of urine until the bottles were overflowing.

'What's this you're on, Billy?' remarked Oscar. 'Boddington's best draught?'

Titch, however, was still having problems producing the goods.

'You see,' he explained, 'when I was a little kid and my mam wanted me to do a wee, she always sang that nursery rhyme – the one about this little piggy . . .'

'You're not suggesting we sing it now?' exclaimed Billy incredulously.

'And why not?' said Oscar. 'Anything if it helps to hurry things along.'

Titch's five companions began to sing in unison:

This little piggy went to market,
This little piggy stayed at home,
This little piggy had roast beef,
This little piggy had none,
But this little piggy cried, wee-wee-wee-wee-wee,
I can't find my way home.

Success. It worked – Titch filled his jar.

Triumphantly, they presented the doctor with their precious gifts.

'I merely wanted a small specimen,' he wailed. 'Not a flagon of piss from each one of you.'

Doctors! they thought. They're never satisfied.

Finally, they had their ears checked and it was here that the examiner found an old lesion on Billy's eardrum dating back years to when his mother had accidentally poured water down his ear whilst washing his hair. He had a perforated eardrum of which he'd been unaware – his hearing was something he'd always been proud of.

'Though you've a small perforation on the eardrum, it seems to have healed,' the physician said, 'and I can see no reason why you shouldn't do your service in the army or the air force.'

But that small act of his mother's all those years ago dramatically changed Billy's life. It's truly food for thought when one reflects how the tiniest, apparently insignificant incident can alter the course of a personal history. Even the history of a nation, who knows? 'For want of a nail, the battle was lost . . .'

A couple of weeks later when Billy had returned home after a hard day in the 'Pill Hall' slaving over a snooker table writing out names and addresses, he found a letter in a buff envelope waiting for him behind the tea caddy on the mantelpiece.

Billy wasn't keen on receiving letters like this. His previous experience of them had not been happy and he'd long ago learned never to build up his hopes.

With trembling hands, he tore open the envelope and began to read. As he did so, the bile of disappointment rose in his throat.

'Well, Billy, what does it say?' his mam asked anxiously.

He handed her the letter. She read:

Dear Sir,
NATIONAL SERVICE ACTS
Re. Your recent National Service medical examination held at Ardwick Barracks.
I am directed by the Secretary of State to inform you

that following your recent medical examination to determine your fitness or otherwise to serve in His Majesty's forces, you were classified as Grade IV and will not therefore be required to serve a period of National Service.

I should like to take this opportunity of thanking you for your attendance and for your co-operation.

I am, sir,

Your obedient servant,

Clifford Whitehead

For the Minister of Labour and National Service.

'Well,' said Mam, 'that *is* good news!'

'How do you make that out?' asked Billy bitterly. 'It's the same old story. As soon as I raise my hopes, they're dashed to pieces. I was looking forward to becoming an officer in the army. This letter is telling me I'm a right weakling. I feel like a cripple. Not even fit to join the army.'

'Nonsense,' she said. 'You've got a slight perforation of the eardrum, that's all, and even that's healed up. If there'd been a war, they'd have taken you right enough. Anyroad, I read in the paper the other day that that singer you're always going on about – Frank Sonata – was turned down for the American army because of a punctured eardrum. So you've got something in common. Look on the bright side – this is a piece of good luck.'

'Good luck! How can being told you're a wimp be a piece of good luck?'

'I believe in fate,' she answered. 'Who knows? You might have been sent to Palestine or some place like that and got yourself shot. No, count yourself lucky. Somebody up there is looking after you.'

Gradually Billy came to accept this latest turn in his destiny. Maybe his mam was right. At least his future was clear – no wasting time in the forces. There was some consolation perhaps in the news that Oscar, too, had been turned down, but not much. After all, he had a nasty-sounding deformity. But Oscar had always claimed that one day his arthritic disability would pay off.

The others of their group, Titch, Nobby, Ollie, Pottsy, were drafted into the Royal Army Education Corps. Not as officers – which was another crumb of comfort – but as sergeants.

There was another twist of fate shortly after Billy had his news about National Service. It may have been a coincidence but Adele decided that Duggie Doyle was her Prince Charming after all. A month later, they announced their engagement. Poor old Duggie, Billy thought, had fallen for her wiles and been lured into the honeytrap.

The Sherman's job came to an end and Titch went off to London to stay with relatives. It was a long summer holiday and there were still six weeks to fill. Billy was left at a loose end and was almost back to his adolescent game of dropping plums from the veranda on unsuspecting pedestrians below when he received a card from Titch. 'Pack your bags, lad,' it said. 'There are jobs galore down here. You can stay with me at my aunt's.'

Billy was off like a shot.

He caught the bus from Lower Mosley Street to Victoria where he found Titch waiting.

'I've found us two jobs already,' he shouted excitedly.

The jobs were as building labourers with Percy Bilton's, constructing a training centre in Perivale, not far from the Hoover factory. The foreman, a huge strapping Irishman, looked them up and down.

150

'You,' he said pointing to Titch, 'don't look strong enough to lift the latch of a gate let alone a bucket of mortar or a hod of bricks. You can have a job in the stores.'

Billy stuck his chest out and tried to look muscular.

'And as for you, you don't look much better. You remind me of that American crooner who's always going on about his daughter Nancy with the laughing face. But I'll give you a try on the gang digging a foundation trench.'

He handed Billy a huge pickaxe and fourteen-pound hammer and told him to join a line of Irish labourers. It was glorious weather and he stripped off his shirt to be like the rest of them.

'Will you take a look at this bag o' bones,' said Shaun, one of the labourers. 'How do you expect to do any digging with those muscles? Sure you could get a job in a circus as one o' them there freaks – you could go as the walking skeleton.'

This brand of sarcasm caused a great deal of mirth amongst his fellow Hibernians.

'Anyway,' he continued, 'the first thing we have to do is dig through the hard core of stone and cinders till we reach the clay underneath. Then we dig a trench four feet deep. Do you understand all that?'

'Got it,' Billy said, eager to show what he could do.

He lifted the big hammer which nearly wrenched his arms from their sockets. After five minutes, the sweat poured off him and he was exhausted.

'For God's sake, take it aisy,' said Shaun behind him. 'You'll not last an hour at that rate.'

Billy slowed the pace but he was still worn out, his back ached and his hands began to bleed.

'Shaun, if you could help me get through this hard core,'

he pleaded, 'I'm sure I can do the digging with a spade and my boots.'

'I'll do nothin' of the sort,' said Shaun. 'Sure I won't be gettin' your wages and so I won't be doin' any digging for you. You yourself will be collectin' the money on Friday. So stop your snivellin' and get on with it.'

'But my hands are bleeding,' Billy said.

'Ah, your hands'll get used to it in the end as it did for the rest of us. Piss on your hands to harden them up.'

At the end of that first day, Billy was in a state of collapse and every bone in his body screamed out for rest. But Shaun was right. After ten days, he had become used to the routine and his hands had toughened up.

After a while he was promoted to operating a piece of highly technical machinery – a wheelbarrow. He was entrusted to carry loads of liquid cement from the rotating mixer, across a narrow bridge of planks, and there to upend the squelchy mess into the trench.

And when the first morning tea break came round, what joy! He was so weak with hunger and thirst that he swooped ravenously on the huge pint pots of tea and the pavement-thick sandwiches which were brought round on a trolley at eleven o'clock and at dinnertime. Oh, sweet ambrosia and nectar, he thought. Whatever they tasted like to the Greek gods must have been something similar.

As the weeks went by, he became filled with admiration at the skill the labourers demonstrated getting a job done with the utmost economy of effort, and their ability to time a job to perfection.

One Friday afternoon, the foreman ordered Shaun and Billy to move a quantity of heavy paving stones, about ten in number, from one end of the site to the other. It was 4 p.m. and Billy reckoned they could move them in half an hour. They hoisted the first one into the wheelbarrow and Billy – now a skilled operator – started off with his load to the other side of the site. He was soon back for the next. Shaun, who was sitting by the stones, frowned at Billy and said, 'Sure don't be in such a feckin' great hurry. No need to break your feckin' back.' He set the timing of the operation and demonstrated the truth of Parkinson's great law, which stated: 'Work expands to fill the time available for its completion.'

Billy moved the last one into place at precisely 6 p.m. as the hooter was sounding.

'Time to knock off,' Shaun announced.

At the end of four weeks, Billy had become fitter and healthier than he had ever been in his whole life. He had acquired a deep tan and he glowed with health. Poor old Titch looked sallow, weedy, and positively ill after his incarceration in the windowless stores where there had been little to occupy him.

'Much to my surprise, I passed the army medical,' he said in his usual lugubrious tone. 'I must be better than I feel.'

Every evening, when the work was done, it was off to the local pub with Titch's aunt and uncle plus numerous Cockney cousins. There they consumed copious quantities of ale and Billy acquired a taste for gin and orange. This was indeed a happy time and the conversation and the jokes flowed easily and more noisily as the evening wore on. On one of these occasions, Titch's aunt looked at the two young men through an alcoholic haze and remarked, 'Look at the two of them there. There's my young nephew classified for the army as Grade One – he's as pale as a ghost and looks as if he should be in a TB hospital. And Billy sits there swilling his gin and orange and looking the

153

picture of health with his golden suntan – he's Grade Four. It's a mad old world. I think the government has got its gradings mixed up. Are you sure you boys didn't switch the specimens of pee?'

Sadly, the holiday came to an end and it was time for the Damian gang to take their different paths – a true parting of the ways. With the rest of them, Titch went off as a sergeant instructor in the Royal Army Education Corps to teach illiterate soldiers the rudiments of reading. There were no exotic postings involved and he spent the whole period with the rest of them at Buchanan Castle in the north-east of England. As for Billy, it was time to start looking for a job. The prospect hung over his head like the Sword of Damocles and even the thought of it was enough to give him goose pimples.

Chapter Fourteen

He who can, does. He who cannot, teaches.

George Bernard Shaw

When he got back from London, Billy went looking for a teaching job. He was contracted to Manchester Education Authority as he had taken out a loan of forty pounds with them to get through college, and it had to be paid back from his salary.

Billy went to see his old head, Gus Thomas, at St Chad's for advice about which schools to apply to and Gus gave Billy his preferred order of schools – first St Aidan's, second St Anselm's. Billy arranged to see Mr Muldoon, the head of St Aidan's, but there was nothing doing there as the vacancy had been reserved for Potts pending the result of his Army medical. Obviously Muldoon had not got the news or perhaps Potts's dad, the puppeteer, was still hoping to fix an exemption for his son. Disenchanted, Billy took the bus across to Longsight and went to see St Anselm's school manager, Father Kelly. There was no interview as such.

In the private sitting room, Billy could smell a heady mixture of cigar smoke and malt whisky. Rosy-cheeked

Father Kelly gave every appearance of being comfortable.

'I see,' he began, 'that you have attended an Anglican college. What was wrong with our own college, St Mary's at Strawberry Hill, may I ask?'

Billy told him that the college had soon become full and no one from Damian College had secured a place that year.

'I trust you are a good Catholic,' he said. 'And that you attend Holy Mass and the sacraments regularly.'

Billy reassured him on these points.

Finally he said, 'You will have to pass the Catholic Teachers' Religious Certificate before we confirm your appointment. We don't want you teaching Protestant heresy to our children in the parish, now do we?'

Billy agreed with him of course and assured him that he didn't know any heresies to teach and even if he did, he wouldn't teach them – not to the children in his parish at any rate. He had become confused by the googly the priest had bowled him.

Father Kelly seemed satisfied by this garbled answer, for he said, 'Very well, I'll take you provisionally until you pass the Religious Certificate. You may start at the school next Monday. The school is on holiday at the moment but you should present yourself to the headmaster, Mr Francis Wakefield, on the first day of term.'

Billy's starting salary was £300 a year. He was delighted.

As Billy was about to leave, the presbytery doorbell rang and the housekeeper announced the arrival of a female visitor. She was a middle-aged woman, expensively dressed, decorated with lots of dangly jewellery, and wafting an aroma of exotic perfume. As he escorted Billy over the threshold, Father Kelly introduced her as Miss Andrews, the headmistress of the infants' school at Salop House.

'Mr Hopkins here is going to teach in the senior school,' he said.

'Ah, so you'll be working under Wakefield,' she exclaimed in a plummy voice. 'You have my sympathy. I wish you all the luck in the world – you're going to need it.'

'Thank you for those kind words,' Billy said as he departed.

What was he walking into? he wondered.

On the Saturday before he was due to start, Billy decided to do a recce of the route he would take and of the district itself – the so-called catchment area. He cycled over to Longsight and dismounted at Nelson Grove. As he strolled round the area pushing his bike, he noted the little two-up, two-down, privy-in-the-yard terraced houses – street after street of them, each named by some imaginative city planner after long-forgotten historical events and people. Hougoumont Grove, Waterloo Court, Blucher Street, Bulow Street. Illustrious names that seemed out of place in such squalid surroundings. He turned into Duke Street and was accosted by a young lady heavily made up and wearing an extremely short skirt.

'Lookin' for a short time?' she asked wearily.

'Short time?' Billy asked, puzzled.

'Yeah,' she said. 'A quickie, you know. I can show you a good time. Only a quid.'

'I don't think so,' he replied, getting the point. 'I'm not looking for a short time. I'm looking for St Anselm's School. Do you know it?'

'Know it?' she answered. 'I should do, it's my old school and my young sister still goes there. I think she's in the top class – name of Irene Moody. Look out for her, she'll eat you for breakfast. But there's no school building there now. Jerry put a bomb on it in nineteen forty-two. The best thing

157

he ever did. Anyroad, I think they're now in the Industrial School on Wellington Grove – best to ask there.'

Billy left the young maiden and walked along High Street, past the Corporation baths, past dingy shop fronts and cafés, second-hand furniture shops, a garage, until he finally reached Wellington Grove. At least he now had a rough idea of the district and the location of the school.

On the way back, he took a different route. He cycled some distance along Wellington Grove and then made a right turn into Regina Park Hill, a private estate and a different world. The park was a throwback to the Victorian era when prosperous Manchester cotton merchants, anxious to escape the hoi polloi, set up their large, commodious houses away from the common people. The estate retained a toll gate manned by a uniformed collector, no doubt to discourage traffic taking a short cut through the park. If this was the case, it was unnecessary because the state of the roads was an even greater deterrent – the deep potholes seemed designed to break the springs of any car doing over ten miles an hour. As the road climbed steeply, Billy dismounted and walked the rest of the way until he commanded a fine view of the surrounding district and the slums which nestled at the foot of this rich man's territory.

The estate was like an island of prosperity set in a sea of poverty. No two-up, two-down hovels here. Instead, there were wide, tree-lined lanes and large Edwardian and Victorian houses with drives, orchards, and manicured hedges. And the names of the roads and avenues delivered what they promised. Chestnut Avenue – broad and straight – was indeed lined with chestnut trees whilst Birch Grove, Lime Grove, Sycamore Avenue similarly manifested arboreal truth.

Billy doubted if many of the St Anselm's pupils hailed

from this area; no doubt most of the Regina Park kids would be packed off to private boarding schools or fee-paying grammar schools. He thought about his own background – a tenement in Cheetham Hill. Gardenia Court. That was a laugh; there wasn't a gardenia to be seen within a hundred miles of the place. Somehow, Chestnut Avenue became the symbol of Regina Park wealth and he saw his own district and its lifestyle for what they were – poor and restrictive.

Lost in thought, he cycled back to north Manchester.

Chapter Fifteen

Chalk and Duster Brigade

For the whole of the weekend, Billy was on edge. Monday morning came round and in this anxious state, he had no appetite, his breakfast consisting of a mug of tea and a cigarette. What kind of job was he going to? he wondered. What sort of surprises were round the corner?

'You should try to eat something,' Mam said. 'You can't do good work on an empty stomach. Remember that saying: "In the morning, eat like a king; in the afternoon, like a prince; and at night, like a peasant." You've got it the wrong way round.'

'I've got a touch of the collywobbles at the thought of taking my first class. I dare say I'll be better by dinnertime.'

'I've made up some cheese sandwiches, and I've included a nice apple. An apple for the teacher.' She sounded as nervous as he did.

He put on his best clothes, such as they were – a pair of new grey flannels, a white shirt and tie, and a double-breasted jacket borrowed from Les's demob outfit – without his permission, of course.

'Eeeh, you do look smart,' Mam said. 'Fancy! Our kid a teacher! You've done us right proud, son. Here's a little present me and your father clubbed together to get you. When you started at Damian College, I forgot to buy you a satchel. Remember? Well, we haven't forgotten this time for your first day at school.' She handed over a smart briefcase with his initials embossed in gold.

'Gosh, thanks, Mam,' he said, kissing her on the cheek – a rare thing for anyone in their family to do. They weren't the gushing type. 'It can hold my sandwiches and the apple for a start.'

'You make sure you teach 'em proper now. And do be careful on that there bike,' she called as Billy went through the door.

He carried his Raleigh into Smedley Road and pedalled his way through the morning traffic, breathing in bus exhaust fumes along the way. He reached Albert Square, then went along Princess Street to Longsight. He dismounted at Wellington Grove and turned into Grimshaw Street, a narrow back street which led to a massive solid Victorian edifice built in red sandstone. It had a forbidding, unfriendly aspect, as did the dilapidated noticeboard displaying the title: ST ANSELM'S INDUSTRIAL SCHOOL FOR BOYS 1888.

This can't be it, he thought. He had been led to believe that the school was a much smaller affair. He crossed a large quadrangle and found a smaller broken-down outbuilding labelled 'St Anselm's Elementary School'. Through the gateway came a beefy, rosy-cheeked lad. He has the map of Ireland written across his features, Billy mused. The boy was dressed in corduroy trousers, a threadbare shirt, and a cardigan that had seen better days. He was chewing gum vigorously.

'Can you tell me where I can find the head?' Billy asked.

'You mean Mr Wakefield? Yeah. His office is at the top of the fire escape,' he replied, his jaws working overtime. 'I'll show you where it is.'

'Right, thanks,' Billy said. 'What's your name, by the way?'

'Joe Duffy. Why? I haven't done nothing.'

'I didn't say you had, Joe. But why aren't you in class?'

'We haven't got no teacher – so I'm acting as Wakefield's monitor, like.'

'What does that involve, Joe?'

'Running his errands and that. Put on a bet. Go for his cakes or his fags, you know.'

Together they climbed the fire escape, their feet resounding metallically on the iron steps. At the top of the stairway there was a dirty brown door from which the paint was peeling and on which was pinned a card bearing in green ink the instruction: 'Headmaster's Office. Knock and Wait.'

Joe Duffy did as it said.

'Yes, yes, come in,' called an impatient, tobacco-cured voice.

'Someone to see you, sir,' Joe Duffy announced importantly.

The head looked up from the letter he was writing. 'Who is it, Joe?' he asked irritably.

'Don't know, sir. He didn't say,' Joe answered, glancing impishly at Billy.

'Tell him to come in, for God's sake. And Joe, you can go for my messages. Here's half-a-crown – get me twenty Players and three cream buns. And don't be all day about it.'

'Right, sir. Do you want me to put a bet on for you while I'm out?'

'Not now, Joe,' the head replied testily. 'See me at dinnertime.'

Joe gave Billy a conspiratorial wink as he departed on his errand.

Billy entered and found an extremely small office, bare except for a small table, behind which sat a powerfully built man with a pockmarked, weather-beaten face in which were set two protruding eyes like two poached eggs, and a small, misshapen pug nose. He'd have won no prize in a beauty competition but he was a perfect model for a Toby jug.

Frank Wakefield stood up and held out his hand. Billy felt the firm grip and the rough, flaky skin of his palm.

'You must be Mr Hopkins,' Wakefield said warmly as he settled back in his chair. 'Father Kelly told us to expect you. I'm Mr Wakefield, the head.'

'Pleased to meet you. Yes, I met Father Kelly last Friday. He's offered me a provisional appointment to be confirmed when I pass the Religious Certificate.' Billy was still unsure of himself.

'The Religious Certificate indeed! What nonsense! Just teach the catechism and you'll have no problems.'

'I had a good grounding in the catechism at my elementary school.'

'Very well,' he said, smiling with his eyes. 'What is prayer?'

'The raising up of the mind and heart to God.'

'Right! What is God?' He was still smiling that funny smile.

'God is the supreme spirit who alone exists of himself and is infinite in all perfections.'

'You'll do,' he said, nodding his head. 'Father Kelly doesn't live in the real world. Doesn't know what a shortage

163

of teachers there is. As far as I'm concerned, you've just passed the Certificate.'

'I also met Miss Andrews, the head of the infants' school,' Billy added, still a little puzzled by the lack of formality. Wakefield scowled when he heard the name.

'Andrews! Don't mention that name in my presence. All top show and no substance. All fur coat and no . . . never mind. Best to change the subject before I blow a gasket. Anyway, welcome to the school. I'd ask you to sit down if we had another chair and even if we did, there wouldn't be enough room. Sit down on the edge of the table for the time being.'

Reassured by the warmth of his welcome, Billy sat down as directed. Offering a cigarette which Billy readily accepted, the head gave him a rundown on the school.

'We're a small school of two hundred pupils in eight classes. No school building as such, only a bomb site at present but there are big plans for the future.'

'Big plans?' Billy asked, leaning forward. It was the first he'd heard of them.

Wakefield puffed on his fag. 'The nineteen forty-four Education Act has decreed that we shall drop the Elementary School title and our senior department will become a Secondary Modern whilst the junior section will be housed in a brand new building which is still on the architect's drawing board.'

'Sounds exciting, Mr Wakefield. Will you be the head of one of these new schools?' Billy looked round for an ashtray but could see none. The ash on his cigarette was becoming embarrassingly long.

Wakefield's face became serious. 'Hope so. Miss Andrews has her eye on the junior school but I don't think she stands a chance. Who wants a headmistress that smells like the Gaumont cinema? Anyway, that's in the future. Today we have no building.' Noticing the long ash of Billy's cigarette, he pushed forward the lid of a tobacco tin. 'Use this – it's all we've got.'

'What were the huge buildings I passed on my way in?' Billy asked.

'Not ours, I'm afraid. They used to be the famous, or infamous, Industrial School but now they're about to be taken over by the NFS – the National Fire Service.'

'So we are restricted to this small outbuilding?'

'We are split between this building and some new prefab huts. Half the school is here in this dump and it's a damned dangerous place to teach kids – we've got dangling wires and loose timbers everywhere. The other half is about ten minutes' walk away in the prefabs which were originally intended for domestic science. As you can imagine, we're not popular with Wellington Grove School since we've taken over their nice new huts but we have no choice. I suppose you'd still call us an All-Age School – our children range from seven to fourteen, though the school leaving age has, as you know, been raised recently to fifteen.'

Billy stubbed out his cigarette on the make-do ashtray and then raised the question uppermost in his mind. 'Which class did you have in mind for me, Mr Wakefield?'

'You will be given the top class of fourteen to fifteen-years olds – boys and girls.'

Billy's heart skipped a beat. He couldn't believe what he was hearing.

'The top class! Do you think I have enough experience, Mr Wakefield? I mean, I'm new to teaching. I'm nineteen years of age.'

Wakefield smiled warmly. 'Perfect,' he replied. 'You'll be only four years older than some of the pupils. You'll understand and relate to 'em better than any of us old 'uns.'

Still not sure, Billy asked, 'Which subjects will I be teaching?'

'All of 'em,' he replied, looking intently at Billy. 'Except art, which I shall take, and science – such as it is, since we don't have a laboratory – taken by Mr Grundy. This will give you two double periods free each week to get on with your marking and preparation. Now I'm going to be busy over here this morning and the rest of the week, so I'll let Joe Duffy, my monitor, take you over to the prefabs and show you where your new class is. I'll come over later and see how you've got on. You'll find books and stationery in the storeroom cupboard. Joe'll show you.' He stood up to indicate the discussion was over. Billy moved towards the door.

Wakefield stopped him for a moment. 'Here is a new register for you,' he said. 'Make sure you treat it with the greatest respect as His Majesty's Inspectors will want to examine it, if and when they come to see us. Fairly straight-forward. Simply fill in the details. By the way, are you in the Boy Scouts?'

'No. Sorry,' Billy said, disappointed in himself as he wanted to please his new boss.

The Toby jug frowned his regret. 'Rugby? Do you play rugby?'

'No. Sorry,' he said again, feeling that in some vague way he'd let the side down by not being a rugby-playing scout.

'Pity,' Wakefield replied.

Billy wondered if he had any more strange questions or surprises in store for him. He had.

'One last thing. I have no office in the prefab annexe. I

166

hope you don't mind but I've set up my desk at the back of your class and will work from there.'

'You mean you'll be sitting in on all my lessons?' asked Billy, aghast.

'Not all of 'em but many of them. Maybe I'll learn something from you.'

The thought flitted through Billy's mind that he could still apply for another job since there was a general shortage. Some of the other schools in middle-class districts like Didsbury or Fallowfield had better buildings, better equipment, better facilities. St Aidan's had a vacancy as Potts had gone into the army. He dismissed the thought of changing as unworthy and decided to take his chances.

Still in a state of mild shock, he found Joe Duffy, back from Wakefield's errand, listening at the door. Joe had a ring of cream round his mouth and, after depositing the head's shopping and his change on the desk, joined Billy outside the office.

'Right, Joe, let's go,' Billy said, trying to muster some semblance of authority. 'Did you enjoy the cream bun, by the way?' Billy asked.

'Me? Cream bun? Not me! I haven't had no cake. The buns were for Mr Wakefield.'

Billy smiled to himself. It wasn't so long since he'd been an adolescent himself.

There was a drizzle in the air when they got outside. As they crossed the playground, they met a hefty, corpulent, bearded teacher dressed in a smart military raincoat. He was holding up a large umbrella and was surrounded by thirty children who were awaiting his instructions.

'Right,' he boomed, addressing the gang of kids, 'all of you, to that wall – run!' He pointed to a wall about four hundred yards away. 'You must be the new teacher,' he bellowed, spotting Billy. 'I'm Gregory Callaghan, class teacher to Junior Three. The kids here call me Calor Gas but you can call me Greg. For our sins, my brother Alex and I teach at this academy of learning. Nice to meet you.'

Billy accepted the firm handshake happily.

'You'll like it here,' Greg said, making it sound like a command. 'We're fairly easy-going. Don't stand on ceremony.'

'You're the PE specialist here, are you?'

He gave a loud guffaw. 'Good God! Me, PE specialist? We don't specialise here, old man. We are Jacks-of-all-trades. Polymaths. You name it, we teach it.'

'Doesn't the rain bother you?' Billy asked.

'Not at all. Doesn't bother any of us. We do our drill in all weathers. Toughens the kids up.'

By this time, his PT class was back, clamouring around him, waiting for the next order.

'Right! To that wall over there – go!' he barked, indicating the opposite wall about five hundred yards distant. Whooping like Red Indians, the class ran pell-mell to their objective. Billy wondered if Greg had ever studied the 1933 Syllabus on how to take a PE lesson.

'You'll find Wakefield is firm but fair, but don't get on the wrong side of him,' he roared. 'It would be a distinct advantage to your career prospects if you joined the Boy Scouts or played rugby for Wigan. Which class has he given you?'

'The top class, I think,' Billy answered diffidently.

'He's handed you the poisoned chalice! And may the Lord have mercy on your soul!' Greg bawled. 'Talk to you later in the staffroom at break.'

His wards were back tugging at his sleeve. Joe Duffy and Billy left them to it.

'Yes, yes,' they heard him growl. 'Now run over to the main gate and back.'

The objectives he set them appeared to be more and more challenging, more and more distant, and obviously designed less to provide health-giving exercise than to give him a longer period of respite from their clamouring demands.

They walked a little way down Wellington Grove, and Billy began to feel more and more nervous the nearer they got to the school annexe. He could feel his heart thumping against his ribs. He talked trivialities to Joe Duffy to hide his inward fear, his confidence ebbing with every stride he took. Greg Callaghan's benediction was the second time he'd been warned about what he had let himself in for. Would he be able to cope? he wondered. This wasn't any old teaching practice. This was for real. And what did he mean by 'he's handed you the poisoned chalice'?

They reached a small back entry, and veered left until they came to an open space and the prefabs. There were two buildings, one long, one short, but both resembling army barracks. Both were fully populated, the longer building by young children and their teachers, all of whom seemed hard at work. Through the windows of the smaller, it was a different scene, and it was into this that they now turned. As they opened the door, the racket of twenty youths bawling and shouting assaulted their ears. The young hooligans who were to make up his class were engrossed in their own occupations: two boys rolling on the floor appeared to be practising Sumo wrestling, another group had formed a pontoon-playing quartet; a couple of boys played hangman at the blackboard; several girls were employing the time primping up each other's coiffures whilst others simply sat around, feet on chairs, manicuring nails, reading comics like *Film Fun, Dandy, Girl's Crystal* or simply browsing through back numbers of *Picturegoer*.

As Billy entered the room, one or two pupils looked up lazily from their games, yawned, and resumed their activity. The word 'pupil' gave the impression they were children but young adults would have been more correct.

The young rowdies were not wearing school uniform and yet there was a sameness about their dress and appearance. For the boys, short, quiffed hair styles, T-shirts and corduroys were the order of the day, whilst the girls had adopted their own distinctive mode of tight skirts and jumpers with identical hairstyles based on the Hollywood heart-throb of the day, Rita Hayworth. There was one exception – one deviant girl had modelled herself on Veronica Lake with a peek-a-boo hairstyle.

The class continued to ignore Billy.

'Right,' he ordered. 'Sit down and be quick about it.'

The class looked up but made no move.

'Are you deaf or something? I said sit down!'

'Why should we?' a red-haired lad asked.

'Because I said so!' Billy yelled. 'That's why. Now move. Or maybe you'd like to go and see Mr Wakefield.'

'I'm petrified,' he said, grinning cheekily.

'I didn't catch your name,' said Billy.

'That's because I didn't throw it,' he answered, smirking.

Billy saw that he couldn't win this competition.

It was Joe Duffy who commanded their attention. 'Hey! Quiet, you lot! This is our new teacher.'

A plump girl detached herself from her manicuring clique and addressed Billy. 'Are you permanent or supply? Only we had enough of bloody supply teachers last year. Most of our teachers only come here for the money.'

Some money, Billy thought. Twenty pounds a month.

Five pounds a week – that's my salary.

The rest of the class now noticed his presence and abandoned their activities for the moment to examine him. Suddenly they were firing questions and comments.

'How long are you here for?'

'You're too young to be a teacher!'

'Are we having you instead of Grumpy Grundy? That'd be great.'

'If we'd got that bastard Grundy,' observed the red-haired boy, 'I definitely would not be coming to school. I'd play wag every day.'

Billy wondered if obscene language was a normal part of their vocabulary. On this occasion, he said nothing. He walked over to the single-seater high desk but did not sit down. He gazed out over the faces before him and waited until he had their full attention. Ever so gradually, the groups began to break up and return to their places, girls on one side, boys on the other. When everyone had settled down, Billy addressed them, hoping that his jittery nerves were not too obvious. He cleared his throat.

'I'm your new teacher. You'll address me by my name – Mr Hopkins – or if you prefer it, sir.'

'You mean you're called Sir Hopkins?' said the grinning ginger-haired lad.

'Very funny, I'm sure,' said Billy. 'Anyway, this is the way you spell it.'

He printed out his name on the blackboard, ignoring the dictum they'd drummed into him at college – 'Never turn your back on the class'. But he couldn't see the point in showing distrust so early in the game. He seemed to have judged right, for nothing happened. It's going like clock-work, he thought. Well, almost.

'Let me make one thing clear,' he continued. 'You will

171

cut out bad language and you will never make that bar-
barous row in my classroom ever again.'

They stared back at him defiantly.

'Who the bloody hell does he think he is?' somebody
said in a stage whisper.

'No talking,' Billy commanded.

'Get this guy,' said another lad. 'He's going to play the
hard man.'

Billy ignored the remark.

'Occupy yourself with something more worthwhile than
I have seen up to now,' Billy commanded. 'Then each of you
come up to me one by one and give me your personal details
for the register.' This isn't so bad, he thought. I'm handling
it OK up to now. Playing it by the book.

He spent the first part of the morning collecting their
names, addresses, and dates of birth, and entering them in
the new register, thinking to himself that calligraphy was
the one skill in which he could boast a great deal of
experience after his purgatorial period filling out con-cards
in the Inland Revenue office. He discovered that most of
the pupils hailed from the Napoleonically named streets
along Wellington Grove (with a mysterious concentration
in Victory Street) and that all had been born in the year
1932–3, making them fourteen to fourteen and a half years
of age.

When this chore had been completed, Joe Duffy raised
his hand.

'Mr Wakefield made me the class monitor.'

'Yeah, Wakefield's lap dog,' someone called.

'Enough of that,' Billy said sternly. 'What does class
monitor mean, Joe? Surely not more bets and fags?'

'I sit near the Aga boiler here at the back, and I have to
keep it going by putting in coal every hour.'

The Veronica Lake girl with the sleepy eyes raised her hand.

'And I'm the tea monitor,' she said. 'I make the tea for the staff at playtime and at dinnertime.'

'Your name is?' Billy asked.

'Irene Moody,' she answered huskily, giving him the glad eye. 'I'd better go and put the kettle on.'

'How old are you, Irene?'

'Old enough, sir,' she leered salaciously, flashing her eyes and grinning to her friends.

I can see the family resemblance, Billy thought, remembering her short-skirted sister who had propositioned him with a 'quickie' the previous week.

'Very well, Irene,' Billy answered, ignoring the innuendo. 'You may go and make the tea. I don't want to earn the hostility of the staff on my first day.'

It was an unusual classroom to say the least – well-equipped but not with the kind of equipment he could make use of. Along one wall were a number of sink units complete with running water and draining boards. On the other side of the room were four gleaming electric cookers spaced at equal intervals, and at the back in a small fenced-off section was the large boiler Joe Duffy had spoken of. It was obviously Joe's pride and joy. The classroom had been custom-built for domestic science and one could well understand the frustration of Wellington Grove School at being deprived of this state-of-the-art facility. But as a normal teaching classroom, it left much to be desired.

After filling out the register, he took out sheets of card from the storeroom cupboard, and spoke to the class.

'You know my name but it will take me some little time to learn yours. You can help me by filling in a card with your name and placing it on your desk like business

173

executives. Fold it in half so it looks like a Toblerone chocolate bar – if you've ever seen one. Make sure you print clearly the name by which you like to be known.'

A forest of hands went up.

'Got no pen.'

'No ink.'

'Got no blotting paper.'

'Write in pencil.'

'Got no pencil neither.'

They're just trying to be awkward, Billy said to himself. Fortunately he had anticipated this eventuality and prepared a set of emergency pencils ready sharpened. He congratulated himself on his forethought. I'm in control of the situation, he told himself, but this lot really do need to be spoon-fed.

'Don't forget to return the pencils,' he reminded the recipients.

All heads bowed as they filled out their cards. Some frowned and bit the ends of their pencils. One or two had considerable trouble writing their names. They stuck out their tongues, screwed up their faces into Quasimodo expressions, and squirmed uncomfortably in their seats as they painstakingly printed out their titles. Like my dad, thought Billy, when he's writing one of his rare letters.

While they were busy, Billy sketched a quick plan of their desk locations, intending to memorise them that night as soon as he got home – one of the invaluable tips he'd picked up at college. At least he could avoid addressing them as 'you' or the 'boy in the blue shirt'.

He looked at his watch. It was ten thirty.

'Break time!' Joe Duffy suddenly called. 'I have to ring the bell.' He produced a large heavy hand bell from under

174

his desk and without more ado went outside where he began swinging it up and down.

'Now would one of you show me the way to the staffroom?' Billy said, addressing the class.

'Yes, Mr Hopkins sir. I'd love to show you the way,' said a pretty girl winking at her cronies.

'Your name?' Billy asked.

'Vera Pickles and no relation to Wilfred before you ask.'

Billy dismissed the class. 'OK, Vera,' he said. 'Let's go.'

Chapter Sixteen

Meet the Staff

Billy opened the door of the staffroom and was met by a smell like that of a saloon bar on a Saturday morning – a mixture of stale tobacco smoke and body sweat. There was clutter everywhere. Several tables were heaped with untidy stacks of exercise books seemingly abandoned in despair by their markers; in a corner lay discarded sports gear – soccer boots, a half-inflated football, a collection of odd gym shoes, table tennis bats, and a couple of broken hockey sticks. Confiscated comics and overflowing ashtrays dotted the room, and on one wall there was a row of coat pegs on which hung an assortment of coats, hats, and umbrellas. Piles of textbooks perched perilously on the edge of a central table, round which were arranged four wooden chairs, and about the room were scattered five or six rickety armchairs.

Being the first to arrive, Billy opened a window, and with a sigh of relief sat in the nearest easy chair.

'Not there, old man,' bellowed a stentorian voice which he recognised as that of Gregory Callaghan, the erstwhile running instructor.

'Why not? Is there something wrong?' Billy asked.

'I'll say there is. That's Grundy's chair. He'll play merry hell if he sees you in it.'

Anxious to please and not antagonise Grundy, Billy changed chairs quickly.

'Who's Grundy?' he asked.

'You'll find out soon enough,' Gregory said ominously. 'Now let me introduce my older brother. Our mother had ambitions for us and named us after popes. Anyway, this is Alexander. Older brother but not wiser. And certainly not Great. Alexander the Sixth, the poisoner, is more his style.'

Alex gave Billy a big smile and a firm handshake. His horn-rimmed spectacles gave him a faintly disdainful, intellectual look but his facial expression was cheerful and hearty.

'Welcome to St Anselm's,' he said. 'Call me Alex. I'm in charge of the remedial class. When I came to the school, they took one look at me and could see I was the remedial type right away. Take no notice of my brother there. He's planning to get married early next year and the thought of bedding a woman has affected his brain. And don't be put off by his sergeant-major voice. I always said it was a mistake to send him for those elocution lessons – thinks he's addressing a multitude the whole time.'

Alex's warmth and sincerity came through easily and Billy took a liking to him immediately.

'In our family,' said Gregory, 'the only way to get heard is to shout. One needs a loud-hailer or a public address system.'

'Thanks for the welcome, Alex,' Billy said, laughing. 'I'm finding it a bit daunting but everyone assures me I'll get used to it.'

'You will in time – that's the trouble,' Alex smiled. 'But what do we call you? We can't refer to you as Mr Hopkins, that's too formal.'

'Well, my family calls me Billy but my friends call me Hoppy.'

'Then Hoppy it is,' he replied, offering a cigarette from his case.

Gregory said, 'Better take it, Hoppy. It's the only one he'll ever offer. Notice how the moths flew out of the cigarette case. As for me, I prefer an intelligent man's smoke.' He took out the meerschaum pipe on which he was endeavouring to shape his personality. Now Billy knew why the staffroom smelt so musty.

The door opened to admit a white-haired, bespectacled lady, elegantly dressed and with her hair coiled matriarchally at the nape of her neck. She carried the inevitable portmanteau which seemed to be an indispensable accessory for the schoolmarm role.

'Good morning,' she said softly. 'I'm Miss O'Neill, the deputy head. We are so pleased to see you here at this school. We count ourselves lucky to get you as there's still such a desperate shortage of teachers in the country.'

Before Billy could respond, a short middle-aged woman, around fifty and of mannish appearance, strode into the room. Her plain face was free of cosmetics, and her grey hair was cut in a short style, which matched her severe two-piece suit. She stood with legs apart, hands on hips.

'Let me introduce Miss Elizabeth Logie,' said Miss O'Neill.

'Pleased to meet you. Call me Liz,' the newcomer barked.

'Likewise. I mean, pleased to meet you. I'm Hoppy,' Billy answered.

178

'You'll have to speak up as she's a little deaf,' said Miss O'Neill.

'Nonsense,' snapped Miss Logie, lighting up a small decorated pipe which gave off the pungent aroma of Turkish tobacco. 'I can hear perfectly well when my deaf-aid is switched on. Besides, I can lip-read.'

Billy wondered how she coped in a school like this. The girls in the top class, he thought, would make mincemeat of her.

Next came Mrs Sybil Melton-Mowbray, tall, angular, hearty and bespectacled, with a red, scrubbed-looking face.

'I'm pleased to meet you,' said Billy offering his hand. 'Isn't your name—'

'A town in Leicestershire,' she said. 'My hubby's name is Melton and mine's Mowbray. When we met, he said it was fate had thrown us together and we were destined to be joined together. A marriage made in heaven. Jolly romantic, what?'

'Certainly unusual,' said Billy.

'Jolly nice to have a new face,' she chortled. 'Don't be put off by the staff comm – it's not very homey-from-homey, what? I know when I first came here I was jolly depressed when I saw it. The whole place is in need of a spot of jollification, if you ask me. Not like my old school – we had a spiffing den there.'

She seemed so out of place in St Anselm's, Billy wondered how she had come to be there.

She seemed to read his thoughts, for she said, 'Emergency trained, don'cha know. Ex-ATS and all that. Used to work in Cheltenham but moved up North when my dear old hubby was posted here. Came a year ago when old Wakefield interviewed me and appointed me as his third mistress. I teach Senior One and take the gals for netters.'

179

'Finally, let me introduce Miss Mackenzie,' continued the deputy head, moving on.

Billy turned to look at the young lady before him and his heart skipped a beat. She was the most beautiful girl he had ever set eyes on. A kind, gentle face, neat nose and mouth, dimples, and there was about her a quiet, refined elegance. Her soft nut-brown hair was tied back with a red ribbon. But it was her large, round, hazel eyes with their faint hint of sadness that captured Billy's attention – they seemed to reflect inner calmness and tranquillity. The kind of eyes that brought out his protective instincts.

'Laura is fairly new here,' whispered Miss O'Neill. 'She started at the end of last term when she was kind enough to help us out by taking Junior Two.'

Laura Mackenzie turned to Billy and gave him a warm, friendly smile. 'Nice to meet you and welcome to the school.' She held out her hand. 'I hope you'll be happy here.' She had a young, fresh voice with a hint of a Scottish lilt.

Like Dante's meeting with Beatrice, it was love at first sight. A hackneyed phrase but nevertheless true. Billy fell without a shot being fired and in that instant, all thoughts of Adele, ballroom dancing, worries about the new job and his unruly class were consigned to limbo.

He swallowed hard, and almost forgot to take her hand. 'So pleased to meet you,' he mumbled. Her hand was soft and warm. 'How do you like it here?' he asked. It was the best he could manage.

'I've only been here a short time,' she said quietly, 'but I like it very much – I've found the children and the staff easy to get on with.'

'You'll have to be careful what you say to Laura,' Liz

Logie said, laughing. 'Her father is a school governor.'

'Merely a nominal post,' said Laura Mackenzie. 'I don't think the governors have even met yet.'

Irene Moody entered the room carrying a large heavy teapot. Remembering college lectures on 'Teacher and the Law', Billy thought if she had an accident and scalded herself, there'd be hell to pay and this school would be sued for all it had got. Irene, however, didn't seem worried and even found time to give Billy the sleepy, slinky look he had seen earlier. That one could be big trouble, he said to himself.

'Help yourself to tea,' said Miss O'Neill.

'Any drink you want,' bellowed Greg, 'as long as it's tea.'

Billy went up to the table and joined the queue for tea. He looked over the selection of mugs and picked out an attractive one bearing an outline of Winston Churchill – it was one of the few not chipped.

'Not that one, old man,' bellowed Greg Callaghan.

'Don't tell me,' Billy said, a little exasperated. 'It's Grundy's cup.'

'Got it first time,' Greg laughed, slapping him on the back.

'How can you be so sure it's Grundy's cup?' Billy asked, his hackles rising.

'Because it says so underneath, old man. Look under the cup.'

Billy did so and there, printed on an Elastoplast strip, were the words: GRUNDY'S CUP. HANDS OFF.

Billy chose another cup – a chipped one. He wondered if he dared take a biscuit. Perhaps they were Grundy's. He decided to chance it and opted for a chocolate variety.

'Sorry again, old man,' said Greg, this time quietly – that

is, quietly for Greg, which was in fact loud.

'Grundy's biscuits?' Billy sighed resignedly.

'No, just for once. You have to join the biscuit club – chocolates are an extra threepence a week over the digestives. Sixpence a week will cover it. You have to tell Miss O'Neill which kitty you wish to join. You'll soon learn the routine.'

Billy was learning fast. Decisions, decisions, he thought. He determined to lash out and join the ChocBikky group.

He looked around for a teaspoon.

'There's only one spoon,' chuckled Alex, handing him a tannin-stained spoon. 'You have to wait your turn. Grundy has one of his own but he carries it with him in his waistcoat pocket.'

Billy wondered if it was the right time to inquire about arrangements for dinner.

'Most of the staff go out for dinner,' Miss O'Neill told him, 'but Mr Wakefield and I have sandwiches in the staffroom. You're welcome to join us.'

Then in he came – Grundy! The capitalist who had cornered the market in chairs and cups.

Billy didn't know why but he'd expected a big hairy man who would tower over everybody. He couldn't have been more wrong. Grundy was a diminutive man with a pencil moustache and a nervous tic. He smiled, showing a set of ill-fitting false teeth the colour of Cheddar cheese. Obviously needs a new set of dentures, Billy thought.

Grundy picked up his Churchill mug of tea, stirred it with his personal spoon, then collected a chocolate biscuit and flopped down in his chair.

'They're all daft,' he bayed. 'I don't know why we bother trying to teach 'em anything. Science – that's what I'm supposed to be selling. Waste of time.'

'What's happened now?' asked Greg.

'I've been trying to get across Archimedes' principle to Senior Three. I asked 'em why big heavy ships at sea don't sink. Tracy McFadden reckons it's because the sea is so deep and strong it holds them up. So I asked her how come that they float when they're in shallow dock. That's why they have to tie them up, she says. To stop 'em from sinking. We may as well try to teach nuclear physics to a bunch of chimpanzees.' He sniggered at his own wit.

He noticed Billy.

'Hello, hello,' he murmured. 'What have we here? New blood. Fresh meat?'

'I have been given a provisional appointment,' Billy said.

'Appointment, by George! Not an ordinary job like ours! And provisional, he says. Why provisional?' he asked.

'Provisional until I obtain a Catholic Teachers' Religious Certificate.'

'What nonsense! Wakefield doesn't mind what you teach as long as you remember to clear up the milk bottles and put the chairs on the desks at the end of school.'

'Why is that?' Billy asked.

'So that the caretaker can sweep the classroom. You can teach the Koran and the Torah if you like but whatever you do, don't forget to put the chairs up and to clear away the bottles. Wakefield's more scared of the caretaker than of HM Inspectors.'

'Understandably,' said Liz Logie, puffing heartily on her pipe. 'The caretaker has power over life and death. Get on the wrong side of him and there'll be no heat in the school and the wastepaper baskets won't get emptied.'

'Anyway,' continued Grundy, 'our new friend here has the

183

top class, so I've been told. What a bloody waste of time that is, raising the school leaving age for that dumb lot. Officialdom seems to forget that we are part of the elementary school system – the dustbins of the educational world. Our job is to keep the lids firmly closed on the bins and to keep the rubbish off the streets. The bright kids go to grammar or technical schools and we're left with the dross.'

Billy wondered how the staffroom would have reacted had he rushed at Grundy, tipped his chair backwards, gouged his eyes out, and plucked out the bristles of his revolting miniature moustache one by one with a pair of tweezers.

'Surely you're not serious,' Billy exclaimed.

'Oh, aren't I?' replied Grundy, a sneer curling his lips. 'Your college taught you that these kids are no good at academic things but they're good with their hands. Twaddle! We know what these kids would like to do with their hands all right. So some bright civil servants in Whitehall thought up these places and hired idiots like us to sit on the lids and keep 'em quiet. That's your job – keeping the lid on. Better to kick 'em out at fourteen and make 'em earn their living in the jungle out there is what I say.'

Rather than tear out his hideous moustache, thought Billy, it might be better to yank out his revolting false teeth and flush them down the toilet.

He resisted the temptation and instead said, 'People said the same thing when the government raised the school leaving age from twelve to fourteen in nineteen eighteen. Factory owners reckoned they needed the tiny hands to keep the wheels of industry turning. There was even a deputation of actors who claimed that Shakespeare plays requiring child actors would no longer be possible if the age was raised.'

184

'That was for children of twelve – now it's a different kettle of fish. They're fourteen.'

'Surely at fourteen they're still kids,' Billy protested. He could feel himself getting hot under the collar. 'They'll stand a much better chance of getting on in the world if they've had a better training, a better education.' What a surprise, Billy thought. Taffy's lectures on the philosophy of education are beginning to pay dividends at last!

'Watch out, watch out!' Grundy whinnied. 'Here he comes, the idealist straight out of college with his new-fangled ideas. I've only been teaching twenty years and so what do I know? Why, the ink on your certificate isn't even dry yet, mate. You wait till you've had Senior Four for a year, you'll change your tune.'

'If he ends up anything like you,' snapped Liz, her eyes flashing, her nostrils flaring, 'heaven help us. You keep your ideals, Hoppy. God knows we need a few people with ideals in this world of ours.'

'Huh, we know your teaching ideals, Liz,' sneered Grundy. 'Send out the kids to do your shopping for you on Friday afternoon. Practical maths, she calls it. It'll be God help you if one of 'em gets run over.'

'At least I don't belt the living daylights out of them like you do with that strap of yours,' Liz Logie snorted. 'You should have got a job in a concentration camp. And even with your whippings and your beatings you can't control your classes.'

'You know what they say,' Grundy retorted. 'Spare the rod and spoil the child.'

'That went out in the eighteenth century about the time we stopped drawing and quartering people,' said Miss O'Neill sweetly.

185

'A great pity they ever did,' said Liz, looking pointedly at Grundy.

'I can't believe the kids are anywhere as bad as you're making out,' Billy said, addressing Grundy. 'You have to give them a chance.'

'Great,' replied Grundy. 'By all means, give 'em a chance but never turn your back on them, that's all.'

'Well, I did this morning,' said Billy, 'and I'm still here to tell the tale.'

'Beginner's luck,' said Grundy. 'You took 'em by surprise – they weren't ready. Wait a day or two.'

'Take no notice of him, Hoppy,' said Liz Logie. 'He exaggerates and he's trying to frighten you. You've got to adjust your teaching methods to suit your pupils and you'll be fine.'

'That's a laugh,' said Grundy. 'There's no teaching or learning in this place. Our pupils don't want to learn. It's every man for himself. Survival of the fittest.'

'Or as Oscar Wilde put it,' said Alex, 'survival of the vulgarest.'

'I'm optimistic,' said Billy. 'I think adolescents respond to the right approach.'

'And the best of British luck,' said Grundy. 'How on earth did you end up in a dump like this, I'd like to know.'

'Influence,' said Billy.

This intellectual debate ended with Duffy's bell-ringing.

'The bells of hell go ting-a ling, ling. For you but not for me,' Greg sang. 'You see, I have a free period,' he added.

'Don't ask for whom the bell tolls,' declaimed Alex. 'It tolls for thee.'

'Best of luck with your class, Hoppy,' Laura Mackenzie called in a warm, friendly tone.

Billy's heart skipped a beat.

186

'Thanks, Miss Mackenzie,' he said. 'From what people have been telling me, I'm going to need it.'

Chapter Seventeen

Cold Reception

After break, Billy stood in front of Senior 4 and waited until they had settled down. I'll treat them as equals, he thought. Adopting a friendly, informal approach, he addressed them.

'As you know, I'm new to the school – new to teaching – and so I hope you'll have patience if I put my foot in it or say the wrong thing. I don't know anything about you and if I'm to teach you properly, I need to find out what you can do and what your abilities are. So I propose to give you some short tasks which will give me an idea of your capabilities.'

One of the boys, a tall, athletic lad, raised his hand. Billy consulted the cardboard tag on his desk.

'Jim Mitchell. What's your question?'

'Look, let's get one thing straight from the start. We hate this dump. Nearly everyone in this class would have left school this year if it hadn't been for this sodding government raising the leaving age to fifteen. My dad had a good job lined up for me as a decorator's apprentice and now I've got to waste another bloody year doing the same old thing. We're sick of it. We've learnt nowt at this school.'

This short speech prompted a series of shouts, cries, and catcalls which threatened to get out of hand.

'Quiet, quiet!' Billy called.

Vera Pickles, the pretty dark-haired girl, joined in the protest. 'I had a good job at Lewis's as a shop assistant and now I've lost it. We can't see the point in staying another year in this dive.'

There was a general murmur of agreement amongst the rest of them.

'OK, OK,' Billy said. 'Keep your shirts on. I get the point. But what do you want me to do? I don't make the laws of the country. But who knows? You might get an even better job at fifteen than at fourteen. No more arguments. Right now, I want to see what you can do.'

Jim Mitchell gave a deliberately loud yawn.

'Let's try reading for a start,' Billy said a little desperately. 'I notice you have copies of *Gulliver's Travels* in the stockroom. Joe, give them out.'

Joe Duffy got out twenty-five tatty, dog-eared books.

'Right, cop for this,' he shouted, flinging books along the rows. There was an opening and banging of desk lids, calling out of names and general mayhem ensued. Once again, the situation was getting out of control.

'I said give them out not throw them,' Billy shouted, taking the books from Joe.

Billy noticed a boy in the front row. He was smiling an idiotic, vacant smile and he stared back at Billy blankly.

'What are you grinning at?' asked Billy irritably. 'See something funny, do you?'

The lad continued smiling.

'What's your name?'

189

'Dempsey. I haven't done nothin'.'

'Well, Dempsey. What's the big joke? Why are you grinning like a jackass?'

'He grins all the time,' said Mitchell. ' 'Cos he's not all there.' He tapped his temple with his index finger. 'Nobody at home upstairs.'

'That's right. No use asking him,' added Tessie Shea, the tubby one. 'He's as daft as a brush. All the boys in this class are thick. Better to ask a girl.'

'Shut your ugly face, Shea,' bawled Mick Lynch, the red-haired lad with the pink eyes. 'You girls make us sick. All stuck up. Can't think of anything except doing up your hair.'

'Grow up, Lynch,' shrieked Nellie Wallace, a tall, gangly girl. 'You boys are like a bunch of snotty-nosed kids.'

Billy thought it time to intercede in this inter-sex slanging match. 'That's enough of that. If you're going to survive in this rotten old world of ours, you must learn to tolerate each other. Now I want to hear for myself what Alf Dempsey can do.'

Alf began hesitatingly and stumbled through each word by sounding it out syllable by syllable. It was painful to hear.

'HE p-u-t – PUT th-i-s – THIS en-gi-n-e – ENGINE to TO ow-er OUR ear EAR.' For Alf, reading was like stumbling through a minefield – every word an explosive danger. He had the reading age of a kid of six.

'How old are you, Alf?' Billy asked.

'Fourteen and a half, sir,' he replied.

'Did you have a job planned like the others?'

'Yeah. I was going to be a body builder and a boxer.'

There was a howl of laughter from the class.

'I think he means car body builder, sir,' said Des Bishop. 'And the only boxing he'll do will be in a biscuit factory.'

Billy tried two other boys' reading, Duffy, then Horner. They were equally bad. Every attempt was greeted by howls of derisive laughter from the rest of the class. He finally chose a bright-eyed, intelligent-looking girl by the name of Anne Greenhalgh.

She got to her feet, picked up the book and began reading clearly and fluently, her voice modulating beautifully to the sense of the passage. The rest of the class fell silent.

' "He put this engine (a watch) to our ears, which made an incessant noise like that of a water-mill, and we conjecture it is either some unknown animal, or the god that he worships; but we are more inclined to the latter opinion." '

'That's how it should sound,' Billy said quietly when she'd finished.

He had found out what he wanted to know.

He switched next to written English by giving them a simple dictation from the same book.

'This is an abridged version of *Gulliver's Voyage to Lilliput* by Jonathan Swift,' he announced. 'You'd enjoy reading about Lilliput,' he added.

His remark seemed to cause amusement, especially to two boys at the back who were convulsed with laughter. Billy wondered what he'd done that was so funny. He checked his flies – rule number one in college teaching practice sessions. He shrugged his shoulders. Perhaps the boys were simply moronic.

He read out the excerpt carefully in short phrases. ' "He,

191

the emperor, is taller by almost the breadth of my nail than any of his court, which alone is enough to strike awe into the beholders." '

Billy noted the great differences in the facility with which they did the exercise. For some, it was purgatory as with contorted facial expressions they twisted and turned in their seats in their effort to transcribe the passage. When they had finished, he collected the papers for marking that evening. The first of many home assignments to come.

Billy had half an hour left to dinnertime and he utilised this with a simple mental arithmetic lesson, using examples from everyday shopping.

'I went into a shop,' he began, 'and I bought a cabbage for sixpence ha'penny—'

'Then you were bloody well robbed for a start,' said Mike Lynch, interrupting him. 'Cabbages are only fourpence on my dad's barrow.'

The class rewarded his comments with the usual guffaws.

'Your dad's a costermonger?'

'A what? Wait till I tell him what he is. But yeah, I suppose that's what you'd call him. He's on Market Street, and I help him every Saturday, and God help me if I give the wrong change.'

'Don't question the prices, Mike. Simply add up the bill and calculate the change.' Billy continued with the arithmetic exercise.

Mike Lynch, whose reading was sub-standard, was like greased lightning when it came to working out a bill and the change due. Faster than Billy and there was a pause each time until he had caught up with him. This caused much amusement but Billy didn't mind. On the contrary, it was a cause for rejoicing that one of his learners could add and subtract so rapidly.

He kept them thus occupied until Duffy rang the dinner bell.

Lunchtime!

Deo gratias. Thanks be to God.

Billy told the class to stand for the Angelus but before he could begin, he saw that the two gigglers had raised the flap of their desk and were pointing out something inside to their immediate neighbours, causing great hilarity. Billy walked over and made them open the desk lid fully. The source of the helpless laughter was a copy of *Lilliput* magazine opened up at a picture of a nude with impossibly large breasts.

'We was only looking at our copy of *Lilliput*, sir,' leered Roger Horner, obviously the leader of the pair. 'You told us to take a look at Lilliput.'

'Put that disgusting magazine away,' Billy said severely, 'and I don't want to see anything like that in this class again. Otherwise . . .'

He left the threat unsaid. Mainly because he couldn't think of a suitable punishment and he also found it difficult in his heart to reproach Horner as sternly as he deserved. Billy had no room to talk – only five years earlier he had been going through a similar phase of adolescent development.

The class said the Angelus. 'The angel of the Lord declared unto Mary . . . And she conceived by the Holy Ghost . . .'

When the class had finally departed, Billy sat down at his high desk and put his head in his hands. What a morning, he thought. Resistance to his authority in his first encounter with the class. Could he last the pace?

Could he survive in this hostile environment?

Chapter Eighteen

Lunch Hour

In the lunch break, he walked over to the staffroom and found that Miss O'Neill had made dinner arrangements with a true woman's touch, having spread an embroidered cloth over the table and provided a small vase of flowers. She had laid three places with cutlery, plates and china teacups.

'Beautifully done, Miss O'Neill,' Billy remarked.

'Why, thank you,' she said. 'We try to make lunch a civilised affair and not like the free-for-all we seem to have at morning break.'

They sat down to lunch. Billy unwrapped his sandwiches and placed them on the small plate Miss O'Neill had provided. He lifted the top slice and was gratified to note that Mam had given him not only cheese but slices of tongue, specially bought for his first day.

Shortly after, they were joined by Frank Wakefield.

'Sorry I couldn't get across this morning,' he said, addressing Billy. 'Well, how did you get on with Senior Four?'

'Oh, not bad,' he replied. 'I know it's early days but I found out two important things about them.'

'And what are those?' he asked, now very interested.

'Well, first, there's tremendous resentment at being made to stay on at school for an extra year. I can well understand the way they feel.'

'Right,' he said, opening up his lunch box. 'And the second thing?'

'There are vast individual differences in their levels of intelligence and achievement. Some of the class are extremely bright but one or two of them are practically illiterate and innumerate. They'd have problems coping in the modern world. They could hardly read the instructions on the side of a can, or an electrical appliance, like a toaster or an iron. Could be dangerous in certain circumstances.'

'Some of them can't read very well because they have bad attendance records,' said Miss O'Neill as she poured the tea. 'It's hard to teach them anything if they're not here. When they come back after a long absence, the class has moved on and they're left way behind.'

'Everything you say is true but it's no good simply wringing our hands, we're stuck with the situation,' said Wakefield, slicing a tomato. 'More important, what do you propose we do about it?'

'Look, Mr Wakefield,' Billy said, 'I'm the beginner round here. I don't want to be thought arrogant trying to teach my grandma to suck eggs. Mr Grundy's already accused me of being an idealist with a head full of useless training college theories.'

'Never you mind what Grundy says,' retorted Wakefield. 'He's got problems of his own, has that one. He lives at home with only his aged sister and a cat for company. No wonder he's bitter and twisted. Sorry, Miss O'Neill, I wasn't implying that being unmarried makes you doolally but . . . well you know what Grundy's like. He's happy if he can make it to Friday at four o'clock without a confrontation. As for you being an idealist, Mr Hopkins, I'd take that as a compliment,' he said, munching his sandwich. 'But let's get back to the problem of Senior Four and their individual differences. Any ideas?'

'One thing's obvious,' Billy said. 'Class teaching is out. We have to devise a system which allows us to cater for the wide differences in their abilities. Whole class teaching means it's too easy for some and too hard for others.'

'I agree,' said Miss O'Neill, 'but we can't go round giving thirty separate lessons to each one of them. That would mean many of them would get too much attention and some would get none.'

'There's a plan I remember reading about at college . . . but I don't want you accusing me of trying to foist new-fangled ideas on you. It'd be hard work for me because it means drawing up an individual programme for each child – at least in the basic subjects of the three Rs.' Billy wondered if he was giving the impression of being a know-all.

He need not have worried, for Wakefield said, 'Sounds great. Can you work out some details for me to take a look at? To start things off, you'd better have a look at the syllabuses for your class – I'll let you have copies of them later.'

'Meanwhile,' Billy said, now warming to his subject, 'I'll give the class a few standardised tests in the basics and then go to work on producing work schedules for each pupil. I can see it will mean burning the midnight oil.'

'Great,' Wakefield said. 'Now let's stop this formality business of Mr Wakefield and Mr Hopkins. Call me Frank. What do we call you?'

'Hoppy,' chimed in Miss O'Neill. 'I heard Alex talking to you at break. And you can call me Norah,' she added bashfully.

'OK, Hoppy,' said Wakefield warmly. 'What about the other problem? Senior Four resentment. More intractable, I'd say. It's a case of motivation and low morale.'

'I may have one or two ideas on that but I'd rather hear your notions of what we can do to get them interested.'

Wakefield offered him a cigarette and they lit up together. Miss O'Neill began clearing away the dinner things.

'I'm not going to give you a sermon on education but I have definite views on what it's about. Education is so important. We've finished a world war and we know that to defend a country, you need an army, but to defend civilised values you need schools. Many of our kids come from poor homes where they're knocked about. I don't think we should simply continue this practice and so we keep corporal punishment down to an absolute minimum. Grundy, though, is the exception and I think he's too free with the strap. I know that kids can sometimes get up to serious mischief, in which case I don't hesitate to deal with it, but I think we should be sparing in the use of corporal punishment. The one piece of advice I want to give you is this. In the early days of your teaching, be strict. Be firm. Don't stand any nonsense from them. Show them who's boss from the start and you can relax the reins later.'

'The iron hand in the velvet glove?' said Billy.

'More like the velvet hand in the iron glove,' Wakefield laughed. 'Absolute firmness hiding a mild approach. These kids have to stay on an extra year and it's no use our doing the same things all over again. They have a right to expect something different, something more interesting and exciting. The word education comes from the root *e*, meaning out of, and *duco*, I lead. It means a leading out. For me education is a leading out of what is already there in the pupil's soul.' He offered Billy another cigarette and a light.

'I'm going to owe you a fortune in fags,' said Billy.

'Don't worry about it,' Wakefield replied. 'I know what it's like to be a young teacher starting out. For Grundy, education isn't drawing out but putting in something that's not there, and that's not education. If anything, it's intrusion from the Latin *trudo*, I thrust. Grundy's method is to thrust in a lot of data into the pupil's head as if they're empty vessels needing to be filled up; mine is leading out of knowledge, and that is true education.'

'In other words, developing their potential, bringing out the best in them,' said Billy, drawing on his cigarette.

'Exactly,' he replied. 'School isn't simply a place for stuffing their heads with facts and figures – which they'll soon forget anyway. No, it has more to do with preparing them for life on the outside and that includes their social and spiritual, as well as their intellectual, development. We've got to release their full potential, not just their mental abilities. In this sense, education is everyone's business and involves everything that living itself involves. Our job is to give them guidance in the greatest of all problems – the problem of living.'

'That's a pretty tall order,' said Billy, frowning a little in perplexity. 'How do we do all this in one year?'

'I'm not saying we can do it in a year but we can make a start by taking them out of the classroom and involving them with the world outside – show them the beauties of nature, the practices of other occupations, get them involved in the process of creating something, not merely imbibing useless information. There's more to teaching than mere instruction. The old idea was that children were so many receptacles and it was our job to cram the facts in.'

'Like Mr Gradgrind in *Hard Times*,' Billy said. ' "Now, what I want is, facts . . . facts alone are wanted in life. Plant nothing else and root out everything else." '

'That's it,' Wakefield laughed. 'What I should like to see with the top class is a situation where we take them beyond these four walls and out into the world – hiking in the hills, cycling in the country, visiting factories, and so on. Take them out into the community and bring the community in.'

'Wow!' Billy exclaimed. 'Are you sure I'm the man to do it, Mr Wakefield – Frank? I mean, I'm still wet behind the ears.'

'You're young and you're enthusiastic. I know you can do it,' he said earnestly. 'You're an idealist,' he added with a glint in his eye. 'And that's what we need, an idealist.'

'I hope I can come up to your expectations,' Billy said. 'From what you've been saying, it looks as if we need a two-pronged attack. First, individual work schedules, and secondly a programme of visits. This is going to keep me busy.'

'But very fulfilling,' said Wakefield. 'Now, this afternoon, I shall take your class for art in order to give you a chance to have a tour of the school and find your way around. I'm sure other members of staff will be glad to show you what's what.'

At least, thought Billy, I get a temporary stay of execution before I have to face that bunch of savages again.

Chapter Nineteen

Grand Tour of the School

In the afternoon, as Frank Wakefield had suggested, Billy made a grand tour of the school by walking over to the NFS annexe. First on his list was Miss Logie.

'By all means, come in,' she cried when she saw him. 'Meet Senior Two. Show how polite you can be. Say good afternoon, Mr Hopkins.'

The class obeyed her instruction and Billy responded in kind.

'This lot are the daftest in the school,' she announced, looking affectionately at her pupils.

The boys and girls in the front row grinned good-humouredly.

'What are you?' she asked.

'Daft, miss. That's why we've got the daftest teacher,' one of them called loudly.

'That's enough from you, Morgan,' she replied. 'That one should have been a pirate like his namesake,' she said in an aside to Billy.

Liz obviously had an easy-going relationship with her wards.

'Here, Buccaneer Morgan,' she said suddenly. 'Show

Mr Hopkins that you're not a pirate and not as daft as you look. Go with Nancy there on to Stockport Road and do my shopping. Here's the list and the money. And make sure you get the change right. And don't get knocked down!'

The two pupils left the classroom with her shopping basket.

'As for the rest of you,' she shouted, looking from one side of the room to the other, 'get on with your compositions, "What I'd do if I won the Treble Chance", whilst I have a talk with Mr Hopkins here.'

'Don't you worry that the two shoppers might have an accident?' Billy asked.

'Accident? This lot? They're quicker-witted on the streets than the two of us put together. No, I believe in practical arithmetic. When they come back, we'll put the shopping list on the blackboard and they can calculate it as an exercise. Last week, I had them reading imaginary gas meters and calculating the bills.'

'You seem to have a good relationship with them,' said Billy, and he meant it.

'True, but don't let that fool you. I can be strict with them as well if necessary. What you saw is the result of many years' experience. I can be friendly with them but they know how far they can go. You see, I was brought up in this district myself and there's nothing they can tell me about it. Now you've got a tough job on your hands taking the top class. My advice to you is to sit on them right from the start. If you let them step all over you at the start, you'll find it hard to get control later. Whatever you do, don't try to curry favour with them or try to win the popularity stakes. Show them who's in charge and if you win them over, you can always ease up later on.'

'That's exactly what Frank Wakefield said,' Billy remarked.

'Great minds think alike. Be on your guard, though, especially with the girls – they're practically grown women and they know the ropes. You're a young, good-looking man and they'll try to take advantage. One last thing. Never, never lay a finger on any of them or they'll have you in court before you can say Sugar Ray Robinson.'

'I'll try to remember it,' said Billy as he left her classroom. 'I'll go and have a word with Mr Grundy.'

'You'll find Grundy's nasty with the kids. But one thing I'll say for him, he's always fair.'

'How do you mean, Liz?'

'He's equally nasty with all of them.'

Billy walked along the corridor until he reached Mr Grundy's classroom. As he opened the door, he noted the strange atmosphere – the absence of noise. Complete silence in a school classroom was not merely rare, it was unknown, unnatural even.

'Mind if I come in?' he called.

'Not at all!' replied Grundy. 'Always glad to put a newcomer straight and get him on the right track.' He turned to the class and hissed, 'Right, you lot, do Exercise Sixteen on percentages and I don't want to hear a word from any of you.'

At the front of the class, three boys were kneeling on the hard wooden floor before the blackboard. Another had his arms raised sideways as if playing at aeroplanes – though it was evident that he wasn't enjoying himself by the way his aching arms wobbled.

'Get those arms up,' Grundy commanded.

'What have they been up to?' inquired Billy.

'This quartet,' said Grundy pointing to the penitents, 'were talking when they should have been working. So, for their sins, they can experience a little inconvenience.'

'I see,' said Billy, meaning that he didn't. 'You believe in running a tight ship, as it were.'

'Too true. I'm a great believer in original sin – there's a lot of badness in these kids and it's up to us to knock it out of them. Some mornings I begin the day by strapping everyone in the class – one stroke each.'

'Irrespective of what they've done or haven't done?'

'Why not? It's just to let them know what'll happen if they try it on. You've got to keep on top of them, show them who's master if you're going to survive. Teaching in this school is like working in a zoo and these kids are like wild animals. The only way to keep control is by means of the whip.'

'You mean like dealing with a pride of lions?'

'More like a bunch of vultures watching a thirsty man in a desert. Turn your back and they'll have you. They can smell fear on a new teacher and so you have to stay on top if you're going to survive. Be tough from day one. They may not like you but they'll respect you and that's worth a lot more. Most of them come from broken homes and what they're lacking is firm discipline. They get belted at home but it's inconsistent. They never know whether they're going to get a pat on the head or a clip round the ear. It's my job to see that they get strict but predictable discipline.' He turned to the wobbly armed sinner. 'Arms up, I said,' he yelled at him. 'Excuse me a moment, Mr Hopkins,' he said suddenly.

'Hamilton!' he roared. He strode quickly across the room

and clouted a fair-haired lad across the head. 'I said no talking! I'll teach you to disobey me when I give you an order. I'll stand for no nonsense in my class. Is that understood?'

The luckless Hamilton went to the front of the class.

'Right,' Grundy snarled, 'now hold out your hand.' He produced a tawse from a drawer of his desk and proceeded to deliver a stinging blow to Hamilton's left hand. 'Now get back to your place, and remember to do as you're told. And another thing, Hamilton, if you're going to chat to your companion, try to speak English and not that diabolical Glasgow dialect of yours. And it's about time you bought yourself a satchel for your homework. What are you going to carry your books in, laddie? Your kilt? And we don't want the grease of your fish and chips all over the exercise books either.'

Grundy turned to Billy. 'There's a spare strap in my desk which I'll let you have. Only, when you use it, there are a few finer points to keep in mind. First, make sure they've got their fingers stretched right out and their thumbs out of the way. Don't let the strap touch their thumbs or you'll leave a mark. Next thing you know they'll be running home complaining to their parents. Another thing, always strap their non-writing hand unless they deserve more than one stroke – in which case you don't have any choice.'

Billy declined the offer, feeling he'd rather try more humane methods to keep class control.

'That Hamilton is a new boy,' Grundy explained. 'Straight from the Gorbals. We certainly get 'em at this place.'

'How do you like teaching?' asked Billy suddenly though he felt he knew the answer already.

'Like it! Like it! That's an irrelevancy. We're not paid to like it. In my opinion, it's a job and it helps to pay my mortgage and my gas bills. As I see it, kids are nasty, brutish, and short. They're evil, smelly little animals who must be trained in the ways of civilisation. Left to themselves, they would soon return to the savagery of the jungle.'

'Don't agree with you there,' said Billy. 'I believe with Jean Jacques Rousseau that man's nature is fundamentally good, that children are by nature moral beings, and it's our job as teachers to bring out the best in them.'

'I hope you succeed in finding something good in that class you've been lumbered with,' he sniggered.

'If you don't like it teaching here,' said Billy, 'why not get another job?'

'I tried once or twice in the early days,' he whined. 'But no use. Once you're employed in the elementary system, you're stuck. Like being a prison guard in Strangeways or Alcatraz.'

'Surely school isn't like a prison. You're dealing with youngsters with fresh, lively minds. Don't you find it rewarding to see their eyes light up when they have insight into something or when you awaken their understanding and interest in science?'

'Personally, I don't give a damn whether they're inter-ested or not. They might not care a toss for Boyle's Law or for the bones of animals that have been dead ten thousand years. All I want them to do is to shut up and listen.'

'Maybe it'll rub off on some of them one day,' Billy said in an attempt to inject a note of optimism.

Grundy snorted derisively. 'In my twenty years at the coal face, it's not happened. As for that class they've dumped on you, you've got real problems. Hewers of wood and drawers of water, that's all they'll ever be. None of them wants to learn, all they're interested in is getting out and earning some money which they'll waste in the dance halls or the pubs. By eighteen, they'll be married and by nineteen, parents. The girls will look like ugly old washerwomen by the time they're twenty-one. Let 'em leave school as soon as possible is what I say.'

'That's easy to say but I'm faced with a *fait accompli* and so I have to get on with it.'

'True, true,' he guffawed. 'But I don't fancy your chances with that bunch of morons. I'll give you six months.'

'Anyway, thanks for your time,' said Billy and he moved towards the door.

'No problem,' called Grundy.

Billy left Grundy's class thoroughly depressed and wondered if he, too, would end up with the same pessimistic view of human nature after a few years in the job.

So that's the general advice from the old hands, he reflected. Be a hard-nosed bastard – wear a tough mask no matter how you feel inside. The trouble is you can become so harsh, you forget you're a teacher and you end up bitter and twisted like Grundy. No, playing the hard man wasn't his style. He desperately wanted to be a good teacher with a relaxed, easy-going manner, whose teaching was a pleasant and enjoyable experience, not a petty dictator or a prison guard imposing his will on a lot of youngsters who were forced to come to school by law.

His next visit was to the remedial class taken by Alex Callaghan.

'Hoppy, great to see you!' was Alex's greeting. 'Come into my kingdom.'

The atmosphere in the room was a complete contrast to the last one. This is more like it, thought Billy. The children were smiling and looked happy. They were involved in a variety of tasks. Some were counting on an abacus, some absorbed in assembling simple jigsaw puzzles, others building models of Plasticine, still others trying to cut card with the monstrously blunt standard school scissors, and a few were struggling their way through a simple reader.

'As I said at the break this morning,' Alex whispered, his eyes twinkling, 'Frank Wakefield took one look at me and knew my calling right away. The backward class.'

'What exactly does that entail?' asked Billy, gazing at the class of children.

'Well, one big advantage is that the class is small – only fifteen children – but they require constant individual attention. The ages in this class range from eight to fourteen. Teaching them requires incredible patience and even the smallest advance is a reason for celebration.'

'How remedial are they?'

'Let me give you an example.' Alex called to a dreamy-looking girl in the first row. 'Norma, come here to the front for a moment.'

She came forward with a fixed smile on her lips, and stood before Alex's desk.

'Tell Mr Hopkins here your name.'

'Norma Johnson,' she answered shyly.

'And how old are you, Norma?' asked Alex.

'Don't know, sir. I think I'm fourteen.'

'How many buttons are there on your coat, Norma?'

'Don't know, sir.'

'Let's count them together.'

Norma and Alex counted off each button. 'One – two – three – four.'

'Now, how many buttons, Norma?'

'Four, sir,' she replied with a triumphant smile.

'Well done, Norma. Now sit down and go on with your building bricks.' Alex turned to Billy. 'That may give you a rough idea, Hoppy. We progress in very small steps. If we were to ask Norma again in a few moments how many buttons are on her coat, she'd probably have forgotten, and we'd have to do the exercise again.'

'Are all the kids as remedial as this?'

'Not quite. Norma is probably the most retarded but all are fairly backward. If we can teach them the absolute basics, we count it as a success. One or two might even manage to read simple text and do simple calculations.'

'Will they get jobs when they leave school, do you think?'

'The less retarded might but for the severely retarded, prospects are probably bleak.'

Billy left Alex's class with much to think about. Maybe the task of teaching the top class wasn't so bad after all.

Last port of call at the Fire Service annexe was Miss Norah O'Neill's needlework class. As he stepped into the room, he noted the atmosphere of quiet industry. About a dozen girls were seated in a circle engrossed in their various sewing tasks. A couple of the girls were engaged in trying to thread their needles, with one eye closed, face screwed up, tongue darting in and out like a snake as they summoned up all their reserves of concentration. Another girl had been deputed to read aloud from *Anne of Green Gables* to the rest of the group. At the exciting bits, many of them had pricked their thumbs and, not wishing to waste the heaven-sent opportunities which had fallen into their laps, had utilised the drops of blood to adorn their work with interesting red-spotted patterns.

Miss O'Neill came forward smiling broadly when she saw him. 'Welcome to our sewing circle,' she said. 'Say good afternoon to Mr Hopkins,' she instructed the class.

They looked up from their work. 'Good afternoon, sir,' they dutifully chorused, smiling coyly at Billy.

'Good afternoon, girls,' Billy replied. He felt like a visiting bishop.

'These girls will never have to do any elaborate sewing,' Miss O'Neill whispered. 'The most challenging things they will ever have to do in real life will be darning socks and sewing shirt buttons for their husbands.'

'They seem to be doing well as far as I can see,' Billy said. 'If I need any little mending jobs on my clothes, I'll know where to come.' On Les's clothes, that is, he thought.

'I teach them the fancy stitches,' Miss O'Neill said, 'as it's part of the syllabus. Back stitch, hem stitch, single stitch, double stitch, and so on. In the end, I usually have to unpick their efforts and do them over again. Take this piece of work.' She picked up an example from one of the girls. 'The gussets are gigantic and her necklines not nice. Last week I had to unpick her tucks. Nevertheless, they like this class – it's one of the few places they can find a bit of peace in their lives.'

'My own class, Senior Four, could learn a thing or two here,' said Billy.

'We're so glad you came here,' she said. 'We consider ourselves lucky to get you. You're young and enthusiastic so you'll have a better understanding of the needs of the top class than anybody. I do hope you get on with them.'

'I've got my fingers crossed,' Billy replied.

He left the NFS annexe and as he crossed the play-ground he espied Sybil Melton-Mowbray – a whistle suspended from a lanyard round her neck – and her 'netters' class.

'No, no, you silly pie!' she called as she leapt after her 'gals'. 'Pass the ball to Janet! Now shoot, girl! Shoot!'

Billy gave her a cheery wave which she returned with great enthusiasm.

'You see what I have to put up with,' she called. 'No team spirit.'

Billy returned to the prefabs and found the classroom of the person in whom he was most interested. Junior 2 and the class of Miss Laura Mackenzie.

He knocked gently on her classroom door and entered. He was met by the quiet hum of activity – of thirty children busy at their various tasks. Laura Mackenzie was seated at her desk and was listening to a young boy read. She smiled brightly when she saw Billy, and signalled him to come to the front of the class.

'Well done, Mark,' she said, addressing the child. 'Now sit down at your place and go on with your reading.'

'I hope I'm not disturbing you,' said Billy, 'but Mr Wakefield suggested I might walk around the school and acquaint myself with the lie of the land.'

'You're most welcome,' she said. 'And I know how you must feel in a strange place for the first time. I felt exactly the same when I came last term.'

'Your class seems busy.'

'They're a bright bunch and I try to keep them at it. At

211

the moment, some of them are getting on with their Janet and John books and some are practising their Marion Richardson patterns.'

'Marion Richardson patterns? What are they?'

'They are lines of patterns which prepare the children for what they call "real writing".'

'They look like lines of squiggles to me,' he said, glancing at the blackboard. 'Wavy lines that go up and down, and up and down again.'

Laura laughed. 'I suppose they do but at the end of the day, they produce beautiful handwriting – genuine calligraphy.'

'You obviously enjoy your work,' said Billy. How easily and happily she laughs, he thought.

'I love it,' she said warmly. 'And I also like this school a lot, both the children and the staff.'

'The staff,' Billy smiled. 'There's a fascinating subject. Quite a few characters amongst them. One or two seem to have stepped right out of Dickens.'

'True,' she said, her eyes sparkling, 'but no Daniel Quilps or Bill Sykes among them, I'm glad to say.'

'I won't say who but we do have a Micawber and a Gradgrind,' Billy said.

'True,' she laughed. 'But apart from the friendly staff, another reason I like this school is that it's so handy for me. I live only a short distance away in Regina Park.'

'Don't tell me you live in one of those mansions on Regina Park Hill!'

'Yes, I'm afraid I do,' she said light-heartedly. 'Why, is that bad?'

'No, no, not at all,' Billy stammered. 'I cycled over there recently and I was most impressed with the estate.'

'Ah, so you're a fellow cyclist,' she said. 'I come to

school on a bike every morning – much against the wishes of my boyfriend.'

Boyfriend. This was like a thump in Billy's chest. She already has a boyfriend, he thought, and furthermore she lives in one of those posh houses. Out of my league. He banished any thoughts of dating this wonderful creature. He felt the disappointment rise in his throat.

'Yes,' she was saying. 'It takes me ten minutes to come to school as it's downhill but I usually push my bike back as I find the climb up the hill a bit too much.'

'Your boyfriend disapproves of cycling, you said. Why is that?'

'Oh, Hamish thinks the traffic is dangerous. Anyway, you can ask him yourself if you like as he's coming to meet me when we finish at four o'clock. Come over to the school gate and say hello.'

'Sure thing,' said Billy, lying through his teeth. 'I'd like that very much.'

After four o'clock, Billy collected his bike and his brief-case, said goodnight to Frank Wakefield and walked over to the school gate where a large crowd of parents were waiting to collect their children. As he approached, Billy thought he'd play a little game with himself and try to guess which one was Hamish. To have won Laura he must have special qualities. Did they show? Would these qualities be written on his face? Would he be tall? Dark? Handsome? There were several men who could have fitted the bill. He spotted Laura talking to a Robert Taylor type near the fence.

That's me out, he thought. I've no chance against opposition like that. I'll simply have to tough it out.

He adopted a cheerful smile and waved to Laura. She

waved back and beckoned him over.

'Let me introduce Mr Jarvis,' she said. 'Father of Tony in your class and Francine in mine.'

Billy shook his hand warmly. 'I'm truly glad to meet you,' he said. 'Tony is one of my brightest pupils.'

After a brief exchange of pleasantries, Laura suggested they go and meet Hamish. 'That's him over there,' she said, pointing.

Billy was five feet eleven but Laura's boyfriend was a good five inches taller. He was thin and couldn't have weighed much more than eleven stone. He had a long face with high cheekbones, bushy eyebrows, and mousy-coloured hair. His severe facial expression seemed locked in a permanent frown of disapproval. His dark clerical suit, buttoned up at the front, looked expensive and was smart enough but didn't seem to go with the bright Fair Isle cardigan he was wearing underneath.

Laura said, 'Let me introduce Hamish Dunwoody. Hamish meet Hoppy.'

'Glad to know you, Hamish,' said Billy, offering his hand.

The hand remained hovering in mid-air.

'Pleased to make your acquaintance,' said an unsmiling Hamish, 'But if you don't mind, I won't shake hands at this time. Influenza germs can be easily passed through hand-shakes, did you know that?' He had an unexpectedly high-pitched voice, out of place in such a long body.

'I didn't know that,' said Billy, returning his hand to his side. 'But I'll be careful in future.'

Hamish assumed control of Laura's bicycle and then took her free arm possessively, more in the manner of a police officer than a boyfriend. Together, the three of them set off, pushing their bikes along the pavement.

Hamish continued, 'I take a leaf from Louis Pasteur, the French chemist who pioneered the idea of pasteurisation. He was careful about his own hygiene and refused to shake hands because he knew better than anyone that you often carry cold viruses in the palms of your hands.'

'Is that a fact?' said Billy. 'But I always thought that a germ is not necessarily dirty or harmful – it's the name given to any small scrap of life.'

'Aye, that's true, but about seventy per cent of the living organisms in the world are bacteria and I don't believe in taking chances.' He released Laura's arm for a moment and, taking out a Vick's inhaler, sniffed noisily into each nostril in turn.

Laura said, 'Hamish's early studies make him wary of risk-taking. Tell Hoppy about them, Hamish,' she added proudly.

'I did three years of medicine at Glasgow but then decided it wasn't for me.'

'What made you change your mind?' asked Billy.

'I found work on the wards depressing and you can pick up all kinds of ailments in hospital,' he replied. 'They're like huge warehouses stocking a vast array of diseases. You can pick up anything from a common cold to an exotic tropical disease.'

Billy laughed. 'Like leprosy, smallpox or elephantiasis, for example.'

'It's no laughing matter, believe me,' said Hamish, cutting him short with a withering glance. 'It's well-known that as many as seventy-odd thousand patients develop a life-threatening disability as a direct result of being in hospital. The same goes for doctors' surgeries.'

'It sounds as if you've been lucky to escape with your life,' Billy replied politely. What on earth did Laura see in this moronic hypochondriac? 'What are you doing now?' he asked.

'Now I'm studying to be an actuary – I'm in my final year at Glasgow.'

Glasgow! That means he'll be away much of the time. That's a relief.

'Actuary?' said Billy. 'That's a new one on me. What does an actuary actually do?'

'An actuary,' said Hamish, as if reciting from a textbook, 'is one who calculates insurance risks and the probabilities of the occurrences of various contingencies, such as birth, marriage, sickness, accidents, retirement, and death. Give me a few simple indices of a person, like his social class, occupation, religion, and I can predict certain things about him.'

'Such as?' asked Billy.

'Which part of town he lives in, which newspaper he reads, what illnesses he's prone to, and the age at which he'll probably die.'

'Like fortune-telling?' said Billy.

'A lot more accurate than that. We rely on statistics, not reading tea leaves. I'm always telling Laura that travel by bicycle in Manchester is risky. Did you know, for example, that in Manchester alone, one person is knocked off his bicycle every three hours?'

'I'll bet this bloke's getting really fed up with it,' said Billy.

Laura's eyes twinkled and she began to giggle.

'No, no, you don't understand,' said a frowning Hamish. 'Not the same man, for God's sake. I'm speaking statistic- ally, do you see?'

'Oh, sorry.' Billy smiled.

They had reached the Regina Park toll gate.

'Well, this is where I leave you,' said Billy, mounting his bike. 'I'll chance it across to Crumpsall. I hope I don't become that three-hourly man.'

He pressed down on the pedal of his cycle and with a cheery wave, set off for home.

As he turned the corner, Billy dropped the act. His heart was sinking. So that's her boyfriend, he said to himself as he cycled down Stockport Road. A real neurotic if ever I saw one – obsessed with his health. Sounded as if he were worth a bob or two. Three years at Glasgow University, eh! And now studying to be a high-flying executive! What chance do I stand against that kind of competition? Laura's the most beautiful girl I've ever clapped eyes on but maybe she's way out of my class, belongs to a different world. Compare my Gardenia Court with her Regina Park estate.

She probably has a servant or two to run her bath and wait on her hand and foot. What've I got to offer a girl like that? A bike, my old stamp album plus a lousy teacher's salary, that's what. Maybe Dad's right, best to stick to your own kind and not get ideas above your station. Best to know your place. Nah, *I* don't go for this know-your-place and stick-to-your-own-kind rubbish. S'too late anyway for that 'cause I think I've fallen for the girl. But will she ever take a peasant like me seriously, I wonder?

He was so absorbed in these thoughts, he forgot to give a signal as he turned right at Devonshire Street and came perilously close to being knocked down by a 92 bus.

The driver slid his window back. 'You silly sod,' he yelled. 'Watch where you're going, can't you? What's a matter with you? Somebody stole your girl, or something?'

'Sorry, mate,' Billy called back. 'Must've been dreaming.'

Stole my girl, he thought? Not on your life. Then adopting a John Wayne drawl, he said aloud to an invisible audience, 'I don't wanna worry you, Hamish Dunwoody, but I'll give you till sun-up to git out o' town.'

Chapter Twenty

The Two Cultures

The longcase clock in the hall of the Mackenzie household struck five. For the umpteenth time that day, Grandma Mackenzie adjusted the silk mobcap on her silver hair as she sat rocking in her chair by the kitchen range in the capacious kitchen. In the corner, old Aunty Aggie snored gently as she dozed in her high-backed armchair. Her spectacles had slipped from her nose and the copy of *The People's Friend* had fallen from her lap.

Grandma, a small, wrinkled old woman shrivelled by her eighty years, her hands knotted with arthritis, was feeling out of sorts and impatient for her food – it had been three hours since she'd had that cup of tea and the arrowroot biscuit. But there was another half-hour before Duncan, the head of the house, got home and it was unthinkable that they could begin without him. From time to time her bird-like eyes shot accusing glances at Jenny, her granddaughter, who sat in the large winged chair at the other side of the hearth, daydreaming.

'You'd better not let your father catch you in that chair, young madam,' the old lady rasped. 'You may be eighteen years old but that doesn't entitle you to sit there.'

Jenny continued to stare into space.

'Did you say something, Grandma?' she asked eventually.

'Oh no. I'm a senile old fool and I like blabbing to mysel'. You must be half asleep, child. But you dare to stay in that chair, my bonnie wee lass, and your father'll soon give you a rude awakening.'

'Dinna fash yoursel', Gran'ma,' Jenny answered. 'I'll be out of it soon enough when I hear him come in.'

Louise Mackenzie entered from the scullery, carrying a large plate of freshly baked bread, a dish of butter, and a board containing a wide selection of cheeses. She was in her early forties and an attractive woman with her auburn hair, large brown eyes, and rosy complexion.

'You'd better stir yoursel', Jenny, and set the table afore your father gets home. Hurry now.'

Jenny tossed her head impatiently, causing the ringlets in her red hair to dance for a moment. She got out of the chair reluctantly and began laying places for eight.

'That lentil soup you're making smells awfu' good, Louise,' said Grandma.

'It should do, Grandma. It's good rich stock made from the lamb we had at the weekend. With food rationing getting tighter every day, we've got to make the most of everything we get.'

'I'm so hungry, I don't know if I can wait another half-hour. And that fish you're steaming makes the waiting even harder.'

At that moment, old Aunty awoke. She looked over her spectacles at Grandma.

'Do you think of nothin' but food, Meg?' she murmured. 'If you had my constitution, you wouldna be so bothered. I mind a time when I could eat an oatcake with the best of

220

them. But now . . . well, I'm not long for this world.'

'You've been sayin' that for the last twenty years, Agnes,' said Grandma. 'If you're on your way out, you're certainly takin' your time about it. But I'm that peckish, I think I must have the appetite of a twenty-year-old.'

'You'll have to wait, Grandma,' said Louise. 'It isn't ready and you know how Duncan would react if he found we'd started without him. As for the fish, you ken full well that's for Duncan's sensitive stomach.'

They heard the front door open and close, and for a brief moment they tensed.

'It's all right,' said Louise. 'It's only Laura home from school.'

Laura came into the kitchen.

'You're home later than usual, Laura,' said her mother. 'Did you have extra work at school?'

'Sorry, Mammy. We didn't get out until four fifteen. We don't finish at half past three like nursery school teachers,' she said, flashing a smile at Jenny.

'I'll bet she's been blethering to Hamish Dunwoody at the gate,' Jenny said peevishly.

'No, Hamish and I have been talking to a young man who's joined the school staff, that's all,' she answered.

'A young man?' asked Jenny, pricking up her ears. 'Is he handsome?'

'Yes,' laughed Laura. 'He's young, handsome and he's free, as far as I know. But I think you'd have to move quickly, Jenny – he's the type that will be snapped up quickly.'

'Some hopes,' replied Jenny. 'I'd have to get Daddy's approval first. My last boyfriend didn't come up to scratch because he was only a railway clerk.'

'You're both too young to be thinking about such things,'

said Grandma. 'In my day, we didna walk out with a young man until we were twenty-one and even then we were closely chaperoned.'

'It's nineteen forty-seven now, Grandma,' answered Jenny. 'Things have changed. My friends don't have fathers who vet their boyfriends and check their bank accounts before they're allowed to walk out with them.'

'Your father only has your best interests at heart,' said their mother. 'Anyway, enough of this blethering, it's nearly half past. Laura, go and call the others and tell them to get washed before Daddy comes in. Quickly, quickly, he'll be here any minute.' Louise made a quick survey of the table for any impropriety of detail which might reflect on the thoroughness of her preparations. 'Let's see, bread, butter, soup plates, side plates, knives, spoons. Fish knife and fork for Duncan.' She made a few minor adjustments to the arrangements. All seemed in order.

Meanwhile Laura had gone into the hall and called, 'Hughie! Katie! Time for tea! Daddy'll be home soon! Better get washed right away!'

A young boy's voice called back from the drawing room, 'On my way, Laura! Just finishing my homework.'

This was followed by a little girl's voice from a bedroom. 'Coming, Laura!'

A few moments later, the three came into the room. Hughie was sixteen years old and tall for his age. He was a striking contrast to Laura, his eldest sister, for, like Jenny, he had blue eyes and red hair. Katie, on the other hand, was a pretty twelve-year-old with light-brown eyes and hair which cascaded down her back – a miniature version of Laura and her mother.

'Come along now, all of you,' Louise ordered. 'To the table.'

She glanced at the clock on the wall and having satisfied herself as to the exact time, poured the boiling water into the warmed teapot. Then she joined the others at the table.

The seven people sat at their places and waited. As the clock in the hall began striking the half-hour, there was the noise of a car in the driveway, and five minutes later they heard the lock of the front door turn. Next, the clatter of an umbrella being placed in its stand. Footsteps followed, the kitchen door opened and in came Duncan Mackenzie.

He was about fifty years of age, a tall man with red hair, blue eyes and a healthy, ruddy complexion. He was wearing a black jacket and striped trousers – the standard dress for a senior inspector in the service of His Majesty's Inland Revenue.

His entrance was greeted with a respectful silence. He walked silently over to the fireside chair, sat down, removed his shoes and put on the carpet slippers which had been left warming at the hearth.

'Shall I take your coat, Daddy?' asked Jenny. She helped remove his coat.

'Hang it up carefully in the hall wardrobe,' he said.

'I always do,' replied Jenny.

Mr Mackenzie went into the scullery and washed his hands. The rest of the family waited in silence. He emerged from the scullery and went over to the table and sat down in the carver chair.

'Let us say grace,' he said.

All bowed their heads.

'Bless us, O Lord, and these Thy gifts which we are about to receive from Thy bounty, through Christ Our Lord.'

'Amen,' they said.

Louise poured his tea into his special cup which he received with a curt nod of the head. These preliminaries completed, Louise got up and brought in a large tureen brimming with hot lentil soup, which she deposited in front of Duncan, along with a ladle and seven deep plates. Carefully – clinically – he doled out the soup which was passed from hand to hand round the table. Louise returned the tureen to the scullery. Duncan commenced eating, which was the signal that it was now permissible for the others also to begin. This first part of the meal was consumed in reverential silence, with Duncan indicating his need for bread or pepper by simply pointing at the item in question. Six pairs of willing hands reached out to meet his requirements. The only sound to be heard was from Grandma as she slurped her soup with obvious relish.

'Must you make that row, woman, when you take your soup?' Duncan snapped. 'Can you no' eat like a civilised human being?'

'I'm always telling her that,' said Aunty. 'God knows I have little appetite now without havin' to listen to that racket.'

'It's my old dentures, Duncan,' Grandma whined, ignoring Aunty's comment. 'They dinna fit as well as they used to.'

'Then you should buy yoursel' a new set,' said Duncan. 'God knows you've got a good pension and you live cheaply enough here.'

'I'm waitin' on the new National Health Service,' she replied. 'We're told that false teeth and spectacles will be free.'

The soup course finished, Louise collected the plates and took them into the scullery. She now spoke for the first time.

'I've managed to get you a nice piece of hake, Duncan. I've steamed it the way you like it with a thick parsley sauce. We've got to be careful of that stomach of yours.'

'That's good, Louise,' said the great man. 'You know how fond I am of a bit o' fish.'

Grandma was eyeing his plate covetously.

'And I suppose you like fish, too, you old glutton,' Duncan said facetiously. 'Here, pass your side plate.'

He scraped off a small portion of his fish onto her plate.

'I only wish I could manage to eat like her,' said Aunty plaintively. 'But I'm no' long for this world.'

The company ignored her.

'Oh, thank you, Duncan,' Grandma simpered. 'You're a good boy. I've always said that.'

Judging the mood of the master of the house was not usually an easy matter but this act of generosity gave a clue as to his present humour which appeared to be amiable. It was all right for everyone to talk.

The rest of the family tucked in to the bread and cheese. While they did so, Louise took it as an opportunity to instil a little discipline.

'Katie, I hope you're going to eat up your crusts. We cannot abide waste in this house. There's many a poor family would appreciate the lovely bread you're leaving on your plate.'

'Yes, Mammy,' Katie said.

'And Jenny, don't slouch like that,' said Louise. 'Pull your shoulders back, girl. You're getting a terrible stoop. And you know your father doesn't like to see you hunched up like that. And you, Hughie, take your elbows off the table. How many times do I have to tell you?'

'Yes, Mammy,' the two Mackenzies chorused.

Duncan looked at his youngest daughter and his features softened as he said, 'Well, young Katie, are you still the brightest lassie in the class?'

225

'I don't know, Daddy. You'll have to ask Laura,' Katie answered shyly.

'She's doing well enough,' said Laura. 'Katie's holding her own but we don't have such fierce competition in the junior school.'

'Then you should,' snapped Duncan. 'The world out there is a competitive place and only the best come to the top. Have ye no read your Charles Darwin?' Then turning his attention to Hughie who had been trying to lie low, he asked sarcastically, 'And how's my genius of a son been getting on at school?'

Hughie flushed and looked uncomfortable. He shuffled in his seat. 'Not bad, Daddy.'

Duncan gave him a withering glance. 'NOT BAD! What does that mean, laddie? You're still first in class, I trust.'

'I'm still first in the sciences, Daddy – physics, maths, chemistry, and biology. Third in English and Latin but I'm having a struggle in French. It's all those irregular verbs and accents.'

'Then you'd better get your head down, laddie. If you want to get into medical school, you must have matriculation and that includes a modern language. Do you hear me?'

'Yes, Daddy.'

'You'll stay in every night and do your studying. I'll have none of this gallivanting off to the youth club, prancing about to that jazz music. Your career must come first. I'd be disappointed in you if you failed to get the necessary grades.'

'Yes, Daddy.'

'If he doesn't get into medical school, Daddy,' said Laura softly, 'he could become a teacher perhaps instead.'

'I'll not hear that defeatist talk in my house,' bellowed

Duncan. 'Teaching! Pah! All right for a woman – a nice respectable occupation until she finds a husband, but not for a man, not for the breadwinner.'

'There's nothing wrong with a man being a teacher,' replied Laura defiantly. 'It's a noble profession.'

'You hould your whisht. It's not nice to argue with your father like that,' said Grandma ingratiatingly. She was hoping she might get the remainder of the fish that Duncan appeared to be abandoning.

'I mind a teacher we had in Kirkintilloch many a year ago . . .' Aunty began.

The family took no notice of her soliloquy. They'd heard it before.

'Teaching – a profession! I've never heard such rot,' Duncan shouted. 'The only professions worth talking about are medicine, law, accountancy. They're the only ones with decent salaries. Now that boyfriend of yours, Hamish, has got his head screwed on the right way. An actuary is one of the best paid jobs around. You'll never starve if you marry him.'

'There's more to life than money,' protested Laura. 'There are things like caring for others, dedication.'

'You try paying the grocer with those,' scoffed Duncan. 'Perhaps you've heard the saying, "When poverty comes in at the door, love flies out at the window." ' With that, he rose from the table. 'I'm off to the study for a smoke,' he announced. 'Where I can get some peace from a lot of nagging women and their jabbering tongues.'

Before he left, he turned to Hughie and said, 'You remember, laddie, what I said. You'll stay in every night and do your studying. Get some work done on your French – your life and career depend on getting at least a credit.' He stalked out of the kitchen.

'You shouldn't have provoked him like that,' said Jenny. 'It's best to agree with him and do your own thing anyway.'

'He's always going on about money and security. As if they're the only things that matter,' Laura said.

'I mind a man in Dumbarton many years ago. Now he had lots of money but he wasna happy despite his wealth . . .' Aunty rambled off on a solitary stroll down Memory Lane.

'I'm all for keeping the peace,' said Louise. 'You've got to try and avoid rubbing him up the wrong way. You were talking a minute ago about altruism, service, and dedication. Here's your chance to put them into practice. The dishes are waiting for someone to wash up.'

Jenny and Laura laughed, went into the scullery, and rolled up their sleeves.

The rest of the family took up their own pursuits. Grandma dozed by the fireside, dreaming of the next meal of cocoa and cream crackers, Louise took up her embroidery, and the two youngest continued with their homework. Duncan smoked his Three Castles cigarettes, read the *Daily Telegraph*, and listened to the wireless. Around eight o'clock, he rose and went up to the bathroom, emerging fresh and ready for a night with his cronies at the Knights of St Columba on Princess Road. First he went into the kitchen where he found the Mackenzie womenfolk about their various activities.

'I'll just pay a visit to the club, Louise,' he said. 'I said I'd take a look at their accounts for them and there's a man I have to meet there to discuss some business.'

I know his business, thought Louise, it's a discussion of Manchester United's chances in the FA cup and the quality of Younger's bitter.

With Duncan's departure, a cloud of repression was lifted

from the house, and the family heaved a collective sigh of relief. For the first time that evening, the sound of laughter was heard in the kitchen.

Billy was exhausted when he reached home after his first day at school. Bike on his shoulder, he climbed the stairs to their tenement flat, taking in the familiar stale stench wafting from neighbours' open doors – boiled fish, sour cabbage, and yesterday's stew. There was the usual screeching and bawling from the Pitts family in the flat below as they fought another round in their never-ending dispute.

Before he had turned the key in the lock, Mam opened the door.

'Well,' she said eagerly. 'How did it go?'

'Tea first,' he said, depositing his bike in the spare bedroom. 'It's a long bike ride from Longsight.'

'Already brewed,' she answered triumphantly. 'I saw you coming from the veranda.'

Seated a little later at the table, cup of tea in hand, he recounted the day's happenings.

'First, they have no building and I've been given a domestic science room in a prefab with the top class of fourteen- to fifteen-year-olds.'

'You seem to spend your life in these here domestic science rooms. If I remember rightly, you were in one when you were evacuated to Blackpool. But what about the other teachers? What are they like? Are they friendly? Do you think you'll like it? What about the kids you'll be teaching – are they well-behaved?'

'Whoa, Mam!' he exclaimed, holding up both hands. 'One thing at a time. In reverse order. The kids are a bit bolshie but I think I can talk them round. They're hopping mad because they've been made to stay an extra year at

229

school. I like the staff, though. The head's OK, a rugby-playing scoutmaster, and there are two brothers named after popes, a big woman with one of those posh, double-barrelled names – a jolly-hockey-sticks type – a deaf woman who smokes a pipe, and a bloke who thinks he's commandant of a concentration camp.'

'It sounds like a Prestwich loony bin, or the inside of a cuckoo clock, if you ask me,' said Mam, shaking her head. 'Do you think you're going to be all right?'

'I know I'm going to be all right for I've fallen head over heels in love with one of the staff.'

'Not the deaf one with the pipe,' she said with a straight face. 'Your father'd go mad if you brought her home.'

'No, this one is the loveliest creature I've ever clapped eyes on, a Miss Laura Mackenzie.'

'And I suppose you're going to tell me she smokes cigars and has a beard.'

'No, nothing peculiar about her. Simply beauty unadorned, a vision of loveliness straight out of a Gainsborough painting. You know, like the one you see sometimes at the cinema at the start of the big picture.'

'I hope her clothes are more up to date than that woman with the big hat. But you sound as if you've been struck by lightning,' she said.

'I have,' he said. 'But no need to worry. She's my ideal but unattainable – unreachable. In a higher class. Anyway, she already has a boyfriend from a rich family – Hamish Dunwoody. I don't stand a cat in hell's chance.'

He was hoping Mam would contradict him and she did.

'Well, you know what they say,' she replied, looking right at him. 'A faint heart never won a fair lady. Is she engaged to this Hamish fella?'

'Not that I know of.'

230

'Then there's always hope.'

'And a cat may look at a king,' he said. 'Or in this case, a queen.'

Mam drank it all in, enjoying the experience vicariously.

After Billy's account of his first day, she said, 'Well, anyroad, apart from that – falling in love, and deaf women smoking pipes – your dad and me are right proud of you. It's a real feather in our cap to have a teacher in the family. You should have seen their faces in the corner shop when I told them our lad was a teacher. Green with envy, they was. "Oh, he'll be that rich," the neighbours said. "Teachers get good wages, good holidays, and a big pension at the end. You're a lucky woman, Mrs Hopkins." So there you are, I feel as if we're somebody at last.'

'Why does everyone keep telling me about my pension? I've only just started the job. I don't plan to retire for another forty years,' he laughed.

But Billy was glad she was happy about his new status. He himself was less sure. He had that top class to deal with and he could smell trouble.

Chapter Twenty-One

Trouble in't Classroom

The next morning, Billy was up bright and early, ready to face his first real day of teaching. The euphoria and the excitement he felt were shared by Mam as if she were undergoing the experience with him. As she pushed his packed lunch into his hand, she gave him a big hug and said, 'Go and make us proud, our kid.'

Now where had he heard that before?

He reached school forty-five minutes later after the usual struggle weaving through the Manchester morning rush hour. As he crossed the grass between the prefabs, a leather football shot through the air, narrowly missing his head.

'You stupid bugger, Horner,' he heard a voice call.

'Piss off, Lynch. You should get out of the way, you fat get!' Horner replied.

'Hey up, here comes bloody Hopalong Cassidy!' another one cried.

So he'd been given a nickname already.

He entered the classroom, his head still buzzing with Wakefield's pep talk from the day before. His idea was to tread water until he had formulated some firm plans for his pupils. He decided to spend the first part of the day testing their level of English. The quickest way was to get them to write something.

'I'm going to start today with composition.'

There was a loud groan from the class.

'All right! All right!' said Billy. 'Take out your pens. I want you to write on this subject, not in your books but on the paper I shall give out.' He turned to write on the blackboard. As he did so, a pellet struck him on the back of the head. He knew it was a waste of time to ask for the name of the culprit. He ignored it but continued to write – sideways: WHAT I THINK AND WHAT I HOPE.

'OK. Start writing and let's see what you can do. One further thing, tell me what you really feel. No one else will see what you write except me.'

'Got no pen,' Mitchell yelled.

Billy had anticipated this and quickly supplied him from the spares he had ready.

'Need a new nib,' shouted Horner.

'Right, cop for this,' called Joe Duffy, throwing one across the room.

'You stupid bastard!' yelled Irene Moody. 'Look what you've made me do. I've spilled ink over my book.' She threw her exercise book at him.

'You crazy cow!' bawled Alf Dempsey. 'That bloody well hit me.' He threw the book back.

'You gormless git,' screeched Nellie Wallace. 'Now you've spilt my inkwell over my desk.'

Billy blew his top. 'Stand up, all of you!'

Slowly they dragged themselves out of their seats, scraping their chairs noisily across the floor. There was a banging of desk lids. They glowered back at Billy insolently.

'Did you throw a pen, Duffy?'

'Me? Me?' he said, protesting his innocence and appealing to the rest of the class. 'I haven't done nothing. Don't pick on me.'

'Right,' said Billy, exasperated. 'That's enough of this nonsense. Now get on with it.'

The class sat down and scowled at him. One or two of the brighter ones – Tony Jarvis, Anne Greenhalgh – got down to work but the rest were determined to have some fun by riling him, questioning his authority and generally causing as much trouble as they could.

'We can't write with this bloody ink, Duffy,' complained Mick Lynch. 'It's like bloody water.'

'Shut your gob, Lynch,' hissed Duffy. 'You're always moaning about something.'

'Get stuffed, Duffy,' Lynch retorted.

'You wait till break, you red-haired get,' snarled Duffy. 'I'll kick your balls in.'

'You and whose army?' growled Lynch.

So the lesson continued. A disaster.

At the end of the morning, Billy collected their efforts, such as they were. During the lunch break, he took a quick look at their writing. Most of it was execrable – a hotchpotch of blots, scratchings-out, misspellings, for the most part the work of illiterates though there were exceptions. Ignoring the messy style, he skip-read through them to see if there were any nuggets of gold to be mined from so much dross. He noted that there was a common theme running through them all. Without exception, they complained about the harsh methods of Mr Grundy. A typical example was that of Mick Lynch.

I cannt wate to get out of this skool

I reely haite skool and have allways hatied this dummp. Speshially Grumpy Grundy who shud get a job in 1 of Hitlers consentrashun camps, he is crooel and likes belting us, if he ever trys to hit me agen, like he did last turmm Ill thump him 1 in the gob. I hope he brakes his legs on the way home from skool, the new teecher Hopperlong is allrite but I think hes two soft.

And from Irene Moody:

I think are new teachers dead smashing but hees not tuff enuff, not like other teachers who our dead rotten. The worst of the lot is grundy as hees all ways giving us the strap even the young girls, I think hees a saddist and get pleshur from it an I hope that 1 day he will fall down a manwhole, I think he secrettly would like to get off with 1 of the girls. We sing a song about him: mister grundys a very good man, he goes to church on Sunday, prays to god to give him strengt to belt the kids on Monday.

The morning session had set a pattern of rowdiness for the day and the rest of the lessons continued in the same vein. The class were set on wrecking all his efforts. At dinnertime, Billy did not report their behaviour to Frank Wakefield.

This is my problem, he said to himself, and I must solve it for myself. But one thing is obvious, Grundy is not very high in the popularity stakes, and if the pupils' hopes and wishes come true he will be spending a considerable part of his life in traction. But I've got to find some way of getting through to these kids, something that will make them see sense and start behaving like civilised human beings. But what?

Next day, there was a change in their behaviour. They were talking when he took his first class in the morning but they went to their desks at once. The room became silent immediately. Silent as a tomb.

Great, he thought. That's the way I like it. They've come to their senses.

'OK, Joe,' he said. 'Give out the *King's English* books.'

Duffy distributed the books quietly and efficiently.

'I want to check up on some of the common mistakes in English that I've heard you making. When I know where your faults are, I should be able to help you. Speaking correct English can be important to your job prospects.' He spoke frigidly and without emotion.

He waited for the usual repartee from someone – 'What, me – a bricklayer? What good's correct English to me?' But no one spoke. They continued to stare at him wordlessly.

'The questions are pretty easy and I'm sure you'll have no problem with them. Turn first to page thirteen and look at Exercise Seven. It says, "Fill each space in the sentences with the correct word from the list." Got it?'

Nobody answered. The quiet was somehow strange and unnatural, and Billy was finding it disconcerting to be met by this wall of silence. But then, he supposed, that was the general idea.

He continued regardless. 'The first example is done for you. "When he met the lady he (rise, rose, raised) his hat." The answer is of course "raised". Now, Mitchell, do number two, using the correct part of the verb go.'

Mitchell pushed his chair back, scraping the floor noisily,

and stood up. He studied the sentence for a while and said: 'She had went for a walk.'

Billy glared at him. Then he saw the light in the eyes of the rest of the class as they exchanged glances. Still no sound.

'No, that's not right, Mitchell. The answer is "She had gone for a walk".'

Mitchell shrugged his shoulders impassively.

'Vera Pickles, try the next one.'

'He seen his uncle yesterday,' she replied.

A few members of the class snickered.

'If you go on answering like this, I'm going to create a scene all right. Next one, Lynch.'

'The old man has fell asleep in his chair,' he answered coldly.

' "Fallen",' said Billy wearily. 'Try the next, Tessie Shea.'

She answered the instant she heard her name. 'He was awaked by the noise,' she said, looking round the class triumphantly.

Billy saw what they were up to but there was nothing he could do about it. They had switched their tactics from rowdiness to bloody-mindedness. He listened to the rest of their botched answers.

The bell rung just after I had wrote the letter.
The picture was drew by a famous artist.
I have knew him since he was small.
The tree had fell across the road and many of its
    branches were broke.

'Obviously,' said Billy, 'you find correct English usage difficult. So I want you to finish the rest of the exercises at home tonight. I shall mark them tomorrow when you bring them in.'

This announcement was greeted with a howl of protest. For the first time that day, the silence was broken.

'Can't we just write out the answers?' Anne Greenhalgh asked.

'No, you will write out the complete sentences. Each and every one of them.'

'But there are forty of them,' protested Tony Jarvis.

'Good, it'll be good practice for you.'

'I've got to do my paper round,' Roger Horner called. 'I can't do it.'

'Got to help my dad on his barrow,' cried Mick Lynch.

'I serve in a shop,' said Tessie Shea.

'I've got to deliver my mam's washing,' screeched Nellie Wallace, 'I haven't got no time for no homework.'

'You should've thought about that when you were planning to ruin my English lesson,' said Billy.

I'm building a barrier, a wall of hostility between the class and myself, he told himself, but there seems to be nothing I can do to demolish it. The process seems to have a momentum of its own. I desperately want to teach and teach well but this lot won't give me a chance. I have to find a way of breaking this chain of events.

In an all-out effort to win their interest, he spent the whole of Wednesday evening at home drawing a colourful, detailed map of the school district showing the important landmarks and places, and – very important – the streets where his wards lived. This ought to attract their attention, he thought, if anything will. He rolled up the map and inserted it into a cardboard cylinder, ready for school next day.

'I hope you're not going to spend every night working,' said Mam when she saw him poring over the dining-room table. 'All work and no play makes Jack a dull boy.'

238

'This isn't work,' Billy replied. 'It's more than that. It's survival.'

Next day, he proudly unfurled his work of art in the geography period. There was a gasp of admiration as he pinned it up on the board. There was an immediate response.

'Hey, there's our street.'

'And the corner shop and the chippy.'

'There's my dad's pub,' exclaimed Mitchell.

'And our house!' squealed Nellie Wallace. 'And there's the houses where I take me mam's washing.'

It's working, thought Billy. At last they're interested in something.

At the afternoon break, as he went off to the staffroom for tea, there was still a small crowd of pupils around the map identifying various features in their little world.

When Billy returned ten minutes later, he found the classroom strangely hushed. They sat in their places expressionless and quietly waiting for him. He soon discovered the reason for their unusual demeanour. His map was a mess. During his absence, someone had ruined it by throwing a bottle of red ink over it. Billy looked despondently at his masterpiece, over which he had laboured for so many hours. Turning his attention to the class, he lowered his voice and spoke quietly and menacingly. The kids at the front could see how he narrowed his eyes and tightened his lips.

'You morons! I won't ask who did this because I know it'd be a waste of time. I'll simply say that if I ever find out, I'll take the law into my own hands.'

The class continued to gaze back at him coldly. On some faces, there was a look of stubborn defiance, on others a look of sad regret.

On Thursday evening, as Billy cycled home, he took stock of his first four days of teaching. Catastrophic. The class seemed to have gone through several phases. First, the bloody-minded phase with the slamming of doors and desk lids, followed by the awkward squad stage with many of them losing their pens, pencils, rulers, exercise books; next, the dumb insolence stage where every request or command was met with a scowl or an impudent reply. The last straw had been that afternoon, the vandalisation of his visual aid. He was in despair and ready to give up teaching for good. Maybe Grundy was right in his assessment. Perhaps they *were* unteachable.

At home over a cup of tea, he outlined his problem to Mam.

'These kids I'm trying to teach are angry, not with me but with Rab Butler and his Education Act. With the government for raising the leaving age and stopping them from going out to work. But they're taking out their anger on me and I'm having a bumpy ride. I really want to teach but they won't let me. There's nothing worse than a bunch of bolshie adolescents.'

'Eeh, I'm right glad,' she said, 'that you grew up before they invented all this adolescence. Most of your scholars are nearly grown up, nearly as old as you. I left school at the age of ten but today they're young adults not school-children.'

'They don't act like adults, Mam,' said Billy.

'P'raps that's because you don't treat them like adults,' she said. 'Give a dog a bad name and hang him. If you treat 'em like kids, don't be surprised if that's the way they behave.'

'Maybe I'm too young for them, Mam. Maybe they should have someone older and tougher.'

'P'raps you are too easy with them,' she said. 'They might be better off with that fella Grundy you're always going on about. I'll bet he'd give 'em what for.'

'That's pipe-dreaming, Mam. They're my class and they're my problem. I must admit, though, I don't know how to get control of them. Punishment is no good – that'll only make them into enemies. But there must be some way, some *thing* that I can hold over them. They must have a pet hate, something they detest. Something that'll scare the daylights out of 'em.'

'Well, whenever you or any of the lads gave me trouble, I always threatened you with your father. "Wait till your father gets home," I used to say. It always worked.'

'That's all very well, Mam, but I can't threaten them with that.' Suddenly, Billy had an idea. Vague at first, no more than a glimmer of light, but the more he thought about it, the more it seemed that it might be the answer. 'Wait a minute though, I think I can see a solution. Mam,' he said, kissing her on the forehead, 'you're brilliant. A genius. I think I know how to bring my young savages into line.'

'If it was something I said,' she replied, 'I'm sure I don't know what it was.'

'You know, up to now, I've been treating them with kid gloves. It's time they learned how it is when I come out fighting. If it's a scrap they want, they're going to find out they're up against the kid from Collyhurst. So they'd better watch out.'

241

Chapter Twenty-Two

The Ultimatum

Friday was the last day of the week and Billy could hardly wait to get to school to talk over his idea with Frank Wakefield, for its success would require his co-operation. He would have to play his cards right because today could be a very important day. Make or break day.

The first period of the day began with the usual insolent behaviour from Senior 4 – noise, raucous laughter, sullen looks, glowering and sulking. At the mid-morning break, Billy sought out Frank Wakefield.

'I've been giving a little thought to the problem of Senior Four, Frank,' he began, seriously understating the time he'd lain awake in the early hours, his pre-occupation at breakfast and along the route to school, 'and I think I may have the remedy.' He explained his plan of action.

The head readily agreed to give it his fullest support.

After the tea break, Billy returned to class. His pupils slowly returned to their places with their customary rowdiness and shuffling of chairs. Billy bided his time. Then he went into action. He banged his fist on his desk. He began pacing the front of the room like a nervous leopard in a cage. Every pair of eyes in the class followed him.

'Look, you bad-mannered louts!' he thundered. 'I've had it up to here with the lot of you. Everyone has advised me to get tough with you. "Give 'em hell," they said. But I'm not like that. This is my first year of teaching and I looked forward to teaching you – the top class. Top! That's a laugh! The dregs, more like it! This class should be setting the example and the pace for the rest of the school but look at yourselves. A bunch of ragamuffins. I tried treating you like adults and what was my reward? You've acted like hooligans ever since I got here – banging doors, desk lids, throwing books, swearing, scowling. But when you threw ink on my map yesterday, that was the last straw. I've had enough of you and so I've decided to ditch you. DO I MAKE MYSELF CLEAR?'

The class went quiet and, for the first time that week, were all ears. The boys glowered but some of the girls looked enraptured. Irene Moody gazed at him admiringly.

'You've done your best to sabotage everything I've tried to do for you. I've tried to treat you as responsible beings and your response has been that of a bunch of apes. Well, that's it, I've run out of patience. I've spoken to Mr Wakefield and he has agreed that starting on Monday morning, this class will be taken by Mr Grundy and I shall take his class, Junior Four.'

Silence. The class looked shell-shocked.

Then Jim Mitchell was up on his feet. 'Wait a minute, you can't do that to us. We hate Grundy. I for one won't be coming to school if we get Grumpy Grundy.'

'You will have to come to school, that's the law,' answered Billy calmly. 'Play truant and your parents will be prosecuted.'

243

'You don't mean it,' said Anne Greenhalgh, smiling nervously. 'You're bluffing. You wouldn't do that to us!'

'Try me,' Billy replied. 'I can assure you, it's been agreed. There's only one solution, I'm afraid.'

'Well what is it?' Tony Jarvis demanded. 'I tell you, the idea of spending my last year with old Grundy sends shivers down my spine.'

'Here it is,' said Billy. 'I'm leaving this class in about ten minutes and I shan't be back until one thirty after dinner. It's up to you. Here's your first exercise in taking responsibility. You've got to decide for yourselves. I want a solemn undertaking from each and every one of you that the hooligan behaviour I've seen in my first week will cease for good, starting Monday morning. Everyone must agree – no exceptions. Otherwise, I walk. And I mean it. It's been settled.'

Senior 4 was still in shock.

Billy left the room and walked over to the staffroom. His hands were shaking. He lit a cigarette and marked books until dinnertime.

As he ate his sandwiches with Frank Wakefield and Miss O'Neill, he wondered if he had done the right thing.

'Don't you worry about it, Hoppy,' said Frank. 'If they don't come round to their senses, I'm moving Grundy in with them, whether he or they like it or not. After all, he gets paid as a senior teacher. He can damned well earn it for a change. But this is Senior Four's first taste of democracy and somehow I think you'll find they see the light.'

'Hope so,' said Billy. 'Things came to a head when they destroyed my map. Obviously we couldn't continue along that course. Something had to give and it's not going to be me. They're up against Billy the Kid and I'm going to come out fighting.'

'That's better. That's the way to talk,' said Frank, adopting a Wild West tone. 'Them's fightin' words, pardner.'

At half past one, Billy returned to class. He found them in their places. He walked to his desk and sat down.

'Well,' he demanded. 'What have you decided?'

The class looked at him with cowed respect. Jim Mitchell stood up.

'The lads and me have talked it over and we're agreed we've been giving you a rough time lately and they want me to say we're sorry. If you'll give us another chance, we'll try to behave and do as you say. We don't want Grundy as our teacher. Anything but that. Tell us what you want us to do.'

The boys nodded their affirmation of what Mitchell had said.

'OK. Fair enough,' said a much-relieved Billy. 'Now, what about the girls?'

Anne Greenhalgh was on her feet. 'The girls in the class have elected me as their spokeswoman,' she said, 'and like the boys we want to apologise for our disgusting behaviour. We want you as our teacher and we're willing to stop messing about and do as you tell us. Only don't send in Mr Grundy or we won't know what to do. We'll do anything you say to stop that.'

There was a murmur of agreement from the girls.

'Right,' said Billy. 'Apologies accepted. From now on we all turn over a new leaf and start again. Pretty soon, you'll be leaving school and taking jobs. You'll be expected to behave like adults, which is what you are. So let's start right now in this class. I'll treat you not as kids but as grown-ups. After all, I'm not much older than you myself.'

The class laughed good-humouredly.

'These are some of the things I want you to do. First, no more swearing in my class. I don't want to hear the obscene words that have been thrown about in the last week. Secondly, treat each other with respect. I don't like this war between boys and girls as if you hate each other's guts. From now on, you call one another by your first names. When you start your first jobs, you'll find that the people in the workplace have respect and friendship for one another and they usually refer to each other by first names. So, we'll do the same.'

'What about you?' asked Tony Jarvis. 'What do we call you?'

'I'm your teacher and the office I hold should be respected. Call me Mr Hopkins or sir – take your pick. You should also have respect for other teachers in the school.'

'You don't mean old Grundy, surely, sir,' exclaimed Mick Lynch.

'I do indeed,' said Billy. 'What he does in his classroom is his own business, not ours. He is a teacher and has his own methods. No more nasty remarks about him, got it? Now, I have an obligation to you to try to make my lessons relevant and worth your while. You have the right to expect that from me. But on the other hand, you have the duty to pay attention and give of your best. Start behaving like grown-ups and that's the way I'll treat you.'

As he was speaking, the door shot open and Nellie Wallace burst in and sat down at her desk.

'I had to deliver me mam's sodding washing – that's why I'm late,' she announced to the class. She looked around the room. 'Why's everyone so sodding miserable?'

The rest of the girls frowned meaningfully in her direction.

246

'Here's our first example,' said Billy. 'Nellie, go out of the room and come in properly.'

'What the hell's going on?' Nellie shouted.

'Just do it!' snapped Irene Moody.

Nellie shrugged her shoulders, got up and went out of the room. A moment later, she walked back in with a book on her head and with the deportment of a Christian Dior model.

The whole class burst into spontaneous laughter. Then applause.

'Sorry I'm late, sir,' she said curtsying. 'I had to do some errands for me mam. May I please sit down?'

'By all means, Nellie,' said Billy, laughing despite himself.

Nellie's tomfoolery helped defuse a tense situation.

By special concession granted by Frank Wakefield, Billy dismissed his class early at 3.30. As he cycled home at the end of his first week, he was elated.

'I've cracked it! I've cracked it!' he repeated to himself all the way up Cheetham Hill Road.

Chapter Twenty-Three

New Deal

That weekend at home, Billy burnt the midnight oil working out a programme for his recalcitrant class. By Sunday night, he had the details clear.

If this works, he reflected, teaching the top class is going to be a joy instead of a penance. He went to bed happy but with a bonnet buzzing with a billion bees. He had a restless night with so many ideas turning over in his mind. Next morning, he awoke still tired but nevertheless looking forward eagerly to putting his scheme into action.

Monday morning began with the usual hymn-singing practice for the whole school, but when Billy faced his class in the second period, he noted a different atmosphere. Somehow they looked tidier and their faces shinier. All eyes were focused on him. He had their full attention.

'Well, Senior Four. For us, this is a fresh start – the first day of the rest of our lives. We shall see how it goes till Christmas. Then we'll review the situation.

'Remember this: you are the senior class in this school, the so-called top class. It means you must set an example at all times. The youngsters look up to you and their little eyes are watching everything you do and say. If you swear and curse, they'll do the same; if you push and shove, so will they; if you come to school looking like tramps, don't be surprised if they imitate you. Up to now, you've not set a very high standard but from today, all that's going to change. Starting now, you've got to show that you are indeed the top class in every way – in behaviour, manners, bearing, and actions. If I'm to be your form master, I want to be proud of you. From what I've seen of you, I know you've got it in you to be a great class – the finest this school has ever seen. It's up to you.'

Jim Mitchell had raised his hand. 'This is all very well, Mr Hopkins – sir – but you've got to see it from our point of view. We should have left this year and we don't want to go on doing the same old things we've been doing for the past three years.'

Billy noticed the respectful 'sir'. Things looked promising.

'I hear what you're saying,' said Billy, remembering his college lectures on counselling. 'I have a programme which I think you'll like. It's different from anything you've ever done before. When I drew it up, I was thinking that you'll soon be leaving school and it was time that we started to take that into account by preparing you for it and teaching you some of the things you'll need. In other words, a preparation for life.'

'What kind of things will we be doing, sir?' asked Anne Greenhalgh, intrigued.

'As I see it,' Billy continued, 'the mornings will be devoted entirely to work in the basic studies – reading, writing and arithmetic plus history and geography. But with one difference, the lessons will be designed for your individual needs. Each of you will have a specially tailored programme to suit your own particular requirements. I'll show you what I have in mind a little later.'

'Did you say the mornings for the basics?' asked Tony Jarvis. 'But what do we do in the afternoons?'

'Afternoons will be given over to social and recreational skills.'

'What are those, sir?' asked little Josey Parker.

'Well, for example, Monday afternoons will be for games as usual, the boys go to football or cricket, and the girls to netball – those parts of the timetable will remain. The other afternoons will be different. They will be given over to some aspect of learning about life outside school. Tuesday afternoons, we shall go out to visit the local library to do our own study and research.'

'Research – us?' asked Nellie Wallace. 'What kind of research? I mean, do we wear white coats and that, like they do in a Frankenstein picture?'

There was general laughter, which Billy joined.

'No, Nellie. It'll be research into books and encyclopaedias. But one thing at a time. On Wednesday afternoons, we'll either go out to visit some place of interest, like a factory, a hospital, or the fire station, or even a police station, to see the people at work.'

'If we go to the police station, some of us might not get out again,' said Roger Horner.

More laughter.

'I live in a pub,' said Jim Mitchell. 'My dad could fix up a visit to a brewery.'

'I'm not sure about that,' said Billy. 'Some of you might not want to go home.'

More merriment. The pupils of Senior 4 were enjoying themselves.

'Anyway,' Billy went on, 'sometimes, we shall bring in an expert to talk to us, like a doctor, or a policeman, or a nurse, or an engineer, people who can tell us about their jobs. Thursday afternoons, we shall learn some of the social graces and the time will be given over to ballroom dancing.'

There was a gasp of amazement from the class. They turned to each other in excitement. Billy gave them a moment to digest this news.

'But who will teach us, sir?' asked Irene Moody when order had been restored. 'Most of us can't dance – especially the boys.'

'I shall have that honour,' said Billy. 'I've taught dancing for a few years. Mr Wakefield has given us permission and the school will lend us its gramophone, and I can arrange to borrow a few records.'

'Fantastic,' exclaimed Tessie Shea.

The class was having difficulty in taking all this in. So different from anything they'd experienced before at school.

'That leaves Friday afternoon and you'll be free to pursue your own activity provided you've reached your target and finished your programme of work.'

'You mean we could play football in the yard?' asked Joe Duffy incredulously.

'If you've done all your jobs, yes.'

The class looked stunned by this revolutionary curriculum.

'Look,' said Billy. 'You'll get into the swing of things as we go through the term – it'll become routine. Right now, let's have a look at one of our basic subjects. Arithmetic. What is it and why do we need it?'

'Who knows and who cares?' replied Mick Lynch, causing the usual ripple of merriment around the class.

'Arithmetic! How I hate it!' exclaimed Vera Pickles.

'Why do you hate it?' Billy asked.

'Because I'm no good at it. I'm hopeless.'

251

'Look,' Billy said, getting hot under the collar. 'Let's have one thing clear in this class. You never, never say "I'm hopeless" or "I can't do this or I can't do that". If you keep feeding yourself with negative thoughts, telling yourself you can't do something, how do you expect to be able to achieve anything? You've already made up your mind you're no good at it. Always tell yourself positive things like "I can do it" and "I will do it". Then we'll get somewhere.'

'Yes sir,' she answered, 'I'll try to remember it. And, sir, I like it when you get mad.'

Billy sighed. This wasn't going the way he'd planned.

'OK,' he said. 'I'll try to get mad to please you. Now, what about arithmetic? I need to know how much you know about it so I can start teaching you at the right level.'

'It's about numbers, adding and subtracting, measuring things, and that,' said Tony Jarvis.

'Good answer,' Billy said. 'And why do we need it?'

'So we can get the sums right and not cheat each other,' replied Anne Greenhalgh.

'Right. Give me some examples.'

'When I'm working on my dad's barrow in Market Street,' said Mick Lynch, 'God help me if I don't give the right change when I'm selling someone potatoes or apples.'

'Good. Let's look at money.'

Billy tested them on money tables, pennies in a shilling, shillings in a pound, shillings in a florin, shillings in a guinea, pennies in half-a-crown. They seemed to know their tables well enough.

'What other things do we measure?'

Joe Duffy raised his hand. Good, Billy thought, we don't get many answers from him.

'Please, sir,' said Joe, 'it's time to put coal in the boiler. I have to do it every hour.'

'OK, Joe,' Billy said disappointed. 'Do your job.'

At this point, Wakefield came into the room and began working at his desk at the back of the room.

Billy had been led to believe that the classroom was the inner sanctum of a teacher, a private place not subject to scrutiny and observation except by inspectors or by invited guests. He'd have felt nervous teaching in the presence of any of his colleagues or of an outsider. But the head! A hundred times worse. He felt he was destined to have a permanent critic weighing up every word he uttered.

'Now, as I was saying,' Billy continued uneasily, 'what other things do we measure?'

'How heavy things are,' answered Vera Pickles.

'Right – weight. What do we measure weight in?'

'Tons, hundredweights, pounds, ounces,' she answered.

'There you are. And you said you didn't know arithmetic.'

He checked their knowledge of weights – most of them had a firm enough grounding.

'How do we weigh people?'

'In stones,' answered Tessie Shea, the tubby girl. 'Don't I know it!' The class rewarded her with the usual laughter and Billy couldn't help joining in. It was good that she was able to laugh at herself.

'How many pounds in a stone?'

'Fourteen,' Tessie answered gloomily.

'If anyone here is worried about their weight,' said Billy, 'be comforted by the fact that the heaviest man in recorded history is an American called Hughes who weighed seventy-six stone.'

The class was suitably impressed.

'What's the lightest any grown-up has ever been?' asked Josey Parker, the small slip of a girl.

'I believe it was once again an American – this time a woman. She weighed forty-nine pounds. How many stones is that?'

'That's only three and a half stone,' Anne Greenhalgh gasped.

'So much for weighing things. What about measuring liquids? They can change their shape so easily.'

'Gallons, pints, gills,' Jim Mitchell said right away.

'He should know, sir, his dad runs the Waterloo Arms,' said Tony Jarvis,

'I'll bet you don't know, sir,' said Jim Mitchell, 'how many tots in a bottle of whisky.'

'You've got me there, Jim. But I'm willing to learn.'

'We measure tots in an optic and we get thirty tots and a bit from each bottle. They call the bit that's over "the barman's tot". Every so often, we get a visit from an Inspector of Weights and Measures who comes round to check our measures. I can show you if you come to the pub some time. You can even have a free pint.'

'Thanks, Jim. I may take you up on the offer. Now these measures we've been talking about are used here in Britain and are called imperial measures. If you ever go abroad to the Continent, you'll find they operate on a different system called the metric. But you won't ever need to worry about that unless you go to live over there. The last thing I want to test you on is time. How do we do time?'

'By going to prison,' Roger Horner called out.

When the giggles had died down, Billy said, 'How do we measure it? And don't say by chalk marks on the prison cell.'

'In seconds, minutes, hours, days, weeks, months, years,' answered Anne Greenhalgh.

'Good. There are twelve months in a year. Why twelve?'

'Hasn't it something to do with the moon going round the earth, sir?' said Tony Jarvis.

'That's correct, Tony.'

'Why do we have leap year every four years?' Irene Moody asked suddenly, giving Billy that look of hers.

'Because it takes three hundred and sixty-five and a quarter days for the earth to go right round the sun. This means that we have a quarter of a day left over. So every fourth year we add a day to February.'

'I remember Mr Grundy telling us about that in science,' said Roger Horner, grinning and looking round the class. 'Wasn't it a fella called Copper Knickers who worked that out, sir?'

'You mean Copernicus, I think,' Billy replied. My wild days in the Upper Fifth are coming back to haunt me, he thought.

'Isn't the leap year the time when a woman can propose to a man, sir?' Irene asked, darting a knowing look at the other girls. 'And isn't the next leap year next year in nineteen forty-eight?'

'Why, yes, so it is,' he said, falling for it.

'I'll be back next year, sir, to see if you're free,' she said, fluttering her eyelids.

Once again, the class enjoyed the joke. They were beginning to see that school could be fun.

'It's rough on anyone who has their birthday on February the twenty-ninth,' remarked Des Bishop. 'They only get to celebrate it every four years.'

The lesson was interrupted when Mr Wakefield sitting at his desk at the back raised his hand.

'What about horses, Mr Hopkins?'

'Sorry, I don't get you, Mr Wakefield. Horses? What about horses?'

'How do we measure them?'

'I believe it's in hands but I don't know much about it.'

'A hand,' said Joe Duffy, making his first real contribution, 'is the width of the hand from thumb to little finger – it's about four inches.'

'Good lad, Joe,' said Wakefield. 'It's exactly four inches by decree of Henry the Eighth. Sorry, Mr Hopkins, I thought you might like to know that.'

'Why thank you, Mr Wakefield. Most interesting. If I need information about horses, I'll know where to come.'

This informative exchange brought Billy's first 'arithmetic' lesson to an end.

'Hey, sir,' said Vera Pickles in a surprised tone, 'I enjoyed that lesson. If they're all like that, I think I'm going to like arithmetic.'

'Well, the way I see it,' Billy said, 'is that you think you've had a raw deal by having to stay at school for an extra year. But give me a chance to prove to you that school is the happiest time of your life. Give me three months, till Christmas, say, and then see what you think.'

The boys and girls of St Anselm's were not accustomed to being spoken to as young adults like this and they didn't know what to make of it.

'The programme you've fixed up for us, sir, sounds great,' said Tony Jarvis. 'We've got to come to school by law and so we may as well make the best of it. At least we don't have Grundy as our teacher.'

Billy finished his first afternoon of teaching by reading the first chapter of their set book, *A Christmas Carol* by Charles Dickens, an old favourite which would take them to the end of term and the start of the Christmas holiday.

When the class had departed, Billy began packing the various papers he'd need to begin lesson preparation –

textbooks, syllabuses, schemes of work, assignments for marking. A chore that was to last more than forty years.

Billy reached home at five o'clock, his new briefcase bulging with papers.

As usual, Mam had already prepared tea.

'Well, Billy, how did it go?' she said solicitously as she poured out his tea.

'Pretty well, Mam. I'm teaching a class that's only four years younger than me and I think I've already had a proposal of marriage from one of my pupils. To be timed for leap year.'

'It sounds as if you've made a good start. They must like you if they want to marry you already.'

'And I've got enough work on my plate to keep me busy till twelve o'clock every night,' Billy said.

'Fancy,' she exclaimed. 'I still can't hardly believe it. Me with a son a teacher. And think how rich you'll be when you get your first pay cheque at the end of the month. That'll give your dad something to think about, him and his rubbish, always going on about you getting a trade in your hands.'

In that second week, Billy initiated the first part of the two-pronged programme for his class. He worked as he had never worked before and was never in bed before midnight. Apart from the vast amount of marking and lesson preparation that the job involved, he drew up individual work schedules to match the attainment level of every pupil. Each one had a custom-designed set of objectives both in arithmetic and English, and each pupil recorded his own achievement on a grid chart after each lesson. The individual programmes involved exercises in arithmetic to be completed correctly, or certain English tasks – learning about conjunctions or full stops, writing a letter or a composition, learning a spelling list. The plan relied heavily on individual or small group teaching. At the end of the week, those who had achieved their objectives were released from the classroom to play football or netball in the school yard.

'How's it going?' Frank Wakefield asked one dinnertime.

'Too early to judge,' replied Billy, 'but one big advantage is that each pupil works at his own pace and even if absent misses no important lessons. He simply takes up where he left off before the absence.'

The pupils began to respond to this new way of working and even the slower pupils worked hard at their own standard to complete their jobs to win free time at the end of the week.

'I like this way of working,' remarked Tony Jarvis. 'I can work at my own speed and I feel as if I'm learning something at last.'

'I'm starting to like school and even arithmetic,' said Vera Pickles. 'Before, I was always being made to look stupid in front of the others. Now I get on with my own work at my own speed and I don't bother about what the others are doing.'

Nellie Wallace and Alf Dempsey, too, began to make progress with their reading as Billy had encouraged other members of the class to listen to their reading efforts. They were both keen to win their freedom on Friday afternoons.

It was the ballroom dancing that was the biggest success. At first, there was a good deal of shyness on both sides but gradually this receded. To the strains of Victor Sylvester, the top class of St Anselm's learned to move gracefully across the floor. Further, there was great progress in the cultivation of social graces and the art of relating to the opposite sex. When it came to inviting a girl to dance, in the early stages boys had simply beckoned a girl onto the dance floor by jerking a thumb, to which the girls responded with a 'Get lost!' The boys soon learned that they got better results by approaching a partner and politely asking, 'May I have this dance, please?'

As time went by, Billy's relationship with his class got better and better. A happy, friendly atmosphere developed and, furthermore, the pupils began to take a greater pride in their appearance and their status as 'senior' class. Their behaviour became less strident and more civilised. They were growing up.

On the way home, Billy got into the habit of walking with Laura Mackenzie up to the toll gates of Regina Park. Hamish had returned to his studies at Glasgow University and so the two of them were able to talk without benefit of actuarial statistics. Their conversation flowed easily and amicably and Billy found Laura had a quick wit and a ready sense of humour. Much of their time was spent laughing about some of the funny happenings at school and the eccentricities of some of the staff.

'I liked the way Greg announced in ringing Gielgud tones to his junior art class: "Dear boys and girls, I prefer you put the paint on the paper and not on your faces," ' said Billy.

'As if Junior Three could appreciate irony!' she chuckled.

'At first I didn't think I was going to like this school but things have settled down and I now enjoy teaching. Senior Four is a delight to be with and I think I'm getting somewhere with them.'

'Somehow I always felt you would,' she said.

But things weren't always plain sailing. One Thursday dinnertime, Nellie Wallace appeared at the staffroom door.

'I've told you that we don't like to be disturbed at

dinnertime. It's the only peace we get,' Grundy barked. 'Well, what do you want?'

'Please, sir,' said Nellie, 'I've come for the school record player and the Victor Sylvester records.'

'The what?' Grundy exploded. 'What on earth's going on?'

'It's OK,' said Billy, coming to the door. 'It's for our ballroom dancing lessons.' He handed the equipment over to Nellie.

'Ballroom dancing lessons!' Grundy shrilled. 'Whatever next! This is supposed to be a school, not a dancing academy. We're here to educate them not mollycoddle them.'

'Depends what you understand by educate,' Billy replied. 'Education isn't simply book-learning and instruction. It involves a wider concept like learning adult behaviour and some of the social graces. Besides, for the eighteenth-century gentleman, dancing was an indispensable part of his broader education. You should try reading Jane Austen.'

'This is an elementary school, mate, not a finishing school for ladies and gentlemen,' he sneered.

'I don't see how you can object to the top class learning useful social skills and good manners,' Billy replied hotly, becoming more and more exasperated by Grundy's sarcasm and derision.

The rest of the staff had been listening to this exchange and now Liz Logie joined in.

'It wouldn't do you any harm to learn some of the common courtesies,' she said to Grundy.

'I've noticed a definite improvement in the dress and deportment of the top class,' said Alex. 'They seem more mature somehow. Less horseplay and fooling about.'

'Whatever you're doing to 'em,' added Greg, 'keep on

doing it. Maybe I'll come over one Thursday and learn ballroom dancing myself.'

'Any success I've had with the top class is down to Mr Grundy,' said Billy. 'Because of him, I was able to establish control and win the co-operation of my class.'

Mr Grundy preened himself. 'I'm glad you listened at least to some of my advice,' he said smugly.

'You'll never know how much you helped me,' Billy replied, smiling.

Chapter Twenty-Four

Plans

On one of the research visits to the local library, Billy had set the class the task of finding out about their own street names and their own locality. They had spent the afternoon delving into the various encyclopaedias and local documents, and writing up their findings in the special notebooks provided. Next morning back in class, they were bubbling with enthusiasm about what they had discovered.

'I live in Waterloo Court, sir,' gushed Josey Parker. 'It's named after a famous battle.'

'And our pub,' added Jim Mitchell, 'is the Waterloo Arms – that's named after the battle as well. Didn't we beat the French in eighteen fifteen, sir? Is that where it got its name?'

'Absolutely right,' said Billy. 'Any other findings?'

'Wellington Grove,' answered Tony Jarvis. 'Named after the Duke of Wellington who led our troops against Napoleon.'

'Our house is in Blucher Street,' Nellie Wallace squealed fervently. 'And Blucher was a Prussian general at that battle as well. And I take my mam's washing to a lot of the streets I found out about.'

'We live in Victory Street, sir,' said Irene Moody eagerly. 'Did it get its name 'cos we won at that battle?'

'That's right,' said Billy, nodding his head earnestly. 'Obviously you've been working hard at the library. I congratulate all of you. First-class research.'

The eyes of his class shone with happiness at their success.

'And I live in Napoleon Street,' said Joe Duffy. 'Trust me to live in a street named after the loser.'

'It must have been a great day after the victory was announced, sir,' said Anne Greenhalgh. 'Like the end of the war in nineteen forty-five when the newspapers had headlines like "Victory in Europe" and "Japan Surrenders".'

'Why don't we do the newspaper like it was?' asked Jim Mitchell, his interest suddenly awakened. 'Pretend, like, that we're living in eighteen fifteen and reporting on the battle and that.'

There was a murmur of approval from the rest of the class.

'Let's do it, sir. It'd be great fun, sir.'

Billy felt the pride rise in his heart. This is what it's all about, he told himself. Ideas coming from them, not me stuffing their heads with things they don't want to know.

'OK, OK,' he said glowingly. 'A few years ago, I worked on the *Manchester Guardian* as general dogsbody and I can show you how we could organise it.'

From that point on, there was no stopping them. Anne Greenhalgh was voted editor-in-chief. In discussion with Billy, she agreed to arrange the editorial staff into special-ised teams. One group of girls opted to cover a 'Woman's Page' and female fashion of the early nineteenth century; two boys, Jim Mitchell and Tony Jarvis, chose to cover details of the battle; Mick Lynch and Roger Horner selected arms and weapons of the period; a mixed group ran a 'Letters to the Editor' column; and two boys who had shown some skill in art settled on cartoons, graphics and maps.

The project sparked off a wave of enthusiasm and participation. Billy found himself inundated with questions on every topic and a new lively atmosphere developed. Often when Joe Duffy got up to ring the bell for break or dinner, a small crowd of pupils, disinclined to leave, lingered behind, wanting to carry on. Sometimes, Frank Wakefield joined in the discussion and added his know-ledge and opinion to the topic being considered. He was pleased to see the new developments and the direction the curriculum was taking. For Senior 4, school had become a happy and a valuable experience.

In the midst of one of these discussions one day, Anne Greenhalgh remarked wistfully, 'It's all very well, writing up about these things, ladies' fashions and that, but all we've got are pictures and drawings. It'd be much better if we could see the actual things themselves. Isn't there a museum or something we could visit, sir?'

Jim Mitchell nodded his agreement. 'It's the same with writing about the battle and the kinds of weapons they used. What does a flintlock look like? And how did they fire it? What kind of bullets did they shoot? What's the difference between a flintlock, a matchlock, and a musket? We'd have a better idea if we could see the real thing instead of just pictures.'

Billy promised to look into it and discuss the matter with the headmaster.

'There's a first-class exhibition at Tatton Hall in Cheshire,' Frank Wakefield replied. Shaking his head doubtfully, he added, 'But the difficulties in taking a mixed group out there are insuperable. First, there's the question of transporting twenty-five adolescents and there's also the little matter of accident insurance. I can't see Manchester Education Committee agreeing to it. I'll look into it but I don't offer much hope.'

Surely, thought Billy, there was some way out of the impasse. It would be a great pity to dampen his pupils' fervour at this stage. But part of the growing up process was the ability to take life's ups and downs. The sensible thing to do was to discuss it with them.

'Tatton Park,' he began when he met them, 'would have been the ideal place to visit but there is the problem of getting there since there is no direct bus or train service there.'

There was a groan of disappointment.

'We could go by bike, sir,' Alf Dempsey suggested.

A great roar of scornful laughter greeted this crazy idea.

'Where are we going to get twenty-five bikes?' sneered Roger Horner, looking round the class for support. 'Use your brain, Dempsey, if you've got one.'

'It's not such a daft idea, sir,' said Tony Jarvis slowly. 'Many of us have got bikes. Some of us have sisters or brothers with bikes. We could borrow them for the day.'

'Sometimes, radical notions pay off,' said Billy thoughtfully. 'Let's have a show of hands. How many have bikes?'

Seventeen hands were raised.

'How many can get an extra bike?'

Five more hands.

'That leaves us three short. Any ideas?'

Silence.

'Either we all go,' said Billy, 'or none of us goes. We can't leave some members of the class behind whilst the rest of us cycle off to Cheshire.'

At that point, Frank Wakefield came into the room. He took one look at their faces.

'This place looks like a funeral parlour,' he said. 'What's happened? Who died?'

'We're short of three bicycles,' Billy answered, 'for our projected trip to Tatton Park.'

'I think I could borrow a bike for you,' Wakefield said slowly, 'but you've a long way to go before you set off on such a hazardous safari. As I said earlier, we have to get permission and insurance. I can't promise anything at this stage.'

Such was the look of anticipation on the faces that it would have taken a heart of stone to turn them down now. And the one thing that Frank Wakefield did not have was a heart of stone.

'I'll see what I can do,' he said, smiling encouragingly.

'I think I know where I can borrow the other two bikes,' said Billy. 'But first I'll have to ask them. The people concerned are not aware at this moment that they are going to offer us a loan of their bicycles.' He had in mind his brother Les and Laura Mackenzie.

'Hey, sir!' said Jim Mitchell warmly. 'You know, I think it's going to work!'

Nellie Wallace raised her hand. She looked distraught. 'Please, sir, even if you do borrow a bike for me, it's no use. I don't know how to ride one. I've never had a bike to learn.'

'No problem, sir,' said a beaming Joe Duffy. 'If we get the bikes, I'll teach her on Friday afternoons.' Irish eyes really did smile.

The pupils of Senior 4 now went into action. The rest of the week saw the appearance of a motley collection of bicycles, bone-shakers and crocks, from the sit-up-and-beg variety to the latest racer with ten gears. Billy expected a scooter, a three-wheeler, or at least a penny-farthing to be brought in any day. Every dinnertime, a team of boys could be seen outside the prefabs repairing, servicing, oiling, greasing and updating the miscellaneous machines which were brought in from back yards and cellars. Several boys, Alf Dempsey among them, showed a marked aptitude for mechanics. Terms like Schrader valve, cotter pin, lubrication points, rod brakes, rim tape, trigger control could be heard being bandied about. Repairs to punctures, gears, brakes, wheels, sprockets were carried out as a matter of routine. Joe Duffy gave Nellie Wallace training and practice every dinnertime until she was reasonably proficient and no longer wobbled about. As their Wednesday afternoon visiting speaker, Billy invited the traffic adviser from the city police, who gave lots of tips about cycling safety.

'As a cycling club, you may cycle in pairs but keep well over to the left, always signal clearly and in good time, make sure your bike is in good order, especially brakes. At junctions, your teacher should control the traffic to let you pass through.'

The class looked expectantly in Billy's direction.

Billy extracted the maximum education value from the projected trip. The form was set the task of planning and calculating the route – distance, time required to reach their destination, places of interest on the way and, most important, what they expected to see at Tatton Hall itself. Jim Mitchell was elected by popular vote as route leader.

'As far as we can calculate, sir,' said Jim, 'it's about thirteen miles from here and it should take us about one and a half hours including stops to get there – maybe longer if we have any mishaps, like punctures or breakdowns.'

Came the day when Frank Wakefield reported the results of his inquiries to Billy.

'Good news and bad news,' he announced, looking steadily at Billy.

'OK, Frank,' said Billy anxiously. 'Let me know the worst.'

'No, I'll give you the good news first. The Education Committee has granted permission provided we can get ourselves insured. That shouldn't present any problem.'

'And the bad news?' Billy asked, searching his face.

'There must be two teachers to accompany the party. One male for the boys, one female for the girls.' His eyes twinkled as he said, 'I thought we might ask Mrs Melton-Mowbray. What do you think?'

Billy couldn't hide a slight grimace. 'Fine,' he answered. 'But I don't think she has a bicycle.'

'Is there anyone else we could ask? Any of our female teachers with a bike?'

'I suppose we could ask Laura Mackenzie,' Billy said carefully as if it had taken profound thought to reach such a conclusion, 'though I was hoping to use her bicycle for one of the girls. But she did say when I mentioned the matter to her that she might be able to borrow her sister's bike as well for the day. But who would take her class while she was away?'

'I think that can be arranged,' Wakefield said, now smiling broadly.

At four o'clock, Billy escorted Laura to Regina Park gates. As they wheeled their bikes along, Billy broached the subject.

'It looks as if our projected trip to Tatton Park is on. And Frank Wakefield has given me his OK to ask you if you'd like to accompany me, I mean . . . that is . . . us . . . Senior Four, on the visit.'

'I'd love to, Hoppy. I feel greatly honoured to be asked. But why didn't you ask Mrs Melton-Mowbray or Liz Logie?' she asked teasingly.

'Well, of course, we thought of them first,' he said in the same vein, 'but they don't have bicycles.'

'Incidentally,' said Laura, changing the subject, 'are you aware that half the top girls have been shadowing us all the way from school and have been doing so every day? I don't know what they're expecting to see.'

'Perhaps they're hoping for some indiscretion one of these evenings.'

She gave him a mischievous look. 'I wonder what kind of thing they have in mind,' she said, deadpan.

Chapter Twenty-Five

Cycle Trip

Next morning, Billy gave the news to the class. There was a loud cheer.

'We shall set off in a week's time, next Wednesday morning at nine o'clock prompt. So no one must be late or they'll find we've gone without them. Remember to bring a packed lunch – sandwiches and whatever you like. I'm glad to say that Miss Mackenzie has kindly agreed to go with us to chaperone the girls.'

'Chaperone! We're not a bunch of kids, sir,' complained Irene Moody. 'Do we have to have a chaperone?'

'Afraid so. Not that I believe any of you need an escort but that's the regulation.'

'Anyroad, I'm glad she's going,' grinned Tony Jarvis impishly. 'She's a stunner. I'll bet you're glad she's going as well, aren't you, sir?'

Billy looked at him quizzically. Was the boy able to read his mind?

'Shut your face, Jarvis,' Irene snapped angrily. 'What do you know?'

'Now, now, Irene,' answered Tony patronisingly. 'Don't get them into a twist. We know what's in your mind.

270

And by the way, it's not Jarvis, it's Tony, if you don't mind.'

On the morning of departure, Billy made the usual trip across Manchester and arrived at school at eight forty-five. As he entered the classroom, he was taken aback by the sight that met his eyes. His wards were already at their desks, packed lunches much in evidence, notebooks at the ready. There was a sense of excitement and a new, radiant look about them. They were truly prepared for the excursion, spruced up, scrubbed, groomed and gleaming, and also dressed as if they were to take part in the Tour de France cycling race. Many of the boys were wearing shorts and jerseys, others had their trousers held by bicycle clips. It was the girls, however, who had excelled themselves with their long skirts and woollen jumpers, their hair tied back in ponytails, looking for the world like a bevy of Hollywood beauties. A few had applied a smidgen of red to their lips.

'I can't believe my eyes,' exclaimed Billy. 'Is this my class of pupils I see before me? Or is it a group of fashion models dressed up for the catwalk?'

The class basked happily in his delight.

'My dad has sent a pile of fruit for everyone,' Mick Lynch announced. 'An apple and an orange each.'

'Hope they're not faded rejects,' retorted Tessie Shea to everyone's amusement.

Billy called the register, to which the class responded clearly and quickly, impatient to be on their way. As he reeled off the names, it soon became obvious that there was one person missing. A person they could hardly forget.

'Wait a minute,' said Billy, looking round the room. 'Where's Nellie Wallace? We can't go without our Nellie. Not after all her practice with Joe there.'

At that moment, the door burst open and Nellie barged into the room.

'Sorry I'm late again, sir,' she panted. 'I had to take Mrs Ormeroyd's dinner round to her house for warming up later on. But I'm ready now, sir.'

'Ready' was the right word. There was a gasp of incredulity followed by happy laughter when they took in Nellie's costume. She was attired in wide pyjama-legged culottes, a thick woolly jersey and a bright red beret set at a saucy angle.

Mick Lynch was first to react. 'We're going to look at old-fashioned clothes,' he guffawed. 'You weren't supposed to get dressed up in 'em.'

'Quiet, Lynch – I mean Mick – you're only jealous,' she rejoined, tossing her head.

'You look fabulous, Nellie,' said Billy. 'But where did you get such a beautiful outfit?'

'Me mam give me it, sir. She used to go bike riding and that when she was a young girl.'

'She must have gone cycling with Victoria and Albert,' smirked Mick Lynch who had to have the last word.

Laura Mackenzie arrived. Many of the boys could not restrain a wolf whistle. She wore a calf-length tartan tweed skirt, a knitted jumper with matching cardigan, and on her head a tammy with a large red bobble.

'Good morning, everyone,' she said brightly, looking around the room. 'I can see everyone is prepared for safari.'

'You look smashin', miss,' exclaimed Tony Jarvis. 'Doesn't she, sir?'

'She certainly does, Tony,' Billy agreed enthusiastically. 'A little touch of Scotland to help us on our way.'

'Why, thank you, kind sirs,' said Laura.

'And did you bring your bagpipes with you, miss?' asked

Irene Moody archly, glancing slyly at her female friends.

'No, Irene,' Laura smiled back. 'Unfortunately they wouldn't fit into my saddle bag, but I did bring a little haggis for lunch.'

'Haggis for lunch?' said Alf Dempsey. 'I always thought haggis was a lot of ugly old women.'

'Maybe that's what she eats,' was Irene's catty rejoinder.

'No, no,' said Des Bishop. 'Haggis is a Scottish musical instrument like a sweet potato pipe.'

'Like an ocarina?' suggested Billy.

'I can see that you've got a lot to learn about Scotland,' Laura laughed.

Frank Wakefield, who had been busy settling Laura's class down to some work, now made his appearance and cast an inspectorial eye over the assembly. He obviously approved, for he said, 'It makes me feel proud to see you dressed so smartly for the occasion. I know that your behaviour for the rest of the day will be exemplary. Remember, you are representing the school. If this visit is successful, there's no reason why we shouldn't arrange more of them. Take care on the road and obey everything that Mr Hopkins and Miss Mackenzie tell you. Now off you go and enjoy yourselves. Oh, and don't forget, this is an educational visit. So make sure you learn something useful.'

The class divided into pre-arranged partnerships. Girls on the inside, boys on the outside. Joe Duffy, who had taken responsibility for Nellie's safety, now made a point of escorting her. Jim Mitchell as route leader rode at the front of the convoy with Laura at his side. Billy accompanied Anne Greenhalgh at the back.

Soon they were moving smoothly through Regina Park and along Birchfields Road towards the two-lane Kingsway. The traffic was light for a Wednesday morning. They were overtaken by the occasional 40 bus and every now and then by a new Morris 8 or an Austin 7.

Lucky blighters, Billy thought. They must be very rich or have special privileges to own a car, especially since petrol is still on ration.

Every now and then they passed a billboard which asked in large letters: IS YOUR JOURNEY REALLY NECESSARY?

In the case of Senior Four, yes! Billy said to himself.

Free from the formality and the constraints of the classroom, Billy found that his pupils unburdened themselves, seizing the opportunity to tell him about the things that were on their minds.

Whenever traffic allowed, Billy moved along the rows like a sheepdog checking that all his wards stayed in line.

As he passed along, Tony Jarvis called out, 'Hey, sir, this is better than school, isn't it?'

'This *is* school,' Billy called back as he came abreast of Joe Duffy and his protégée. 'Joe,' he said, 'could you drop back so that I can talk to Nellie there and see how she's getting on?'

Joe complied and Billy turned to Nellie.

'Well, Nellie, how's it going?'

She beamed happily. 'Everything's fine, sir. I love school now and I'm enjoying this trip out. I'm glad of the rest.'

'You work pretty hard at home, don't you?'

'I'll say, sir. Me dad walked out on us last year – he ran off with a younger woman and left me mam to fend for herself. There's five of us in the family and I'm the eldest. We're always dead short of money, sir, and me mam has to take in washing, ironing, sewing and darning from the neighbours in our street. We even cook for some of them and donkey-stone their steps to earn a few coppers.'

'And you help your mam out?'

'That's right, sir. That's why I'm late for school some-times. But I'll try to do better.'

'You've got a lovely name, Nellie. Do you know you're named after a famous music-hall star?'

'Yes, sir. That was me gran. She saw her a few times at the Ardwick Empire and so because me dad's name was – is – Wallace, she gave me the same name.'

'Let's hope you become as famous one day,' said Billy, and he cycled on to draw up alongside Alf Dempsey.

'Enjoying yourself, Alf?'

'S'great, sir. I love being out in the open air – hate being cooped up in the classroom all day. But you've changed all that.'

'You're keen on the great outdoors, I can see that. Also keen on sport.'

'Yeah, that's right, sir. Especially boxing.'

'How come?'

'Me dad used to be a boxer, sir. Won dozens of cups and medals, and that. But he drinks a lot, now he's retired from the ring. Comes home every night from the pub drunk. Gets nasty sometimes and turns on me and me mam.'

'Sorry to hear that, Alf.'

'S'all right, sir. He doesn't do it so much now – I'm getting too big for him. And if he tries to hit me mam again, I'll belt him one.'

'So that's why you want to become a boxer!'

Alf grinned. 'Yeah, that's part of it, sir.'

The group had now reached the roundabout on the main Altrincham Road where they had to turn right. Billy rode to the front of the line and ordered everyone to stop.

'OK,' he called. 'We'll adopt the routine we've practised. I'll go on to the main road and stop the traffic coming from

275

your right and when I give the signal, make your right turn towards Altrincham.'

The manoeuvre was executed without a hitch. Not that there was much traffic to deal with anyway. Then it was on through the leafy lanes of Cheshire to Bowden and then Bucklow Hill until they had their first glimpse of Tatton Hall. And what a thrilling sight it was! They felt like Livingstone when he first espied Victoria Falls. Their eyes beheld the magnificent mansion as they approached it through a beautifully landscaped park complete with lakes, woodlands and deer. The boys and girls were mesmerised as if they had entered a fairyland – which they had.

When the bicycles had been parked at the back of the mansion, Billy gathered his class outside the main entrance for an introductory briefing.

'Well, Senior Four, here we are at last. Congratulations on your cycling skills and your road manners and behaviour. Our routine today will be as follows. For the rest of the morning, we shall be taken on a conducted tour of this wonderful building. Ask the guide as many questions as you like. We'll meet again at half past one this afternoon when you'll be free to conduct your own research for our newspaper. We shall leave at three o'clock. We are asked to help preserve this historical monument by not touching any of the exhibits but I'm sure there's no need to tell you that. And Duffy – no smoking!'

When the laughter had died down, Duffy retorted, 'And the same goes for you, sir.'

Billy took his class in to meet the guide who had agreed to take them on a tour of the Egerton home. As if in a dream, the visitors tagged on behind, gazing in silent awe at the paintings, the portraits, the decorated ceilings, the furniture and the furnishings, listening to their guide's animated account and also to the ticking and melodious chiming of the many ancient clocks that were distributed throughout the hall. Billy's chest swelled with pride when he heard the flow of questions being directed at the guide.

'When was this building first put up?'

'How many servants did the Egerton family have?'

'Does the park grow its own food?'

'Is the Egerton family connected with Egerton Road in Manchester?'

Laura circulated among the little groups, directing their attention to unusual exhibits, or pointing to a particular painting or an interesting sculpture. She certainly won over the boys who hung on her every word.

Is this the same group, Billy mused, that was so rebellious only a few weeks ago? Is this the class that Grundy wrote off as useless? Only yesterday in the staffroom he had dismissed the whole idea of an outing as 'rubbish and merely an excuse to get out of the classroom and avoid doing work'. What would Grundy say if he could see them now, completely absorbed in the guide's explanations, questioning, note-taking, drawing, sketching?

Dinnertime soon came round and teachers and pupils had built up healthy appetites. The young students wandered off to discuss their reactions to the visit and, no doubt, thought Billy, to enjoy an illicit smoke. He decided to let it go this time. After all, in seven or eight months' time, they'd be masters and mistresses of their own fate.

At some distance from the mansion, Laura and Billy found a picnic spot giving a panoramic view of the undulating parkland. At a table near a fountain containing a statue of Cupid, they settled down to eat their lunch.

'This is an idyllic spot,' Laura said as she unwrapped

her sandwiches. 'Thank you so much for inviting me, Hoppy.'

'You're the one doing the favour,' he answered, pouring coffee from his thermos. 'Incidentally, Hoppy is a nickname my pals at school gave me and I got stuck with it. OK for school and for my cronies but I'd be glad if you would call me Billy.'

'Then from now on, Billy it is,' she said warmly.

He felt a tingling of his scalp when he heard her use his first name like that.

'That's that settled. You know, Laura, it's funny how an outing like this, when we're away from the formality of school and playing the role of teacher, we relax and simply be ourselves. We stop acting a part, as it were. On the way here, pupils have been pouring out their problems in a way they never would or could back in the classroom. I felt like Sigmund Freud.'

'I know what you mean, Billy,' she laughed. 'Perhaps there's something about you that makes people want to confide in you. But I had a little taste of it too. On the road here, Jim Mitchell gave me his life story and some of the difficulties he has living in a pub. Like the Saturday night knees-ups and the fist fights. Makes you realise that we're not merely teachers but social workers as well. I must say I like the idea.'

'That's right. Not merely instructors but sympathetic listeners too. But then everyone's got problems, I think. Though to be honest, you always look so cool, calm and collected, Laura, I can't imagine you with a problem.'

'Don't take everything at face value, Billy. Maybe I don't have any major problems, but I do have little things which niggle. Only pinpricks, I suppose.'

'Like for instance?'

'There you go, Billy. Playing at Sigmund Freud again. The thing that's on my mind is my younger brother. I'm a little worried about him. He's doing important exams soon, and my father is pushing him a bit hard. Daddy's a wonderful man but he rules the roost with a firm hand, brooks no argument, and knows all the answers. We love him very much but he does tend to be a bit bossy.'

'I know the problem, Laura. I've got a father like that myself. You said "we" just now. Who's "we"?'

'The rest of our family – my mother, younger sisters Jenny and Katie, and my brother Hughie. Oh, and I nearly forgot, my grandmother and old Aunty Aggie.'

'So, four children plus two old 'uns in your family. Almost as big as my own – there are five of us. And I'm the baby. And spoiled, so they tell me.'

'I'm sure you're not,' she laughed. 'But what about your father? You said he was a bossy-boots as well.'

'Bossy only when my mother gives him permission to be so. He's more mellow nowadays though – has to be or my mother would give him what for. On balance, I'd say she's in charge in our family but she's developed the knack of letting my dad think he's in control.'

'She sounds quite a character, Billy. As for my father, he's a creature of his Scottish background, I think. In Scotland the man reigns supreme and he expects everyone, especially the womenfolk, to obey him without question at all times.'

'Surely your dad admits that he can be wrong sometimes. After all, he's only human.'

'Never, I'm afraid,' she laughed, and poured herself a cup of coffee. 'There are two infallible beings to his way of thinking – God and Duncan Mackenzie. Sometimes God is wrong but never Duncan. It's a matter of saving face. If ever he's wrong, he cleverly reverses the argument so that it appears that you were the one who was mistaken.'

Billy chuckled. 'Sounds to me as if he'd make a good politician – even Prime Minister. What does he do for a living, Laura?'

'Senior inspector in the Inland Revenue,' she said apologetically.

'Inland Revenue! Don't mention that term to me!' Billy exclaimed. 'I used to work – I use the term loosely – in an income tax office as a serf. The senior clerical officer was bad enough. He had his desk in the main office and was regarded by everyone as a minor deity but as for the senior inspector! He occupied an office away from us lower mortals and we rarely caught sight of him. If your dad was one of those, then as far as I'm concerned, he is God and no mistake.'

Laura laughed. 'Tell him that and he'll love you forever. The trouble is that he has fixed ideas about education. Once again based on the Scottish system. If you don't have a degree, then you're not fully educated. Preferably a degree with honours written after it.'

'That lets me out,' sighed Billy. 'I'm a lowly peasant with a rubbishy Teacher's Certificate.'

'Same as me,' she said. 'But in my case, it's OK because I'm a woman. I have to wait until a member of one of the acceptable professions with an honours degree falls in love with me.'

'Like Hamish, I suppose.'

'Oh, Hamish! His family and mine have known each other since the beginning of time when we all lived in Dumfries. Hamish and I grew up together and our family have always had an understanding that we'd marry some day when he's qualified. Of course, for my father, Hamish can do no wrong – he's Scottish, he's studying for honours, and his subject is actuarial studies which everyone assures me is very lucrative.'

'Family understanding, you say. What about love? What about Cupid over there,' Billy said, indicating the statue on the fountain. 'Doesn't he come into it?'

'Afraid not. Not unless he's a doctor, a lawyer, or an accountant with a degree and a professional qualification from the University of Glasgow.' She sounded contemptuous of the whole system.

'Don't let yourself get trapped, Laura, into doing something you don't want. Life is too short. There's more to it than having a secure future. Love and happiness are more important. Oops, there I go doing my Sigmund Freud again.'

'I'm sure you're right, Billy, but going against family wishes, especially my father's, is not as easy as you think.'

As the conversation proceeded, Billy's heart sank slowly deeper and deeper into his boots. Honours degrees? Noble professions? Scotland? Bagpipes? Haggis? He didn't stand a chance with this beautiful, beautiful girl with whom he'd fallen in love.

'But we seem to be talking only about me,' she complained. 'What about you? Do you have a girlfriend? I'd be surprised if you didn't,' she added.

'What makes you say that, Laura? I mean, how do you know I like girls?' he said with a mischievous grin.

'My instincts tell me,' she smiled. 'You're quite nice-looking, so I'm sure the girls queue up to go out with you. I've noticed anyway that the top girls have a crush on you. They obviously think the world of you.'

'What's your evidence for saying that?' he asked, pleased by the implied compliment.

281

'I suppose it's the way they genuflect when you go by,' she laughed.

Billy joined in her laughter. Maybe she's not out of reach after all, he thought. She's handing me a small bouquet.

'But you must be careful, Billy. Those girls will eat you for breakfast. Especially that Irene Moody. I've seen the coquettish way she looks at you. That girl could give Veronica Lake a few pointers. There's something about that girl . . . I don't know what it is but she acts a bit too grown up. Anyway, to get back to the subject. I was asking you if you had a girlfriend.'

'Not really,' Billy answered reluctantly. 'There was a girl called Adele but I think she's now engaged to be married to someone else and so I don't have anyone at the moment. I used to do a lot of ballroom dancing and Adele was my partner for competitions.'

'You said you think she's engaged. Is it not definite then?'

'Knowing Adele she could always change her mind. I hope it's definite though,' he laughed, 'or she might come knocking at my door.'

Was it his imagination or did he notice a flicker of concern on Laura's face? He didn't mention the necking in Adele's parlour every weekend. That was in the past. What would she care anyway if he had a string of girlfriends?

'The only dancing I've done,' he heard her saying, 'is Scottish dancing – eightsome reels.'

Billy had a fleeting vision of Laura hopping about with a bunch of brawny Jocks dressed in kilts.

'But the Scots,' she went on, 'are more concerned with educational qualifications than dancing the Highland fling. This Scottish obsession with the great paper chase is enough to drive one round the bend. As I said earlier, I'm concerned about young Hughie. Only sixteen and about to take his School Certificate. He is expected to go in for medicine. He's doing well enough in science subjects but having a struggle with his French which he has to have to complete the required matriculation. My father's putting the pressure on him and I'm getting worried about him – Hughie, that is, not my father.'

When he heard this, Billy saw a faint glimmer of hope – and it was no more than a glimmer. Maybe this was his chance. He heard himself saying, 'French? Maybe I could help him, Laura. I don't have an honours degree but I have studied French and am qualified to teach to School Certificate standard.'

'Oh, would you, Billy? I'd be so grateful. We'd pay you of course.'

'Pay? I don't know what my Jewish friends in Cheetham Hill would say but your gratitude is pay enough. We'll fix up something tomorrow. I'll give him a passage to translate from English to French so I'll know where to make a start.'

'Billy,' she said warmly, 'you're a wonderful person. I could kiss you for that.'

'So what's stopping you?' he said, holding out both hands and adopting his best Yiddish accent.

'Mainly the fact that your class is on its way back for the second session,' she giggled.

In the afternoon, the form divided into their different editorial teams – fashions of the early nineteenth century, sports, furniture, and weapons and artillery. For ninety minutes, they inspected different parts of the mansion like young professional journalists going about their business, writing up notes, discussing findings, sketching items which caught their interest. At three o'clock, it was time to bring the visit to a close.

On the way back, the class was full of it, jabbering away like a cage of monkeys.

'Did you know, sir, that some of the women had pinched-in waists, sir – only seventeen or eighteen inches,' exclaimed Vera Pickles. 'It must've been murder, sir. They used to squeeze themselves into tight-laced corsets and stays.'

'And so did the men!' added Anne Greenhalgh. 'In fact, they used to spend more time than the women primping themselves up.'

'And those dresses they wore! Even the men's clothes! They looked so small,' commented Tessie Shea. 'They wouldn't fit people today. I know I couldn't get into any of those gowns the women wore.'

'Quite right, Tessie,' said Billy as he cycled alongside. 'People were smaller and shorter in the past. For example, the average height of a man in the Middle Ages was only five feet six inches. Today, it's around five feet ten inches.'

'The Egertons had over forty servants, sir,' said Josey Parker. 'And did you see the terrible kitchens they had to work in? Up at half past five in the morning and working till ten o'clock at night – even later if there was a banquet on.'

Further along the formation, discussion was on military matters.

'Wellington's army used grenade launchers, sir,' Jim Mitchell called out breathlessly as they climbed a small incline in the road. 'Many of Napoleon's troops were still using swords and lances against muskets.'

'And Wellington used infantry squares against the French

light infantry,' added Mick Lynch. 'The French were clobbered.'

All along the line of bikes, the pupils pedalled on with a constant stream of enthusiastic chatter about all they'd seen and heard. Billy had now become the final authority in settling disputes and here and there he heard his name being quoted as the last word. 'Hopalong said . . .' 'I asked sir and he said . . .' For Senior 4, Billy had become God.

With a strong wind behind them, they made good time back. Laura left the convoy at the corner of Regina Park Hill and Billy took the rest on to school which they reached shortly after four thirty. The school was deserted. Four o'clock at St Anselm's saw a mad dash for the gates and it was usually a toss-up who got out first, children or staff.

Billy's own class seemed reluctant to depart but he dismissed them and they finally cycled off, still twittering excitedly.

Billy went into his classroom to collect his belongings. A successful day, he said to himself. I think everyone got a lot out of it.

As he was about to leave, he had one last visitor – Irene Moody who had waited outside the classroom until everyone had departed.

'I came to get my things, sir,' she said huskily, giving him her slinky look. 'That was one of the happiest days of my life. And, sir, I want you to know that if there's anything – and I mean anything – I can do for you, you've only to ask.'

Laura was right, thought Billy. I have to watch my step with this one. She's a sensitive adolescent. I like her and I don't want to hurt her by ridiculing her but dealing with her is like walking on eggshells.

'That's nice of you, Irene,' he said tactfully, moving

towards the door. 'I'll remember your offer. And I'm glad you enjoyed the day. We learned a lot. It's been a long day and now I think it's time to make tracks. It's all very well for you, Irene, you live close by. I still have to cycle across to Cheetham Hill.'

'Yes, sir. Goodnight, sir. And thanks once again.'

Billy mounted his trusty mechanical steed and pedalled off.

Chapter Twenty-Six

Model Lessons

The morning after the Tatton visit, Billy arrived a little late for school. The traffic along Princess Street had been particularly heavy that morning, and he cursed the trams, the cars, and the traffic lights as he was held up at junction after junction. If I had my way, he said to himself, I'd ban cars and trams from the city centre and allow only bicycles and pedestrians. Maybe a few buses but that's all.

When he finally pedalled through the school entrance it was five past nine and his pupils were already in their places. As he stepped through the door, the whole class rose as one. There was a smile on every face.

'Good morning, Mr Hopkins,' they chorused.

'Good morning, everyone,' Billy said. 'Please sit down. You're embarrassing me.'

The class grinned back.

There was something about them, an eagerness in their expressions, and from that day forward, there was a different atmosphere. The Tatton excursion had somehow released a new energy and a new spirit of co-operation. Billy was euphoric about this development for it meant acceptance and recognition that he was their teacher and had earned their respect.

The class got down to the job of producing an historical newspaper. They called it *The Morning Post*, and the front-page headline was 'VICTORY AT WATERLOO', followed by an account of the battle by 'our special correspondent' Jim Mitchell. The rest of the paper contained contributions from every member of the class, including Alf Dempsey and Nellie Wallace. Billy's job was to print it, which meant writing it out in Indian ink with the authentic layout of a national newspaper. The result was proudly displayed on the school noticeboard and every break a crowd of children gathered around to read it. The senior class was justly proud of their effort and woe betide anyone who even thought of defacing it.

The class fell into a happy routine. Mornings were devoted to hard graft – the basic curriculum of the three Rs, science, art, and social studies. The afternoons were given over to broadening their horizons through a series of outside visits and invited speakers, plus their weekly ballroom dancing lessons.

One morning, Tessie Shea raised her hand in class.

'Yesterday in our research afternoon at the library,' she said, 'I was reading about a man called Ebenezer Howard who built a new town called Welwyn Garden City.'

'That's good,' answered Billy. 'You happened to see his name in the library, did you?'

'Not really, sir,' she replied. 'I saw his name first on the back of a packet of Shredded Wheat and so I looked him up in an encyclopaedia.'

'So what's your point, Tessie?'

'I had an idea, sir. Why can't we build a model town like his in class, showing the way our town ought to look.'

'I have an uncle and an aunty who live at Port Sunlight,' added Anne Greenhalgh who had obviously been discussing it with her. 'That's a model town as well, built by Lord Lever. We could build our model town on a large board. On one side, we could show our district, all black and dirty, as it really is, and the other as it could be – the town of the future.'

'I like the idea,' said Billy, 'but what do we build it out of? It's a big project and we have little in the way of funds.'

'Out of matchboxes,' suggested Tony Jarvis. 'When I was a nipper in the infants' school, we used to make things out of old boxes. I remember matchboxes were the best.'

'You'll have to show us,' said Billy.

At morning assembly, Frank Wakefield appealed to the whole school to bring in matchboxes. A large cardboard box was placed outside the classroom for this purpose. The response was overwhelming. Matchboxes poured in from every conceivable source and of every shape, size and with every kind of illustration on them – cats, camels, sauce recipes, Red Indians, trains, Russian dolls.

Billy supplied the class with pictures of all kinds of buildings but left the actual construction to the pupils, to their imagination and their handicraft skills.

The class had been divided into groups, each with responsibility for a particular section. The various groups gathered the motley collection of matchboxes – Puck, Captain Webb, Swan Vestas, Bryant and May – onto their desks and puzzled out how to make use of them. They turned the boxes this way and that in an effort to create a house similar to the picture before them. Some houses, like the slum houses of the Industrial Revolution, were relatively easy, but others, like the circular modern houses and public buildings, were more challenging and required much

289

creative imagination. Billy wandered around the class making suggestions and giving help and advice where it was required.

One day, two window cleaners appeared at the windows and as they were polishing the panes, they were distracted from their task by what they saw as bizarre educational practice.

'Hey, Bert,' one of them called to his companion. 'Come 'ere and have a butcher's at this.'

Bert complied and gazed spellbound at twenty-five adolescents playing around with a lot of boxes.

'Bleedin' hell,' he exclaimed, shaking his head. 'It's like a bloody asylum in there. If that's modern education, you can stuff it.'

The result at the end of the term was a magnificent display entitled 'Buildings: past, present and future'. On one side were depicted the slums and factories of the Industrial Age whilst the other provided a contrast illustrating how a modern town could be laid out, complete with roundabouts and ring roads.

This wasn't the end of the matchbox episode. Tony Jarvis discovered not only a new word – *phillumeny*, or the love of matchboxes – but a whole new world and a new interest which was to occupy him for the rest of his life. For the remainder of that term, he went around telling anyone who was willing to listen, 'I'm a phillumenist.'

Billy's classroom became at times like a marketplace. Wakefield had his 'office' at the back of his classroom and there was a succession of visitors to see him during Billy's lessons. Most of them were quiet and peaceful enough, though on one occasion Wakefield had to deal with Alf Dempsey's father who had arrived the worse for wear from drink, which he had no doubt needed to give him Dutch courage. For Senior 4 it made an interesting diversion from arithmetic exercises.

'You kept our Alf behind after school, Wakefield, for being late, di'n't you? We need 'im to 'elp at 'ome, see. Keep 'im behind again, you bastard, and I'll be round to duff you up.'

'Right, on your way, pal,' said Wakefield, helping him forcibly out of the room.

'Oh, so it's a fight you want,' shouted Dempsey senior, taking up a professional boxing stance.

Frank Wakefield was no lightweight and he grabbed Dempsey round the shoulder to push him out. They both fell to the ground, grappling with each other. It was the son who came to the rescue and resolved the contest.

'Get home, Dad, before I belt you one. You're showing me up in front of my mates. Now piss off home.'

This seemed to do the trick, for the older Dempsey looked at his son through his alcoholic haze and some notion of the commotion he had caused penetrated his brain.

'Right, son. I was only looking out for you.'

'Well, don't!' Alf yelled, ushering him out of the room.

The interruption provided an interesting diversion which Billy exploited by instructing his pupils to write an essay describing the event.

Every Tuesday afternoon at 3 p.m., Mr Stanley Cashman, a clerk from the Education Offices, appeared to check and pick up the savings which the Head had collected from the schoolchildren during the week. He stood beside Wakefield's desk at the back of the room reconciling the various sums of money he had come to take away. Most of his attention, however, was given over to Billy's series of lessons on the early explorers and he hardly gave a glance to the accounts books he had come to examine.

Flattered by the attention he gave every week, Billy prepared his best lessons for him and an unspoken mutual understanding sprang up between them. On these occasions, Billy became oblivious of the rest of his class and there were only two people in the room – Billy and the bank clerk. Every Tuesday afternoon they set off together on their perilous journey of exploration and as the weeks went by they became seasoned travellers.

There developed between them a special bond of comradeship, and why not? After all, had they not come through some hazardous journeys together? Had they not sailed together with the Vikings in their longships from Scandinavia to Iceland and points further west; journeyed with Marco Polo across the roof of the world to meet Kublai Khan in Xanadu; in 1487 set out in three caravels and rounded the Cape of Good Hope with Bartholomew Diaz; and in 1497, after a hair-raising voyage round Africa in which they had almost come to grief, finally made it to India in the company of Vasco da Gama. They looked forward to the next episode, to their trip across the Atlantic in the *Santa Maria* when they would discover America with Christopher Columbus at the helm.

Often Wakefield had to bring Stanley Cashman back to reality by reminding him of his purpose in the school.

A procession of tradesmen and artisans also came through Billy's class regularly. Most of them became absorbed in the lessons being taught and occasionally one or two of them would join in, forgetting that they were no longer pupils but had come to fix something or other or to install a piece of equipment.

One morning Billy was taking an English literature lesson and was reading *The Invisible Man* by H.G. Wells aloud to the class. They were engrossed in the story and had reached the point where a villager's snarling dog attacks the Invisible Man and tears his trousers. Fearenside, the owner of the dog, tells his friend of the incident and recounts how strange it was that there was no sign of pink flesh showing but only a black void where the leg should have been. He ends up by referring to the Invisible Man as 'piebald'.

Tessie Shea raised her hand. 'What does piebald mean, sir?' she asked.

Now at college, Billy had been trained never to answer such a question directly. 'Never tell your pupils anything,' he'd been instructed. The correct approach was to engage one's learners in dialogue and encourage them to follow a train of thought, the so-called Socratic method, by which they'd be led along a sequence of questions and arguments until they stumbled on the correct answer – much as Socrates himself had done when he strolled around the marketplace in Athens engaging his young followers in disputation and logical thought.

'Think of the word "pie",' Billy suggested. 'Can anyone think of its use in another word?'

The answers came thick and fast.

'Apple pie.'

'Potato pie.'

'Meat pie.'

'No, no,' Billy said. 'You've got the wrong pie. This "pie" means different colours.'

'Rhubarb pie!' shouted Des Bishop. 'That's different colours.'

'How about blueberry pie?' suggested Jim Mitchell.

Billy was getting desperate. 'Look, think of a man who had "pie" in his title.'

'Ah, now I know, sir,' said Tony Jarvis triumphantly. 'You mean the one Simple Simon met when going to the fair. The "pieman".'

'Sometimes me mam calls me dad that when he comes home blotto,' said Horner.

'How do you mean?' Billy asked, puzzled. 'How does "pie" come into it?'

'Me mam belts him with a rolling pin and shouts, "Drunken bugger! Pie-eyed again."'

Billy was about to give up on the Socratic approach and resort to old-fashioned instruction when Alf Dempsey of all people raised his hand. Most unusual, Billy thought. Alf never answered anything but maybe, just maybe, he had the answer this time.

'Ice pie!' he called.

Billy and the rest of the class were baffled by this contribution.

'Ice pie, Alf? I don't get it,' he said.

'It's a game, sir, that we play at home when there's nowt to do.'

'He means "I Spy",' said Jim Mitchell.

When the guffaws had died down, Billy felt it was time for a more direct approach.

'The word "pie" means dappled or marked in spots, patches, or blotches of a different colour or shade.'

'You mean speckled, sir?' said Anne Greenhalgh.

'That's right,' Billy said.

'The Pied Piper,' she said. 'He was dressed in clothes of different colours.'

'Now we're on the right track,' Billy said. 'And there's a common bird that has the word "pie" in its name.'

'You mean blackbirds baked in a pie, like?' asked Vera Pickles, trying to be helpful.

'No, no,' Billy almost screamed. 'This bird is known for its habit of pilfering and hoarding. Sometimes it's taught to speak.'

'How about "magpie"?' called Mick Lynch. 'That's black and white.'

'Good! Got it at last,' Billy exclaimed with a sigh of relief. 'So now can you tell me the meaning of "piebald"?'

'Excuse me,' said a voice from somewhere under the floor.

Billy looked around bewildered.

The plumber emerged from under the sink and announced in ringing tones, 'Why don't you bloody well tell 'em and have done with it? Piebald means black and white; roan means grey and white; skewbald means brown and white. I know 'cos I place a bet on the horses every dinnertime. I've got a bob each way on one today and it's a piebald. Awright?' With that, his head disappeared back under the sink.

Billy could only mumble, 'Why, thank you very much for that information. We'll try to remember it.'

The class looked at Billy puzzled. Should they listen to him or the oracle from the underworld?

So much for the Socratic method, Billy thought. From now on, I'll simply tell 'em. It's simpler and quicker.

It was not only the general public who joined in. Frank Wakefield sitting at the back of the room couldn't resist putting his oar in from time to time.

In one lesson, Billy had got on to figures of speech – a favourite with the class. They had dealt with similes – as blind as a bat, as fierce as a lion, pleased as Punch, as smooth as velvet, ignoring the smooth as a baby's bottom suggested by Des Bishop – and had finally reached onomatopoeia, the imitation of natural sounds in words.

Billy wrote up the words 'bang, blast, boom, bellow' on the blackboard. 'Look at these words,' he said, 'and tell me what they have in common.'

'They all begin with B,' said Mick Lynch immediately.

'What about these?' he said, writing up 'crunch, gurgle, plunk, splash'.

'They give the sound of what's happening,' said Irene Moody.

'Good. We call this onomatopoeia.' He wrote it up on the blackboard.

'What do we call this figure of speech, Alf Dempsey?'

'Tomatopie,' answered Alf.

Trust Alf to produce the malapropism, thought Billy. He should come and meet my mother some time.

'Not quite, Alf. Can anyone give me the word that indicates the sound of coins?'

'Jingle,' said Anne Greenhalgh.

'Good. Now the sound of heavy chains.'

'Jangle,' said Roger Horner. 'Like in a filum about Alcatraz.'

'Paper being crumpled up.'

'Crumple,' said Alf Dempsey.

'Well done, Alf! And another word for the same?'

'Crinkle,' from Tony Jarvis.

'Excellent,' Billy said. 'Now horses' hoofs on a pavement.'

'Clatter,' said Tessie Shea.

'Yes, well done!' he said. 'Now. . .' Billy noticed that Wakefield, sitting in his usual place at the back of the room, had raised his hand. 'Sorry, Mr Wakefield. Anything wrong?'

'No, no,' he replied, 'but wouldn't "clippety-clop" do there, Mr Hopkins?'

296

Billy thought about it for a moment. He had to be careful here.

'No, not really, Mr Wakefield. Clatter is a better word, I think.'

'Why? What's wrong with "clippety-clop"?'

'Nothing really wrong but it's like saying "gee-gee" for horse.'

'Oh, very well,' he said, 'if you say so.' With that, he went back to his correspondence.

Frank Wakefield did not forget the incident. He bided his time and got his own back a little later. Revenge is a dish best eaten cold, was his philosophy.

Billy was giving a lesson on Christopher Columbus, and was enjoying himself. He had both the class and the bank clerk eating out of his hand.

He had explained how Columbus had sailed across the Atlantic in his ships *Nina, Pinta* and *Santa Maria*, how he had the idea of proving the world was round by reaching Cathay by sailing west, how he hoped to make his fortune and at the same time convert the Chinese to Christianity, how the crews were superstitious and had become more and more terrified as they sailed into uncharted territories. As they journeyed on without any sight of land, they became panic-stricken, imagining the horrors which lay ahead – boiling seas, monstrous sea serpents, the constant fear of falling over the edge of the world into a bottomless void. The idea grew that they would never return to their wives and their families back home in Spain. Billy's story was reaching its climax.

'So there they were sailing where no man had ever been before – into the unknown,' Billy declaimed. 'They'd been at sea for months and still there was no sign of land. The sailors began to mutter amongst themselves. There was murmuring and mumbling and talk of mutiny.'

'If Columbus had hand-picked men, surely they wouldn't mutiny,' said Jim Mitchell, caught up in the suspense. 'They'd be loyal to their captain, surely.'

'Good point, Jim,' Billy exclaimed, nodding his head vigorously.

The bank clerk signified his agreement about the shrewdness of the question and gave a thumbs-up.

'But you must remember,' said Billy, 'that many of the crew were criminals who had been given a pardon by Queen Isabella provided they sailed with Columbus on his hazardous voyage. Apart from that, they had mouldy food, stale water, damp clothes, cramped quarters – life on board was rotten and unhealthy.'

The bank clerk had abandoned the work of accounts and had become an active participant in the lesson, for he now raised his hand.

'How many men were on these ships, Mr Hopkins?' he asked.

Billy had prepared his work well, knowing that Mr Cashman would be in his audience.

'The *Pinta* and the *Nina* were small ships – forty and sixty tons only. On the *Pinta*, there were eighteen men on board, another eighteen on the *Nina*, but on the *Santa Maria*, which was one hundred tons, there were about sixty crew.' He turned back to his class.

'Anyway, as I was saying. The crew were fed up to the back teeth – they had been at sea for six months. On the eleventh of October, fourteen ninety-two, Slit Gizzard Jack, the bosun, yelled to the crew gathered on the foredeck: "I've worked it out, lads, and we'll never get back to Spain. Come on, let's take over the ship afore we fall over the edge of the world."

298

' "Aye," they shouted. "Mutiny! Mutiny! Let's kill Columbus!"

'They began to move towards the captain's cabin but as they did so, from high, high up in the crow's nest,' with a flourish Billy pointed towards the ceiling, 'a voice called out . . .' he paused for dramatic effect and was about to bellow 'Land ahoy!' when with consummate timing Wakefield interrupted with an urgent cry from the back of the room.

'The boiler's gone out back here, Mr Hopkins!'

Touché.

Sometimes, embarrassing situations arose for teacher and pupils alike. Billy could never forgive the writer of one textbook who had devised examples without examining the implications for young adolescents, especially girls, who had to deal with them. The book also taught Billy an important lesson, namely the need to check out material before presenting it to his class.

The English class was employed on parsing and analysis and everything was going well for the first ten minutes.

Jim Mitchell began with the first sentence. ' "John saw the red squirrels." "John" – proper noun and subject of the sentence. "Saw" – active transitive verb. "The" – definite article qualifying "squirrels". "Red" – adjective qualifying "squirrels". "Squirrels" – common noun, object of the verb "saw".'

'Very good, Jim,' said Billy. 'You've obviously done your homework. Next, Vera Pickles. Parse the next sentence.'

The class turned to the next page and to the next sentence. Vera was confronted with: 'Great tits sang in the trees.'

Both Vera and Billy turned a bright red when they realised what was in store. The class stared at the book unbelievingly. Several heads submerged under desk lids.

'Yes, make a start, Vera,' said Billy, determined that they should plough ahead regardless. Vera looked at Billy pleadingly.

'Must I, sir?'

'Yes, why not?'

Vera began. You could have made toast on her cheeks – and on Billy's.

' "The" – definite article qualifying "tits". "Great" – adjective qualifying "tits". "Tits" – common noun, subject of the sentence. "Sang" – intransitive verb. "In the trees" – adverbial phrase of place.'

Needless to say, the class had dissolved into uncontrollable giggling. Billy wished he could find the author of the book so that he could slowly and enjoyably pull each one of his teeth out with a pair of pliers.

However, the most potentially embarrassing predicament was to come. After the morning break one day, Billy returned to class to find everyone in place and ready for the lesson to start.

Nellie Wallace was in the front row and chewing gum vigorously, reminding Billy of a matronly cow chewing the cud. All businesslike, Billy strode into the room.

'Come on, Nellie. You know the rule. Into the wastepaper basket!'

Billy ordered the class to take out their exercise books and he walked down the central aisle, examining their work as he did so. A strange hush fell over the room and his wards stared at something ahead which had captured their attention. Tony Jarvis's head had disappeared into his desk and his shoulders heaved with uncontrollable glee.

Puzzled, Billy turned round and could not believe his eyes.

Nellie had stepped into the wastepaper basket and was standing there, gawky girl that she was, still chewing, the colour mounting her cheeks. She was having trouble maintaining her balance. She looked at Billy appealingly with a look that said: 'I've obeyed your instruction. Now please get me out of this.'

Billy was in a dilemma. He realised that one sarcastic remark, like 'Not you, you silly girl! The chewing gum!' would destroy her and she'd never forgive him. The class waited in anticipation for Billy's response, ready to explode into laughter at the smallest encouragement. Billy was determined not to give it to them.

'OK, Nellie,' he said. 'Step out of the basket. Drop your chewing gum into it. Remember that's where your chewing gum should be. Now go back to your place.'

'Yes, sir. Thank you, sir,' she said quietly.

The class sighed collectively in disappointment. They were not sure whether Billy had intended she step into the basket.

Later, Billy thought, Nellie doesn't understand elliptical speech but by God what discipline! If I'd said, 'Jump, Nellie!' she'd have asked 'How high, sir?' only when she was in mid-air.

Chapter Twenty-Seven

French (Ici on parle School Certificate Français)

The following Monday Billy had his first date with Laura. Not the romantic kind. It was business. He'd arranged to accompany her home to start the series of French lessons for her brother Hughie.

'I think he might be a little nervous at first,' she said as they wheeled their bikes up Regina Park Hill. 'So I hope you'll not be too hard on him if his French isn't up to scratch.'

'He's not the only one who's nervous,' said Billy. 'I feel as if I'm entering the exciting world of the rich and famous, like Beverly Hills.'

Laura laughed. 'You have a slight tendency to exaggerate. We're neither rich nor famous.'

They had reached the top of the hill. There were some open fields and a few large houses set back from the road. In front of them was one of the biggest private houses Billy had ever seen – practically a mansion. They stopped at the front gate, an imposing wrought-iron affair.

'This is it,' she said. 'Home.'

'Not rich and famous, you say? What about this?' said Billy, pointing to the plaque on the wall. It read: LOUISE

MACKENZIE, LRAM, TEACHER OF MUSIC AND SINGING.

'Oh, that's one of Mammy's interests – she takes on a few pupils. She used to be a professional singer in Scotland before she married.'

'Ah, is that all?' He swallowed hard. This was a very different world from his own.

They opened the gate and walked along a winding drive through what estate agents call a mature garden of trees and shrubs – rowanberry, elm and rhododendrons.

'We can leave our bikes in the garage,' she said.

She opened the door of the porch and turned her key in the front door. The hall smelled of lavender and beeswax and there was a large porcelain flowerpot containing an arrangement of chrysanthemums on a half-circular walnut table. He could see the reflection of the flowerpot in the cushion-framed looking glass – the whole setting resembling an illustration from *Ideal Home*. The Persian carpet gave it the finishing touch.

Billy helped Laura off with her coat and then took off his own. She hung them up in the hall wardrobe.

'Hughie!' she called. 'Mr Hopkins is here.'

A tall, good-looking boy appeared from one of the rooms off the hall. He was smiling. Billy wasn't sure whether the smile was one of welcome or a nervous grimace.

They shook hands warmly.

'Nice to meet you, Hughie,' he said. 'Laura has told me about you – all to the good, I might add.'

'Glad to know you, Mr Hopkins,' said Hughie, still smiling. 'Thanks for agreeing to help me with my French.'

'Don't call me Mr Hopkins, it keeps us at a distance. Billy will be fine.'

'We've arranged for you to take the lessons in here,' said

Laura, opening one of the doors. 'In the drawing room, if that's OK.'

'That's fine,' said Billy. Drawing room? Where he came from, they called it 'the parlour', and they didn't even have one of them in the flat.

'Is it OK if I smoke?' he asked.

'Of course,' she answered and brought him a heavy glass ashtray from the other side of the room.

My God, he thought, even the ashtray is a collector's item.

'I'll leave you to it, Billy,' she said. 'If you need anything, I'll be in the kitchen across the hall.'

Billy and Hughie went into the drawing room, and, for Billy at least, into a different domain. Billy looked around him at the Pye radiogram – not only a radio but incorporating a record player that could play 33.3 rpm, a whole symphony on two sides! – the decorated firescreen, and a good deal of elegant period furniture. What caught his attention in particular was the mahogany Bechstein grand piano which stood in front of the large bay window. On the fold-down music stand, someone had left a book of Chopin Nocturnes opened at one dedicated to Laura Duperré. A portrait of Beethoven glowered down from the wall.

'We can work here,' said Hughie, indicating a writing bureau, 'if that's OK.'

'Suits me fine,' said Billy, thinking it's the first time I've ever worked at a Queen Anne bureau. 'How did you get on with the unseen passage I sent over for you?'

'Not bad, I think, I'll let you be the judge, Billy. I should warn you, though, that I'm not very good. Hamish, Laura's boyfriend, told me that my real ability was on the science side and that I have no aptitude for languages.'

'No aptitude for languages! What nonsense!' Billy exclaimed vehemently. 'Everybody's got aptitude for languages. We master our first by the time we're five at our mother's knee. Anyway, let's take a look at your effort.'

Hughie handed over his work and watched Billy's face anxiously as he gave it the once-over. Billy noticed immediately a considerable number of errors but he looked up and smiled.

'Not bad, not bad,' he said. 'Good for a first effort. English into French is never easy. A few errors but I can see no reason why you shouldn't get a distinction by the time the final exams come round.'

'I'd be so grateful, Billy,' he said. 'Daddy has been putting on the pressure lately. Forbidden me to go out at night. I have to get at least a credit to matriculate.'

'You remind me of an American friend,' said Billy. 'He hated school so much he was always saying that every time he passed his old High School, he used to matriculate.'

Hughie laughed for the first time that day.

At that point they were interrupted by Laura bringing tea on a silver tray.

'Oh, it's so nice to hear Hughie laughing,' she said. 'Music to my ears. I thought you'd both like a cup of tea to get you started. And Billy, you're invited to join us for a meal when you've finished, if you have time. You can meet the rest of the family.'

'Love to,' replied Billy, at the same time feeling a little uncomfortable as he wondered if his table manners were up to it.

'Now, let's take a look at some of your basic errors,' he said when Laura had left. 'First, learn to spell *beaucoup* and avoid those *beacups*. I notice, too, that you have written *dans Paris*. I know that in English we say "in Manchester"

305

or "in America" – the word "in" can apply to nearly every situation. In French, not so. They like to distinguish between the different "ins". Learn this sentence: *Quand on est à Paris, on est en France*. The word "in" is *à* for towns and *en* for most countries.'

So the lesson continued and their hour together soon passed.

'I think I've learned more French this evening than I have in the last month,' said Hughie, finishing off his notes.

'Remember all we've said this afternoon, Hughie, and I'm sure you'll soon be producing error-free translations.' Then Billy added, 'The funniest attempt I ever came across was from a boy at my old school who translated *Non, merci, ma chérie, je ne veux pas acheter un appareil cinématographique* (No, thank you, my dear, I don't want to buy a cine camera) as "No sherry for me, thank you, I'm appearing at the cinema".'

Tears of merriment sprang to Hughie's eyes.

Laura appeared once again at the door. 'Time for tea, you two. From the noises coming from this room, it sounds as if you've been telling jokes instead of working.'

'Not at all,' said Hughie. 'Laughing and working at the same time. I think I'm going to enjoy these French sessions.'

'Don't forget, Hughie, to do the second unseen for next week's lesson.'

'Thanks for everything, Billy,' said Hughie.

'And that goes for me too, Billy,' said Laura earnestly. 'Now, perhaps you'd like to freshen up before you come and meet the family. The bathroom is upstairs, along the landing and second on the right.'

As Billy climbed the stairs, he couldn't help noticing the thick red carpet, the stained-glass window on the first landing, the small pictures in their gilt frames hanging on the walls of the passageway. Botticelli's 'Spring', Manet's *'Déjeuner sur l'herbe'*, and a Millet country scene. The only art Billy was acquainted with were the flying ceramic ducks which his dad had acquired with cigarette coupons.

The bathroom was in keeping with the rest of the house, that is to say, large and luxurious. It was fully tiled in pink, had a kingsize washbasin, gold-plated towel rails and taps, a large mirror extending the length of the bath, a separate shower cubicle, a WC and a kidney-shaped basin with taps, which Billy surmised was designed for washing the feet. On the third wall was a large reproduction of Bellini's 'Young Woman at Her Toilet'. Everything was spotlessly clean and smelt of freshly laundered towels and soap scented with attar of roses.

Billy compared it with the little cramped bathroom at home with its one pair of swivel taps that served both bath and washbasin, the noisy cistern that had drying under-clothes forever clinging to it like barnacles, and the narrow windowsill that served as bathroom cabinet. As he saw it in his mind's eye, he became acutely aware of his place in the social hierarchy. The more he thought about it, the more it reinforced his notion that he was inferior. He washed his face, flicked a comb through his hair, and went downstairs to meet the Mackenzie family.

As he walked across the hall to the kitchen, his nostrils were assailed by the smell of freshly baked scones and bread. He knocked and entered when a voice softly called, 'Come in, Billy.'

Laura was at the small kitchen table rolling pastry. She had a smudge of flour on her nose and at that moment Billy fell in love with her all over again – with an overwhelming feeling of tenderness. Like William Cobbett, who had determined on his bride when he first saw her 'scrubbing out a washing tub in the snow', Billy knew that there could never be anyone else in the world for him but Laura Mackenzie.

She put down the rolling pin, wiped the flour from her hands on her pinafore, and came forward.

'Let me introduce my family. This is Billy,' she announced. 'And this is my mother, my sister Jenny, my sister Katie, my grandmother, and Aunty. Hughie you already know of course.'

After hand-shaking all round, Louise said, 'You are very welcome, Billy. And thank you for agreeing to give Hughie tuition in French.'

Not only a music teacher, Billy thought, she has a musical voice as well, like her eldest daughter. Or should that be the other way round?

'No problem, Mrs Mackenzie,' he said. 'I love teaching and Hughie is such a talented student, he is a pleasure to deal with.'

Katie gazed at him shyly. She'd seen him at school along with the other teachers and she was in awe that one of their teachers was here in the family kitchen and talking to her mother and sisters.

'Are you any relation to Douglas Hamilton Hopkins of Kirkintilloch?' asked Grandma.

' 'Fraid not,' answered Billy. 'I think I'm of Irish extraction.'

Grandma didn't reply but looked disappointed that an Irish type had managed to infiltrate the family kitchen.

'This is a lovely big farmhouse kitchen,' said Billy, looking round the room. His eye took in the Servis washing machine, the Prestcold refrigerator, the Aga cooker. 'So warm and inviting.'

'It's big,' said Louise. 'I think too big sometimes. It was all right I suppose when there were lots of servants to do the hard work. Notice we've still got the servants' bells up there on the wall but no servants.'

'Now she's got her daughters,' Laura laughed.

Aunty had been staring at him all this time, wondering if she might chance retailing one of her many anecdotes about the old days. He might listen to her.

'You remind me of my younger brother Jamie,' she began. 'I mind a time, ye ken, when—'

'I'm sure Billy doesna want to hear your stories,' Grandma snapped.

Anxious not to be seen as impolite, Billy began paying Aunty close attention but this was interrupted by Louise who said, 'What would you like for tea, Billy? We are having homemade scones and preserves or perhaps you'd like a couple of boiled eggs?'

'That sounds wonderful, Mrs Mackenzie,' Billy said. 'Boiled eggs would go down very well.' Was that the right thing to say? he wondered.

'I'll put them on now. We always wait for Mr Mackenzie before we begin,' she added. 'He should be here fairly soon.'

The mention of Mr Mackenzie's name sent an involuntary *frisson* down Billy's spine.

They sat down at the large dining table.

'I'm not long for this world, Billy,' Aunty began, 'but I mind a time, ye ken, when my brother Jamie came back from the war and . . .'

Billy nodded attentively but his mind was on the layout of the table as he examined it for unfamiliar implements that might cause him problems. It was not like the table at home. For one thing, the bread was not pre-cut. He noted a breadboard and knife – obviously here one cut one's own. There was a dish of butter and he verified that he had a butter knife. Was one expected to pour one's own tea and, if so, did one put the milk in first? What about the boiled egg? Oh, how he wished he had opted for simple bread and jam. Was it the done thing to cut bread soldiers and dip them in the yolk? Pottsy in his etiquette tutorials at college hadn't covered these matters because they'd never been served boiled eggs.

Aunty was still relating her story of how Jamie had returned after a spell in the trenches, and of her family connections to the great John MacCormack, when her soliloquy was interrupted by the sound of a car coming up the drive.

'That'll be Mr Mackenzie now,' said Louise.

Billy froze but the family went into action. Louise put the finishing touches to the boiled fish she was preparing, and took Billy's eggs from the water. Laura infused the tea, Jenny arranged the great man's slippers before the fire. The hall clock struck five thirty and they heard the key turn in the lock.

A minute later, Duncan Mackenzie entered the room. Billy stood up when he saw him.

'This is Billy,' Laura said quickly.

Duncan looked at Billy intently as if he were assessing a taxpayer for possible tax evasion. After a pause, he gave a curt nod and took Billy's hand in a firm handshake.

'How d'you do?' he said.

'Pleased to meet you,' answered Billy, equally economical with his greeting. It came out as *Pleasetameetcha*.

'Your slippers are warmed, Daddy,' said Jenny.

'Your tea is poured, Daddy,' said Laura.

'And your fish is ready whenever you are,' added Louise.

Duncan went into his evening routine. He removed his coat, put on his slippers, washed his hands while the family waited in silence. He sat down in the carver chair at the head of the table. The rest took their places round the sides – Billy next to Hughie and opposite Laura and Aunty. All bowed their heads as Duncan said grace. 'Amen,' they said when he'd finished.

Billy felt that he was taking part in a James Bridie play.

Louise brought on the cooked meals for the men. Fish for Duncan, eggs for Billy.

Duncan pointed to various articles on the table, first the cruets, then the bread. The rest of the family reached out swiftly to minister to his wishes. Billy had the impression that there was a competition going on to anticipate the next requirement, the winner being the first to seize the desired object. Maybe there were points for the various items and a prize at the end for the one who got most right – six for the salt, five for the pepper, four for a teaspoon. Billy became so absorbed by the family ritual, he found himself trying to guess the target of Duncan's index finger. There was little conversation and what little there was had to be addressed to the head of the table for evaluation. However, there was something in Billy's nature that found long silences painful. He had to say something.

'I'm sure we'll soon have Hughie speaking French like General de Gaulle,' he said.

'As long as it's de Gaulle's accent,' added Hughie, 'and not Winston Churchill's.'

All eyes turned to Duncan for assessment of these remarks. Were they funny? Was it OK to laugh? Were they to be treated seriously or with contempt?

Billy felt that a signboard such as was used to prompt reactions from a studio audience might not go amiss here.

LAUGH! GROAN! APPLAUD! HISS!

Duncan cut short any snickering with a cold stare. 'Hrrumph' was his response.

Billy turned his attention to the eggs and the implements for dealing with them. He had a choice. He could cut the top of his egg in one deft slicing movement with his butter knife. Was that the done thing? Or he could tap the shell with his spoon. Watched by the family, he opted for the latter. It was the wrong choice. It involved peeling off tiny bits of shell and some of these clung unfairly and tenaciously to the thin membrane of the egg. Now there was the question of what to do with the debris. Oh, how he wished he'd chosen the scones and the preserve! The family continued to watch fascinated as Billy struggled to resolve the conflicts in which the eggs had involved him. He realised that bread soldiers were out and he could tell that his decision to go for buttering half slices was the right one by the relieved expressions on the watching faces – though he was aware that he had lost points in his hacking of the bread. How would they have reacted if he'd sliced up the egg and made butties? he wondered. That would blow his chances with Laura and no mistake.

'And so,' Duncan began finally, addressing Billy, 'you've come to give Hughie there a few French lessons. How has he got on?'

Hughie looked at Billy pleadingly.

'An excellent start, Mr Mackenzie. I think he'll get at least a credit next summer, if not a distinction.'

The gratitude showed in Hughie's eyes.

'I'm glad to hear it,' Duncan said. 'I think the laddie needs a kick in the backside to get him working. How much shall we owe you for this tuition? I'm a man who believes in paying his way, ye ken.'

'Nothing, Mr Mackenzie. I'm glad to do a service for a colleague,' said Billy, looking at Laura who smiled and gave him a Gainsborough lady nod in acknowledgement.

No fee, Billy thought. Just the hand of your daughter in marriage.

'That's the kind of fee a Scotsman likes to hear,' said Duncan, grinning. 'Especially one who works in taxes, as I would have to add such a fee to your income for tax purposes.'

'On my pittance,' replied Billy, 'I'm barely within the tax range, despite the fact that I've taken part-time work in a youth centre to supplement my income. By the way, did you know, Mr Mackenzie, that I used to work in the Inland Revenue?'

'Is that a fact? Which district was that?'

'District Three in Sunlight House. I was a T3.'

'Everyone has to start somewhere, I suppose,' he chuckled.

'What's a T3?' asked Laura. 'It sounds like a mysterious job in the Secret Service.'

'Hardly,' said Billy, 'T3 means temporary clerk, grade three, and it's the lowest rank possible, slightly above office cleaner, in the civil service.'

'You're now a teacher,' said Louise encouragingly. 'So obviously you've risen in rank since then.'

'Not by much,' Billy laughed. 'I'm now a junior master in charge of the senior class at St Anselm's. Still at the bottom of the heap.'

'Not quite true,' said Laura. 'By all the accounts that reach my ears, you're a good teacher and you should go a long way one day.'

'All the way to Timbuktu according to the wits in my form.'

313

The family laughed together. An unusual thing for them to do at the dining table.

'You have a degree of course?' said Duncan.

' 'Fraid not,' answered Billy. 'I went to a teacher training college and as it was at the end of the war, they weren't really geared up for degrees.'

'To get anywhere in this world,' Duncan pontificated, 'you need a university degree, especially in teaching. In Scotland, if you were to teach in an academy, that's the secondary school, you'd have to have a degree. Those who teach at the higher levels must have honours.'

'In a secondary modern like St Anselm's, we're not academic,' answered Billy.

'Doesna matter. Things are going to get competitive in the future and only university graduates will stand a chance. Take a leaf out of Laura's boyfriend's book. Hamish is studying for his degree in actuarial studies at Glasgow.'

At the mention of Hamish's name, Billy felt the bile rise in his throat.

'I think Hamish is a bright man,' said Jenny. 'He knows which side his bread is buttered on all right.'

And bread never falls but on its buttered side, thought Billy. I hope Hamish falls on his face.

'Perhaps you two men would like to go into the study for a smoke,' suggested Louise, 'whilst we clear the table.'

'Good idea,' said Billy, thinking it was the best idea he'd heard all night. But there was another word. Study!

Duncan and Billy retired for their smoke.

The study was a long room, with a varnished wainscot and lined with leather-bound books from floor to ceiling. There was a log fire burning in the fireplace. The Parker-Knoll Camden armchairs completed the picture.

314

Duncan took out a box of cigars, guillotined the ends of two with his cutter and offered one to Billy, lighting it for him with his desk lighter. Billy puffed happily at his smoke. This was gracious living indeed. All he needed now was a brandy in a balloon glass and his contentment would be complete. Then I shall have joined the Tory Party, he thought. Wonder what my dad'd say to that.

As if reading his thoughts, Duncan poured two brandies into balloon glasses.

'This can be your fee,' he said, drawing on his cigar. 'Napoleon brandy – the best.'

Billy looked round the room in awe – he had never seen so many books outside a public library. The titles and authors of the volumes were equally impressive: Jane Austen, R.M. Ballantyne, Hilaire Belloc, G.K. Chesterton. He had reached the works of Charles Dickens when the study door opened and Laura joined them.

'I love the smell of cigars – reminds me of Christmas,' she said.

'That and tangerines,' added Billy. Returning to his examination of the books he said, 'You have a fine collection of books here, Mr Mackenzie.'

'Yes,' he agreed. 'Many of them inherited from mine and Louise's parents. But there's one book I feel is better than the rest put together. Which one would you say it was, Billy?'

Now here was a dilemma. Billy favoured the works of Robert Browning but he was sure the answer would be more esoteric.

He hazarded a guess: 'St Augustine's *Confessions*.'

'No,' said Duncan. 'Try again.'

'The Oxford English Dictionary?'

'No,' said Duncan, picking out *The Path to Rome* by Hilaire Belloc. 'This one.'

Billy determined to read it at the first opportunity. Earning the approval of Laura's father was going to be a full-time job. He must try to make Duncan like him and if one way of doing that was to read Belloc's *Rome* book, so be it.

'Would you be prepared to lend me the book for a little while, Mr Mackenzie?' he asked.

'Certainly. Always glad to enlighten a young man like yoursel'.'

Billy determined to study it thoroughly in case there was a *viva voce* exam on it the next time they met.

'I see, Mr Mackenzie, that you have the complete illustrated works of Charles Dickens,' Billy continued.

'Ah, so you like the works of Dickens,' said Laura warmly. 'So do I! We have something in common.'

'Not only am I a fan of Dickens's work but also that of his first illustrator, George Cruikshank.'

'Ah, you mean Boz,' said Duncan. 'All the sketches in Dickens's work were done by Boz. That was Cruikshank's pen name. Did you not know that?'

'Are you sure, Mr Mackenzie?' said Billy, puzzled. 'You must be thinking of Dickens's first novel *Sketches by Boz*, which was published in serial form. Cruikshank illustrated both this first book and *Oliver Twist*. Cruikshank was never known as Boz.'

'I'm surprised that a secondary school teacher – and an English teacher as well – could get a thing like that wrong. Boz was the pseudonym of Cruikshank, I can assure you.'

'I made a study of Dickens at college, Mr Mackenzie,' Billy argued gently, 'and I think you'll find I'm right. I had to write a long essay on him as part of my finals.'

316

Laura was making little danger signals to Billy with her eyes.

'I'm not a betting man,' said Duncan, 'and so we'll not wager on it. But we'll settle the matter here and now with the *Encyclopaedia Britannica*.'

He went over to the reference section and pulled down the volume marked Decorative to Edison.

Uh-oh, thought Billy. Trouble. How am I going to get out of this one? Whatever happens, Duncan mustn't lose face. He looked to Laura for help but she simply raised her eyes to heaven in supplication.

Duncan had found the required entry. 'Ah, here we are. Now, we'll see who's right. I'll read out what it says. "In 1833, Dickens began contributing stories and descriptive essays to magazines and newspapers: these attracted attention and were reprinted as *Sketches by 'Boz'* in February 1836. Illustrations were done by George Cruikshank." So you see, Billy, you were wrong. Boz was the name adopted by Dickens for his first book, d'you see?'

'Ah, now I see, Mr Mackenzie,' agreed Billy warmly. 'Boz was the name for Dickens, not his illustrator. What does the encyclopaedia say about Cruikshank?'

'Let's see,' Duncan said. He began to read from another volume: ' "Cruikshank, George (1792 to 1878) British caricaturist and illustrator whose large output included the illustrations for Dickens's *Sketches by 'Boz'* and *Oliver Twist* where he was known simply as Cruikshank." '

'I stand corrected, Mr Mackenzie,' said Billy, though he was hurting inside.

There was a glow of triumph in Duncan's eyes as he said, 'So, you've learned a thing or two about Dickens tonight, Billy. I'm always glad to pass on a little erudition to a young man like yourself.' Savouring his intellectual 'victory', he turned to Laura and said, 'Perhaps Billy might enjoy our musical evening next Sunday night. What do you think, Laura?'

Laura pursed her lips and looked dubious.

'Well, would you, Billy?' Duncan said. 'We hold a musical "At Home" once a month – it's very informal. Just a few friends and family. I think you'd enjoy it. We usually put on one or two little efforts, bits of music, recitations and the like. You may be able to join in the fun here and there. What do you say?'

I've really got my feet under the table now, he thought. Eating a meal with the family and attending a musical *soirée*. Hamish Dunwoody, you got till sunup to get out o' town. I don't know what this musical evening entails but I can always find out from Laura at school. If it means an opportunity to be near her, count me in.

'Yes, I'd love to come,' he heard himself saying.

'Good,' said Duncan. 'It might give us another opportunity to broaden your education.'

There may have been triumph in Duncan's eyes but in Laura's it was a different look. Not only gratitude but a new bond of understanding between them.

As the Mackenzie clock struck seven, Billy felt it was time to take his leave. He said goodnight to the family and Laura accompanied him to the door.

'Billy,' she said as he went to the garage to collect his bike, 'I don't know how to thank you for all you did tonight – for Hughie and for the way you helped Daddy save face. That took real guts.' She kissed him on the forehead. 'Thank you so much.'

Billy's heart leapt for joy.

On the way home that night, he said to himself, in that

318

argument with King Duncan, I lost the battle but I won the war.

And one piece of poetry suitably modified went round and round in his head.

> *Say I'm weary, say I'm sad,*
> *Say that health and wealth have missed me,*
> *Say I'm growing old, but add,*
> *Laura kissed me.*

Back at the Mackenzie household, Billy was assessed as a 'likeable young man'. But it was Aunty who gave him the highest accolade when she said, 'I think he's a wonderful young gentleman. He's the only one who ever listened to me.'

Chapter Twenty-Eight

If Music Be the Food of Love

In the staffroom next day, Laura seemed highly amused when Billy asked her about the projected musical 'At Home'.

'I don't get it,' he said. 'What's the joke?'

'You,' she answered. 'You do let yourself in for things without weighing up what's involved. Impulsive isn't the word for it. First, tutoring Hughie in French. I'm sure you took that on without thinking about the work it involved. Then you've accepted Daddy's invitation to one of our *soirées*.'

'If I'm impulsive, that's because my astrological sign is the crab. We're supposed to be an impulsive lot. Anyway, I see nothing wrong in volunteering my services to help Hughie. I enjoy teaching. As for the evening, I assume it'll be conversation and listening to a few classical records on your magnificent radiogram. I haven't heard a 33.3 player yet. At home, we're still struggling with an old HMV wind-up gramophone. On that, the music sounds as if it's being performed with a nest of snakes hissing in the background. I've borrowed your father's copy of *The Path to Rome* and I'm hoping we can have a discussion about that.'

'Our musical evenings involve a lot more than that,' she laughed. 'They vary but there's usually poetry reading, piano playing, singing, and Daddy may even perform a Highland fling or a sword dance.'

'Singing? What kind of singing?'

'Some solos, duets, madrigals, part songs – that kind of thing. Whatever takes our fancy. Do you have a party piece, Billy?'

'Not that I'm aware of, though I once danced like Fred Astaire in the infants' school. But surely you haven't got to do something. I'll simply come and watch.'

Laura raised both eyebrows. 'Perhaps you're right,' she said. She didn't sound sure.

'Who'll be there, Laura?'

'The family and an old friend of ours, Monsignor Guerin. And oh, I almost forgot, Hamish. He expects to be home for half-term.'

When he heard the name Hamish and the news that he'd be there, Billy felt a pang of anguish like a knife in his heart. He hid his feelings.

'Laura, please find out what the programme is likely to be so I can start inventing my excuses.'

Greg sidled up puffing a great cloud of nauseating smoke from his hideous pipe. 'You two look as if you're hatching up a plot,' he guffawed. 'You'll have people talking.'

'Do keep it quiet,' whispered Billy. 'We were thinking of putting a bomb under Grundy's chair.'

'Not a bad idea,' Greg roared. 'I came over, Hoppy, to enlist your help,' he continued. 'As you know, I'm getting married, and Emily and I have managed to find an apartment in High Lane, Chorlton, but it's in a poor state of repair. Flats are as rare as gold dust and so we don't have much choice. I wondered however if you'd be willing to help Alex and me decorate the place.'

'Sure thing,' laughed Billy. 'Why not? I can see that fate is guiding me into my true vocation – painting and decorating. It might be a good career move. I'm sure it would mean better pay.'

'I'll hold you to that pledge,' said Greg. 'When we get the key to the flat we might roll up our sleeves and get to it.'

'OK. Count me in,' said Billy.

'There's the crab in you again,' remarked Laura. 'Don't you ever say no?'

'Yes,' Billy answered.

The following Sunday, Billy cycled over to Regina Park for the Sunday *soirée*. He took off his cycle clips, deposited his bike in the garage, and rang the doorbell. Jenny answered it.

'Good evening, Billy,' she said warmly. 'Everyone's already here and we've been waiting for you with bated breath.'

'That's what comes from eating too many bates,' he replied. What a weak joke, he thought.

Jenny laughed. 'Laura told me you're something of a comedian,' she said as she showed him into the drawing room where they were all waiting – the Mackenzie family plus Hamish and a priest wearing the purple vest of a monsignor.

'I think you know everyone here,' said Laura, 'except Monsignor Guerin who is a long-standing friend of the family.'

'Though at the present moment, you're sitting down,' Billy joked. He was nervous.

Monsignor Guerin acknowledged the greeting and the drollery by shaking hands and laughing heartily.

Duncan glared at Billy. 'Hamish here was telling us about his university course,' he said, ignoring Billy's attempt at wit, 'and an interesting course it sounds. It should lead to a good, well-paid job. Deservedly so.'

'I think I have a job lined up already, Mr Mackenzie, with the Caledonian Mutual in Edinburgh,' Hamish simpered. 'They're offering me nine hundred pounds a year to start.'

Billy thought bitterly about his own paltry salary as a young teacher at the bottom of the scale.

'Fantastic, Hamish!' enthused Jenny, and she could not prevent herself from exclaiming, 'Lucky Laura!'

'Excellent, Hamish,' Duncan purred, glancing in Laura's direction, 'and I suppose you'll have big plans if you pull that off.'

The significance of these exchanges was not lost on Billy.

'I've no doubt that I'll be coming to see you then about a serious matter, Mr Mackenzie,' Hamish said. Looking at Laura, he asked, 'How does the idea of living in Edinburgh appeal to you, Laura?'

Laura flushed. 'I'm not sure about that, Hamish. Manchester's where my home and my job are and I'm loath to leave them at the present. But we can cross that bridge if and when we come to it.'

Good for you, Laura, thought Billy. Don't let them push you into something you don't want.

'Enough of this serious talk,' said Louise brightly. 'We're here to enjoy ourselves. It's a musical At Home, not a debating club.'

'Quite right,' said Duncan. 'I thought we might start the

323

evening's entertainment off with a part song. I found a beautiful Victorian piece by Walter MacFarren when I was browsing in the Henry Watson Music Library at lunchtime on Friday. His name sounds Scottish and so it's bound to be good.'

Huh, Billy thought.

Duncan handed out copies of a composition entitled 'You Stole My Love'.

'Before you came, Billy,' Duncan said, 'we agreed that Louise aided by Katie will sing soprano; Laura and Jenny, alto; Hamish and Hughie, tenor; and Billy, if you wouldn't mind singing bass with Monsignor. Our two senior members over there will act as observers and critics.'

Billy looked enviously at Grandma and Aunty, who sat comfortably by the fireside having been granted exemption because of their age.

'I used to sing alto in a choir, Billy,' Aunty croaked, 'but that was many years ago. Now, I'm not long for this world. I'll no' last another year.'

'Sing us another song, for heaven's sake,' snapped Grandma. 'And besides, when you were in a choir, I ken you had a terrible squeaky voice.'

Billy had already asked Laura to pass on the message that he couldn't read music but either there had been a breakdown in communication or his protestations had been swept aside.

He looked at his copy. The black squiggles on the paper were no more than a collection of lower case ds and ps – some upright and some upside down like a series of clay pipes in a shooting gallery. From his early musical training at St Chad's Elementary School, though, he knew that some of the notes went up and some down but the crucial question was exactly how much up and how much down. He was relieved to notice that there were no passages of solo bass singing.

The priest was standing behind the piano, and Billy joined him, thinking it was going to take every ounce of his working-class guile to get through this one.

Louise struck a chord. There was a droning sound like the humming of a swarm of angry bees as the singers cleared their throats and found their notes.

Duncan raised his long index finger which seemed to have been specially designed as a pointing stick and a symbol of his authority. Billy was half tempted to grab the finger and bite it but resisted.

Duncan held the digit aloft and with a 'One, two, three', brought it down smartly, and they were off, singing with gusto:

> *You stole my love. Fie upon you fie*
> *You stole my love fie, fie ah.*
> *Guessed you but what a pain it is to prove*
> *You stole my love, fie fie ah*
> *Fie, fie, Fie upon you fie.*

Billy found that by singing a milli-second behind Monsignor he was able to create the impression that he was sight-reading the music. For his part, Monsignor had the strangest feeling that he was in an echo chamber but being a courteous cleric, said nothing. The group continued in this fashion for a good ten minutes and Billy lost track of the number of 'fies' he had sung.

As they flicked over the pages, the pace quickened, the volume rose and the stream of 'fies' multiplied until they reached the last sheet, when the instruction *accelerando e fortissimo* released a flood of angry 'fie

325

upon yous' from the whole company. Hamish seemed to be especially vehement in his denunciation of the Victorian Lothario as he raised his high tenor voice to fever pitch, and Billy had the distinct impression that his particular 'fie upon yous' were being directed at him personally. In the final bars, the 'fies' flew thick and fast and furious, bouncing off the walls and ceilings until Duncan's commanding forefinger was raised aloft and then swept sideways in a scything movement to bring the performance to a smart and unified conclusion. That is to say, almost unified. Billy had been so intent on watching Hamish's angry accusations that he missed the signal and when everyone snapped their mouths shut in disciplined fashion, he found himself singing one extra 'fie' not provided for in the music.

The whole company collapsed in laughter. Everyone seemed well satisfied and flushed by the entertainment, adjudging it 'great fun'.

'Excellent,' enthused Duncan. 'A perfect performance except for the supplementary 'fie' at the end but that's best forgotten.'

'Sorry,' said Billy, 'there were so many "fies"! I lost my way.'

Louise now took over the proceedings.

'I'd like to sing a song specially dedicated to my son and to the memory of his first day at school – which seems like only yesterday to me. A day I'll never forget.'

Accompanied by Laura on the piano, she sang 'Wee Hughie' in a soprano voice. But beautiful as Louise's voice was, Billy's attention was riveted on her accompanist and the graceful way her hands moved across the keyboard as her mother sang:

He's gone to school, wee Hughie
And him not four
Sure I saw the fright was in him
When he left the door.
But he took a hand of Daddy
And a hand of Dan
Wi' Jo's ould coat upon him,
Och the poor wee man.

Jenny was second in the programme with a wistful rendering of a Chopin Nocturne. She played slowly and sensitively, leaving her audience sad and thoughtful.

'That was a beautiful performance, Jenny,' said Hamish. 'You seem to get better and better each time I hear you.'

Flatterer, Billy thought.

'Why, thank you, Hamish,' murmured Jenny warmly. 'I never realised you were listening so closely. But it's Mammy's teaching you should be praising.'

For Billy, however, it was Laura's rendering of Haydn's song 'My Mother Bids Me Bind My Hair' that provided the highlight of the evening. Her gentle, lilting voice seemed to go to the core of his being and he felt an overwhelming love for her.

'Magnificent,' he said, when the polite applause had died away. 'Mr and Mrs Mackenzie, you really do have a most talented family.'

'Why, thank you, Billy,' said Duncan. 'But wait, there's more. You have yet to hear the younger end. Hughie, let's hear your piece.' It sounded like a command.

Hughie stood up, looking nervously towards his father. 'I can't sing but I've learned a poem, Daddy. I hope it's all right.'

327

'Yes, yes, Hughie. No excuses now. Let's hear your effort.'

Hughie cleared his throat. ' "The Charge of the Light Brigade" by Alfred, Lord Tennyson.

> *Half a league, half a league,*
> *Half a league onward,*
> *All in the valley of Death*
> *Rode the six hundred . . .'*

As Hughie recited, Billy rummaged through the jumble in his mental attic for a suitable ballad which would go down well with this company. He knew a few lines from a similar military verse but all he could remember was that each stanza ended with 'Sam, Sam, pick up tha' musket'. Then again he half knew a Lancashire monologue called 'Albert and the Lion' but it was not quite the thing for this distinguished assembly. As for the bawdy poem he'd heard in the college common room, all about the exploits of a certain Eskimo Nell, that was definitely out. He had in his inside pocket a possible contribution but he would use it only as a last resort.

Hughie completed the Tennyson ballad without a mistake.

'Well done, Hughie!' Billy called. 'You have a remarkable memory. I thought you might have given us a poem in French. But nevertheless, well done!'

'Not bad, not bad at all, I suppose,' said Duncan grudgingly. It sounded as if it had cost him great deal of effort to make the admission. 'Time for one more before we pause for a break. Any volunteers?'

Nobody moved. Nobody spoke. Billy shuffled uncomfortably in his seat. He could feel the net closing in. The situation was saved by Monsignor Guerin who now stepped forward into the breach both literally and metaphorically.

'I could give you the famous speech from *Henry V* if that would be acceptable,' he said.

The cries of 'By all means' and 'Yes, let's hear it' gave him sufficient reassurance to walk to the centre of the room and begin declaiming with arms outstretched to an invisible audience.

'Once more unto the breach, dear friends, once more;
Or close the wall up with our English dead! . . .'

'First class, Monsignor,' Duncan called when the priest had finished, 'though when you speak of English dead, I take it you mean British dead. British citizens object to the use of the term English when it means the whole population of Britain. Remember that in *Henry the Fifth*, we had a captain from each nation: Fluellen, Gower, Jamy, and Macmorris.'

'You're right there, Mr Mackenzie,' Billy exclaimed, anxious to earn a few points after his *faux pas* in the 'Fie Upon You' madrigal. 'During the war I always thought that Ivor Novello's patriotic song "There'll Always Be an England" excluded the Welsh, the Scots and the people of Ulster. Hardly fair when all Britain was fighting the Nazi menace.'

'I agree,' Monsignor Guerin said. 'But I think the word England is used in a loose sense to include all the people of Britain.'

'Then they should say so,' grumbled Duncan. 'There's nothing wrong with "There'll always be a Britain, and Britain shall be free." '

'Sorry to interrupt this high-falutin' debate,' said Louise. 'It's time for a break. The ladies will retire to the kitchen and bring on the tea and buns, though I don't see why one of these nights the men can't take over that particular chore. After the break, perhaps we can hear what the rest of our company can provide in the way of entertainment.'

When he heard this, Billy felt a pang of alarm. He wondered how he could get out of it. Perhaps if he announced some excuse for having to depart suddenly, like 'I've just remembered it's my mother's sixtieth birthday today and the family's arranged a special surprise party – they're expecting me at home. Slipped my mind.' Somehow it didn't ring true. He'd have to think of something else.

'If anyone would prefer a glass of wine,' Duncan announced, 'I have a Blue Nun in the fridge.'

Billy didn't bat an eyelid when he said, 'That should liven things up good and proper.' If the nun was in the fridge, was it any wonder she was blue? Anyway to him, 'Blue Nun' sounded distinctly lewd like the title of a pornographic movie.

The ladies filed out to fetch the food.

While they were gone, Billy hoped the conversation might switch to a discussion of Belloc's *The Path to Rome* which he had spent the week studying in the hope of winning credits with Duncan for diligence. He was ready to submit to an oral examination on the subject, but no luck. The half-time discussion took a different direction.

'That was indeed a fine rendering of the *Henry the Fifth* speech, Monsignor,' said Duncan. 'Worthy of Laurence Olivier in the recent film.'

Ah, good, thought Billy, here's a subject I know some-thing about. Perhaps in lieu of Belloc, I can earn a little credit on this new subject. He spoke up confidently.

'Olivier's *Henry the Fifth* was one of the finest films to come out of Pinewood Studios. Interesting the way Olivier brought Shakespeare's poetry to life within the Globe itself and on the rolling hills of Agincourt.'

'Of course,' added Hamish not to be outshone by this working-class peasant, 'since it was made as a morale booster during the war, it could not be shot at Agincourt itself. It was filmed in Hampshire in nineteen forty-three, forty-four.'

'Quite right, Hamish,' agreed Duncan. 'Agincourt itself was impossible, Billy,' he explained patiently, 'because of the war. As Hamish said, Hampshire was the actual location.'

'Sorry,' said Billy, 'but at college we had to make an intensive study of *Henry the Fifth* and I can assure you the film was shot not in Hampshire but in Ireland of all places, on the Enniskerry estate, to be exact. So the English bowmen were really Irishmen and the English soldiers falling out of trees onto the French were straight from the bogs of Ireland. While showing his Irish extras how to drop twenty feet from a tree to attack passing horsemen, Olivier sprained his ankle. I read somewhere that he directed one hundred and eighty horsemen and five hundred footmen from the Irish Home Guard.'

'Nonsense!' bayed Hamish. 'Where did you hear such drivel?'

'It never ceases to amaze me,' added Duncan, 'how people can pick up such wild ideas. We can soon test it out, however. Hughie, go to the study and bring me the book entitled *Fifty Years of Cinema*. We'll settle it once and for all.'

Billy remained quiet. He was in a spot. Again. He knew he was right but he was a guest in the Mackenzie home and it would be the height of discourtesy to cause Duncan loss of face. Hamish he didn't mind about. It was time he was taken down a peg. But what was the use in winning a debating point if it meant embarrassing Duncan and losing Laura?

Hughie returned with the film book already opened at the section on films of 1944.

'It says here,' he said, hardly able to keep the glee from his voice as he read from the book, ' "The film Henry V was produced and directed by Laurence Olivier and the film was dedicated to the Commandos and Airborne Troops of Great Britain, the spirit of whose ancestors it has been humbly attempted to recapture in some ensuing scenes.

' "Interior scenes were shot at Denham Studios but the actual battle of Agincourt gave the film-makers severe problems. In the early stages, an attempt was made to shoot the film on location in Hampshire but there was so much disturbance from the noise of the warplanes passing over-head that Olivier decided to move the location to Ireland where he employed many Irish extras who were cheaper as they were non-union men. Thus many of the English warriors and bowmen were in fact Irishmen." ' Hughie looked up triumphantly.

'Ah, so we were right,' said Duncan. 'The film was originally shot in Hampshire as we said. It was only later that the film-makers moved it to Ireland. Now do you understand our argument, Billy?'

Billy realised that he could never win a debate with Duncan.

'Ah, now I see,' he uttered diplomatically. 'I'd no idea that the film was shot at first in Hampshire. Thank you for pointing that out, Mr Mackenzie.'

'Always glad to pass on the wisdom of age,' said Duncan, never for a moment accepting that he'd changed his argument.

If ever Laura and I marry, thought Billy, I shall remind her that the price I had to pay to win her was the surrender of my intellectual pride.

'It's always best to be sure of your facts before entering into a debate,' added Hamish sententiously.

'My thoughts exactly,' said Billy, bringing the verbal jousting to a swift if unsatisfactory conclusion.

The smell of hot, buttered home-baked scones and ginger cake heralded the approach of the Mackenzie ladies who arrived with two trolleys laden with tea, crockery, and scones, along with a new delicacy of their own creation. 'Nutty nibbles' they called them.

'Ah, here comes the food at last,' said Grandma. 'About time too. I'm famished.'

'All very well for you,' whined Aunty. 'I don't think I could eat a thing – my digestion isn't up to it.'

'I'm sure I can cope with your share,' rejoined Grandma eagerly.

'These nutty nibbles,' said Billy, 'look most appetising. What exactly are they?'

'They're a sweet biscuit made from oats and syrup,' answered Laura.

'I think you should patent them,' said Billy, biting into one. 'You might make a fortune. You must give me the secret formula, though, and I'll pass it onto my mother.' He wondered whether it was the done thing in the Mackenzie household to dunk them in his tea.

Billy's mind went back to the time when in his etiquette seminars Pottsy had dealt with the subject thoroughly. How long should one dunk a biscuit to achieve the perfect consistency and to avoid its collapse into a gooey mess in one's tea? Research physicists, using an X-ray machine, an electron microscope, sensitive weighing equipment, a little gold and a complicated mathematical formula, had worked out that most biscuits would survive 3.5 seconds, though this varied with the viscosity of the drink. There was also a correct way of holding the biscuit as it was dunked, namely a shallow angle with the imprinted surface down.

The dilemma now facing Billy was whether to dunk at all. To dunk or not to dunk, that was the question. The matter was resolved when Grandma took her nutty nibble between two fingers and thumb and dunked. That was good enough for Billy. He imitated her and was relieved to see that the whole company had begun dunking.

The break was soon over and the second half began with crunch time coming a little nearer for Billy. He could feel the noose tightening.

Duncan stepped forward when the tea things had been cleared away.

'I'm no singer as everyone here is aware but I'll start the ball rolling,' he proclaimed, 'with an old Scottish ballad.'

Duncan's admission as to his lack of singing ability was the under-statement of the evening. In unmelodious tones Duncan cackled his way through 'Wee Cooper of Fife':

> *There was a wee Cooper wha lived in Fife,*
> *Nickety Nackety noo, noo, noo.*
> *And he has gotten a gentle wife*
> *Hey Willy Wallacky, hoo John Dougal*
> *A lane, quo Rushity, roue, roue, roue.*

For Billy, Duncan's rendering of this ditty was not only tuneless but also pure gibberish. Nevertheless he joined in the applause when Duncan finally sat down.

The queue's getting shorter, he thought. Nemesis is at

hand. Like waiting to be executed and no chance of a last-minute reprieve. Could he feign a sudden attack of laryngitis or perhaps throw an epileptic fit? On balance, not a good move; it might get him out of the present predicament but he'd lose any chance he might have with Laura. The family wouldn't welcome a schizoid hypochondriac in the family – though if Laura married Hamish, that's what they'd be getting.

'Well, that's the finish of the contributions from the Mackenzie family,' Duncan said. 'Now perhaps we can look to our guests for a contribution.'

'Wait a minute though,' said Billy. 'What about young Katie here? We haven't yet heard from her.' Anything to put off the dread moment.

'Very well,' said Duncan, eyeing Billy balefully. 'I dare say young Katie there can show us how it's done. Come along now, Katie, the family honour's at stake.'

'Yes, Daddy.' Katie whispered, 'but I'm too shy and so I'll have to say it from under the piano.'

What a splendid idea, thought Billy. Now why didn't I think of that? Wonder if I'll be allowed to perform from the same vantage point.

Katie settled herself under the Bechstein and recited softly the William Blake verse:

> *Little Lamb who made thee*
> *Dost thou know who made thee*
> *Gave thee life and bid thee feed?*

Her brave performance was rewarded by spontaneous approval.

'Well done, Katie!'

'Brave little girl!'

'Beautiful recitation!'

Hamish now threw his hat into the ring. He gave Billy a look of triumph as he said to the waiting assembly, 'I suppose there's no getting out of this. So I'll sing a song of Robbie Burns.' He took out a throat spray and began squirting a loathsome mist into his mouth.

This should settle his hash, Billy said to himself. I'll bet he can't sing a note on key.

Hamish began singing of all things Burns's 'Ae fond kiss'. To Billy's chagrin, Hamish demonstrated a pleasant tenor voice, if a little too sweet. Billy noted with quiet satisfaction that his voice had a touch of vibrato, poorly controlled. His choice of song, too, hardly seemed appropriate given his phobia about the transmission of diseases by coughs, sneezes and kisses. He finished with ringing emphasis:

> *Ae fond kiss, and then we sever;*
> *Ae fareweel, and then for ever!*

The applause and acclamation with which the end of the song was greeted was meat and drink to Hamish's ears but poison to Billy's. Hamish sat down with a look of elation in his eyes. He glanced triumphantly in Billy's direction. 'Beat that,' his expression said.

'Magnificent,' said Duncan.

'You've obviously had your voice trained,' said Louise. 'It shows in your breath control – no doubt about it.'

Hamish preened himself.

'You'll have me greetin' in a minute, Hamish,' said Jenny warmly. 'That song went straight to my heart.'

'That was good,' said Laura warmly.

Apart from Grandma and Aunty who had now dozed off

before the warm fire, there was only one person left. Billy prayed fervently that the floor would open up and swallow him but God ignored his plea. Why can't they force the two old ladies up from their chairs? he wondered. Wake 'em, shake 'em and make 'em do something.

'Well now,' said Duncan, 'that concludes our evening at home, I think, unless . . .' He looked towards Billy.

'What about Billy there?' said Hamish slyly. 'Is there not something he could do to amuse us?' He laid stress on 'amuse'.

Billy heard a voice saying, 'I think I could perhaps offer a little party piece to the company now.'

It was his own voice doing the speaking.

'I'm not sure if my contribution is suitable,' he said diffidently, 'but anyway I've brought the music for it.'

'Let me see it,' said Laura eagerly. 'I'll be glad to accompany you.' She looked at the music and smiled broadly. 'This should make the party go with a swing,' she said.

Billy stubbed out his cigarette, went to the middle of the room, and cleared his throat. Laura played the introductory chords and Billy began to sing. It was a modest enough opening, all about how nice it was to go roaming, how the sun was shining and the birds singing until the wanderer got further away from home . . . then he would have only one thing on his mind . . .

The audience watched fascinated, wondering what was coming next.

Billy then broke out into his best imitation of Larry Parks imitating Al Jolson singing 'My Mammy' in *The Jolson Story*. With great feeling he sang the refrain about his mammy until he reached the middle part of the song. At this point he dropped to one knee and with great expression

337

added his own dramatic recitative.

'Mammy! My little mammy. It's my mammy I'm singing about, nobody else's!' Then pointing to an imaginary mammy in the sky, he implored: 'Mammy, look at me! Ah, don't you know me? Don't you recognise me? It's your little baby boy – Billy, the Collyhurst kid, come home to see you once more.'

The song finished with a great flourish with Billy down on one knee and hands outstretched in supplication as he sang with great emphasis:

> *I'd bike to Argyle*
> *To see your smile*
> *My mammy!*

The silence which followed was deafening. All eyes turned to the Emperor for final judgement. Would it be a thumbs up or a thumbs down consigning Billy to be eaten by the lions? The silence was not more than twenty seconds but to Billy it was eternity as he gazed anxiously at Duncan for evaluation.

Then it was over. Duncan's face lit up with a dazzling smile.

'That was stupendous!' he exclaimed.

The rest of the company took the cue and applauded enthusiastically. Hamish's face clouded over but who cared about him.

Billy was in!

Nobody was willing to follow the Mammy song and so the evening's proceedings came to a close.

Laura and Jenny accompanied the two young men to the door.

'Thank you both for a lovely evening,' Laura said and

planted an affectionate kiss on both men's cheeks. 'It's an evening I shall treasure forever.'

'The same goes for me,' said Jenny, imitating her sister's actions.

Hamish appeared to have forgotten his kissing phobia.

When the door had closed behind them, the visitors walked down the path, Hamish to his parked Morgan sports car, Billy to his bicycle in the garage.

'You don't stand a chance with Laura, you know,' Hamish hissed. 'Duncan would never accept a tyke like you.'

'I see. Duncan! Don't Laura's wishes come into it? But what makes you say that, Hamish? Why are you so nasty?'

'I didn't like the way you were looking at Laura this evening. Making sheep's eyes at her. I'm giving you fair warning. Stay away from her. If you're looking for a girlfriend, why not try Jenny? Laura's *my* girl – you just remember that.'

'You make her sound like a piece of property, a chattel.'

'You may think what you like,' Hamish snarled, 'as long as you bear in mind that Laura belongs to me. We've been going around with each other for a long time and there's been an understanding between us and our two families for years. In other words, it's not just a flirtation but a serious match. Laura and I will marry in two or three years' time when we've got enough money together. I doubt if you on your teacher's salary can afford to keep her in the style to which she is accustomed. Anyway, steer clear. You'll only create trouble for yourself and for Laura as well. Think about it.'

'I'll do my best to keep it in mind,' said Billy, 'but you make it sound like a political alliance rather than a love match. As for keeping away from Laura, I can't promise anything.'

On that sour note, they parted company.

It was drizzling when Billy cycled off but he didn't notice the wind against his cheeks and the rain in his hair. To the rhythm of his pedalling and the theme of Tchaikovsky's Fifth Symphony, he hummed the same phrase over and over again, 'I love you, Laura. I love you, Laura,' all the way home.

Chapter Twenty-Nine

Billy Hopkins, RA

A week after the *soirée*, Billy took up painting. The decorating kind. At Greg's flat.

Tennyson has said that in the spring a young man's fancy lightly turns to thoughts of love. In the case of Greg Callaghan, his thoughts turned to decorating his newly found apartment – which amounted to the same thing, for his wedding date had been fixed for the coming July.

After school one evening, the two brothers and Billy cycled over to the Alexandra Park district of Whalley Range.

'First, we'll go and meet my folks and have a bite to eat,' said Greg, 'and then we'll wander over to High Lane and start splashing on the paint.'

The Callaghans lived in a Victorian semi-detached house in Demesne Road. The house had large rooms and lots of them but the family spent most of their time in the spacious kitchen-cum-dining room.

Greg introduced Billy to his mother and father.

'Very pleased to shake your hand, Billy,' said Greg's father. 'Any friend of my sons is welcome in my house. You may call me Packy as everyone else does.'

341

'And the same goes for me,' the mother said, 'though indeed my name is Edna and not Packy. Wait now while I wet the tea and we'll soon have a brew ready for you boys. I'm sure after all that talking you do at the school you'll be ready to moisten your dried-up tongues.'

Edna infused the tea in the biggest teapot Billy had ever seen. He wondered why it had to be such a size. His question was answered when he saw the giant mugs which were each big enough to empty a normal teapot.

Alex offered his cigarettes round and everyone lit up except Greg who ignited his foul-smelling pipe.

'Now, young Billy,' began Packy. 'That name Hopkins is a common one in the west of Ireland. Are your parents Irish, by any chance?'

'I believe my maternal grandmother came originally from the old country,' Billy replied.

'Is that a fact now,' said Edna, thrusting a great mug of tea into his hands. 'What was your grandmother's name?'

'Lally.'

'Well, would you believe that?' she exclaimed. 'When I was a headmistress of a national school in Limerick, wasn't the school superintendent himself named Lally? Now that's a coincidence.'

'Most interesting, Mrs Callaghan,' said Billy politely.

'Hopkins is a much respected name in the west of Ireland,' continued Packy. 'My old friend Patrick Hopkins was once evicted from his cottage by an evil English landlord.'

'Ireland has had a troubled history,' Billy commented.

'Sean Lally, his name was,' said Edna. 'A grand man he was too. Proposed marriage before Packy came along.'

'Amazing, Mrs Callaghan,' said Billy.

342

'Some of our Irish peasants suffered terrible persecution at the hands of the English aristocracy,' Packy continued, ignoring his wife. 'Now Patrick Hopkins, there was a man for you.'

'Glad to hear it,' said Billy.

'Sean Lally was a handsome fellow,' Edna went on. 'I wonder sometimes if I made the right choice marrying Packy here.'

'The flat we're going to paint,' said Greg, blowing noxious clouds in every direction, 'is at the bottom of High Lane in Chorlton. Emily and I were lucky to get it.'

'Flats are not easy to get nowadays,' said Billy agreeably.

'You know, young Hopkins,' Packy continued, 'Benjamin Franklin visited Ireland in seventeen seventy-two and remarked on the opulence and affluence of the English noblemen and gentlemen of the time.'

'Anyway, Packy came on the scene and won my heart,' said Edna. 'He had no money but we were young and we thought love was all-important.'

'I asked Frank Wakefield today if he could give me a greater allowance for the retarded class,' said Alex, now joining in. 'We urgently need extra money for equipment for backward children.'

'Emily has chosen a class of green paint for the walls,' said Greg. 'I'm not too sure about it myself.'

'Franklin was appalled by the straitened condition of the bulk of the people who were tenants and extremely poor.'

'I think Sean Lally broke his heart when we parted,' said Edna dreamily, holding her steaming mug of tea with both hands. 'I don't think he ever married.'

'You know there are three more brothers that you haven't met,' Greg announced suddenly. 'Clement works for an

343

Irish shipping line here in Manchester. He doesn't get home till around seven o'clock.'

'That's been the problem of Ireland for the last three hundred years,' said Packy. 'Impoverished peasants and absentee landlords. A polarised society.'

'Frank Wakefield is tight with the allocation of funds,' said Alex.

'The other two brothers are Sylvester – he's a Benedictine monk and probably the only one who stands any chance of becoming Pope – and Calixtus who is the eldest and lives in Dublin.'

'I sometimes wonder if I might have prospered better if I'd married Sean Lally,' sighed Edna.

Billy looked from one to the other, trying to digest four conversations at the same time. It's like watching a Mozart opera, he thought, where the performers are intent on singing their own particular recitatives. Not easy to follow and even more difficult to respond to each separate speaker. A conductor might have helped, co-ordinating the performances, bringing each speaker in on cue.

The four-sided conversation continued throughout the delicious meal of bacon and eggs which Edna conjured up, a cigarette dangling from the corner of her mouth.

'I suppose you'll be wondering where we get bacon and eggs in these times of austerity.' Touching her nose, she answered her own question. 'Sure, we have special contacts across the water.'

'The peasants lived in the most sordid, wretched conditions,' Packy was saying. 'In dirty hovels of mud and straw, and clothed only in rags. Is it any wonder the lower orders considered themselves plundered and kept out of their own property by the absentee land-owning aristocracy?'

'We'll begin by painting the ceiling white,' said Greg, 'and we'll go for green on the walls.'

'It's impossible to teach a class of backward children without the necessary equipment,' Alex continued.

Everybody smoked throughout the meal.

Finally it was over.

'I felt you had a most sympathetic ear,' said Edna. 'With a name like Lally in your background, is it any wonder?'

'It was grand talking to you, young Hopkins,' said Packy. 'Come again – any time. You obviously have sympathy for the downtrodden. It's a long time since I had such an intelligent conversation.'

Alex, Greg and Billy cycled across Chorlton to High Lane.

They climbed a narrow staircase to Greg's flat and changed into their old togs. It was comfortable, if basic, accommodation comprising a large lounge, a small kitchen, a bathroom, and a large bedroom which Greg described as 'the most important room in the house'. Maybe some day Laura and I could start off with something like this, Billy thought.

Every night for a whole week after school, Billy slapped the paint onto Greg's walls and a goodly proportion onto his furniture. The colour chosen was *eau de nil*, a pale green colour supposed to resemble that of the Nile but for Billy it bore a closer resemblance to the water in a horse trough. The pungent smell of gloss paint turned his stomach and he came to hate the colour so much that he made up his mind never to visit the Nile if he ever won Littlewood's Pools. Not that there was much chance of that since he didn't bet on the pools.

Towards the middle of the week, as Alex and Greg were busy wiping up the sploshes of paint which had somehow missed the walls and landed on the carpet, the conversation turned to the subject of marriage in general.

'I have no intention of ever marrying,' said Alex. 'Your friends like you and they accept you for what you are; your wife loves you but is forever trying to change you into somebody else.'

Billy had to have his say. 'Didn't some sceptic say: "Marriage is the price men pay for sex, sex is the price women pay for marriage"?'

'You're a couple of cynics,' said Greg. 'Remember the old saying: it's better to marry than to burn.'

'Not everyone would agree with that,' answered Alex. 'Burning might be preferable.'

'And what about you, Billy?' said Greg, ignoring his brother. 'I have the distinct impression that you have your eye on Laura Mackenzie.'

'What makes you say that?' said Billy, flushing. So people had begun to notice!

'You must be joking,' Greg guffawed. 'Why, it's obvious, man. The way you look at her, the way you hang on her every word, that soulful expression that appears on your face whenever she enters the room.'

'I had no idea I was so transparent,' said Billy.

'The whole staff is aware of it,' added Alex. 'The question now remains, what are you going to do about it? We're waiting on tenterhooks.'

'I don't think I'm going to do anything about it,' Billy replied. 'Laura Mackenzie is out of my class.'

'You're worried about that tall Scotsman she goes around with,' said Greg. 'What's his name?'

'You mean Hamish? I suppose I am in a way. He talks down to me. He called me a tyke the other day. Thinks I belong to the peasantry.'

'He shouldn't be a problem – he's studying at Glasgow University, isn't he? You should get in there while he's away. Besides, I think the reason you don't like him is plain jealousy,' Alex said.

'I suppose you're right. I don't like the way he considers that he has a natural right to claim Laura as his own. She goes about with him because there's some kind of long-term understanding between the families. I'm not so sure that she goes along with all that. I think I might stand a chance with her if I tried.'

'Then for God's sake, do something about it!' bellowed Greg. 'Phone her, ask her out. She's not engaged to this Hamish fellow and you're still a bachelor. So what's the problem?'

'I'm afraid I might be rejected, sent away with a flea in my ear.'

'Nothing ventured, nothing gained,' said Alex. 'You sound as if you're in love with the girl.'

'And how's that supposed to sound?' Billy asked.

'For one thing, you talk about her as if she's a mysterious being; you've surrounded her with a mystical aura and put her on a pedestal.'

'And another, you sound as if you want to take her to bed,' added Greg.

'I don't think of her like that,' said Billy quickly. 'I wouldn't dream of trying it on with Laura. If it's love at all, it's the romantic, chivalrous variety – the courtly kind like Lancelot and Lady Guinevere, like Abelard and Héloïse. I believe that perfect bliss is found only in unattainable love, when it's just out of reach.'

The two brothers roared with laughter.

'We've heard that one before,' boomed Greg. 'You've been reading too many books about King Arthur. Look,

347

our knight in shining armour, we'll set it up for you. We'll arrange a hike during the Easter vac – just the four of us – to the Peak District. We'll make sure you get plenty of opportunity to talk to the girl about chivalry and gallantry.'

Greg was as good as his word and approached Laura in the staffroom.

'I'd love to go,' she said. 'A chance to get away from it all and I'm fond of walking in the Derbyshire hills.'

The four of them arranged to meet one Monday morning during the Easter holidays at Lower Mosley Street bus station to take the bus to Hayfield.

The agreed time was nine o'clock but Billy made sure he was there at half past eight. Laura turned up just before nine o'clock. She was wearing the same outfit she had worn for the school bicycle trip, including the tammy with the large red bobble. She looked more beautiful than ever and Billy told her so.

'Greg and Alex aren't here yet,' he said. 'I hope they're not too late as there's a bus leaving at nine thirty. The next one is an hour later.'

They hung around the bus stop glancing anxiously in the direction from which they expected the brothers to appear. Nine thirty came and went and so did the bus.

At ten o'clock, Billy said, 'Well, Laura, it looks as if they're not coming. They don't have a phone so there's no way we can reach them. What shall we do?'

Laura didn't hesitate. 'I think we should go without them. I'm all set for a ramble in the country. I have my sandwiches and my flask and, well, I don't feel like going home again.'

'Do you think so?' Billy said, trying not to sound too

eager. He suspected she knew what Greg and Alex were up to.

They caught the next bus and ninety minutes later were in Hayfield.

'Let's walk to Jacob's Ladder,' Laura suggested. 'There's a glorious view of Kinderscout and Hope Valley from there.'

Together, they set off and the conversation flowed easily as if they had known each other all their lives.

'I loved the way you did your Al Jolson act at our musical evening. It brought the house down,' she said, chuckling at the memory of it.

'I thought at the end it was going to bring the house down about my ears.'

'Daddy loved it. It was such a contrast to the other efforts. You saved the evening from becoming stuffy.'

'When your dad said he had a Blue Nun in the fridge, I could hardly keep a straight face,' Billy laughed.

'I noticed,' she giggled. 'I don't think the rest of the company cottoned onto the double meaning though.'

'I was nervous about coming at first but I enjoyed the evening. You have a talented family.'

'Why, thank you, Billy,' she said. 'One thing I should tell you though. You've made a big hit with Aunty Aggie.'

'Only with Aunt Aggie? I'd rather make a big hit with you.'

Laura flushed.

They were passing Edale Cross and Billy pointed towards Kinder Downfall. 'That's the place where my closest friend Robin Gabrielson died in nineteen forty-five,' he said sadly. 'Only a week before we were due to go to college.'

'I heard about that. How tragic it was. The kind of

349

thing in your life you never get over.'

'None of the Damian gang ever did. When we reached college in Chelsea, his name was still on many of the administration lists. He was even due to get the room next to mine.'

'How sad it must have been,' she said, taking his hand.

They walked on together hand in hand until the path seemed to come to an abrupt halt. Laura ran ahead a little.

'My heavens! Come and take a look at this, Billy.'

They had reached the Jacob's Ladder escarpment and together they gazed at the panoramic view of the Peak District spread out below.

'It's breathtaking,' said Billy. 'Have you ever seen such magnificence?' He pointed to the distant scene. 'Over there to the left is the majestic Kinderscout and to the right Rushop Edge.'

Laura rested her head on his shoulder. 'It really is beautiful,' she murmured, nestling into him. Billy looked down into her eyes. 'And so are you,' he whispered and kissed her on the lips. Not a long kiss but a soft, gentle touch. 'I love you, Laura,' he said quietly. 'I love you very much. Ever since that first day when I set eyes on you in the staffroom, I have loved no one else. You were wearing a blue dress and your hair was tied back with a red ribbon. I didn't sleep very well that first night and haven't many nights since.' A feeling of unutterable sweetness and tenderness swept through his being. The lines from Keats echoed through his mind: 'O, the sweetness of the pain! Give me those lips again!'

For a while they stood at the top of Jacob's Ladder clinging to each other so closely they could feel each other's heartbeats.

'The same goes for me, Billy,' she said. 'I think I've

loved you ever since that day when Miss O'Neill introduced us in the staffroom.'

'But why didn't you give me some hint of how you felt?'

'A respectable girl doesn't go up to a man and say simply "I fancy you". When we were at Tatton Hall, you talked about ballroom dancing competitions and your partner – Adele, I think you said her name was. I imagined a glitzy, glamorous world of beautiful girls in shimmering, sequin dresses. Girls by the dozen at your beck and call.'

'I should live so long,' he said, holding out his upturned hands. 'I imagined you dancing the Highland fling surrounded by big, porridge-eating, caber-tossing Scotsmen. What chance did I stand against that kind of competition? Besides, you were going around with Hamish, the family favourite!'

'Hamish!' she exclaimed. 'I'd forgotten about Hamish! I don't know how he'll take it. But we'll cross that bridge when we come to it.'

Hand in hand, they set off back to Hayfield.

Chapter Thirty

Coppélia

Later that week, Billy walked to the public telephone box at the corner of Gardenia Court. He picked up the phone, listened for the gentle purr, inserted two pennies, then rang Laura's number. It was Jenny who answered.

'Rusholme two seven six four,' she answered brightly. Billy pressed button A and heard his coins drop. 'Could I speak to Laura, please?' he asked.

'Oh, it's you, Billy. What have you been doing to Laura? I've never seen her so bright and so chirpy. She's going around the house singing. She's in the shower at the moment and she's still singing.'

The image of a naked Laura singing in the shower flashed through Billy's mind. Attractive though it was, he dismissed it quickly. He didn't want to think of her in that way. For him, she was Lady Guinevere, Maid Marian and Snow White rolled into one. Laura was sexually desirable but despite the cynical comments of Greg Callaghan, his love for her was more spiritual than carnal, more Agape than Eros.

'Wait a minute though,' Jenny continued. 'Here she is. She must have heard the phone and come running.'

'Billy,' Laura said breathlessly. 'I thought it might be you.'

'Laura. It's twenty-four hours since I saw you last and every hour has been painful. Can we meet at the weekend? I can get two tickets for *Coppélia* at the Opera House for Friday, if you'd like to go.'

'Billy,' she said, 'is it really twenty-four hours since we last met? Of course I'd love to go. I'll meet you in the foyer at seven o'clock.'

'What about Hamish? Have you given him the good news yet?'

'Look, I'll tell you about it when we meet. Daddy's just coming and so I'll ring off for now.'

'Very well, Laura. I understand. One thing at a time, eh? I'll count the hours till Friday. I love you.'

'Me too,' she said hurriedly. 'Goodbye till Friday, Billy.'

Billy put the phone back in its cradle. What was happening? he wondered. Why did she sound so worried about the appearance of her father? If Laura was his fairytale princess, perhaps there was a dragon or two to slay. There was Hamish of course but he was a minor threat in the lexicon of dragons. There was probably a more fiery example in the person of Duncan, her father. He hoped there were no more.

On Friday night, Billy got to the Opera House in Quay Street at six thirty and anxiously paced the thick red carpet of the foyer. He was there with borrowed things – Les's demob raincoat and ten shillings from Mam for the five-shilling seats in the stalls. There remained a few bob in his pocket in case they had a drink at the interval.

'I don't think the ballet is a nice place to take a respectable girl,' Mam had said when he'd told her. 'All those men in tights prancing about and showing all they've got.'

'It's not that sort of show,' he'd explained patiently. 'This is a story about a toy shop and how the dolls come to life.'

'I hope you're right,' she'd said doubtfully.

Billy glanced around him. There was something about the atmosphere of a luxurious theatre that made him feel uncomfortable and inferior. Perhaps it was the smell of Havana cigars and the exotic perfume, perhaps it was the other theatre-goers who always looked and sounded so posh, as if they belonged there by right – the burly men in their Reid Brothers suits and their plump, bejewelled wives in their fur coats, gloves and hats. He was expecting to be unmasked at any moment by the big commissionaire in the Cossack uniform who seemed to be eyeing him suspiciously.

He wandered over to the display of photos advertising previous productions – Ivor Novello's *Perchance to Dream*, Noel Coward's *Private Lives*. He hoped Laura wouldn't keep him waiting too long. A horrible thought struck him. Maybe she wouldn't turn up. Maybe Duncan had put the kibosh on their meeting and forbidden her to go out with him. It had been obvious that he preferred Hamish as a suitor. After all, what could he, Billy Hopkins, offer his daughter? Nothing but a life of drudgery and penury. He was an impecunious, non-graduate teacher in a secondary modern school. Some prospects!

As these maudlin thoughts ran through his brain, suddenly she was there smiling at him, radiantly beautiful and wearing a new hat – a velvet, plum-coloured affair. Her appearance gave him confidence and security, for she looked as if she belonged naturally in this milieu. She was his admission ticket to this élite theatre society.

354

'Laura,' he exclaimed, taking both her hands and kissing her on the cheek. 'Am I glad to see you! For a while there I thought you weren't coming.'

'Sorry I'm late,' she said. 'I had to wait a long time for a bus. But wild horses wouldn't have kept me away. I haven't forgotten our walk in the Peak District. My memory isn't that short.'

'Anyway, you're here now, that's all that matters.'

As they went into the theatre, he said, 'It's a ballet about Charles Lamb's policeman brother by a bloke called Leo Debility.'

She looked puzzled for a moment. Then her eyes sparkled and she burst into laughter. '*Coppélia* by Leo Delibes. You are a bit daft, aren't you?'

'At last you've realised it,' he grinned.

The theatre lights dimmed, the orchestra struck up and they sat enthralled by Delibes' music and the superb choreography of the visiting Sadlers Wells company. From time to time, Billy glanced at Laura's enraptured face as she followed every movement of the dancers and took in every nuance of the music. A shiver of joy ran down his spine and he felt a bliss he had never known. If only time could stand still. Making this girl by my side happy, he thought, will be my life's ambition.

At the interval, they went to the crowded, smoke-filled bar.

'Isn't this expensive?' she asked. 'Seats in the stalls and now drinks in the bar.'

'No problem. I took out a mortgage before we came out. What is your pleasure, mademoiselle?'

'A pineapple juice would be fine, Billy.'

'A nice inexpensive drink. I'm beginning to like you more and more.'

Billy managed to push his way through the throng at the bar and soon came back with two Britvic juices. They had cost a bob each which he thought was daylight robbery.

'Now, tell me what's been going on. Have you given Hamish the good news?'

'Yes. I phoned him on Monday and told him that our courtship was over.'

'And how did he take it?'

'He sounded angry. Said he'd suspected that you'd had designs on me and that you'd taken advantage of his absence.'

'Do you agree with that, Laura?'

'Of course I do, Billy. Thank God you did have designs on me, and as for taking advantage of his absence, if Hamish and I had truly loved each other, absence would have made the heart grow fonder. But it didn't. One strange thing though. My sister, Jenny, seems pleased about developments. I think she's set her cap at Hamish and, well, who knows? The only trouble is, Daddy hasn't accepted that Hamish and I are through. And you know better than anyone how he likes to get his own way.'

'I hope that on this particular occasion he doesn't get it.'

'No need to worry on that score, Billy. As far as I'm concerned, Hamish is the past. You are the present – and the future,' she added.

'I'm so happy to hear you say that, Laura. Your father could be a problem though. I think he's of the opinion that I'm the poor man at the gate. He's the emperor, you're the princess and I'm the swineherd daring to have ideas above my station.'

'But you'll remember from the Hans Andersen story that the swineherd turned out to be a prince in the end. I think Daddy'll come round eventually. He thinks money's the most important thing for a secure marriage and that Hamish is a sound commercial proposition. I happen to think there's more to life than money. Anyway, you're not going out with my father, you're going out with me, and don't you forget it,' she said, giving Billy a friendly dig in the ribs.

'OK, boss,' he said. 'I defer to your orders.' But the talk of her father and his ambitions for her had sewn disquiet in his heart.

'On a different subject,' he said cheerfully, 'how do you like the ballet?'

'I love every moment of it. How the ballerinas manage to pirouette so gracefully on the points of their toes, I'll never understand.'

'I think they must have hammer toes to execute those fouettes and maintain those arabesques.'

She laughed. 'You sound knowledgeable about ballet, Billy. Have you seen many?'

'This is my first. But I looked up one or two ballet terms in *The Bluffer's Guide to Ballet* in order to impress you. Anyway, if you say my name carefully, it sounds like Ballet. Only one vowel different.'

They enjoyed the second half of the show even more than the first. It ended with tempestuous applause and cheering. Billy and Laura clapped with the rest until their hands grew tired.

'You know,' Billy said, 'one day, I shall invent a pair of automatic hands, like a football rattle, which will do the clapping for us. We'll simply press a little button and sit back.'

They collected their coats from the cloakroom and Billy helped her on with hers. She linked her arm in his and held onto him tightly as they walked to Albert Square to catch the 89 bus.

At the gate of her home, they stood talking for a while,

about this and that, about school, about their families, about anything – the subject didn't matter. Simply being together was all they needed. They were aware of Jenny, Hughie, and Katie watching them from an upstairs window.

'They're hoping to see something,' Laura murmured.

'Let's not disappoint them,' he said and kissed her lightly on the lips.

At that precise moment, Duncan came upon them suddenly. He was returning from his nightly visit to the Knights of St Columba.

He nodded curtly at Billy and, addressing Laura, he said, 'Don't you be too long out here. It's time you were indoors. Has neither of you got the brains to notice the weather? It's raining.'

'Goodnight, Laura,' said Billy quickly. 'And goodnight, Mr Mackenzie,' he called.

'Hrrmph,' came the reply.

That weekend, Billy wrote a letter to Laura.

My dearest Laura,
Thank you for the most wonderful night of my life. Why must you torment me so? You have invaded my brain and I can think of nothing or no one but you. Everything I do is for you. I wash in order to please you; I spend hours cultivating waves in barren hair for your delight. I eat for your edification. I listen to music for you. You have inhabited my soul. May your residence be permanent.
You looked so beautiful in your new hat, I felt I had to mark the occasion with a verse. Forgive my puny effort.
All my love,
Billy

AN 'AT FOR AN ANGEL

Cities quake;
Bells peal;
Houses shake;
Dogs squeal;
Babies cry;
Sun blushes;
Birds fly
Into bushes;
Bells clang;
Buses crash;
Doors bang;
Windows smash;
Sinners pray;
Women shriek;
Horses neigh;
Mice squeak;
Cats spit;
Pups growl,
Throw a fit,
Start to howl;
Cars stop;
Pets escape;
Eyes pop;
Mouths gape;
Oh begorrah
Gossips chat;
They see on Laura
A bran' new 'at.

Chapter Thirty-One

Walking Out

They became sweethearts in a tender, old-fashioned way. They met each weekend and spent their time walking in Fletcher Moss Gardens, boating on the Mersey and on Heaton Park lake. Billy was becoming a proficient oarsman.

'Do you think Oxford would have me in the next boat race?' he asked.

'I'm sure they would,' she said. 'After a little more practice perhaps. And if they reject you, I'll have you on my team.'

They attended performances of the Hallé conducted by Sir John Barbirolli in the King's Hall, Belle Vue; on Saturday nights, they went to the Apollo cinema on Ardwick Green, cuddling on the back row as they half watched Spencer Tracy and Katharine Hepburn doing their stuff in films like *The World and His Wife*. They made love but not the wild passionate kind – they hugged, kissed, and embraced, and that was it. To sit on a park bench with Laura's head on his shoulder was for Billy perfect happiness. Not that they didn't desire each other physically; but the idea of snatched, furtive sex in a dark corner held no appeal for them. Such goings-on would have made her unhappy and

Laura's happiness was the most important thing in the world as far as he was concerned. Besides, there was always the possibility of an unwanted baby and the disgrace that that would entail. Physical love would wait until after they were married. For the present, simply being with each other was enough.

Frank Wakefield took a cigarette from the packet, put it between his lips and lit it from the one he'd just finished. My God, he thought, I'm becoming a chain-smoker. He sat in his little cramped office in the NFS annexe.

'Come in, Hoppy,' he called when he heard the knock. 'Come in and sit down, if you can find room, that is.' Wakefield smiled nervously. He wasn't looking forward to this – not one bit.

Billy wondered what it was about. At the end of his lesson before break, he'd received a message that the head wanted to see him. Most unusual, he'd thought, as he always saw Frank Wakefield at lunchtime when they shared their sandwiches. Have I gone wrong somewhere? he wondered. Done something I'm not supposed to?

'Coffee?' asked Wakefield, plugging in the kettle. 'It's only Camp coffee but I think you'll find it a little higher standard than that noxious brew they have over there in the staffroom.'

'Thanks a lot, Frank.'

'Cigarette, Billy?' he said offering his Players.

'Thanks again, Frank.' Billy didn't like the sound of this. What was this strange preamble leading up to? As far as he knew his record was OK.

Wakefield pulled on his cigarette and swung his chair sideways so that he was looking at the chart on the wall.

'You've been with us a year now, Hoppy. I thought it was

361

time you and I had a little private chat to review things. You've settled in here wonderfully well.'

'I made a false start, Frank, but then I think I got the hang of it,' Billy replied, still puzzled.

'More than the hang of it, Hoppy. Your projects and your organisation of visits have been exemplary and the HMIs have said as much in their probationary reports.' He stubbed out his fag in the ashtray and began playing with the ruler on his desk. He didn't look at Billy. He was finding it hard to say what he had to say.

He cleared his throat and said in a rasping voice, 'This school is not like other schools, though. Mind you, things are not as strict as they used to be. Why, before the war, if a woman married, she had to leave the profession. It was the same in the civil service. Did you know that?'

'No, Frank, I didn't know that.' Where was all this leading?

'You have to remember it's a Catholic school, Hoppy, and we have to set the highest example at all times.'

What the devil was he getting at? Billy asked himself. Surely he wasn't referring to his torrid affair with Adele. That had finished a long time ago.

'You have to bear in mind, Hoppy,' Wakefield went on, 'that this is a small parish and gossip easily goes the rounds, becoming more and more exaggerated as it does.'

'Sorry, Frank,' Billy said anxiously, 'you've lost me. Has someone been complaining about me?'

'No, no,' he exclaimed hurriedly. 'Nothing like that. It's just that . . .' He hesitated and hawked again. 'After a recent school governors' meeting, Father Kelly did happen to mention to me that he'd heard on the grapevine that there was a romance going on between two of his teachers in the school.'

Billy's heart skipped a beat. So that was what this was about! His romance with Laura! He felt his hackles rise.

'So what! I would have thought that that was a private matter between the two teachers concerned and not a matter for idle chatter.'

'Yes, yes, I agree with you, Hoppy,' Wakefield said quickly. 'But in our profession, we've got to be careful not to create scandal. We're like members of the clergy. The adolescents we're teaching are very impressionable.'

At that point, Greg Callaghan knocked lightly on the door and entered.

'Could I see you for a moment, Frank, about the playground duty roster?' he asked, glancing quizzically from one to the other.

'I'll see you later about that, Greg, if you don't mind.'

Greg withdrew diplomatically.

Wakefield turned to Billy and looked him straight in the eyes for the first time. 'The top class thinks the world of you, Hoppy, and if they saw or heard anything untoward between you and Miss Mackenzie, it wouldn't go down too well.'

'But there isn't and never has been anything untoward, as you put it, in our conduct. Look, Frank. I'm a bachelor and Laura Mackenzie is, as far as I'm aware, a spinster of this parish, to coin a phrase.'

'Look at it another way,' Wakefield said. 'Suppose you two fall out, have a lover's tiff. What happens? You're both not talking to each other and you create an uncomfortable, tense atmosphere in the school. Why, one of you might even decide to leave the school and then we're short of a teacher. School romances usually mean problems for everyone all round. Why, we'd be at sixes and sevens if we all started falling in love with each other. Take it from me,

Hoppy, it doesn't do to form close relationships in school, they nearly always lead to trouble.'

'Trouble? Laura Mackenzie and I are very much attracted to each other. Where's the trouble in that? I think you have a vivid imagination, Frank, and you're anticipating things that will never happen.'

'I'll tell you where the trouble might be, Hoppy,' he said, his hands visibly shaking. 'You have to be very discreet. You're young and inexperienced in the ways of the world. Your prospects – and mine as well for that matter – at this school are in the hands of the managers. They have the power to hire and fire, and the power to promote and demote. It's not a matter of whether you've done anything wrong or not, it's a matter of the way *they* see things. I've found it's best to keep your nose clean if you're going to get anywhere in the world of education. Look, let me be blunt. If you're looking for a girlfriend, why not pick someone from outside the school?'

Billy bristled. 'What business is it of yours or of anyone else who I choose for my girlfriend! And by keeping your nose clean, you mean doing exactly what the managers dictate. Is that it? And isn't Mr Mackenzie on the management board? He's a big noise in the KSC and the Catenians. I think I see what's going on here.'

'Whoa! Hold your horses, Hoppy!' Wakefield exclaimed, holding up both hands as if warding off an assault. 'Who said anything about Mr Mackenzie? I'm simply talking about a chance remark from Father Kelly, that's all. I'm not even sure he was serious. Don't go jumping to conclusions.'

Billy's rage, however, was on a roll. 'Look, Frank, I wasn't born yesterday. I can put two and two together. When you talk about promotion, I suppose you're thinking of your own chances and the new headship. The whole thing

364

stinks. It makes me sick. You can tell Father Kelly – and Mr Mackenzie, if he's somewhere in the background – that they can take a running jump. What Laura Mackenzie and I do in our private lives has nothing to do with them. As for promotion, they can stuff it.' He got up to storm out of the office but Frank Wakefield stopped him.

'Hold it right there, Hoppy. Take it easy! I knew you'd react the way you did. I'd have been disappointed in you if you hadn't.'

'I can assure you, Frank, that my intentions towards Laura Mackenzie are entirely honourable,' he said, cooling down a little. 'I have a sneaking feeling that Duncan Mackenzie is somewhere behind this attempt to put me off. He thinks I'm not good enough for his daughter.'

'What rubbish! Perhaps he doesn't see the potential in you that I do.'

Billy began to laugh. 'I think he'd like a kilted, bagpipe-playing Caledonian with a first-class honours degree for a son-in-law. Instead he's maybe going to get a gormless Lancashire lad from Collyhurst.'

'That's more like it,' said Wakefield, joining in the merriment. 'You go ahead and live your own life and I'll back you to the hilt.'

Billy returned to the staffroom where he found Greg alone, puffing on his ubiquitous pipe.

'What in God's name was that about, Hoppy?' he bawled. 'Has the old man had you on the carpet? Hauled you over the coals? Read the riot act? I must say, he looked more nervous than you did. What was he going on about this time?'

'Giving me advice on affairs of the heart,' replied Billy.

'He's the last person I should go to for advice,' said Greg.

365

'Well, there's only one thing to do when you're given good advice,' said Billy.

'And what's that?' asked Greg.

'Pass it on to someone else as soon as possible.'

'Fine,' said Greg, 'as long as you don't have me in mind.'

Chapter Thirty-Two

Farewell

The end of Billy's first year of teaching came round all too soon. There was little formal teaching in the last week at school. Frank Wakefield was heavily involved in issuing Leaving Certificates and school references and Billy found himself at a loose end. Youth employment officers came to visit the school to talk to the class about openings and opportunities in the local district, mainly in the building and motor trades for the boys, shop work or clothing work for the girls. Much of the time was taken up with interviews, though many of the pupils had already secured jobs through their own families.

For much of the term, the class had been talking excitedly of leaving school at last, of going out into the big, bad world, of getting a job, earning money, buying the latest gear, and generally enjoying themselves. In the final week, though, the atmosphere was quiet and their enthusiasm muted as they realised that D-day was fast approaching. How would they fare, they wondered, and would they be able to cope?

Mick Lynch was fixed up to help his father in the costermongering business on Market Street. Jim Mitchell had finally arranged to take up the job in a decorating firm – postponed from the previous year. Vera Pickles found her post at Lewis's store was still open. Tony Jarvis landed a plum job as a messenger in the GPO, Joe Duffy would be a trainee bricklayer, and Alf Dempsey an apprentice motor mechanic. Nellie Wallace was going to be a machinist in a raincoat factory. Billy hoped that she'd remember not to obey orders literally and so avoid stepping into any more wastepaper baskets. Des Bishop signed up as a junior in a seminary with a view to joining a foreign mission later on. Irene Moody was undecided as to her future career.

'I don't want to spend my life in a boring job, sir,' she said huskily. The Veronica Lake persona seemed to have become a permanent feature of her character. 'Standing behind a counter at Woolworth's or being a waitress in a café – they're not for me. Besides, the wages in those jobs are terrible. No, I want to have plenty of cash in my pocket when I leave. To buy nice clothes, have nice holidays and that. My sister has her own little business and she said she might show me how to make some real money after school. So, I might join her.' She obviously didn't know that Billy was aware of the nature of her sister's business.

He couldn't help thinking what a strange job this teaching business was. There was no way of judging the effect one's teaching was having, if any. People in jobs which involved production of goods could see the results of their labours. At the end of the day, there was something to show for their exertions – a motor car or a bicycle – and they could say, 'I helped to make that.' Even doctors could say, 'I cured that person,' or if the patient died, 'I failed that time.' There was something concrete to see or to measure. But in teaching, no such thing – it was impossible to gauge the results. If one of the pupils made good, did a teacher claim him or her as a success? If so, what about the failures? Did he disown them and say, 'Nothing to do with me – not my fault'? In the case of Bishop, the school had helped produce a missionary priest. Did they claim him as one of their triumphs? If so, what about Irene Moody who looked as if she was about to join her sister in the oldest profession? Did they wash their hands of her and say, 'Too bad, it was her environment that caused her downfall'? A nice alliteration, he thought, a priest and a prostitute from the same form.

In the final week, everyone was present every day, as if they felt it was their last opportunity to share in something that they had taken for granted all year. On the last day but one at school, the class began recording everything that happened as 'The last time we shall . . .' Billy called the register. 'Do you realise,' said Nellie Wallace, 'that this is the last time Sir will call our name in the register?' They drank their milk: 'The last time we shall have our milk at school.' The boys played football at the break. Their last football in the school yard. The girls went for their needlework class. Their last needlework with Miss O'Neill. No wonder there was an air of gloom about the place. As if they were to be executed the next day.

On the morning of the last day itself, there was a final assembly of the whole school. Miss O'Neill and Laura played one of Schubert's *Marches militaires* piano duets as the various classes filed into the NFS hall. When everyone was in place, Frank Wakefield awarded money prizes from his own pocket for various achievements in class: half-a - crown for first place; two shillings for second, and one shilling for third. Various other awards were made, such as Best Effort, Best Attendance, and Best Improvement. Wakefield called out the names and shook the hands of the

369

lucky individuals and congratulated them on their success. The whole school applauded.

Billy felt sorry for the children who came away with nothing. Had it been left to him, he'd have awarded a prize to everyone.

Then came the sad moment when the head distributed the Leaving Certificates. As he called their names, the leavers came forward to receive their piece of parchment. Every girl wept copiously as she walked up onto the stage, and even the boys looked as if they were having problems holding back the tears.

What a contrast, Billy thought, to the class he had taken over less than a year ago. Then they'd been angry at having to stay on an extra year and ready to take it out on him. Now here they were, sad and weepy at the thought of being released.

How appropriate, Billy thought, if Wakefield had used the line from a Hollywood police film at this point: 'Hey, you guys. Be careful! It's a jungle out there, I tell ya!'

Wakefield settled instead for the singing of a goodbye hymn:

> Sweet Saviour, bless us ere we go,
> Thy word into our minds instil;
> And make our lukewarm hearts to glow
> With lowly love and fervent will.

Throughout that term, the top class had been collecting for their farewell party, arranged for the evening of the final day. After assembly, there was a great deal of coming and going, and Billy spent much of his time in the staffroom, deeming it best to keep out of the way.

The boys were seen with sweeping brushes, mops and

370

buckets, and there was a great deal of moving of furniture. The buffet tables were put in place, the record player and a wide selection of records were taken over in readiness for their big shindig.

At six o'clock, the festivities began and the whole staff attended – including even Grundy who had spent much of the term whingeing about the waste of time it was and how 'education was going to the dogs'.

The pupils began arriving a little after six and Billy's heart swelled with pride when he saw them. The boys were a joy to behold in their best suits, collars and ties, gleaming shoes, and their hair slicked down with brilliantine – though it failed to hold down Joe Duffy's errant locks. Tony Jarvis and Mick Lynch sported tiepins and cuff links, and Alf Dempsey boasted a carnation in the buttonhole of his lapel.

'I hope you're not going to try and put coal into the boiler tonight,' remarked Frank Wakefield to Joe Duffy. 'Not in your best suit.'

'Only if you order me, sir,' he replied, 'and if it's in the middle of Mr Hopkins's lesson.'

'Here, Joe,' Wakefield said, taking out his packet of cigarettes, 'I know you smoke – have known for the past year. Have a decent one after those dimps you've been dragging on.'

'Thanks, sir. They were usually your dimps I smoked anyway.'

The arrival of the girls in a bunch caused a great stir. Their entrance was worthy of a Busby Berkeley parade and the eyes of the staff – and many of the boys – popped out of their heads. The girls had spent considerable time at each other's homes primping themselves up for the big party and the results were delightful. Their bouffant hairstyles, the judicious use of cosmetics, their New Look dresses and high heels – all had blended together in such a way as to transform them from gawky, leggy schoolgirls into young debutantes. No longer school kids, thought Billy, but highly attractive young ladies.

'I hope none of them are wearing those copper knickers Hopalong was telling us about,' Horner whispered to Dempsey.

The dancing began with the music of Victor Sylvester and Billy's pupils demonstrated what they could do.

'Well, I never!' exclaimed Grundy. 'I can see the education this class has been getting and it's not the academic variety.'

'Somehow, I think they'll find ballroom skills of more value in their world,' Wakefield rejoined.

It was Nellie Wallace who stole the show. Her dark hair was combed high on the back of her head and tied with a red silk ribbon. Her black silk dress must have meant many laundry chores for her mother.

'That girl has turned out to be a real swan,' remarked Laura. 'I'll have to watch my step with some of these girls. I think I may have competition.'

'Hardly,' said Billy, squeezing her hand. 'They're beautiful all right but young kittens and hardly in your league.'

The music started up with Sylvester's 'You're Dancing On My Heart' quickstep and Nellie came over to Billy's table.

'May I have this dance, sir?' she said.

'My pleasure,' answered Billy and together they glided across the floor in perfect time in strict tempo.

'You know, sir,' she said, 'when you first came to the school, we decided to give you a hard time. But after that bike ride to Tatton Park, well, things seemed to change. This has been the best year of my life and it's one I'll never forget.'

'That's fine, Nellie,' said Billy, 'but remember, don't obey orders literally by stepping into wastepaper baskets.'

'That's something I do want to forget,' she said. 'And thank you, sir, for not embarrassing me in front of the class. They were waiting to laugh at me and you didn't let them.'

The rest of the evening slipped by quickly and soon it was time for parting. The party had been fixed to end around ten thirty, and as that time approached, Frank Wakefield stepped to the front of the room and called for attention.

'I want to say how much we on the staff have enjoyed tonight and I hope all of you – former members of the top class – feel the same. You have been a great class and we're proud of you. We only hope that the next top class is half as good as you. Remember that although you are leaving us, you can always come back to see us any time. Now I think Jim Mitchell has something to say.'

Jim Mitchell came to the front. 'I'm not much good at making speeches but we're sorry we gave Mr Hopkins a hard time at the start of the year. Anyroad, we're grateful for all he's done for us and the top class has had a whip-round and we've got him a little present.' He nodded to Nellie Wallace who came forward with a package. Billy went forward and received it from her. He was overcome with emotion.

'I don't know what to say,' he mumbled.

'Then it's the first time!' Tony Jarvis called out. 'Open it, sir.'

Billy removed the wrapping and found a pewter tankard

with the engraved inscription: TO OUR TEACHER. THANKS A LOT, HOPALONG.

Billy looked up, his eyes moist. And for the first time in his life, he really was stuck for words.

Chapter Thirty-Three

Absence Makes the Heart Grow Fonder

When the summer holidays came round, the staff of St Anselm's departed in all directions to their holiday destinations, Greg to his mysterious honeymoon and the rest to various places on the continent. Laura, along with her sisters, Jenny and Katie, had fixed up to stay a month with an uncle in Ayr, while Alex Callaghan and Billy had arranged to take a three-week cycling holiday round Ireland. In many ways, Billy was not looking forward to it for it meant a whole month's absence from Laura.

'I don't know if I can stand being away from you for a whole month,' Billy told her the night before departure. 'But I suppose your dad will be glad to see us apart for a lengthy period.'

'I shouldn't worry about Daddy. He hasn't fully grasped yet that the understanding between Hamish and me is over for good, but he'll come round to it slowly but surely.'

'I hope and trust that he does. Whatever happens don't let him persuade you to go back to Hamish while we're apart.'

'Don't even think about it,' she said, taking both his hands. 'Hamish is history. You're the only one for me and

I'll make sure Daddy gets the message whilst you're away. Anyway, you've gone up in his estimation lately.'

'Oh, and why is that?'

'Hughie has just learned that not only did he get his Higher School Cert but also his credit in French giving him the modern language he needed for matriculation. He's been accepted by Sheffield's Medical School after he's served his National Service. We're all very grateful to you, Billy.'

'Aw, shucks, I didn't do nothin',' Billy drawled in his best John Wayne accent. 'But ah tell ya, pardner, ah'm sure gonna miss you like hell these next few weeks.'

'Absence makes the heart grow fonder,' she murmured, putting her head on his shoulder.

'As long as it's not a case of absence makes the fond heart wander,' he said. 'Have you ever noticed that for every one of these sayings, there's an opposite? For example, "Look before you leap" but "Faint heart never won a fair lady" and "He who hesitates is lost".'

'What about "The early bird catches the worm" and "Better late than never"?' she laughed.

'And as for absence making the heart grow fonder, remember also "Out of sight, out of mind", but that will never happen to us. The idea of not seeing you for four weeks fills me with heartache. I shall write to you every day.'

'The same goes for me, Billy,' she said, 'but I can't write to you as you will be on the move the whole of the time. But you'll be in my thoughts every moment of every day that we're apart.'

'There is one saying which is so true, there is no opposite, and that is, "Parting is such sweet sorrow".'

They kissed goodnight at the doorstep. If the rest of the

family was watching from an upstairs window, Laura and Billy were past caring.

The Gladstone Dock in Liverpool was a hive of activity when Alex and Billy arrived there to take the night ferry to Dublin where they were to spend the first leg of their travels with Calixtus, Alex's eldest brother. They reported to the customs shed and an officer came out to examine their luggage and their bikes to assure himself that there really were two bikes and that the two suspicious characters before him were not smuggling contraband to the Emerald Isle. Though what goods England might have that were worth smuggling across the water, they couldn't imagine.

Having run the gauntlet of immigration and passport control, they arranged for the cycles to go into the hold, after which they boarded the steamship *Pride of Erin* and established themselves on deck.

'I've always found it best to stay on the top,' Alex advised. 'That way, you avoid seasickness as you won't feel the ship's roll half so much.'

This was Billy's first adventure abroad and he felt a great sense of excitement as, leaning over the rail, he watched the boat cast off.

A big red-faced Irishman chose this moment to start an argument with a fellow national on the dockside.

'You have a donkey's arse for a face, so you have,' the big man bellowed, 'and if this boat weren't goin' out, I'd knock your feckin' head off into the middle of next week, so I would.'

'You thank your feckin' lucky stars the boat *is* going out,' the docker yelled back, 'otherwise I'd have your guts for garters, you feckin' ignorant bogtrotter.'

The two knew perfectly well that there was no chance of

either of them carrying out the threats as the distance between them was widening with every moment.

The boat ploughed along the Mersey and soon the Liver birds were silhouettes in the distance.

They found a comfortable cubbyhole and settled down for the night. The gentle rocking of the boat soon lulled them to sleep and they looked forward to a peaceful crossing.

It was not to be. About midnight their peace was shattered. The giant of an Irishman, with the red face and shock of matching hair, a bottle of Guinness stuck in each of his jacket pockets, and shirt wide open to reveal a colourful tattoo of His Holy Mother The Church, began serenading the sleeping deck passengers.

The lament he had chosen contained around ninety-six verses, each of which ended with the invocation: 'Glorio, glorio to the bould Fenian men!'

As if disturbing the slumber of the travellers wasn't enough, he proceeded to go around the deck demanding alms, for what charity or cause he didn't say, and his requests were couched in such terms that no one had the temerity to ask. Like the rest, Alex and Billy dug into their pockets and made a contribution. As a reward for their generosity, the minstrel treated them throughout their journey with all verses of 'The Boys of Wexford' several times over.

It was a tired and baggy-eyed pair of travellers that finally reached the Kingstown Harbour in Dublin where Calixtus was waiting to take them home for their overnight accommodation. Calixtus lived with his wife and two children in a comfortable semi-detached in the suburb of Blackrock, just south of the city.

After a breakfast of bacon and eggs – why was it called a

full English breakfast, Billy wondered, when no one in England had the wherewithal to provide it? – they pushed back their chairs and everyone lit fags. Sweet Afton was the name of the cigarette produced – why the Irish had adopted the name of a poem by the Scottish bard as their most popular brand was another puzzle. Pointless trying to find a rational explanation to these conundrums. Calixtus's children sat at the table with them and Billy remarked how well-behaved they seemed. They didn't, however, come up to Calixtus's exacting standards and he spent much of his time hitting or threatening to hit them with a rolled-up newspaper.

'Will you stop picking your nose, Patrick, or do I have to hit you again with this?' he called, brandishing a cylindrically shaped copy of *The Irish Times*. Or, 'Mary, give over biting your nails or do you want a taste of the front-page news?'

Fascinated, Billy drank it in. All part of cultural learning.

Their first day in Ireland was one of rest and sleep in preparation for an early start next morning.

At eight o'clock they set off, past Phoenix Park and on their way to Cork – 160 miles distant. After thirty minutes of hard pedalling, they reached Clondalkin on the outskirts of Dublin. They stopped at the first post office so that Billy could pen a postcard to Laura in Ayr. It was to be the first in an endless stream of cards that would land on her doorstep. All with the same message of love.

'At the rate we're moving,' said Alex, 'it'll take us maybe two days to reach Cork but we're in no hurry.'

At that point, a small open truck roared past and screeched to a halt about a hundred yards down the road. The driver got out of his cab and beckoned to them.

'Where are you headed, lads?'

'Cork,' answered Alex.

'Hop on the back, lads, I'll have you there in two shakes.'

They caught up with him quickly and clambered aboard, bikes and all.

The truck set off like a rocket. With the wind rushing through their hair, they watched the Irish countryside shoot by. Naas, then a short time after, Portlaoise. On through Tipperary to Cashel and an hour after that they hurtled into Cork. The whole journey had taken a little over two hours.

Billy and Alex got out of the truck elated.

'I think you were trying to break the land speed record,' said Billy to the driver. 'Can we buy you a pint of porter to show our gratitude?'

'I don't see any reason why not,' their Irish Sir Malcolm Campbell said. 'Haven't I a mouth like a dry crust?'

They went into a nearby bar and ordered three pints of porter and stood there talking about their driver's chances in a round-Ireland truck race. After a short time, he left and Alex and Billy remained at the bar where their unorthodox cycling dress of open shirt and baggy white shorts attracted the attention of their fellow drinkers.

'Are you on a cycling holiday, lads?' asked an inquisitive bystander sipping his pint and pulling on his clay pipe.

'That's right. We're cycling right round Ireland,' Billy replied, sticking out his chest and drawing on his Afton. He couldn't resist boasting a little.

'Now, is that right?' said an old man in the corner of the room. 'How far have you come today, lads?'

'From Dublin,' answered Alex nonchalantly.

'That's a fearful long way on a bike,' said another. 'What time did you set off yesterday?'

'We left this morning at eight o'clock,' said Billy truthfully. 'We came at a good speed.'

'Bejabers!' said the speaker. 'And it's only half past eleven now by the bar-room clock. You must be cycling champions. Will you take a pint o' porter with us?'

At two o'clock in the afternoon, the two travellers rolled out of the bar to find a boarding house for overnight accommodation.

Cork turned out to be a popular town and every place they approached was full. They tried St Christopher's Boarding House, St Patrick's, then St Agatha's but there was no room at the inn.

'I appreciate how St Joseph and Mary must have felt,' remarked Alex.

They sought help in a corner shop.

'Have you tried St Finbar's?' said the owner.

'We've tried the whole litany of the saints,' said Billy.

They eventually secured places in Mary O'Shea's lodging house: 'Clean rooms guaranteed,' the sign said. They deposited their luggage, locked up their bikes, and went out to get a meal and explore the town.

'This is a beautiful little spot,' remarked Alex. 'Like a picture postcard.'

That was the wrong thing to say for it triggered the need in Billy to send a card winging its way across to Scotland. They retired to Skiddy's Almhouse where Billy wrote his message:

My dearest Laura, I'm here in this beautiful little town but without you here to see it, it doesn't mean a thing. If I spot something lovely, my first thought is that I want you here to share it with me. Missing you every hour of the day. Alex talks but I hardly pay attention as I'm lost in thought about you. As you know, we're men of few words and so tomorrow, we

381

go to Blarney where we shall kiss the stone and see if it helps us to get over our shyness and our taciturnity. All my love, Billy.

There was a strong wind blowing when they left Cork the next day heading west for Glengarriff via Bantry Bay. They made slow progress and as a distraction from the struggle with the elements, they sang, or rather panted, all the Irish songs they knew. 'Shake Hands With Your Uncle Mike, Me Boy' and 'Star of the County Down' with its chorus line:

> *From Bantry Bay up to Derry Quay*
> *And from Galway to Dublin Town,*
> *No maid I've seen,*
> *Like the brown colleen,*
> *That I met in the County Down.*

'It's about sixty-five miles,' said Alex, 'and if we go through Skibbereen it's going to take us all day to reach Bantry at this rate.'

'Is it any wonder?' Billy gasped. 'We're cycling into the teeth of an Atlantic gale.'

Four hours later, they reached Skibbereen exhausted.

'Time for a break,' said Alex, pointing to Molly Malone's Tea Rooms. 'I think we deserve a cup of tea and a smoke. It's been tough going so far, Billy.'

'We need another racing driver like the one yesterday,' laughed Billy. 'Have you noticed, by the way, that nearly every place we've passed through since we came to Ireland has either had a mention in a song or had a whole song devoted to it?'

'I have indeed. Like Dublin, Tipperary, Blarney, Cork, Bantry.'

382

'And later, we'll be going through Tralee, Killarney, Derry, and Galway,' added Billy. 'Why haven't our own towns in Britain had songs written about them?'

'Well, a few have. Like places in London or Glasgow. But who would want to write about Salford or Wigan or Manchester or Dukinfield?'

'I suppose you're right,' said Billy. 'Imagine a song about "Rose of Salford Docks" or "The Star of Trafford Park". Hardly places of great beauty like the ones we're passing through.'

'That explains it. Is it any wonder they're commemorated in music – we've come through some glorious scenery.'

'I'm afraid I've not been good company in this respect,' said Billy. 'If I see a wonderful scene or view, I want to share it with Laura Mackenzie and without her being present to see it with me, I can't fully appreciate it.'

'Instead of sending her these picture postcards, why don't you phone her and describe the places to her?'

'I'd love to, Alex, and I have her phone number in Ayr but so far I've not seen a single phone box. Do they have phones in this part of the world?'

'Of course they do,' he laughed. 'Ireland's not as backward as that. Since every Irishman is born with a silver tongue, they have to have phones to accommodate their vast vocal output. Probably best to try a hotel in the next town.'

'I will at the next opportunity,' Billy said eagerly. 'I don't know why I didn't think of it before.'

'You've fallen for that girl, haven't you?'

'Ah, so you've noticed,' Billy grinned.

'Noticed! You must be joking! You light up like a neon sign when you hear her name. The whole staff has noticed. We'd have to be blind as bats not to. She's a lovely girl.

You'll be a lucky man if you win her.'

'Were you never attracted to her yourself, Alex?'

'I was and I am but we're too much like each other.'

'I always thought that being alike and having things in common was a good thing.'

'True, true. You must share common values and interests, have a similar level of education, have a similar outlook on important things like religion, how to raise kids, and that type of thing. Otherwise you'd never be attracted to each other. The more things like that you have in common, the better. But when it comes to personality and temperament, that's a different matter.'

'What makes them different?'

'Take you and Laura. You couldn't be more different and that's why you're ideally suited.'

'How do you mean, "ideally suited"?'

'I have a theory about what makes a good match. Not everyone agrees with me – in fact some people think it's daft but I believe that opposites attract.'

'I suppose you're going to say next that she's beautiful and I'm grotesque. She's Esmerelda and I'm the Hunchback.'

'Be serious for a minute. I reckon some people are natural talkers and others natural listeners. When two people with this combination get together, you've usually got a good match. Each partner's happy, talking and listening the amount that suits their personality.'

'You reckon then that Laura and I are a match made in heaven?'

'Well, made at St Anselm's at least.'

'A great theory. You ought to write a book on it.'

'Maybe I will one day. Now, I've done more than enough blathering to fill my day's quota. If we're going to make

Bantry before dark, we'd better get a move on.'

The road took a northerly direction but the gale did not let up. After five miles of it, cycling with heads down, they turned into a hedge, and lit up their fags. They had been there only five minutes when an old farmer came along with a solitary cow. From time to time he struck it lazily with a long cane. When he saw the two cyclists sheltering in the hedge, he stopped and in a loud voice inquired, 'Where are you headed, lads?'

'Bantry,' Billy announced.

'Are you going on through the storm?' he asked in ringing tones that would have done justice to a Shakespearean actor at the Globe.

'We are!' proclaimed Billy in the same vein.

'Ah, ye'll never make it! Ye'll never make it!' he trumpeted, raising both his arms to heaven. With a sudden movement, he stuck a cigarette butt in his mouth and lowering his head close to Billy's ear, muttered, 'Have you got a light there?'

Billy obliged him with a light, and asked, 'Which is the best road to Bantry, would you say?'

'Well now, if I were trying to get to Bantry myself . . . well, in the first place I wouldn't start from here. But you see that road to the left?'

'We do,' they said.

'Well, don't take that one – it goes nowhere.' With his half fag ignited, he strolled off into the wind, still striking the unlucky beast.

'That man would knock John Gielgud and Donald Wolfit into a cocked hat,' remarked Billy as they watched the farmer's retreating figure.

Two hours later, they rode into Bantry Bay, found a cheap boarding house, and collapsed onto their beds completely tuckered out. An hour's rest and they were ready to explore the town.

'First, I must find a phone,' Billy said. 'It'll be so wonderful to hear Laura's voice again.'

'It's only a few days since you saw her,' Alex protested.

'To me it seems like eternity.'

They asked their landlady, Mrs Kathleen Quinlan, if she knew of any place that might have such a thing as a telephone.

'Ah, now,' she said, 'there's a very interesting question. I myself wouldn't have such a contraption in the house. I don't hold with such dangerous technology. Did I not read in the *Bantry Gazette* only yesterday that putting an electric gadget like that to your ear can give you every class of disease.'

'That's news to me,' Billy said. 'What kind of disease?'

'Deafness, for one thing,' she replied. 'And then the radiation passing through your head is sure to soften the brain and cause madness. Apart from that, you could pick up some terrible infection from the earpiece. Who's to say that the last one to use it didn't have leprosy or some such thing. Anyway, you could try the Tim Healy Hotel across the road – last I heard they'd installed one of them new-fangled inventions.'

The hotel looked a likely bet. At the reception desk, they found a leprechaun of a man – the image of Barry Fitzgerald. Billy gave him details of his requirements and the number in Ayr. 'We do have a telephone,' he said, eyeing them suspiciously as if they were English spies. 'We don't get much call for it, you understand, but I'll check with Bridget O'Hara, the town telephonist.'

He cranked the handle on the telephone vigorously and blew into the mouthpiece.

'Is that yourself there, Bridget?' he asked. 'How are you, me ould flower? And the family and the wee bairns? Good, that's good. Now I have a couple of Englishmen here who want the use of the telephone to talk to someone in Scotland.' He made Scotland sound like the Kremlin. 'Would that be possible now?' They heard Bridget squawking some kind of answer.

'She said it might be possible though she'll have to look up the procedure and the cost of such a long-distance trunk call,' he answered eventually.

'I take it the call will be private,' Billy said. 'Only I want to talk to my girlfriend in Scotland without the whole of Ireland listening in.'

'Jabers, how could you ask such a thing! Do you think we've nothing better to do with our time than eavesdrop on your idle chatter? Of course your call will be private.' This is going to provide me with a story for the regulars in Houlihan's Bar tonight, the midget thought. 'Twill be worth at least two pints, maybe three.

After a fifteen-minute wait, the phone rang again and Bridget made contact with Billy.

'I have Scotland on the line for you, caller,' she said. 'Hould on, please whilst I try to connect you.'

There followed a series of weird noises which sounded as if a tornado was raging at the other end of the line, then a succession of blips, burps, farts, and whistles, finally a chain of tut-tut-tut-tuts. Then silence. Billy was about to give up when over the ether he caught the faint sound of a human voice. It was Hamish.

'This is Ayr two oh eight five,' he called querulously. He seemed to be a million miles away. 'Who is this?' he kept repeating.

Heart pounding, Billy called, 'Hamish, this is Billy. I'm

speaking from Ireland. Could you put Laura on, please?'

There was a pause. The tornado over in Scotland seemed to be getting worse. Then Hamish's voice came back.

'Billy, you're no' welcome here. Laura is out walkin' with her sisters and I'm sure she doesna want to speak to you. You're no' wanted here. As for me, I dinna want to hear your voice ever again. Is that clear?' There was a clicking noise and the phone went dead.

Bridget came back on. 'I take it your call is now finished,' she said. 'There was no call for him to talk to you like that. None whatsoever. He had the tongue of an adder.'

Billy turned his anger and his frustration onto Bridget. 'I thought my conversation was supposed to be private,' he barked.

'Of course it was private,' she said. 'I didn't hear a single word that was said. All the same, he'd no right to speak to you like that. The bad-mannered, bad-tempered ould bugger. Let me try again.'

Bridget made several more attempts but to no avail. Hamish had taken the phone off the hook.

The call worried Billy to the core. Why was Hamish back on the scene? Had Duncan's views prevailed? Was Laura back with him? He felt like abandoning the whole tour and somehow getting across to Scotland. Hardly fair on Alex, though, he thought. This was his summer holiday and he'd so looked forward to it.

Before they set off for Tralee the next day, he sent off his daily postcard. He tried to make light of the phone call but deep down he was hurt.

My dearest Laura, Alex thinks you and I are ideally matched because we're so different in temperament etc. that we complement each other. For example,

388

I'm a man and you're a woman; you play the piano
and I do not; you like marmalade and I do not; you're
like Maureen O'Hara and I'm like Charles Laughton.
I won't elaborate. Every moment without you is
painful. Tried to phone you but all I got was Hamish.
What's going on? All my love, Billy.

The rest of the tour took them through some of the most
picturesque places in Ireland and in every one of them,
Billy sent a picture postcard to Ayr. In every town he
tried to find a phone but they were as scarce as haystack
needles.

For the sake of Alex, Billy pushed his worries to the back
of his mind and lustily joined in the songs about the places
they were passing through. In Killarney, it was,

'By Killarney's lakes and fells/Em'rald isles and winding
bays.' Then on to Tralee: 'I strayed with my love near the
clear crystal fountain/That stands in the beautiful vale of
Tralee.'

On the tenth day of the tour, they arrived in the city of
Limerick. They found a lodging house as usual and then
explored the town – the magnificent cathedral and King
John's Castle with its five drum towers. As they crossed
Sarsfield Bridge, Billy turned to Alex and said, 'I must try
to phone Laura again. I'm really concerned about things.
What was Hamish doing in Ayr? I'm sure her father is trying
to push me out of the picture. The trouble is, Laura can't
phone or write to me as we don't know where we're going to
be from one day to the next.'

At Cruise's Royal Hotel, there was no difficulty contact-
ing the operator and getting through to Ayr, but the number
was reported as unobtainable. Now to Billy's anxiety was
added the frustration of a breakdown in communication.

'Sorry to be such a wet blanket, Alex,' he said. 'It's the not knowing that is driving me crazy. It's like a sword over my head.'

'No news is good news,' Alex replied. 'Don't jump to conclusions. I'm sure there's a good explanation for Hamish being there. Why not wait till you get home?'

'Right, Alex. I'll try to cheer up. But the thought of Laura over there in Scotland with Hamish or surrounded by a bunch of young, brawny Scotsmen . . . I'm afraid I might have lost her.'

'You've got too much of a vivid imagination, Hoppy. Try to forget it and look at the beauty of this town we're in.'

Billy was so taken by the glorious sights of the city that he was prompted to write two cards instead of the usual one. One of them read:

> Dearest Laura, We're here in Limerick and there's something in the air that makes me go about spouting verse. Here's one for you.
>
> There was a young fella called Billy
> Whose face looked stupid and silly.
> When asked why it was,
> He said it's becoz
> I'm in love with a beautiful filly.
>
> Don't groan when you read it. I did warn you that I'm mad. Still can't get through to you on the phone. Hope everything's OK. All my love, Billy

Before they left England, everyone, that is to say the Callaghan family, had insisted that they visit the Cliffs of

Moher, 'The grandest coastal stretches in the British Isles,' they'd said. So after their two-day sojourn in Limerick, they headed towards the town of Ennis on the road to the cliffs. The town was a 'twister' of streets, many of which were named after Irish patriots, like Parnell and O'Connell. They noted, too, the statue in the main street and its dedication to 'the Manchester Martyrs who were judicially murdered by the English Government'. It was Fair Day and all available accommodation had been booked up. The only lodging they could find was over a shop and it meant sharing a large Victorian double bed in a vast bedroom which boasted three washbasins.

Before turning in, they visited the local hostelry, the Fergus Inn, and sank a few pints of porter. At half past ten, the landlord called out: 'Come along now, gentlemen, time to close up the place. So finish up your drinks and go home.' Billy and Alex swallowed the last of their pints and made ready to depart. They returned their glasses to the bar and wished the barman goodnight.

'If you'll hang on a few minutes, young sirs,' he whispered, giving them a wink, 'there'll be an extra drink for you.'

The lights were switched off and candles lit, giving the bar a mysterious conspiratorial atmosphere.

'Sh-sh,' hissed the landlord, finger on lip.

He proceeded to draw the illegal pints for his customers. Billy and Alex had not intended drinking more but the air of intrigue made extra drinks irresistible.

'Two pints of porter,' Billy whispered, handing over his money. Stolen sweets are always sweeter, thought Billy.

There was a sudden movement outside the window. The whole bar froze like a tableau in a West End play.

'Quiet. It's the Garda,' gasped the barman.

There was the sound of voices outside the door. The landlord came in with a uniformed police officer.

Caught in the act, he thought. Now we're for it.

'Give Michael here our best pint,' the landlord said to the barman. 'On the house,' he added, slapping Michael, their Garda guardian, on the back.

There was an audible sigh of relief from the regulars of the Fergus and everyone went back to their secret drinking.

Around midnight, Billy and Alex got into the big double bed, settled down, and, as a result of the porter and a hard day's biking, were soon fast asleep. At three in the morning, the room was suddenly flooded in bright light, and half a dozen big, rubicund Irishmen burst into the room and began shaving at the three washbasins.

'Mornin', lads,' called one of them cheerfully, as if it was the most normal thing in the world to begin their ablutions so early in the day. ' 'Tis a grand morning and the sun'll soon be up.'

The two cyclists felt there was no use in trying to go back to sleep and so they arose and began shaving along with their fellow lodgers.

'When in Rome . . .' said Billy wearily. 'But right now, like W.C. Fields, I'd rather be in Philadelphia.'

Three miles west of Liscannor, the Cliffs of Moher stretch for five miles – giant black rocks which far off in the mists of time had thrust themselves out of the sea in a massive primeval cataclysmic convulsion. Of all the sights they had beheld in Ireland, this was the most awesome and the most terrifying. From the top of O'Brien's Tower, they gazed across the wide expanse of the Atlantic Ocean and watched the rippling waves dash themselves angrily against the jagged rocks below.

392

'If you were ever thinking of committing suicide, this would be the place to choose,' said Billy in hushed tones.

'I'll remember that,' said Alex, 'if ever there's another Wall Street crash, not that I own any shares. But a sight like this fills me with a sense of foreboding and makes me think of the great power and majesty of God.'

This pious thought must have penetrated deep into Alex's subconscious for when they reached the little town of Lahinch on the Saturday night, he suggested that it was time he went to confession. It was in this little town that the close association between Church and secular organisations was so dramatically demonstrated. Billy agreed to join Alex at confession and, after finding the usual five shillings B and B lodgings, they went together to St Patrick's.

Three priests were hearing confessions and there were long queues for two of them. The third, however, Father Sean McCabe, seemed to have no one waiting and it was to him that Alex presented himself. It would be hard to say whether his choice was made out of compassion for the poor unpopular priest whom no one seemed to want or whether it had more to do with the fact that they were in something of a hurry to sample the local hostelry. Whatever the reason, Alex was in with the McCabe cleric for a good ten minutes and when he finally emerged he looked distinctly discomfited and flushed.

Strange, thought Billy, they don't come any more innocent or guiltless than Alex.

Apprehensively, Billy entered the box.

'Bless me, Father,' he began, 'for I have sinned. It is three months since my last confession.'

'As long as that!' the priest snapped. 'You should get to

confession more often than that! Suppose you'd been struck by lightning yesterday. It would have been straight to hell with you. Now tell me your sins.'

'I have given way to impure thoughts.'

'Tut-tut,' muttered Father McCabe through the grille.

'I've neglected prayer and the sacraments and I've been uncharitable in thought and deed.' Billy didn't get any further.

'You know that Christ gave the instruction to his apostles: "Whose sins you shall forgive, they are forgiven. Whose sins you shall retain, they are retained." This means I have the power to refuse you absolution.'

'I know that, Father.'

'Well, I don't believe you are contrite,' the priest hissed.

'I'm as contrite as I've ever been,' Billy replied.

'That's not saying much. Anyway, I don't believe that you are truly contrite. And so you must leave the confessional immediately and pray to God for forgiveness.'

Bewildered, Billy left the box, looking, he supposed, like Alex had when he'd emerged a few moments ago. He tapped Alex lightly on the shoulder.

'Let's go,' he said, 'before they throw us into the dungeons.'

'Gladly,' replied Alex, executing a quick genuflection.

Outside the church, they took one look at each other's mortified expression and broke into laughter.

'I feel as if I've had a session with Torquemada, the monk in the Spanish Inquisition,' chuckled Billy.

'Instead of burning at the stake, I think we deserve a drink,' Alex said.

They repaired to Gerry Hanlon's Bar and over two pints swapped notes.

'The blighter refused me absolution,' said Billy. 'Said I

wasn't sorry. So he quoted the bit about "Whose sins you shall retain, they are retained".'

'Oh, he forgave me,' said Alex, 'but he gave me one helluva penance. Two hundred Hail Marys and a hundred Our Fathers. He made me feel like Old Nick himself.'

'You're lucky,' said Billy. 'Me, he refused to forgive at all. So if I get hit by a bus tomorrow, it's the eternal flames of hell for me. Maybe I should chuck myself over the Cliffs of Moher.'

'I think the problem was that you sounded too English.'

'What's my nationality got to do with it?'

'You sound too matter-of-fact, too stiff-upper-lippish, cold and unemotional. The priests like to hear the true penitent strike his breast and proclaim: "Jesus, Mary and Joseph! God help me! I'm a terrible sinner and I deserve to burn in hellfire," etcetera.'

'You mean talk like that old farmer with the cow on the road?'

'Exactly.'

'Drink up,' said Billy heartily. 'Time for another, I think – that is, if you don't mind drinking with a sinful soul like myself.'

'The way I'm feeling,' said Alex, 'I'd drink with Beelzebub himself.'

'Perhaps you are drinking with him,' Billy rejoined. 'But don't forget you need a long spoon.'

They stayed drinking and discussing their sinfulness in Gerry's Bar until ten o'clock when the grumbling of Billy's digestive system reminded him that they had not eaten for some time that day.

'Most cafés will be closed at this hour in a little town like this,' said Alex. 'We could try the big hotel over the road, I suppose. Perhaps we can get something over there though it's a four-star hotel.'

'Who cares how many stars! Surely they wouldn't turn away two miserable pilgrims like ourselves.'

They crossed the road and entered the richly carpeted foyer of the hotel. The reception staff eyed them with suspicion but, fortified with Dutch courage, they entered the restaurant. It was a grand affair and several of the tables were still occupied by late-night diners. An obsequious waiter came forward, showed them to a table and hovered over them, ready to take their order.

'I think coffee and some cream crackers would suit me fine,' said Billy. 'What about you, Alex?'

'The same.'

'I take it you are residents of the hotel, sirs?' inquired the waiter.

'But of course, my man,' Billy assured him.

The waiter went off to get their order.

'Liar!' hissed Alex.

'I've already been shown today to be an unrepentant sinner doomed to be cast into the outer darkness for all eternity. So what difference will a little white lie make? We'll own up when we've eaten and then pay the bill.'

The waiter soon returned with the coffee and biscuits and a form asking for their names and room numbers. They ignored the request and tucked into the small snack hungrily.

Billy signalled to the waiter who had been watching them from a respectful distance.

'We're not resident. We were so hungry that we told you a fib. We're ready to pay the bill.'

The waiter looked angrily at both of them in turn as if they'd told him his mother was a whore and he was poncing off her.

'Can you wait here for a moment, sirs, whilst I consult the manager. This is most irregular.'

The manager, a little runt of a man, came waddling over and they could see from the way he was belching steam that he was not pleased.

'You have no right to come in here with your lies and your deceit. This restaurant is for residents only. Can't you read the sign on the main doors?'

Billy couldn't explain that through their alcoholic haze, they had failed to notice the sign.

'Look, give us the bill and be done with it,' growled Billy.

The manager did as asked and slapped down the bill on the table.

Alex took one look at it and turned white. 'He wants ten shillings each,' he said. 'That's more than our lodgings. It's daylight robbery.'

'Not really,' said Billy. 'It's now eleven o'clock and so it's night-time robbery.' Turning to the manager, he said, 'Ten shillings each for a coffee and a couple of cream crackers is outrageous. We refuse to pay. You may call out the Garda if you wish, but I'd sooner spend a night in jail than submit to such a bare-faced swindle.'

'That goes for me too,' said Alex.

They folded their arms and prepared to sit and wait for the police.

'Get out! Get out!' the manager exploded. 'I don't want to see either of you in this hotel again.'

The pair thought it best to depart whilst the going was good.

It was a shamefaced Billy and Alex that turned up at St Patrick's church the next morning for eleven o'clock Mass. They went into the porch and joined the small queue of

397

worshippers who were introducing themselves to a church warden sitting at a table in the doorway.

'Terence Dugan, diocese of Galway, two shillings,' the apparitor called out. It sounded like an entrance fee.

'Mary Feeney, diocese of Cork. Two and six.'

When they got nearer, they saw the warden was no other than the manager of the hotel.

Billy and Alex signed the visitors' book.

'Hopkins and Callaghan, diocese of Salford. Ten shillings each!' the little manager called. 'That'll be one pound, if you please.'

The pair paid up without a murmur.

Touché, Billy thought.

The rest of the Irish holiday went by quickly, with flying visits to Galway and Connemara where Alex issued dire warnings not to reveal their English origins.

'Connemara is a Gaeltacht where Gaelic is the accepted language,' he said, 'Best to let me do the talking or these fellas will push you into the Corrib as soon as look at you.'

From Galway, Billy made his third attempt to contact Laura but with the same result. Number unobtainable. He sent off his last postcard, a picture of a sunset on Galway Bay.

My dearest Laura, You will be happy to know that this is my last postcard – you should have enough to paper a whole room. Soon I shall be on my way home to Manchester and to you. I count the days and the hours. It's been a great holiday but throughout I've experienced the constant heartache of missing you. Some day, we shall tour Ireland together. What's happened to your phone? Has your uncle forgotten to pay the bill?

Hope you don't find any spilleng mistakes in this. Sometime I think I'm seffuring from lysdexia. All my love, Billy

Then it was the tedious ride across the girth of Ireland, through Athlone and back to Dublin docks and the night boat to Liverpool. Billy left Ireland with mixed feelings – regret that a wonderful holiday had come to an end and yet elation that he'd soon be back with his Laura. But the elation was tinged with concern, and he hoped and prayed he hadn't lost her to Hamish. One thing was sure – he knew beyond the shadow of a doubt that there could never be anyone else for him but Laura Mackenzie.

Chapter Thirty-Four

Home Sweet Home

Billy hated Gardenia Court from the first day he'd laid eyes on it – its squalor, its malodorous stairwell, the rough neighbours and their constant blasphemous bickering. But now after the holiday in Ireland, after having gazed on the panoramic views of Kerry and the magnificent mountains of Mourne, Billy loathed the tenement with a new disgust. Sometimes, he wondered about the so-called benefits of going away on holiday, of seeing new sights, having new adventures, meeting interesting people. All very well, but when it was over and one had to come back to a dump like this, it seemed infinitely worse than when he'd left it three weeks ago. In some ways, it would have been better not to have gone. How he missed Honeypot Street and the house they had had there before the Luftwaffe put a bomb on it.

He climbed the stairs gloomily, bike on his shoulder. Mam was in the kitchen as usual preparing Dad's tea of tripe and onions. This flat of ours, he thought, as he went through the door, may be in a slum tenement but Mam keeps it so neat and tidy, it's like an oasis in a desert.

'Welcome home, son,' she called as soon as she saw him. 'Kettle's on.' It was good to hear her voice again. Always cheerful and welcoming.

Three mugs of tea later and after he had related his adventures, he said, 'Now I have something good and something bad for you. Which do you want first?'

'Definitely the good,' she said. 'Always think positively, is what I say.'

Billy handed her the present he'd carried all the way from Limerick – the one the Liverpool customs had wanted to confiscate.

Smiling in pleasure like a little girl with a Christmas toy, she unwrapped the gift carefully so as not to spoil the silver paper.

'Oh, Billy,' she exclaimed. 'You shouldn't have. You can't afford it.' It was a set of antimacassars in Irish linen.

'We've got an Aunty Cissie and an Aunty Hetty but I've always wanted an Aunty Macassar. And you're always going on at me about Brylcreem spoiling the backs of the chairs.'

'Oh, they're much too good to use. I'll put them away for a special occasion. Now, what's the bad news?'

'Only this,' he grinned, and he handed her his bag of dirty washing.

Billy had to wait a whole week before Laura came back from Ayr and it seemed like forever. The days of the calendar were marked off, oh so slowly. The week of purgatory ended when they met again in Fletcher Moss Gardens.

'I missed you every hour and every minute of the day,' he said, holding her close. 'So much so that I could not enjoy the holiday and there was a dull ache in my heart the whole of the time. The one thing that came out of the parting is that absence really does make the heart grow fonder. I love you now more than ever.'

'The same goes for me, Billy,' she murmured. 'Not for a single second were you out of my mind.'

'What a burden for your mind to carry around!' he murmured. 'Your companions in Ayr must have thought you slightly mad.'

'I think they did at times when I seemed lost in thought.'

'I was desperate to talk to you but I couldn't get through. And when I heard Hamish answer the phone, I thought I'd lost you.'

'That will never happen, Billy.'

'What was he doing there? Is he still hanging around?'

'He was there for only one day,' she answered. 'He came down from Glasgow.'

Billy felt a pang of jealousy strike at his heart. 'Does he think he's still in there with a chance?' he asked hoarsely.

'No need to worry on that score,' she said, hugging him tightly. 'Guess what? It looks as if Hamish and Jenny have hit it off. They spent a lot of their time together and they seem to have a special affinity.'

What sweet relief to hear those words! Laura was still his. His torment had been for nothing.

'I'm happy that things are turning out for the best,' he said. 'Maybe Hamish and Jenny are made for each other. I suspected that at your musical evening. The way he sang about "ae fond kiss" and the way Jenny looked at him, and how she reacted to his news about a possible job in Edinburgh. But I wonder what they have in common? Perhaps they're both hypochondriacs and study the medical encyclopaedia together.'

'You may be right,' she laughed. 'But remember that even hypochondriacs sometimes get ill. I think Hamish's career prospects may have more to do with it.'

'Anyway, here is my gift from Ireland to you,' he said, and he handed across a tablecloth in Limerick lace. 'It's big enough to cover a six-foot table,' he said proudly.

'Wonderful, Billy. I'm sure it'll look good on the Mackenzie table.'

'I wasn't thinking of the Mackenzie table,' he said. 'I had in mind the Hopkins table.'

'Sorry, Billy. I don't understand,' she said. 'Have I misunderstood? Is the cover for me or your mother?'

Should he ask her now? he wondered. He'd been thinking about it all the way round Ireland. What if she said no or demurred? His whole world would collapse round his ears. It was a risk he had to take.

'No, Laura, I meant for us, for our table.'

She looked puzzled. 'Our table?'

'What I mean to say,' he stammered, 'is, will you marry me?'

Laura burst out laughing.

He looked at her nervously. His life was in her hands and here she was laughing at him.

'Our table! No joking, being with you is like trying to solve a crossword puzzle sometimes.' She smiled warmly. 'Of course I'll marry you. I've been wondering when you'd get round to it or, should I say in your language, when you'd start talking table linen.'

He took her in his arms and they stood together overwhelmed by the emotion of it all. Then Laura laughed.

'That must be the most original proposal ever. You give a girl a linen tablecloth and then ask if she'd like to share your table when you get one.'

'You didn't want me to go down on one knee, I hope, and do a Charles Boyer,' he grinned.

'Don't see why not.'

He knelt on one knee and said in his best Boyer imitation. 'Laura, come away with me to the kasbah. Together, we shall escape from the world and love each other forever.'

'Right,' she answered, 'you've swept me off my feet. When do we leave?'

Chapter Thirty-Five

Meet the Folks

Laura and Billy's romance took up where it had left off
before the holidays. At weekends in the hours they were
away from each other, Billy watched the clock, waiting
agonisingly for the time when they'd meet again. Every few
minutes he checked his watch – the hands hadn't budged.
Time stood still. When at last they met, they went on their
usual long walks and boating outings, with Laura sometimes
opting to take the oars.

'Laura, you're so strong,' he kidded. 'I know you'll look
after me and protect me from harm.'

'Come off it,' she said.

It was after one of the rowing sessions at Heaton Park
that Billy took her home to meet his folks. When he told
his mam he was bringing Laura home, it was as good as an
announcement in the *Manchester Evening News*, for there
was an unwritten if not unspoken rule in the Hopkins
household that the one you took home to meet Mam was
the one you were going to marry. No exceptions. It meant
that the liaison was serious. Taking the intended home
sealed it.

Billy had planned it with military precision. It was a

405

Sunday afternoon and that meant his dad would be having his nap after his dinnertime boozing session in the Junction Hotel. If he timed it right, he could take Laura round to meet Mam, have tea and be out before Dad appeared.

It had often occurred to him that the sight of Dad emerging from the bedroom after one of his drinking bouts was enough to terrify the bravest heart. His face resembled the ugliest gargoyle on a church buttress: red-rimmed eyes, dentures absent, giving his features a collapsed Frank Randle look, his braces hanging down loosely, the top of his long johns showing. And to round it off, possibly a foul temper as well. Billy was anxious to avoid a confrontation; all his protective instincts came to the fore. Apart from that, Laura might even believe, God help us, that when she viewed his dad, she was gazing at a possible future Billy.

Laura looked particularly pretty that Sunday; the rowing had brought colour to her cheeks and given her a fresh, country-girl look.

'You look so attractive,' he said. 'You must take me rowing more often. But when I see you against the background of these dreadful tenements, you remind me of the phrase about a beautiful flower growing on a dunghill.'

'Thank you, Billy. But right now I feel nervous as if I'm going to be examined under a microscope, as it were.'

'No need to worry,' he replied. 'They'll love you. As I do,' he added.

They got to Gardenia Court around half past four. Billy was acutely conscious of how it must look to Laura. There was a dog barking from the ground floor flat. On the various verandas of the block, were the usual sights and sounds: a window frame stuffed with cardboard; the Pitts having their usual screaming match; curious women in pinnies and curlers leaning over the balconies, cigarettes dangling from

406

their bottom lips. From the windows of the four storeys above them, poles stuck out with ropes supporting drying clothes.

As they mounted the stairway, Billy became aware more than ever of the odours emanating from the other flats: the privy smell on the first floor, the pickled herrings from the Finkelsteins, the sauerkraut from the Weinbergs. An assortment of stenches, individual foetid malodours mingling with carbolic as they reached Billy's home where they halted. Billy opened the Yale lock with his key.

'Well, this is it,' he said anxiously. 'Welcome to the Hopkins residence. One day, Laura, I hope you will take me away from all this,' he joked in an attempt to hide the tension.

Mam came to meet them when she heard the key turn in the lock. She, too, looked edgy.

'This is my mother,' he said. 'Mam, meet Laura.'

'Very pleased to meet you,' Mam said, reaching out her hand. 'Billy's told us all about you. He talks about nothing and nobody else. You're every bit as pretty as he's said.'

'Thank you so much, Mrs Hopkins, and it's so nice to meet you at last,' Laura said, her voice soft and mild. 'What a beautiful flat you have here. It looks so cosy and inviting.'

The flat looked immaculately clean. It ought to, thought Billy. Mam has been scrubbing it from top to bottom for the last week in anticipation of this visit. Good old Mam, she never lets me down.

'I've got a nice tea ready for the two of you,' Mam said. 'Would you like a swill before we sit down, Laura?'

'A swill?' Laura inquired gently, looking to Billy for an explanation.

407

Somewhere we've played this scene before, Billy mused, thinking of the time his sister Polly had brought home Steve Keenan, her future husband.

'A swill,' explained Billy in typical schoolmaster fashion, 'is a Lancashire expression meaning a little wash, a gentle rinse. When we were boys, it meant a little dash of water on the face but not the neck, as opposed to a full-scale wash which involved the turning in of the shirt collar and a thorough dousing, including the neck. Important to distinguish between a wash and a swill. Having a swill is what the middle classes would call freshening up.'

'You'll have to excuse our Billy,' Mam said. 'Sometimes I think he's not right in the head. If you'd like to freshen up, Laura, as Billy puts it, the bathroom's there at the end of the hall.'

'Thank you, Mrs Hopkins.'

'Well, what do you think, Mam?' Billy asked when Laura was out of the room.

'I think she's a lovely girl.'

Laura returned from her swill and they settled down at the table where Mam had prepared a high tea consisting of an egg salad: lettuce, cucumber, tomato, spring onion and beetroot, plus a red middle cut of West's salmon, and miscellaneous condiments, including pickles and piccalilli. As a dessert, she had gone up-market and, instead of the usual pineapple chunks, had invested in a tin of the more expensive peaches and apricots. And of course the buttered bread had been cut diagonally as was usual and appropriate for Sunday tea.

They were joined by Les who had been reading in his bedroom.

'We don't stand on ceremony here,' Mam said. 'Help yourself to whatever takes your fancy.'

'Thank you very much,' Laura replied. 'What a beautiful spread, Mrs Hopkins. You really have gone to a great deal of trouble.'

'It's only what we allus have on a Sunday,' Mam said. 'I believe in getting in something tasty for our high tea.'

'And in your honour, we're to have peaches and cream instead of chunks,' said Les. 'If you marry our Billy, Laura, it'll be back to chunks if you can afford even them.'

'Now, our Les,' said Billy. 'Don't you go making out that I'm poor and can't afford things.'

'Poor!' he replied. 'Has he told you, Laura, that he goes to school wearing my demob jacket?'

'Yes, he has,' Laura laughed. 'He says you never wear it.'

'That's right,' added Billy. 'I've got to keep up appearances. I belong to the noble profession of teaching.'

'It may be a profession but the pay is lousy,' Les rejoined, helping himself to copious amounts of piccalilli. 'Do you know what his monthly take-home pay is, Laura?'

'Not precisely,' she said, 'but I know it's not great. Remember, I'm a teacher too.'

'His net pay,' said Les, warming to his subject, 'is twenty pounds, no shillings and threepence.'

'And that goes on his upkeep, and his cigarettes,' said Mam, unable to resist adding her bit to the financial debate.

'At least I'm left with the threepence,' Billy joked. 'But you've forgotten about the few pounds I earn from the Youth Centre work.'

'His pay is more than mine,' said Laura. 'I get only nineteen pounds. I'm a woman, you see.'

'I've noticed that,' said Billy, 'and it meets with my strongest approval. But if you and I joined forces, Laura,

409

why, we'd have forty pounds a month. A prince could live on that.'

'Sure,' chuckled Les, 'provided the prince lived in a tent. I'm a watchmaker by trade and I earn nearly forty pounds by myself.'

'And is your mother a teacher like you, Laura?' Mam asked, changing the subject.

'She's a private teacher of music, Mrs Hopkins. She teaches singing and the piano.'

'Our Billy could benefit from a few singing lessons, Laura,' said Les. 'You should hear him in the bathroom. Reminds me of Jerry Colonna, that film star with the foghorn voice.'

'It must be nice to have a mother a teacher of music,' said Mam wistfully. 'I've allus been fond of a bit o' music myself. My favourite's Handel's Lager.'

'I'd rather have Boddington's bitter,' said Les, chuckling. 'But talking of Handel, I saw a notice on a billboard outside Cheetham Town Hall the other day. It said: "Tonight. Handel's Organ Works". Somebody had written underneath, "So Does Mine – Every Night".'

'These two lads are allus trying to get me confused,' Mam said. 'Our Les sent me to Lewis's last week to book tickets for that big Italian fella, the one they call Benjamin Giggly. I felt proper daft when I asked for the tickets – the girl started laughing at me.'

'Laughing or giggling?' asked Les.

'I think they're called malapropisms,' laughed Billy. 'She calls the American crooners Kerry Pomo and Bim Crosby.'

'Well, I nearly got them right,' Mam chuckled, joining in the fun.

This brand of conversation helped to relieve some of the early tension and Laura laughed and began to relax and enjoy the company. The banter would have continued in this vein but their voices must have carried through to the adjoining bedroom for sounds of movement heralded the imminent arrival of Billy's father.

Uh-oh, here comes trouble, Billy thought.

Mam rose quickly from the table. 'Leave him to me,' she said. 'I'll tidy him up a little before his public appearance.'

She met Dad as he emerged from the room and steered him off to the bathroom.

'If you are so foolish as to marry our Billy here,' continued Les, obviously enjoying himself, 'I should warn you that he's a Cancerian, that is, subject to sudden changes of mood.'

'In what way?' Laura asked.

'One moment he's jolly and joking, and the next he can be crabby or in a melancholy mood.'

'I'm a Gemini, born under the sign of the twins,' Laura answered. 'We're supposed to have changeable personalities too, so we should get on well together.'

'Well said, Laura,' Billy replied. 'Anyway, I'm only crabby when Les won't lend me his jacket and I have to pinch it.'

'Whatever you do, Laura, if you do decide to take him on as your husband, make sure you have a cigarette for him first thing in the morning. Otherwise, he's like a bear with a sore head. Now, if you wanted to swap him for a handsome, even-tempered man, I'm available.'

'Huh! Laura is a woman of taste and discernment, which is why she has chosen me,' Billy replied.

At this point, Mam guided Dad into the room. Whatever she had done, she'd made him reasonably presentable. He had washed his face and, in the terminology that public

411

toilets sometimes couched their sartorial request, he had 'adjusted his dress'. His dentures were in place.

'This is our Billy's girl, Laura,' she said.

Billy liked that phrase 'our Billy's girl'.

Dad said how pleased he was to meet her and, after shaking her hand, sat down at the table where he proceeded to prepare a massive salad butty containing everything on the table. By some gigantic movement of the jaw, he managed to make his first assault on the mountainous sandwich. Billy's nightmare was taking place before his very eyes. Should he take Laura by the hand and make a quick exit before matters got worse or should he hang on and hope things might improve? He opted for the latter.

As Dad continued to champ on his butty, he struck up a conversation with Laura.

'So what does your father do, Laura?'

'He's an Inspector of Taxes, Mr Hopkins,' she said modestly, unable to hide her feeling of awe at his lusty eating style.

'I'll bet he earns good wages at that job,' Dad commented. Then he added, 'But I'll bet it doesn't go down too well with his pals.'

'I don't think he brings his work home with him,' said Laura, springing to the defence of her father.

There was a momentary silence whilst Dad ransacked his mind for something to say. His eye alighted on the beetroot.

'During the war,' he said, 'young ladies used beetroot in place of lipstick. Did you know that, Laura?'

'No, I didn't know that, Mr Hopkins. That's most interesting,' Laura said bravely.

'There was such a terrible shortage of everything,' Dad

went on. 'A bath, if you had one, that is, couldn't be more than five inches of hot water.'

'I was too young to remember most of that,' said Laura, 'but I can still recall that we were allowed only one little bar of soap a month.'

'Things was bad,' Dad continued. 'Why, women even used soot for eye make-up and there was such a shortage of silk stockings, they used gravy browning to paint their legs and pencilled in a black line down the middle for a seam.'

'You shouldn't have been looking at women's legs,' was Mam's contribution to the discussion of wartime deprivation.

'Still, I'll bet the gravy-stained legs attracted an enthusiastic following amongst the neighbourhood dogs,' said Billy in a brave attempt to introduce a little levity into the conversation.

There was a lull in the debate as Dad constructed another gigantic gastronomic delight.

By some strange convoluted process of reasoning, he got it into his head that Laura, being a member of the middle classes and a teacher in a Catholic school, was in some way connected with the Church because his conversation now acquired a singularly ecclesiastical flavour.

'I see that St Thomas of Canterbury Parish in Salford is holding a Mass for the sick and the housebound next Sunday,' he announced suddenly.

The company didn't know how to respond to this disclosure and so there was silence as they absorbed it and tried to assess its significance.

'I notice too in the paper, Laura,' he proclaimed, 'that the Bishop of Salford will be giving confirmation at St Dunstan's Church in Moston next Sunday.'

413

Laura took in this news as if it was the most fascinating thing she'd heard that day.

'That's very interesting, Mr Hopkins,' she said warmly. 'That'll be Bishop Heenan, won't it?'

As the name of the bishop had not been given in his copy of the *Evening Chronicle*, he was unable to give an intelligent answer and so responded by making inroads into his pavement-thick sandwich. He soon followed it with other equally intriguing pieces of news.

'Did you know that Pope Pius the Twelfth spoke fluent German, Laura?'

'I didn't know that, Mr Hopkins,' she said politely.

'Many people say that he was on the side of the Germans during the war, but I don't believe it. He hated war and in nineteen forty he tried to stop it.'

It suddenly dawned on Billy that his dad had prepared for this meeting by memorising choice morsels of church news to impress Laura – despite all his protestations about being against the middle classes. Though the morsels were inappropriate, Billy was touched by the fact he'd made such an effort.

He could see though that he was ready to offer yet more intriguing titbits of information about the clergy from his store of information on the church calendar and Billy decided it was time to make a move.

'We'll have to go now, Dad,' he said. 'I promised to get Laura back home at a reasonable hour tonight. We both have school tomorrow.'

'Thank you, all of you,' Laura said. 'I've enjoyed meeting you. I do hope we can get together again soon.'

Billy helped her on with her coat and they were ready to depart.

'Goodnight, everyone,' she called. 'And thank you once again.'

'Goodnight, Laura,' they said in chorus.

As they descended the stairway, Billy asked, 'Well, Laura, what did you think of 'em?'

'I think they're wonderful,' she replied immediately. 'Really entertaining – all of 'em.'

On the second landing, she turned to Billy. 'Well, how did I do? Am I accepted?'

'Laura,' he responded, 'you were stupendous. The soul of tact and I know they liked you a lot. But now I'm not sure we should get married – I didn't know you had such strong connections with the Church.'

'Very funny!' she said, digging him playfully in the ribs.

After school the following day, Billy faced both his parents over a cup of tea, anxious to have their reactions to their meeting with Laura.

'I think she's a lovely girl,' said Mam. 'She talks real posh like the toffs. Mind you, I thought she was a bit on the quiet side.'

'She could hardly get a word in, with you lot talking so much,' Billy countered. 'Anyway, you have to remember she was nervous, meeting all of you like that.'

'I suppose you're right,' Mam said. 'But you're such a noisy devil with so much to say for yourself, I wonder how you'd get on, that's all.'

'But that's just it,' he said. 'We're perfect for each other. One counterbalances the other. According to my friend Alex at school, it wouldn't do if we were both big talkers or we were both quiet. Anyway, God made us with two ears and one mouth which is about the right proportion we should use 'em. More listening than talking.'

415

'I'm sure you know what you're doing,' she said. 'Remember the saying though: "Marry in haste, repent at leisure." '

Dad had remained silent up to this point but he now felt it was time to deliver his judgement.

'You don't often ask my opinion, Billy,' he said, 'but choosing your life partner is a bloody serious business and you've got to think about it very carefully. Marriage makes or mars a man, they say.'

These weren't the answers Billy wanted to hear. He said, 'Look, we can all go on quoting proverbs about marriage. "Marriages are made in heaven" or "There's more to marriage than four bare legs in a bed" or "Marriage is a lottery" but what I want to know is what you really think.'

'Laura is a real fine-looking lass,' he said slowly. 'But she's not of our class. Why, her father's a high-up civil servant, an Inspector of Taxes, for God's sake. The sort I've been up against all my life. As I see it, the world is like a building made up of different storeys and different rooms – some above and some below, some big and some small. Everyone has his place and position in the building and the parts don't mix together.'

'That's out of date, Dad. You seem to see the world as made up of Us and Them. Those who are not with us are agin us. According to you, there's only two levels in society, like in that old Protestant hymn "All Things Bright and Beautiful":

> *The rich man in his castle,*
> *The poor man at his gate,*
> *God made them, high or lowly,*
> *And ordered their estate.'*

416

'Too bloody true,' he replied vehemently. 'The rich are all in a click and they're out to do the working man down. When you went to college, I had to go to one of them there tax offices. They made me sit on a hard wooden bench for a couple of hours. They treated me like muck.'

'But Laura isn't like that,' Billy protested.

'They're all in it together, son. Take gambling, for example. When our Jim was alive, he used to play pitch and toss with the other lads but let the police catch 'em and they were for it. If I want to put on a bet, I have to break the law by going to a backstreet bookie. But I'll bet if this Mr Mackenzie fella wants to bet, he's only to pick up the phone.'

'So because of your problems about putting on a bet, I'm not to think of marrying Laura?'

'It's not only that. Can't you see? She leads a different life from ours. They're not the same as us, I tell you. They're brought up differently, they eat different food, and are not governed by the same laws. The Mackenzies live in Regina Park, the snootiest district in town, where the wealthy cotton merchants used to have their big houses. Why, we couldn't afford to live in their garden shed. The nearest our class ever gets to them is as labourers or servants.'

'By gum, that's true,' Mam agreed. 'I spent my early adult life in service, so I ought to know.'

'The classes don't mix, it's a law of nature,' Dad argued. 'Oh, you can marry all right but you'd soon find that you don't do things the same, don't think the same. You'd have nothing but trouble, Billy, I'm telling you.'

'You're about a hundred years out of date, Dad. This is ninety forty-nine. I think you're talking rubbish. Of course we'd get on.' Billy was feeling less sure of himself.

'She's used to having nice things about her. You couldn't

afford half the things she's used to. Why, I bet her father's even got a car and a piana. You take my advice, son and marry your own kind.'

'I don't know what you're getting so het up for, Tommy,' Mam said. 'We're a respectable family in this house, we keep ourselves to ourselves, and we've never been in trouble with the police or owt like that. We don't owe nobody nothing and we can hold our heads up anywhere. So I think our Billy's good enough for any girl – posh or not.'

'I'm not saying he isn't,' Dad answered. 'I'm only thinking of what's best for him. Why can't he find a nice working-class lass who'll make a nice home for him and bring his kids up nice? Why does he have to go mixing with the bloody middle class? That's what I want to know.'

'Maybe you've forgotten,' said Billy, vehemently, 'that I've gone over to the bloody middle class myself by becoming a teacher. I've joined the enemy.'

'No need to talk like that, Billy,' said Dad. 'You're young and you can't always see what's best in the long run. It's only your happiness I'm thinking of.'

'I give up!' Billy exploded, and flounced out of the room and into his bedroom.

Quivering with anger, he lay back on his bed, arms behind his head. What bloody, bloody nonsense! he said to himself. The very idea that I should give Laura up because I might be marrying out of my class. It's medieval.

But Billy's dad had given voice to a feeling of inferiority he had harboured ever since he'd set eyes on Laura's home in Regina Park – a feeling he was reluctant to admit even to himself. Nevertheless his dad had planted a small seed of doubt in his mind where it began to germinate.

That night he slept fitfully, tossing and turning in his bed.

Chapter Thirty-Six

Parting Is Such Sweet Sorrow

It was the first day of the new term. Billy's reputation as a lively, exciting teacher had preceded him and the new Senior 4 sat at their desks looking at him eagerly. Unlike the first class of pupils that he'd faced, this fresh set had come to accept the idea that they were to stay at school until fifteen. They also knew that this Hopalong character taught not only the usual subjects but had introduced activities like ballroom dancing, cycle trips, and outside visits to places of interest. On the first morning, however, they were disappointed because it was a tired-looking Billy who turned up at school. He got through the morning somehow but his teaching was dull and uninspired.

At break time, Laura noticed the drawn, careworn expression.

'Billy,' she exclaimed solicitously, 'you look worn out. Are you feeling all right?'

'I'm fine, Laura,' he replied. 'Didn't sleep too well last night. Got things on my mind.'

'What sort of things? I hope I didn't put my foot in it yesterday when I met your family.'

'No, no. Nothing like that. I worry about money matters sometimes, that's all.'

'We're going to the flicks on Friday night, Billy. So we've got that to look forward to but if you're worried about money, we can go in the less expensive seats. And we can go Dutch. I'll pay for the seats if you're broke.'

'There's more to it than that, Laura,' Billy said evasively. 'We'll talk about it on Friday when we've got more time.'

'It sounds serious,' she said, now looking concerned.

'We'll go to the early show at the Apollo. It finishes around nine o'clock and so we can walk home and talk things over.'

'It sounds very serious,' she said. 'Can't you tell me now what's on your mind?'

'Best to leave it till Friday.'

The feature film at the Apollo was *Brighton Rock*, an adaptation of one of Graham Greene's best novels featuring Richard Attenborough, but they hardly noticed this detail. They sat in their usual double seat in the back row but Laura noticed painfully that Billy neither put his arm round her nor held her hand as he always did. Something was troubling him and she picked up his misery like a cold.

After the show, Laura put her arm through his and they walked in silence for a while along Stockport Road.

'Billy,' she said, 'you look so unhappy. What is troubling you? Why so sad?'

'I've been thinking things over,' he said slowly, 'and I'm no longer sure that you and I are meant for each other. Perhaps we're not suited.'

Laura went white and her heart skipped a beat.

'Not suited!' she faltered. 'How do you mean, not suited?'

'It's like this. You and I live in completely different worlds. You come from a well-to-do family and I'm from . . . well you saw on Sunday where I'm from. I don't think it's going to work out.'

'Is it something I've done? Something I've said?' she gasped.

'Nothing like that, Laura. I still think you're the most wonderful person in the world.'

'Well then? What's wrong? What's changed? I don't understand.'

'Laura, you're used to a certain lifestyle. One that I couldn't even begin to offer you. To paraphrase Churchill, I have nothing to offer you but tears, toil, sweat and penury.'

'Oh Billy, Billy. I don't care about lifestyle. It's you I want. Can't you see that?'

'That's all very well, Laura. You know the saying, when poverty comes in at the door, love flies out at the window.'

'Only too well,' she said ruefully. 'My father's always quoting it. But there's another saying which I prefer – love conquers all. Billy, we have something good here. Don't throw it away.'

'To put it bluntly,' he said, 'we belong to different social classes. You are middle class and I'm working class. I don't think the two mix easily.'

'I don't understand that. I thought the notion of social class was dead. Surely that's what the war was about – to end social class divisions.'

'Class is very much alive and kicking, Laura. Britain is a class-ridden society. It's everywhere. Think about the jubilees and coronations when the different orders and ranks are on display for all to see. Why, you'll find social class even in the cemetery.'

'I think you're making too much of this social class

thing. We're different personalities and that's good. But we have so much else in common. We have similar tastes in music and literature. We both like children. And, most important, we have the same sense of humour and that means a lot. What does that "you're middle class" business mean?'

'It means that you inhabit a different world from mine. There are so many things in your life that you take for granted as if you and your family possess them by some God-given right.'

'For instance?' Her hackles were beginning to rise.

'A Bechstein piano, a telephone, a motor car, beautiful paintings on the walls, grapes on the sideboard when there's nobody ill, a Pye Black Box gramophone. I could go on. If we marry, I can offer you practically nothing, except a penny-pinching existence. I'm a non-graduate, elementary schoolteacher and we'd have to eke out a living on a pittance.'

'But Billy, I don't give a damn for these material objects you're listing. Are we to part because we happen to have a piano, a telephone, and a Pye Black Box? They're not my fault. Am I to be jilted because we have flowers and fruit on the sideboard? That's ridiculous.'

They had reached Laura's gate. The faces at the bedroom window would see no kissing tonight.

'I'm sorry, Laura,' Billy said. 'I'm not happy with this but I think it's for the best in the long run. One day, you'll find a man with more money and better qualifications who'll provide for you in the manner to which you are accustomed. That should make your father happy at least.'

Laura broke down and began to weep. 'Billy, Billy. You couldn't be more wrong.'

With that, she ran into the house crying. Billy made his sorrowful way to the 53 bus and back to Gardenia Court.

Laura was absent from school the following week. There was a haunted look about Billy, and those around him could sense that something was amiss.

'I anticipated this,' Frank Wakefield said at lunchtime. 'I saw it coming when you and I had our little chat. You two have had a lovers' tiff and now Miss Mackenzie's off sick.'

'It's more than a tiff, Frank,' replied Billy. 'We're definitely through. At last I've come to my senses.'

'Oh,' he said, 'and what does that mean?'

'Laura Mackenzie and I inhabit different planets. I live in Cheetham Hill and she lives in Regina Park. And ne'er the twain shall meet.'

'That sounds like a lot of sociology claptrap, if you ask me,' he replied.

'But it wasn't so long ago that you were warning me off.'

'You will remember that my concern was for the school's reputation and harmony in the workplace, not your social status with regard to Miss Mackenzie. If you want my opinion, and you probably don't, if I were in love with Miss Mackenzie, I'd move heaven and earth to win her. In life you get only one chance at happiness and you must seize it with both hands when it presents itself. *Carpe diem!*'

'That's all very well, Frank. But love doesn't pay the grocery bills. You know my salary. What could I offer her?'

'Love will find a way,' he said.

'If anyone else quotes another proverb about love,' exclaimed Billy, 'I shall throw a fit. For every proverb, as I keep telling my English class, there's one that contradicts it.'

'You are in a prickly mood,' he said. 'All I know is that

423

this new development in your amatory relationship means I'm a teacher short and I'm having to take Junior Two myself. So please come to some conclusion quickly so we can all get on with our work.'

Laura returned to school the following week but she looked pale and drawn. She had obviously spent much time weeping and there was a grief-stricken air about her as if she was in mourning for someone close.

They could not avoid each other in the staffroom nor did they wish to. They nodded to each other politely and exchanged the usual greetings and pleasantries as they did with other members of staff. Billy tried to go about his business normally, teaching, conversing, joking with colleagues, but in his innermost being, he felt a great sense of despair and of loss.

It was around this time that Titch came home on Christmas leave. Naturally they had to celebrate the furlough with a few pints in the Sawyer's Arms.

'Well, Titch, your National Service is up soon,' Billy said when he'd got the drinks in. 'Time has certainly flown.'

'It may have flown for you, Hoppy, but it certainly hasn't for me and the rest of the gang. But it's right, thank the Lord, we finish in summer – provided we don't get put on a charge that is, because for that they can add another three months.'

'You'll all have to keep your noses clean, then.'

'Too true. We're all watching our step.'

'So, what's everyone got planned?'

'Pottsy has decided to join his father in the retail business. When he saw what teachers get paid, that was enough for him.'

'Pottsy never had his heart in teaching,' said Billy. 'I

think he came to college just for the fun of it. What about the rest of them?'

'Ollie, too, has come to the conclusion that the classroom is not his scene. He's been studying for the ALA examination while in the army and he's obtained a librarian's job in Dewsbury.'

'And the other two?'

'Nobby's taken a commission in the Army Education Corps. It seems he was right about the uniform pulling the birds. He has them queuing up to get into his bed. At least, so he says. But you know Nobby and his slight tendency to exaggerate.'

'Typical Nobby. And Oscar?'

'As you probably know, Oscar found a post last year in a boys' boarding school in Yorkshire. Last I heard, he was happily settled there.'

'All great news, Titch. And what are you going to do with yourself?'

'I've managed to get a job in a secondary modern in Altrincham. Can't be much of a school though 'cos I was the only applicant.'

'Still the same old Titch,' Billy laughed. 'Always looking on the gloomy side.'

'Prepare for and fear the worst – that's our family motto. How's life been treating you, Hoppy, while we've been living it up in the army?'

Billy gave him a summary of all that had happened since they last met, the initial trouble with his class, the odd characters in school, especially Grundy. He told him about Laura and the way his dad had reacted to their engagement, how they had parted because Billy believed he wasn't good enough.

Titch listened to the whole story with rapt attention and

without saying a word. When Billy had finished telling him about the latest turn of events, he spoke for the first time.

'Hoppy,' he said, 'you're mad. Mad as a hatter. From what you've told me and from the way you've told me, it's obvious that you and this Laura are meant for each other. This is your big chance, you idiot, to achieve happiness. I've never said this before to anyone but this kind of certainty comes but once in a lifetime. Don't let it slip between your fingers. If Laura's the one, don't let her get away.'

'You've become quite philosophical in your old age, Titch.'

'That's what the army does for you.'

They parted company vowing to keep in touch now that they would both be living in Manchester. Later that night when Billy was alone in his bed, he thought over everything that Titch had said. Somehow he'd touched a nerve with his talk about not letting Laura get away. Now he wondered if he could get her back.

Next day at school, he greeted Laura in the staffroom. She returned his greeting but she was remote. She'd been hurt and she wasn't going to repeat the experience in a hurry.

Now Billy began to kick himself for his stupidity and all that nonsense about social classes and hierarchies. He'd let his dad lead him up the garden path all right. Up to now only his pride had stopped him from going up to her and saying, 'Please forgive me. Come back to me.' But Titch's little speech had hit home and he felt he had to do something to win back her love. Easier said than done, for he had the impression that Laura's sorrow had somehow turned to impatience with him and he was fearful that if he approached her again, she'd tell him to take a running jump.

I think I've screwed up well and truly, he said to himself. I doubt she'll have anything to do with me again. I suppose her father will be pleased about that and Hamish the hypochondriac is probably back in the running.

The rest of the term went by in routine fashion and Billy began to be reconciled to a cool, aloof relationship. No use, he thought, I've blown it for good.

Chapter Thirty-Seven

Deep Throat

It was after Christmas and the start of a new term. Billy put his personal problems behind him and poured his energy into his teaching in an attempt to forget his troubles. His new class were an eager bunch.

During a lesson on David Livingstone, Billy was going big guns on the adventures of the Scottish explorer. He had the class in the palm of his hand and they were hanging onto his every word. Stanley Cashman, the bank man, was spellbound and even Frank Wakefield looked up from his accounts from time to time. The atmosphere was electric as everybody in the room, pupils and adult observers alike, paddled their canoes through rivers infested with alligators and hippopotamus, waded through malarial swamps seething with crocodiles, slashed and macheted their way through dark forests and on towards central Africa. They had reached the mighty waterfall which the local tribes called Mos-oa-tun-ya, the smoke that thunders, and which Livingstone christened the Victoria Falls in honour of his queen. Billy hoped that the headmaster would not break the tension he had so carefully built up with some fatuous remark about the boiler needing replenishment.

'Picture the scene,' he said. 'Livingstone has abandoned his steamboat on the Shire River and now, frail and sick, he is being carried on a *kitanda* stretcher by his faithful porters. They come across a slave caravan surrounded by armed men. Livingstone detested the slave trade and orders his men to attack immediately. The guards run away and Livingstone frees eighty-four slaves. On they go, fighting their way through the impenetrable jungle, searching for the great lake which Livingstone believes to be the source of the Nile. They had given up hope when Chuma, his loyal six-foot African servant, pointed through the trees and called.' Billy raised his hand dramatically and pointed to the horizon, calling out, '*Huko bwana – nyasa!* Over there, boss – the lake!' At least, that is what Billy had intended to call but instead of a full-blooded cry, there emerged from his throat, not the roar of the African giant but a high-pitched, mouse-like squeak.

His classroom audience gazed at him nonplussed.

He tried again with the same result. A squeak.

What in God's name was happening? If the truth be told, Billy was proud of his voice – several friends had commented favourably on its rich timbre. He tried a third time and was highly relieved to find that his full voice had returned – but not for long. As he continued his narrative, it changed without warning from baritone to tenor. Perplexed, he decided to ignore the change of key and, clearing his throat, went on with the story. A minute later, it happened again, only this time he modulated to coloratura soprano. Strange, he thought. My voice broke about ten years ago. Perhaps I'm having a second adolescence.

His listeners by now had lost interest in David Livingstone and were finding greater entertainment in the changes of vocal pitch Billy was producing. Enthralled,

429

they thought it was some trick he was employing in order to win their attention.

It was no trick. He soldiered on with his account of the scramble for Africa, alternating as he did so between Paul Robeson and Lily Pons until Sammy McGrath, Joe Duffy's successor as the head's monitor, mercifully brought the lesson to an end with his bell ringing. A bewildered class filed out of the room quietly but once released from control, began a vociferous post-mortem.

'What's gone wrong with old Hopalong?' asked Lily Malone, the new tea girl.

'He's going through a sex change, that's what,' said Sammy McGrath.

'Nah, he's having us on. He'll do anything to grab our attention.' This from Vito Clarke.

Several of the more ambitious pupils began telling each other stories, adopting roller-coaster vocal intonations in imitation of Billy's octave leaps. 'So this bloke Livingstone went down in the valleys and up amongst the mountains, down to the bottom and up to the top.'

Billy was at a loss to explain the phenomenon and there seemed nothing he could do about it – the modulations happened of their own accord. But it could be serious, for without a voice, he was out of a job. Speech was his stock in trade and whilst sudden sound jumps in his narrative accounts might lend a certain dramatic effect to the telling, it could for some listeners prove a distraction.

At home that night he told Mam about it, who as usual was optimistic.

'It's nothing. Just a sore throat,' she said. 'You've been talking too much. Overdoing it. Don't worry. It'll be all right.'

It would have been more comforting if Mam had been a

member of the Royal College of Surgeons or at least had held a recognised medical degree.

'Try gargling with TCP,' she said. 'That'll move the frog from your throat.'

Billy went into the bathroom and did as he'd been advised, the gurgling noises emanating from his throat resembling the coffee percolating machine in Luigi's trattoria on Cheetham Hill Road.

He tried singing. It should be explained here that the Hopkins bathroom had a curious plumbing arrangement. In the interests of economy, some corporation engineering genius had devised a system whereby the hot and cold water taps could be swivelled ninety degrees so as to flow into either the hand basin or the bath. The channel through which the water ran proved to be a perfect resonant amplifier for any would-be crooners or singers who happened to be washing their hands. It was into this improvised device that Billy now tried out his freshly gargled vocal cords with his best rendering of 'Nancy with the Laughing Face'. No use. He was still singing as a duet.

When he came out, his brother Les remarked, 'You know how we've said you sound like Sinatra? Well now you sound like Flanagan and Allen, both of them together.' Les could always be relied on for the encouraging remark.

Something very peculiar was happening to his vocal output. There was only one thing for it, *The Home Doctor*, the fourth volume in a Book Club series entitled 'The Home Expert' which Mam had bought in instalments through *John Bull* magazine. The other titles were *The Home Entertainer, The Home Handyman, The Home Gardener*. These were missing from the Hopkins collection as Mam had decided to discontinue payment mainly because, as a family, they did so little entertaining,

Dad was a useless and expensive handyman, and since they lived in a flat on the top floor, they were lacking a garden.

Titch had once borrowed *The Home Doctor* and returned it in a fit of depression when he had become convinced that he had every disease in the book from Achilles tendon and acne to xerophthalmia and xerosis. He had concluded that he'd been suffering from encephalitis lethargica since childhood.

The Home Doctor covered double vision all right and Billy noted the term for it was diplopia but there was nothing on double voice and unintended key changes. He turned to sore throat – even though his throat was not sore. He read out loud:

> May be result of excessive smoking or talking or may be part of body's early warning system that the throat is being invaded by germs. Antiseptic gargles are usually enough to combat the infection. The throat never becomes sore by itself – something makes it sore and that something could be something danger- ous. If the soreness does not clear up after two or three days, despite gargling, consult a doctor.

'What did I tell you,' said Mam. 'Too much smoking and too much talking.'

'Suppose you're right as usual, Mam,' he said. 'But I don't have a sore throat.'

He consulted the learned tome once again and then he found it. Aphonia. He read on: 'Loss of the voice or of the ability to speak normally, though may be possible to speak in whispers. May result from excessive use of voice or may be caused by paralysis of the vocal cords. Sometimes occurs also as a symptom of Hysterical Reaction.'

'That doesn't sound like you,' she said. 'I've never known you to go historical.'

'I'm sure my class at school would agree with you. Listen to this.' He continued reading: 'Another cause of aphonia is cancer of the larynx or voice box. Removal of the larynx (laryngectomy) may be necessary. Techniques have been developed to retrain people so that they can learn to speak again after such an operation using what is called oesophagal speech.'

'Glory be to God,' she said. 'Let's hope it isn't that, our Billy. Never trouble trouble until trouble troubles you, is what I always say. The best thing you can do is cut down on the cigarettes, try not to do so much talking, and go on with the gargling.'

'Yes, doctor,' he said.

Next day, he cut his fags from ten a day to five. At school, he avoided as far as possible using his voice and when he had to speak, did so in a whisper to avoid strain. This meant organising his teaching so that his classes were required to do an inordinate amount of written work, which didn't please his wards too well.

'I think I'm getting writer's cramp,' remarked Sammy McGrath.

'And my pointing finger is half an inch shorter,' added Vito Clarke.

'Don't you morons understand?' snapped Lily Malone. 'Mr Hopkins needs to rest his voice.'

'OK, OK,' answered Sammy. 'Keep your hair on. We know you have a crush on him.'

'I do not,' she snapped back. 'You lot are so thick, you can't see that he might lose his voice completely if he's not careful.'

433

In the staffroom, his colleagues remarked on his condition.

'From what I've heard,' sneered Grundy, 'you try too hard in class declaiming and over-dramatising things. This is a school, not a theatre. We're teachers not actors. A little more discipline and you wouldn't have to use your voice so much. You should sit on 'em and keep 'em quiet. Then you wouldn't have to rest your voice so much.'

'I wish one or two people round here would imitate Hoppy and give their voices a rest too,' barked Liz, her eyes flashing. 'Speech is silver but silence is golden.'

'And more people have repented speech than silence,' added Alex Callaghan.

'And some wit said that speech was given to man to disguise his thoughts,' said Greg, determined not to be left out of the sententious discussion.

'It's not as bad as that,' replied Billy quietly. 'I'm just trying to give my vocal cords a chance to recover without recourse to the medical profession. If nothing can be done for me, I can always look for another job where vocal gymnastics are an asset.'

'What about a job in a circus as a freak in a side show or perhaps you could join a choir? There can't be many singers who can achieve five octaves,' Greg guffawed.

'And virtually none who can sing both melody and descant at the same time,' added Alex.

'Demand for *castrati* dried up some time ago because of its illegality and cruelty,' said Liz Logie, not to be outdone in the facetious comments stakes, 'but maybe there's still some opportunities for counter-tenors especially as the music of Henry Purcell is becoming popular.'

Laura approached Billy, concern written over her face. 'I do hope it doesn't turn out to be anything serious,' she said. 'I'll get my class to say a prayer that it isn't. And old Aunty, who is a great fan of yours, says she is offering prayers to St Blaise, patron saint of sore throats.'

Billy was deeply moved when he heard this. What a first-class idiot I've been, he thought, to let this wonderful, gentle person get away. 'Thanks,' he said. 'No need to worry. The only ailment I don't have is hypochondria.'

She laughed. 'That's what I've always loved . . . liked . . . about you, Billy, your eternal optimism and your ability to laugh your cares away.'

'I don't believe in meeting trouble halfway,' he said. 'As for its being serious, I try not to think about it. We can make ourselves ill thinking we are ill and the imagination can run riot. Imagined fears are usually worse than reality. Incidentally, did I hear you say a moment ago "that's what I love about you . . ."?'

'I meant "like",' she said blushing. 'That's supposed to be over and done with. We're different social classes, remember.'

'I haven't forgotten,' said Billy ruefully. 'But you used "love" for "like". Your Freudian slip is showing.'

This slight indisposition of mine, Billy thought, is paying dividends. For one thing, there was the attention he was attracting and he'd definitely won the sympathy vote in the staffroom. But now here was the best prize of all, the possibility, faint though it was, that Laura might be coming back to him. Maybe she was willing to forgive him.

Three days passed and the throat trouble had not gone away. Reluctantly, Billy concluded it was time to seek medical advice. On Thursday evening, he called on Dr Reuben Glass, his local GP.

'What can I do for you?' the doctor asked, looking over

his bifocals. Glass had a face that was screwed up into a permanent grimace, a feature no doubt acquired over the years by dint of sharing and sympathising with the pain of so many patients. Billy described his symptoms to him.

'For some odd reason, my voice has begun modulating between basso profundo and coloratura soprano,' answered Billy. 'It's completely unintended and I'm at a loss to explain it.'

'Have you had any throat trouble before?' he asked.

'Not really but when I get a cold, it always seems to go to my throat in the form of tonsillitis.'

Glass placed a spatula on his tongue and a small mirror to the back of his throat. He looked down into the dark depths.

'Can't see anything. Tonsils seem OK. No sign of any inflammation. Do you have any pain or discomfort?'

'None.'

'Do you smoke heavily – I mean, you're not a forty-a-day man, I hope.'

'Nowhere near that many,' said Billy. 'With my salary, I can hardly afford five.'

'Any difficulty in swallowing?'

'None except when I have tonsillitis.'

'Do you sing a lot? Are you a member of a choir, for example?'

'The answer again is in the negative. I sing in the bathroom but my family would say the word "sing" is an exaggeration.'

'There's most likely nothing to be concerned about,' he said. 'Your trouble is probably due to overstraining your voice in the classroom.'

Billy didn't like the sound of that vague word 'probably'. What did it mean? Good grounds for belief? A good chance

436

that there was nothing to be concerned about? Not definitely. Not sure.

.'What about laryngitis or pharyngitis or tonsillitis?' said Billy. I'm being unfair on this doctor, he thought. After all, although he has completed a long course of medical training, he most likely has not studied *The Home Doctor* as I did last night. I hope my suggestions are of some help to him.

'The absence of inflammation leads me to believe otherwise,' said Glass.

'You don't think it's something serious?' asked Billy. 'Like cancer of the larynx?' There, the C word was out.

'I do not think anything of the sort,' replied Glass, giving his grimace an extra tweak. 'Go back to school but avoid overtaxing your voice if you can. Meanwhile, I'll make an appointment for you with a throat specialist at the Ear, Nose, and Throat hospital. There's a good man there – Mr Levy. He has an international reputation and has published many learned papers in *The Lancet*. He'll run a few tests on you.'

Good man at the ENT, learned papers in *The Lancet*? Run a few tests? To Billy, it sounded like the death knell. Do not ask for whom the bell tolls . . .

'What kind of tests?' he asked nervously.

'Don't get alarmed. A few tests a little more elaborate than I can run. It's nothing.'

'If it's nothing, why do I have to go to the ENT hospital?'

'Stop worrying. I want to rule out one or two items, that's all.'

'Like what?'

'Look, it's nothing. Trust me, I'm a doctor.'

Billy reported back to Mam. 'If they take away my voice

437

box. That's it. I'm going to be struck dumb. I don't know what I'll do,' he said.

'But they didn't say they were going to take away your voice box,' Mam said.

'Obviously they're not going to come straight out with it. Nervous types would go to pieces.'

'Not like you. Anyway, I keep telling you, there's nowt wrong with you.'

'If there's nowt wrong with me, why do I have to see a specialist?'

'Look, they want to be sure it's not . . .' she hesitated.

'Cancer,' he said.

'You said it, not me,' she replied.

'I don't mind *saying* it,' he replied, 'because it's my birth sign. I just don't want to *get* it, that's all.'

'I don't know what you're going on about, you don't have any of the symptoms.'

'I have *all* the symptoms – it's a textbook case of a throat tumour.'

At school, Billy continued to keep up the hail-fellow-well-met front in the classroom and in the staffroom.

'I think you're simply amazing,' said Laura at the end of the day. 'The way you keep joking and laughing care away. Everyone on the staff thinks so too. If I were in your shoes, I'd be scared out of my wits.'

'No point in worrying about something that hasn't happened,' Billy lied. 'I once saw a prayer in Chester Cathedral. It went:

> *Give me a sense of humour, Lord,*
> *Give me the grace to see a joke,*
> *To get some happiness from life*
> *And pass it on to other folk.*

438

That sums up my philosophy of life.'

' "Give me the grace to see a joke" – I like that. You should make it your family motto.'

'I believe in looking on the bright side. I'm inclined to hope rather than fear.'

'I agree with you about that, Billy,' she said. 'It's always best to hope. And I know you're not worried about the strange things happening to your voice but, well, Hamish is coming over to meet Jenny. He did three years of medicine at Glasgow and so he might be able to reassure you. I'll ask him to come over after school.'

'That'd be great,' said Billy. He hoped his lack of enthusiasm for the idea didn't show through. Hamish was the last person in the world he would have chosen to talk things over with.

At Laura's request, Hamish was waiting at the school gate.

'Hamish, I wonder if you could give Billy here the benefit of your medical knowledge,' she said.

Hamish glowered at Billy. 'I'm surprised that you should approach me of all people for medical advice,' he said bluntly. 'I'd like to make it clear that I'm doing this at the request of Laura and for no other reason.'

'And I'm listening to you for exactly the same reason,' Billy said quickly. 'Personally, I'd rather have consulted Dr Crippen.'

'That's it,' Hamish exploded. 'You'll no' get a free medical consultation from me.'

'Wait a minute, you two,' Laura said. 'This could be a serious matter. Don't let personal considerations stop us from using our brains. This throat trouble could be nothing but then again it could turn out to be life-threatening. So for all our sakes, calm down both of you and act sensibly.'

439

'OK,' Billy said. 'I'll take it easy though I don't think my throat merits this attention.'

'I'll see if I can be of any assistance,' Hamish said peevishly, sniffing at his nasal spray, 'though I canna help thinking you'd be best consulting a specialist.'

'My GP has arranged for me to see a Mr Levy at the ENT but it may take a little time.'

'I've heard of Levy,' Hamish said. 'He has worldwide standing so you'll be in good hands. Anyway, let's hear your symptoms and I'll offer my opinion.'

This reference once again to Levy's international repute, far from reassuring Billy, worried him even more. Why did he need to see such a celebrated specialist? He briefly explained his condition to Hamish.

'So what do you think?' Billy asked when he had finished describing his strange vocal experiences.

'Could be an inherited weakness or disposition,' suggested Hamish. 'Or it could be due to heavy smoking or overstraining your vocal cords.'

Billy nodded. 'I know that. But that's not so bad, right?'

'I suppose the dark side of the picture could be a malignant tumour on the larynx,' Hamish said gravely.

'Oh, really, you don't say,' replied Billy calmly though his heart was fluttering wildly. 'But I've felt no pain whatsoever.'

'Doesn't matter,' said Hamish cheerfully. 'Tumours can grow slowly and the sufferer may scarcely notice anything at first.'

'Sounds awful,' said Laura. 'I'm sure Billy doesn't have anything like that.'

'So what's the treatment,' Billy asked, 'for a malignant tumour?'

'Radiotherapy or even removal of the larynx, that is a

laryngectomy,' Hamish replied in sepulchral tones 'But sufferers can usually be taught to speak using the oesophagus. I believe there are approximately two thousand cases in Britain each year.'

'What about benign tumours? I suppose they are more common,' said Laura hopefully.

'Afraid not,' said Hamish. 'Oddly enough, benign cases are less common.'

'It's a good thing you're not the panicky type,' Laura said.

'That's right,' said Billy. 'Always look on the bright side, that's me. Anyway, Hamish, thanks for your help and advice.' Billy cycled off.

'Anytime,' Hamish called, smiling sinisterly.

Chapter Thirty-Eight

The Lionised Levy

Several weeks later, Billy was summoned to meet the illustrious Mr Levy at the ENT hospital in All Saints, Manchester. He presented himself bright and early at the reception desk where a pretty young lady wrote down his details – name, address, occupation, name of GP, next of kin, and finally his religion.

'My religion?' he asked. 'Why do you need to know this?'

'In case we have to inform your next of kin of any developments or summon a minister in case of emergency.'

This definitely sounded ominous.

'If you'd go through into the waiting room,' she said, 'the nurse will call you soon.'

Billy went through the swing doors and found a room crowded with pale, sick-looking, hollow-eyed people, all wearing the same rainbow-coloured bathrobes. It resembled the scene from a concentration camp after the Allied forces had liberated it. He sat down on one of the hard wooden benches and looked around at some of the terrible cases which had congregated in this depressing, ramshackle waiting room. All looked in far worse shape than he did and he felt he was something of an impostor being there. Here was a man with a huge mastoiditis; there was another with an unbelievably large swelling of the nose. What was he, Billy, doing here amongst these sick people? There was nothing wrong with him except a newly acquired ability to speak and sing in five octaves.

Poor devils, thought Billy. They're obviously in-patients who've been brought down from the wards for examinations, clinical tests, X-rays, and the like. Since they live here in the hospital, time is not so important to them and I suppose a trip down to the test centre injects a little excitement into the dull hospital routine. That nice-looking receptionist seemed pretty impressed that I was a teacher, though. Probably doesn't see too many healthy specimens in here. No doubt she'll realise I don't have as much time to spare as these other patients. I wouldn't be surprised if I didn't get priority.

He picked up a tattered copy of *London Illustrated* and began reading about the Jarrow marchers. He hadn't read far when there appeared a formidable giant of a nurse in full regalia complete with an assortment of badges and a blue belt (was it for judo?). Her starched uniform squeaked as she walked.

'William Hopkins,' she announced in a Lady Bracknell voice.

I was right, Billy thought. They can see that I'm a professional and I'm to be given a speedy processing through the system.

'Kindly follow me,' the nurse ordered. 'Now go into the changing room and put this on.'

It was a rainbow bathrobe.

'But it's my voice that's to be examined. Why do I need to put this on?'

443

'Kindly do as you are told,' she commanded, 'or the doctor will not see you.'

Billy obeyed the instruction, hung up his clothes, and joined the others in the waiting room. Was it his imagination or were they smiling at him in quiet satisfaction? Now he, too, looked like a concentration camp victim. Two hours later, after Billy had finished reading in the *Daily Telegraph* the full account of Chamberlain's successful negotiation ('Peace for our time') with Hitler at Munich in 1938, the same terrifying nurse appeared, announced his name, and signalled him to go into Levy's surgery.

Mr Levy turned out to be a small man with a funeral director's face set in the fixed smile of one who delivers a mixture of good news and bad news. He was dressed in a black coat and pinstriped trousers and he wore a carnation in his lapel. He could have come straight from a wedding reception – or a funeral – except that growing from his forehead there appeared to be a contraption that looked like a miniature miner's lamp or an alien's antenna.

Billy gave him the rundown on his condition, feeling that through repetitive practice the account was acquiring a certain fluency and piquancy.

'Uh-huh,' Levy said. He was obviously a man of few words. 'Let's take a look and see what we've got. Open your mouth wide.'

Taking a small linen napkin, he took a vice-like grip on Billy's tongue and yanked it out. Up to that time, Billy had never realised that his tongue was made of elastic; it now came out at least a foot like a piece of bubble gum. Levy put a small mirror to the back of Billy's throat and gazed down into the interior with his miner's lamp.

'Uh-huh,' he said triumphantly. 'Curious. Curious. Most interesting.' He released Billy's tongue which recoiled into place with a twang.

'Is it bad, doctor?' Billy asked anxiously.

Levy ignored him and picked up his phone and spoke into it. 'Max, could you come over here? There's an interesting case you should see.' He continued to gaze at Billy as an interesting specimen as if he had found a new species of insect. Perhaps he saw a Nobel prize there.

His colleague, Max Gluckman, a tall thin man in the same civil service dress, appeared within a couple of minutes. As a team, Levy and he could have appeared in the music halls, like Flotsam and Jetsam or the Western Brothers.

'What have we got, Sam?' Max asked.

'A larynx. See for yourself, Max. Take a look.'

Taking Billy's tongue, Max demonstrated that its length was not a foot but a foot and a half. He peered into the depths with his brow lamp.

'Ah-hah,' he said. 'Most interesting. Most interesting.'

'Thought you'd like it, Max,' smiled Sam Levy.

'What is it, for God's sake?' cried Billy, alarmed by their ah-hahs and uh-huhs and their use of words like 'curious' and 'interesting', yet at the same time secretly pleased that he had caused such interest and excitement for these two distinguished gentlemen. Maybe he'd get his name in *The Lancet*.

The two practitioners turned to look at Billy, surprised that their larynx had uttered words. Body organs on the dissecting table were not supposed to speak or ask questions. Larynxes were not normally attached to brains.

'We have detected several small curious growths on your

445

larynx,' Levy said. 'They need investigating.'

Billy's heart leapt. Were these two gentlemen giving him the black spot? God, he was only twenty years of age. Not a very long life.

'Why was my voice jumping around the octaves?'

'The best analogy I can think of,' answered Max Gluckman, 'is that of a musician playing a violin with several knots in the strings.'

'Can you come back this afternoon and we'll take a small sample for a biopsy?' said Levy. 'It will mean a local anaesthetic only. Meantime, don't worry. You may find that the growths are benign. The growths may be papillomas or polyps, harmless and easily removed without ill effects.'

'And the likelihood of cancer?' Billy asked with trembling voice.

'Remote,' said Gluckman immediately. 'Most cases are nearly always in heavy smokers. How many cigarettes do you smoke, by the way?'

'Used to smoke ten a day but am now down to five.'

'I wouldn't describe that as heavy smoking. Thirty a day and upwards I would define as heavy.'

'Is it true that benign tumours are not common?'

'They're fairly common. But my colleague and I were surprised to find them on your larynx. They're more commonly found in the nose. And we usually find benign growths in people like singers who misuse their vocal cords. It's a good thing that you have come to see us so early so we can check any development. Anyway, let's take this one step at a time. We won't make any decisions until we have all the data in front of us.'

'How soon will I know?' Billy asked.

'We shall take a small snick out of your larynx this

446

afternoon and send it to the pathological department of the university for examination. It's not painful and it won't take long. We should have the result in a couple of days. Meantime, you can go back to school and go on as usual.'

Go on as usual! Billy thought. Some hope! Everyone was sure he was laughing boy who never worried about anything. How little they knew him. OK, take it easy, he said to himself. Nobody said you had cancer. They found a few little growths on your larynx. So what? Could be nothing. Stay cool – no need for panic.

He decided not to go home at dinnertime. No sense in worrying his mam and dad. He went for a light lunch in Woolworth's cafeteria but he had no appetite and his toad-in-the-hole was left uneaten.

He tried to suppress any thoughts of malignancies. The idea of being struck dumb was too awful to contemplate. He'd rather die than spend the rest of his life voiceless and unable to communicate except by sign language. He put such notions out of his mind. Best to wait for the results of the biopsy – to put everything on hold until he knew something definite. He'd get by – he'd always got by. After all, he was young and healthy. Then there was the beautiful Laura. He knew that he was in love with her but if the news turned out to be bad, he'd abandon all hopes of winning her back.

It was good news that Levy had fixed up a test so soon, it would avoid a long and painful wait to know his fate – only two days. At the same time though, the fact that Levy was willing to set up a biopsy test so soon must mean that he was concerned. But it was so difficult to get straight answers from these physicians. 'Probably' was the word they were fond of using, or the phrase 'the chances are'. Well, what else could they say? They could only use indefinite verbs like 'may' or 'might' until they had some definite evidence in front of them.

He walked round the streets of the city centre – Oxford Road, Portland Street, Market Street, Cross Street, Deansgate, King Street – until it was time to return to the ENT.

The afternoon session was quick and simple. A local anaesthetic, Levy took a small sample, and that was it. No pain. No problem.

'Let's see,' Levy said. 'Today is Thursday. We should have the result on Monday afternoon. Come back around three o'clock.'

'Let's hope it's good news,' said Billy.

'I hope so too,' said Levy. 'And I must say how much I admire the calm way you have taken it all.'

With that, Billy was on his way home. It had taken forty-five minutes. Now the time of waiting began.

Billy sat on the 62 bus, to all appearances calm and composed. But within his brain a storm raged and a hundred voices called out the word CANCER! His mind was in a turmoil and as the bus crawled up Cheetham Hill Road, he thought he was going to keel over. The world about him was functioning normally and people were going about their normal business unaware, indifferent and uncaring that he was faced with the prospect of losing his voice and his speech. It was unthinkable. Everyone believed he was always cool and collected, little realising the inner fears he often experienced, like when he'd had to face the top class at St Anselm's. Inside he had been sick with dread and apprehension but to the outside world he had presented a picture of tranquillity and serenity.

He reached home at last and entered the flat quietly.

'Well, what happened at the hospital, Billy?' Mam asked anxiously.

'Nothing to worry about,' he fibbed. 'Clean bill of health.'

'Thank the Lord,' she sighed. 'My prayers have been answered.'

'I don't pray much,' said Dad, 'but this time even I said one for you.'

Billy closed his eyes to hide the tears that sprang up when he heard these words. There was no point in making them suffer with him. They'd know soon enough the result of the biopsy.

He retired early to bed that night. He usually turned in around eleven o'clock but tonight he made it ten. As he lay there in the darkness, he was oppressed by the thoughts he'd kept at bay during the daylight hours. He wanted to cry out: 'Everyone sees me as a joking, laughing, care-free individual but I'm nothing of the sort. I'm really a frightened little boy and I'm scared out of my wits at the idea of losing my voice for good. They're carrying out a biopsy to confirm what they already know. I've got cancer of the larynx.'

He gulped hard. Was it his imagination or was there a hint of pain as the saliva slid past his epiglottis? He could feel the tumours on his voice box. He knew now that he had cancer. He'd be speechless and voiceless and he didn't want to go on living. What would be the point?

'Look, God, I'll strike a bargain with you. Take away – something I've got two of . . . No, not those, I might need *them* some day . . . I was thinking more of an eye or an arm but please, not my voice. I don't want a laryngectomy. I'd rather die.'

The hours of darkness passed slowly and not for one second did he sleep or banish the dread which overwhelmed him.

The next day, he went into school as usual and kept up the pretence that everything was normal, and in the staffroom he indulged in the usual good-natured banter. No one suspected the dreadful turbulence which raged within. He listened to the 'Doctor, doctor' jokes of Greg and laughed with the rest but not for a moment did he forget the awful predicament into which destiny had thrust him.

'You've not been eating these last few days,' Mam said. 'Is there something worrying you?'

'Nothing, I tell you,' he replied exasperated. 'I'm not hungry.'

For the next four nights, he did not sleep. He looked pale and sallow, his face drawn.

'Something *is* troubling you,' Mam said. 'I know you well enough to see that you've got something on your mind.'

In the quiet of the small hours, he could see himself in the ENT hospital. Levy was bending over him in the operating theatre. 'Sorry, but we've had to remove your larynx,' he was saying. 'But don't worry, we'll teach you to speak using your throat muscles.'

Then he was in the ward after the operation and patients in the other beds were pointing him out to their visitors. 'See that poor lad over there? Used to be a teacher till they cut out his larynx.'

He saw himself straining to speak but only able to

produce inarticulate guttural noises. No, he'd rather be dead than go through that.

But time and the hour ran through Billy's roughest day.

Chapter Thirty-Nine

Crunch Time

On Monday afternoon, he caught the bus to All Saints and presented himself to the receptionist at the ENT shortly before three o'clock. He hadn't long to wait.

Mr Levy came out to greet him. 'Please come this way, Mr Hopkins.'

They say that a prisoner in court can tell the verdict by studying the jury's faces. If that were true, it was a foregone conclusion because Levy looked serious and sad. He gazed at Billy for what seemed to be an interminably long time and then he smiled broadly.

'Good news. No trace of cancer – you're in the clear. The tumours are polyps which we can remove with a simple operation. Congratulations. I hope you've not been too worried over the weekend.'

Billy stared at him incredulously. Slowly the news sank in to the core of his being and a great wave of elation passed over him. Pure, unadulterated joy!

'Thank you so much, Mr Levy, for all you've done,' he said ecstatically. 'What happens now?'

'You come in next week for a small op, we remove the little growths and you will have your normal voice restored to you. Who knows, maybe an even better voice. It means a week as an in-patient.'

A week later, Billy found himself in a bed between the mastoiditis and the incandescent nose.

'We three are hospital symbols,' he joked to his two fellow patients. 'You're the ear, you're the nose and I'm the throat.'

Next day, he was wheeled into the operating theatre. As the anaesthetist injected his stuff, Billy said, 'Whilst you're at it, how about giving me a voice like Benjamino Gigli or, better still, Frank Sinatra?'

'We'll see what we can do,' he laughed. And that was the last Billy heard that afternoon.

He awoke around six o'clock and tested the result. 'The day war broke out,' he began with his brilliant imitation of Rob Wilton.

A nurse came running over. 'Good news and bad news,' she said. 'Good, you must take a week off work. Bad, you are not permitted to speak,' she said. 'You must rest your voice for at least a week.'

In the afternoon, Mam appeared at his bedside.

'So you're not allowed to talk,' she said. 'For a change, you'll have to lie back and listen.'

He nodded his assent. 'It's not as bad as that. I can talk a little but I have to conserve my voice for a while until it gets stronger.'

'Right. I can do the talking for a change. I think your father was wrong about that girl Laura.'

'Then why did you agree with Dad when he was going on about how we were working class and Laura was middle class?'

'I've found it's always best to keep the peace. It doesn't

mean I don't have my own opinion. We used to have a saying in Collyhurst: When a woman's convinced against her will, she'll have the same opinion still.'

'So you think Laura's the right girl?'

'She's a lovely girl with a lovely personality. If you think you've found Miss Right, you must not give her up, no matter what anyone says.'

'What about Dad? I don't think he'll accept it somehow.'

'You leave his lordship to me. I'll make him see sense. He's always against anything new at first but he comes round in the end. Remember how awkward he was about you going to college. He bought you a watch – no, two watches – at the finish.'

'I hope you manage to talk him out of that daft idea of the classes not mixing. I know Laura's the only girl for me, and his notion about her being upper and me being lower seems like a lot of hooey. The only problem is money and the lack of it. We can't get far without it.'

'If you're short of money, I have a bob or two put aside and it's yours for the asking. It's only sitting there in the Co-op Bank. I'd much rather it was out helping you and doing some good. We'll see you don't go short.'

'I'll remember that, Mam, if Laura and I get back together.' Billy was close to tears; he knew that her 'bob or two' had been accumulated by scrimping and scraping over forty years of marriage.

When Mam had gone, he lay there thinking deeply about his life and the direction it was taking. Somehow life without Laura did not seem worth living.

Later that same day, Laura came to see him.

'Laura, can you ever forgive me for my stupidity?' he said.

'Billy, oh, Billy, don't you know me at all? I've been

454

worried out of my mind about you. I do love you, Billy, no matter what.'

'Even if I'd lost my voice?' he said quietly.

'I said no matter what. I'd even give up the Bechstein piano and the Pye Black Box for you. There, now, that's saying something.'

'But what about the telephone and the grapes on the sideboard?' he joked.

'Those too,' she laughed. 'I've brought you the grapes from the sideboard as nobody in our house is ill.'

'Lying here in the hospital,' he whispered, 'you get to thinking about things, about your priorities, about what really matters.'

'I've never wavered for a moment, Billy.'

'Trust the middle classes to recognise a bargain when they see one,' he jested.

'Rest your voice and listen,' she said decisively. 'I don't want to hear that rubbish again about social classes and that they don't mix. When you get up out of this bed, I think we should tell everyone that we're walking out, that we're courting, or whichever way you want to put it.'

'You mean announce our engagement?'

'I mean exactly that and blow the consequences.'

'What about your father and honours degrees and so on?'

'You're getting engaged to me, not my father,' she said. Her determination impressed him. 'Besides, he's already married.'

Laura talked until the visiting bell rang.

'I have to go now, Billy,' she said. 'When we were apart, I wrote out this poem by Elizabeth Barrett Browning. Read it and think about it. It says more beautifully what I feel than I could ever say it.' She embraced him, kissed him on the lips and was gone.

A little later when the ward had settled down and all was quiet, he turned to the poem.

> *If thou must love me, let it be for naught . . .*
> *But love me for love's sake, that evermore*
> *Thou mayst love on, through love's eternity.*

For the first time since a child, Billy wept for his own stupidity and the thought that he might have lost Laura, had it not been for her sound common sense.

On her next visit, Billy apologised for his puerile behaviour and the shame he had felt for his own background.

'I felt,' he said, 'that I wasn't good enough for you. I've put you on a pedestal and I worship you. You are the princess in an Andersen fairy tale, the heroine in a tale of chivalry, the beautiful maiden in a Lehar musical.'

'I don't like being on a pedestal,' she said. 'It's cold and lonely there.'

'I was so naïve. I shudder to think that I almost lost you. You left me the Browning poem and I found it most moving. Now I return the compliment with my own choice – a poem from *Love's Philosophy* by Shelley.'

Laura read the poem quietly to herself. She stopped at a particular point.

'I love this part,' she murmured, tears sparkling in her eyes. 'I shall treasure it as long as I live. Let me read it so that only you can hear.

> *The fountains mingle with the river*
> *And the rivers with the Ocean*

The winds of Heaven mix forever
With a sweet emotion.
Nothing in the world is single
All things by a law divine
In one spirit meet and mingle
Why not I with thine?'

Every day, Laura went to see him after school to give him the latest happenings and the latest gossip in the staffroom. How Grundy had blown his top when Greg had provoked him by drinking from his cup and sitting in his chair. And every day they planned their future and their love grew stronger.

'When they let me out of hospital,' he said, 'we'll go, you and I, to Saqui and Lawrence in St Ann's Square and choose an engagement ring. We'll tell the world that we're betrothed.'

He had been condemned to be something of a Trappist monk for seven days – an impossible requirement for Billy. No teaching. No school. No talking. Heaven and hell at the same time.

'I suppose,' he managed to add, 'the correct protocol demands that I go and ask your father's approval and he will give me the third degree as to my income and my prospects etcetera.'

'Why not, if it makes you both happy, but I'm sure it's not necessary,' she said.

'One other thing,' he said. 'My old college is having a reunion in London at half term. Do you think he'd let you accompany me to London?'

'You mean for one of those weekends?' she said in feigned coyness. 'If you have designs on me, Mr Hopkins, for that you will definitely have to ask his permission.'

457

'No, I do not mean one of those weekends. Everything will be above board. Have you ever been to London, Laura?'

'Never.'

'Then I want to be the first one to take you on a tour of the capital. We could book one or two shows and get a taste of the high life.'

'Sounds exciting. We'll ask Daddy's permission but we'll go no matter what. We're both nearly twenty-one.'

After his release from hospital, he returned home and continued the period of enforced taciturnity. He managed to get through the period and he suspected that Mam thoroughly enjoyed the respite and a rest from his endless school anecdotes, his moaning about what a rotten day he'd had, his analysis of current events, and his jokes. She was able to tell him what she really thought and he was unable to reply as fully as he'd have liked. However, he was building up a great reservoir of observations and when his day of release came, the words came pouring out like a dam which had burst its banks. He talked non-stop – mainly rubbish – and although he didn't have a Sinatra or a Gigli voice, the resonance and the timbre had returned. He was back in business.

He felt as if he had discovered the perfect ailment – no pain, a minor op, lots of sympathy, and a week off work thrown in. Further, Laura had visited him every day in hospital and there was no mistaking the look of sheer, unbridled happiness that she manifested when she knew he was not to lose his voice.

There was a corollary. Levy maintained that the polyps were the result of voice strain and misuse of the vocal cords. He recommended two courses. First, lessons in voice training and singing, and secondly, a course of speech therapy.

The first part involved going to Laura's mother for an intensive course of singing lessons. In the Mackenzie drawing room, he went through Benché exercises and learned to sing the part of Mozart's Sarastro. First he tackled 'O Isis and Osiris' and 'within these sacred portals' from *The Magic Flute* and as a party piece 'The Hippopotamus Song' which had been made famous by Flanders and Swan. This part of the course was successful in that it introduced him not only to singing but later to the wonderful world of choral music when he joined the Holy Name Choir and met Denis Glynn, the conductor, who was something of a musical genius, utterly devoted to his field. The Holy Name Choir opened doors to a magical world of polyphony. Polyps to polyphony, thought Billy. He came to know the music of Tallis, Palestrina, Lassus, Vittoria, Britten, and, best of all, William Byrd. Choral music became one of the most important aspects of his life.

So, the first part of training recommended by Levy worked. The second, speech therapy, was not so successful.

Billy was sent to the Wythenshawe hospital and was directed to the special voice training unit where he found the therapist waiting. She was about twenty years of age, dark-haired, big blue eyes, gleaming white teeth, and she had the most beautiful reassuring smile. She looked like Ava Gardner.

'Good morning, Mr Hopkins,' she purred. 'Do sit down and make yourself comfortable. It's my job during these sessions to teach you how to project your voice without putting strain on the larynx. Most important, you must learn how to relax. First your whole body and then your throat and finally your larynx.'

Billy crossed his legs and began tracing a complicated geometrical pattern with his right foot. As she spoke, she surreptitiously watched his foot and began taking furious notes. Billy surreptitiously watched her surreptitiously watching his foot. He stopped the foot fidget and began stroking imaginary dirt from the back of his hand. She took more notes. Forcing Billy to relax was going to be uphill work.

'Look,' she said, 'I think the best way of getting you to relax is to provide a quiet, calm atmosphere. Take off your shoes and lie on the couch.'

Billy did as he was told.

She drew the curtains and, in the half-light, she looked even more attractive. She put on a record of Mendelsohnn's Hebridean Overture, *Fingal's Cave*, and began reading poetry about the sea and about how she must go down to it again, to the lonely sea and the sky . . .

The more she read, the more tense Billy became until he was as taut as a bar of steel.

She lifted his right arm to check the level of relaxation achieved. It stayed rigid in mid-air.

'It's no use,' she said. 'It's not working. I think we had better try again on another day.'

She was right. It wasn't working. She little guessed the reason. Billy had removed his shoes as instructed but he'd forgotten that in the right foot of his socks there was a big hole which he had intended bringing to Mam's attention some time. His big toe jutted out like the rock of Gibraltar.

Billy discontinued the speech therapy and concentrated instead on the Mozart arias.

Chapter Forty

Engagement

In the study of his home, Duncan Mackenzie sat in his favourite wing chair with a copy of the *Manchester Guardian*. He had lit his third cigarette of the evening – one more than he normally allowed himself at this time – and the newspaper remained unread on his knee.

In the drawing room, Billy Hopkins was being put through his musical paces by his wife Louise, and the strains of a Mozart aria rang through the house.

Duncan was lost in thought about his daughter Laura. It could not be said that he had a favourite child, though Laura, his firstborn, had a special place in his heart. But when did she grow up so quickly? It didn't seem that long ago since she'd looked up to him – he'd been her hero and whatever he'd said was accepted as Gospel truth. Came the day when she put on her first lipstick, had her first hair-do, and went out to her first dance. That was the beginning of the end. She'd brought home one or two callow youths with spots and weird hairstyles and they were no problem. It was a relief to see that she could attract boyfriends – it would have been more worrying if there'd been none, he'd have wondered what was wrong with her.

The years had flown by unnoticed and she'd grown from the leggy adolescent into the beautiful young lady she now was. For a number of years there had been an understanding with their good friends, the Dunwoodys, that their only son Hamish and Laura would make an ideal match. Hamish was a nice boy with tremendous career prospects even if something of a hypochondriac, but he'd grow out of that. He offered security and she'd never starve if she married him, that was for sure. But then she'd met this Billy Hopkins character at school – a good-looking boy, very polite and he'd certainly helped Hughie with his French, but he wasn't in the same league as Hamish when it came to earning power. This business with Billy had developed so quickly – it was only six months since the night of the musical evening when he'd sung that Al Jolson song. With hindsight, it had been pretty clear then that Laura had set her cap at him but he'd been blind to the obvious. There'd been something about her – she'd looked different somehow, her eyes brighter and aglow, as if lit up from the inside.

At the table, she'd been full of him. It was 'Billy said this' and 'Billy said that'. You'd think this Billy character was Solomon and Einstein rolled into one. It was then that he'd begun to realise that he, Duncan, had been relegated to second place whilst King Billy reigned on high.

He'd tried to put her off him but he'd had to play his cards carefully. Too much pressure would have driven her straight into Billy's arms. No, he'd had to be more subtle about it. A little nod in the right direction, a word in the right ear, and he was sure that Laura would come to her senses and see which side her bread was buttered. Then what he'd hoped for came about.

She'd come home broken-hearted from one of her dates with the new monarch, and there'd been nothing he or

Louise could do to console her. Inwardly he'd rejoiced that common sense had triumphed in the end. Sure, Laura was upset but she'd get over it eventually. But when her sorrow turned to melancholy, and seemed to get deeper, they became concerned. And now they were back together again.

Tonight, things had come to a head. She'd broken the news to him in such an offhand way. He'd come home as usual and sat down at the table. Jenny was late and he'd inquired about her whereabouts.

'She's out on a date with Hamish,' Louise had said.

'She should be here at the table with the rest of my bairns,' he'd said. An innocent enough remark, he thought. But Laura had reacted strangely with a sudden furious outburst. The conversation was indelibly printed on his mind.

'We're no longer bairns, Daddy,' she'd snapped. 'Jenny's nineteen now and old enough even to be married.'

'Nonsense!' he'd said reasonably. 'Nineteen's much too young. Why, I didna marry your mother until I was twenty-six.'

'That was in the Dark Ages,' she'd said. 'Besides, Mammy was only twenty from what I've been told.'

'Then it was different,' Duncan said, but a little less sure of himself.

'Billy said that young marriages have a lot to recommend them. A young husband has a great incentive to work hard and improve himself. Besides, babies are better looked after if the parents are young and healthy.' She had a reply for everything.

'And does this Billy say who's going to support these adolescent marriages?' he'd countered. He thought that was a pretty shrewd remark.

463

'Anyway,' Laura continued. 'Billy and I want to talk to you tonight after his singing lesson.'

'You're no' thinkin' of marrying this pauper?' he said.

'We've talked about it.'

'And exactly when are you hoping to get married?' Louise had asked anxiously.

'We've not decided,' she'd answered. 'That's what we want to talk to you about. We need to give it some thought. It's up to Billy.'

For Duncan that was the last straw! It's up to Billy! The very idea! He blew his top.

'I hope this wonderful Billy of yours doesna think he can keep running to me for money whenever he's short of funds. If he does, he can think again.'

'Look, Daddy,' she'd retorted, 'there's no need to get hot under the collar or play the outraged father. Billy and I are both adults and I'll tell you something. We've got our pride and would rather die than come begging to you for help. Not if we were homeless and starving in the gutter. We'd rather live in a shop doorway than come to you.'

And that had been that. Now he sat waiting for the music to stop and then they'd face the music together.

He heard Louise play the final chord of the aria. He lit a fourth cigarette. I must cut down on this smoking, he thought.

A few minutes later, Laura and Billy came into the room.

'You remember, Daddy, that Billy and I want to talk to you.'

As if he could forget.

'You make it sound mysterious,' Duncan lied, offering Billy one of his Three Castle cigarettes, 'but I have a shrewd idea what it's about.'

464

'Very well, Mr Mackenzie,' Billy said nervously, accepting the light that Duncan offered. 'There are two things we want to ask of you. I'll get straight to the point. First of all, Laura and I love each other very much and we'd like to announce our engagement. Before we do, we'd like your permission of course.'

'I guessed as much,' he said. 'How old are you Billy?'

'I shall be twenty-one next birthday.'

'I think you're both too young to be talking about engagement but I suppose it's useless my saying that. I dare say you'd go ahead with or without my permission.'

The couple said nothing but the expression on their faces gave him his answer.

'More important,' Duncan continued, 'supposing I were to give my permission, when did you have in mind for the wedding?'

'We hadn't got round to thinking that far ahead,' Laura answered quickly. 'But I suppose about two years or so. We'd need to save a fair sum of money.' She looked to Billy for approval. He nodded agreement.

'You never said a truer word,' Duncan said. 'You'll have an uphill job saving the money you're going to need to set up home. I reckon that a minimum of five hundred pounds is necessary nowadays before you can even think about marriage.'

On my salary, Billy thought, it would take forever to save that amount, and as Jimmy Durante says, 'I can't wait that long, I got only one change of clothing.'

'How much do you have at present in the bank, Billy?' he heard Duncan saying.

'Laura and I have opened a joint bank account, Mr Mackenzie, and we have almost fifty pounds saved,' Billy answered proudly.

465

Duncan looked aghast for a moment. Recovering his composure, he asked, 'What's your annual salary?'

'Three hundred and fifty pounds per year. Net I receive around twenty-two pounds per month.'

'Good God!' he exclaimed. 'How can you expect to marry on that? It's hardly enough for a vagrant to exist on, let alone a married couple.'

'We'll have my salary too, Daddy,' Laura chipped in. 'Together we should have about forty pounds a month.'

'And if you had a baby in your first year, as many young couples do,' Duncan argued, 'what then?'

'We'd manage somehow,' protested Laura.

'That seems like a vague answer to me. If you want to start married life in a house, you'll need a substantial down payment and a mortgage. Also furniture. I can't see you doing it on your limited funds.'

'We've worked it out, Mr Mackenzie,' said Billy enthusiastically. 'I could increase my hours at the Youth Centre, and Laura says she'll work at a Play Centre. So we should be able to save about twenty pounds per month, and in two years that would come to enough to make a start. As for furniture, there's always hire purchase.'

Duncan frowned and said, 'Shakespeare knew what he was talking about when he made Shylock say in *The Merchant of Venice*, "Neither a borrower nor a lender be; for loan oft loses both itself and friend".'

Billy didn't think it was the right time to tell him it was Polonius in *Hamlet* who'd uttered the immortal words to his son Laertes.

'Don't worry so, Daddy,' Laura said. 'I'm sure we'll get by.'

Duncan remained unconvinced. 'You said there were two things you wanted to discuss. What was the other one?'

Billy reddened. Laura followed suit.

'Next month I shall be going to London to attend a reunion at my old college in Chelsea,' Billy stuttered. 'I'd like your permission to take Laura with me.'

There was a long pause while Duncan took this in. He looked black. He gave a Beethoven-like scowl.

'You mean take my daughter to London and stay in the same hotel?' He had difficulty in phrasing the question. He managed to make 'London' sound like Sodom and Gomorrah.

'We'd have separate rooms of course,' Billy faltered. 'It's just that, well, Laura has never seen London and I'd like to be the first one to show it to her.'

'The first one to show it to her.' Witheringly. 'Would you now?' Duncan sneered. 'Yes, I'm sure you would. But isn't that courting temptation? I hope you don't have in mind violating my daughter. Jumping the gun, as it were.'

Billy's red face turned crimson. He has a funny way of putting it, he said to himself. 'I have the highest respect for your daughter, Mr Mackenzie. I'd not contemplate such a despicable act, and I resent your even suggesting it.'

'Daddy, I don't know how you can even hint at such a thing,' Laura exploded. 'Billy and I don't think about such things and won't until after we're married.'

No need to phrase it so strongly, Billy thought, but she was right about putting such ideas on ice until after the ceremony.

'I know human nature,' said Duncan. 'St Paul says somewhere, if you meet temptation, run a mile – or words to that effect. Going to London together, well, you're walking straight into it.'

Billy thought this might be an appropriate time to play the Scripture card he had prepared so carefully the night

467

before. He hoped he wasn't overdoing it. 'Doesn't the Bible say, "Blessed is the man that endureth temptation: for when he is tried, he shall receive the crown of life"?'

Laura raised her eyebrows and looked at Billy quizzically.

'Absolutely right,' said Duncan, 'provided he does endure it and does not give way to it.'

'You'll have to trust us,' said Billy.

Once again, Duncan seemed unpersuaded.

As Billy took his leave at the door, Laura grinned, 'I liked the way you got the Biblical quotation in. That was clever, though I thought you were laying it on a bit thick. You were starting to sound like a Jehovah Witness.'

'Sorry about that, Laura, but you didn't do so bad yourself with that stuff about "we never think about such things". I hope you were speaking for yourself and not for me. But when I quoted the Bible to your father, I was only telling him what I thought he wanted to hear. The one thing that concerned me, though, was that your dad agreed with me. And when he does that, I'm sure I must be wrong somehow.'

Duncan wasn't the only one to raise objections to the engagement. Billy's dad was vehemently against it despite Mam's efforts to bring him round.

'I've got to speak my mind,' he said. 'Marriage between different classes is doomed from the start. It just won't work – oil and water don't mix. Laura Mackenzie's a very nice girl and all that, but how can our Billy afford to keep her in the lifestyle she's used to? Oh, they'll be luvvy-duvvy at first but when the gilt's worn off the gingerbread, what then? I'm warning you, there'll be trouble. Billy should marry one of his own kind, a nice, respectable, working-class girl.'

Later, when talking to Flo, Mam said, 'I think deep down your dad's worried about mixing with the higher-ups. He's frightened of them and nervous in their presence.'

Billy, Les and the rest of the family went to work on him but he wouldn't move an inch.

'You mark my words, they'll rue the day,' was all that they could get out of him.

'So be it,' Billy declared. 'It may be a long time before we marry but when we do, it'll be with or without his blessing.'

The week following the interview with Duncan, Billy and Laura went to Saqui and Lawrence in St Ann's Square and chose a beautiful solitaire diamond ring, paid for out of their savings. There was no formal engagement party but there were many cards of congratulations from friends and colleagues. One card was a surprise. It said 'To the two trend-setters, from Hamish and Jenny'.

At half-term, it was a radiantly happy, excited couple that took the train from London Road station to Euston.

They booked two separate rooms at a small hotel in Chelsea.

'Staying apart is going to be difficult,' said Billy, 'but we gave our word to your folks. I shall have to take a cold bath every time the mood strikes me. Perhaps I should simply stay in the icy water.'

'I feel the same way,' Laura said, 'but I think I'll forgo the cold baths all the same. When we get back to Manchester, maybe we should take up rug-making. It'll keep your hands busy.'

'I believe winding wool serves a similar purpose.'

'So I should take up knitting.'

'No. Both of us should take up knitting.'

Billy showed Laura around the sights of London and he himself re-lived the excitement of seeing the famous landmarks for the first time as he watched Laura's euphoric reactions. She was innocent and artless and he loved her for it. She was content and happy with the simplest of things, like a little girl viewing a Christmas tree for the first time.

On the first evening, Billy went off to the Nell Gwynn in King's Road for his men's college reunion. It proved to be a disappointment as most of his year group were serving out their time doing National Service. Billy was not over concerned as he knew that Laura was waiting for him back at the hotel.

Around eleven o'clock, he returned and found Laura reading quietly in her room. At the sight of her lying there so relaxed and content, his heart overflowed with tenderness and love.

She looked up from her book and smiled happily when she saw him. 'You've been away three hours and I've missed you so much,' she said, holding out her arms.

They embraced and held each other tightly. Soon things threatened to get out of control but sensing the urgency of his need, Laura said, 'I love you so much Billy. I want and need you but if we gave in to our passions now, it would ruin everything, spoil our plans.'

'Right now,' he said hoarsely, 'I'm inclined to agree with Oscar Wilde when he said "I can resist anything but temptation", but even though I want to make love to you, I can see the sense of what you're saying. There is one thing we could try, however.'

'And that is?'

'The Welsh have a courting practice which they call *bundling*.'

470

'What on earth is that? It sounds like wrapping up parcels.'

'It has certain similarities. I sleep here in the same bed with you but we are separated by different layers of bedclothes. That way, we can hold each other closely without going all the way, as they say. I promise to stay in my own section though I can't promise the same for my arms and my hands.'

'Sounds a little crazy to me,' she laughed.

'It could be worse. Sometimes it involved tying up the girl in a sheet or even tying her feet together.'

'I think we'll forget this weird Welsh custom and all its variations. Sharing a bed even in this strange manner would simply be tempting providence. I love you, Billy, but I think we'd be better in separate rooms.'

'You're not sure that I can resist temptation?'

'No, Billy. I'm not sure that *I* can.'

Billy gave her a last kiss and a final embrace and, with a sigh of resignation, retired to his own room.

The rest of the weekend was a joy. They visited the Victoria Palace and laughed at the antics of The Crazy Gang in their farce *Together Again*, and revelled in the music of Irving Berlin's *Annie Get Your Gun* at the Coliseum featuring Dolores Gray, but the highlight of the weekend was the performance of *Madame Butterfly* at the Sadler's Wells. As the tragic story unfolded reaching its climax in act three with the suicide of Butterfly, the strains of Puccini's poignant music filled the theatre. The tears ran down Laura's cheeks, and she reached for Billy's hand. He didn't exactly weep but he swallowed hard a couple of times and there was certainly a lump in his throat.

On their last evening, they had supper at a Lyon's Corner

House to the music of a string quartet and served by a 'nippy' waitress in Edwardian uniform. They returned to their hotel and in Laura's room kissed and cuddled as closely as they dared without going fully overboard.

'This weekend has brought home one thing clearly to me,' said Billy as he held Laura closely on the final evening.

'I think I know what you're going to say,' she murmured. 'And on this point we are fully as one.'

'Even if we are not in the flesh,' he laughed. 'I most definitely cannot wait two years before we join forces, as it were.'

'You have a funny way of putting things,' she said.

'Or not putting things,' he commented suggestively. 'Laura, let's get married this year and blow the consequences. I'm sure we'll manage the money somehow or other.'

'And throw caution to the wind?'

'Completely.'

'But we shall require a tremendous amount of money and at the moment that's the one commodity we're lacking.'

'We can take on a few private pupils and with the extra evening work at the Alfred Street youth centre, we should be able to save another hundred pounds. With the savings we already have, that will give us something approaching a hundred and fifty pounds. That's not a bad sum to make a start.'

'And I could do another night at the Ross Place play centre. Oh, Billy, do you think we can do it?'

'I'm sure we can. Together, we can overcome any difficulties. I know that if we have to wait two years, I shall be no use to you because I'll be resident in the lunatic asylum.'

472

'OK, Billy. I don't want to have to spend my life visiting you in the Prestwich Hospital. Let's do it. But be prepared for a storm of disapproval and resistance.'

Chapter Forty-One

Wedding Preparations

As Laura had predicted, there was an unholy row when they announced their intention to marry in the summer. The objections came thick and fast.

Not enough time to make the arrangements. Where will the reception be held? Not enough time to prepare speeches. What about the catering, the drinks, the flowers, the organist, the bridesmaids, the priest, the trousseau, the car hire, the wedding suits, the photographer? Who will pay for it all?

Not enough notice for many of the relatives to attend. Many have already fixed their holidays. What about Hughie who is in Malaya doing his National Service? Not enough time to get our outfits.

What about the children who will demand to come?

Then there was the other school of thought. Are you sure this isn't a shotgun wedding? We'll be counting the months to your first baby. Couldn't resist each other, eh? Nudge, nudge, wink, wink. It was that dirty weekend in London that did it. More elbow-nudging and winking.

The two fathers worried themselves sick.

'You know, Louise,' Duncan said, 'life's a strange thing. I

did my utmost to encourage Laura to marry Hamish as the one with the best prospects, and instead she wants to marry the one with the worst.'

'No need to worry, Duncan,' said Louise in an attempt to reassure her husband. 'They'll get by. They're young, healthy and resourceful, and very much in love. I'm sure they're going to be very happy. And as for Billy's prospects, I think he may surprise you one day.'

'I hope you're right, Louise,' he murmured. 'Only time will tell.'

As for Billy's father, he refused to countenance the marriage.

'This is one wedding I won't be going to,' he said decisively. 'Include me out. I think the marriage will be a disaster. You just wait till the honeymoon's over, that's all.'

'You miserable old devil,' Mam said. 'We'll just have to hold it without you. I know you though. You're just terrified of meeting up with the Mackenzies 'cos you think they're toffs and you'll put your foot in it.'

'Nonsense,' he replied, not too confidently.

For weeks before the wedding, Laura was involved in detailed planning for her trousseau and bridal outfit.

'We've managed to find a dressmaker who will be making my wedding gown,' she told Billy enthusiastically. 'It'll be made of ivory satin crepe with a full train. And we're using real flowers in the head-dress, the same as my bouquet. What do you think?'

'Great – simply great!' a bemused Billy mumbled. 'Sounds really exciting.' He didn't understand a word of it and besides, he had other things on his mind at that moment, for Duncan had raised more important matters.

'In case you're wondering,' he'd said, 'I've arranged a

good dowry for Laura but I plan to give that to you when you're both ready to buy a house of your own. Meanwhile, you just about have enough money to pay for your share of the wedding and go on a honeymoon. In my opinion your top priority is to find an apartment to rent.'

'Don't worry, Mr Mackenzie,' Billy had said, ever optimistic. 'That matter's well in hand. Laura and I have spotted a few likely looking places in the local paper and we'll be going to check them out after school.'

'If you can't find a place to live,' Duncan warned – almost hopefully – 'I think you should consider postponing the wedding until you do.'

Finding a flat wasn't as easy as Billy had imagined. The two likely addresses they had jotted down were situated on Stockport Road. The first was on the top floor of a Victorian mansion. To reach it, they had to climb three flights of stairs, passing rubbish bins on the way. The capacious stairwell not only reeked of the usual cooking odours but was decorated with assorted graffiti written by Kilroy ('Don't clean this hallway – plant something. Keep this hall tidy – throw your rubbish out of the window') and advising readers in choice language where they could go and what they could do when they got there. One look was enough.

'If we came here,' Billy said, 'it would be like home from home for me. Gardenia Court to Stinkwood House.'

The next flat was a little better but not much. Though it was opposite Pownall's massive warehouse, it had the advantage of being situated on the ground floor.

'You have your own kitchen and living room,' the proprietor told them, 'but the bathroom is on the first landing and is shared with the other floors. If you want a bath, you'll need a shilling for the geyser.'

Billy couldn't resist asking, 'Which flat does the geyser live in?'

Laura inspected the minuscule kitchen.

'I couldn't work in there,' she whispered to Billy. 'It's about the size of a broom cupboard and has no windows. When I'm in the kitchen, I like to look out on the world outside.'

'Doesn't look too hopeful,' Billy said when they emerged. 'Flats are like gold at the moment.'

'I do hope we don't have to go in with the in-laws,' Laura said, 'like so many couples do today. It's usually disastrous.'

'We've not found anything yet,' Billy said, 'but I have a Micawber-like faith that something will turn up.'

It did.

A fortnight before the wedding, Mrs Mackenzie reported that her friend, Mrs Sheila Dobson, a nurse at the Manchester Royal Infirmary, had a flat vacant. Whilst it was nothing to write home about, consisting as it did of a large lounge, a bedroom, a small but reasonable kitchen, and a shared bathroom, for them it was ideal. Mrs Dobson had had the first floor of her house converted into a furnished flat for her son and his wife but his job had taken him to the south of England, leaving the apartment vacant – a stroke of luck for Billy and Laura. There was a further bonus in that Mrs Dobson was away on duty most of the time which meant they'd have free run of the place.

The wedding was fixed for the glorious twelfth of August. 'The day when grouse shooting begins,' remarked Billy.

The wedding was to be held at St Anselm's church and would be presided over by the Reverend Father O'Flynn, aged eighty-two.

'Let's make it a quiet wedding with only the immediate families invited,' said Billy.

'Exactly my sentiments,' agreed Laura. 'A nice quiet wedding. I'm all for it.'

'Better still, why don't we simply elope?' Billy suggested. 'We could marry quietly at Gretna Green. Look at the money and the trouble we'd save.'

Laura looked aghast. 'And miss out on the greatest day of our lives! No, we'll organise the wedding at home and it'll be quiet but I'll still need a trousseau.'

'What's that?' asked Billy. 'I know from my French studies that a trousseau used to be a small bundle that the bride carried under her arm to her new home. I think we can run to that.'

'I should like two bridesmaids – Jenny and Katie,' Laura went on, ignoring his attempt at levity. 'They'll need special dresses. And it's customary for you to buy each of them a present.'

'What type of present?'

'Oh, small mementos.'

'I think I can afford a bag of Mintoes each.'

'Not Mintoes. Mementos! Like a pearl brooch each for example.'

Billy could see the hundred and fifty pounds they had saved rapidly melting away.

'What else am I to pay for?' he asked apprehensively.

'Well, it's customary for the groom to pay for things like church fees, the organist, bouquets and buttonholes, and rings.'

'Is that all?'

'I think so, though don't forget the two boys who pump the organ.'

'Can't be much of an organ if it needs pumping,' Billy said.

'I'll ignore that,' Laura said. 'We'll keep the bouquets simple. I should like to carry a bouquet of roses, carnations and cornflowers. And the bridesmaids similar. They shouldn't break the bank. One last thing. At Easter, Mammy and Daddy went to Rome. They've brought back the Papal blessing for us.'

'How much?' asked Billy.

'That's for free – compliments of Pius the Twelfth.'

Billy wondered what the Pope would have made of his experience at the barbers' shop. On the way home, Billy was accustomed to call at a hairdressing salon outside Victoria Station and he'd become a regular at the establishment of Len and Ken. Every fortnight, he swapped stories and the latest jokes with the two barbers. The establishment was the kind of male stronghold that would have interested anthropologists like Margaret Mead.

Ken started the ball rolling as he trimmed a customer's hair. 'Have you heard about the fella who thought that mutual orgasm was an insurance company?'

The regulars waiting their turn split their sides for the tenth time in the past ten minutes. Another great joke – we are all men here. Women just wouldn't appreciate the humour.

When Billy announced he was to be married the following weekend and would appreciate a special haircut, he was treated to a stream of blue stories about bridegrooms on their wedding night.

As he snipped Billy's locks, Len took up the comedian's role. 'Someone told the new husband that in sex it was essential to begin with foreplay – so he invited the couple next door to join them. Then there was this newly married bloke who told his bride, "I must warn you, darling, that I like to get up early every morning." "Yes," she replied,

479

"I've noticed that you're an early riser." '

Once again, bawdy guffaws all round the shop.

Finally, Len turned to serious matters. 'I suppose you'll be wanting a supply of these,' he said, indicating the box of contraceptives on the shelf. 'And not merely as "something for the weekend, sir", but on a regular basis. We can give a good discount for a box of twelve – that would be a week's supply for you, I suppose,' he grinned.

Billy turned a bright pink.

The waiting customers were agog for his answer.

'No, no . . .' Billy mumbled. 'They're against our religion and the Pope won't allow 'em.'

'I see, sir,' Len replied. 'Going in for a family are we, sir?' He made it sound like an investment in shares or the purchase of furniture from Lewis's.

All agreed that it would be a quiet wedding, a small modest affair with only the immediate families attending.

That was before the extended family got wind of the development. On the Hopkins side, there was no chance that a celebration and a family knees-up would be forgone.

'You can't leave out the children,' protested Billy's sisters. 'The wedding of their Uncle Billy is an affair never to be missed. It'll be something that they'll treasure for the rest of their lives.' Flo had three children and Polly four. When Sam in Belfast heard that their children were being invited, he insisted that his two be included as well. More distant family members heard about the planned marriage on the grapevine and since they regarded both weddings and funerals in the same light, namely opportunities to get together for the mutual exchange of news and gossip over drinks, it was vital they be included on the invitation lists.

By the time the list was finalised, there wasn't a skeleton left in the cupboard. The only shadow over things was Dad's refusal to attend.

Similar considerations applied to the Mackenzie family, and remote clans in the Highland glens of Scotland abandoned their mountain goats and sheep and prepared to make the journey South to celebrate the marriage of one of their lassies to a Sassenach. Bagpipes were a *sine qua non* of their baggage.

Duncan Mackenzie was awakened early in the morning by the excited babble of voices and a pattering of feet round the house. He'd slept badly, his slumbers disturbed by wild, worrisome visions. In his nightmare, it was raining heavily; he had lost his daughter Laura and was searching the streets of Manchester for her. He ran hither and thither looking in derelict buildings and back entries but to no avail, there was no sign of her. At last he'd found her, along with Billy, her intended. They were dressed in wedding outfits and were huddled together in the doorway of Lewis's store on Market Street.

'It's raining and you'll catch your death of cold. Come awa' home with me, both of you,' he'd said.

'We'd rather die of starvation here in this doorway than accept your help,' he'd heard her reply.

Still shivering at the memory, he sat up in bed and listened to the clatter. What on earth was going on? He rubbed the sleep from his eyes. Then it came to him. How could he have forgotten after his nightmare? There was to be a wedding.

There seemed to be panic everywhere with people rushing about the place, the house resounding to frenzied female voices demanding use of the bathroom, frantic

481

inquiries as to the whereabouts of various items, calls for help with this and that.

Sounds like pandemonium, he said to himself. Thank God I have my own bathroom *en suite*. He gazed at the neatly pressed kilt in the Mackenzie tartan that was folded over the chair. This is a proud day for the Mackenzie clan, he thought, and it was up to him to uphold tradition.

He washed and shaved, dressed with particular care, and descended to the kitchen. There was chaos everywhere as the Mackenzie females fussed over dresses, flowers, and coiffures. To add to the confusion, a couple of helpers from the local church ran to and fro putting the finishing touches to the buffet breakfast which had to be ready immediately after the wedding ceremony. One table had been set in the kitchen for the many children who would be attending whilst the main buffet was to be in the study.

Finally, the ladies were ready. Grandma and Aunty both smelt faintly of mothballs and were dressed in costume more suited to a Gilbert and Sullivan opera. They twittered their way out to the waiting limousine, where Katie and Jenny in their silk and satin joined them. Louise, in a massive Ascot-type hat, brought up the rear.

Before they drove off, a delighted Duncan gave them the once-over.

'I'm proud of you,' he said. 'You bring honour and beauty to the Mackenzie clan.'

But if Duncan was proud of the advance party which set off for the church, he was bowled over when he caught sight of his eldest daughter. His heart leapt for joy, gladness and tender paternal love.

'Laura,' he said, 'you're truly a bonnie lass. You look wonderful, simply wonderful. When I see you now all ready to be married, you mind me of your mother and the day we wed. She looked so bonnie too.'

'Thank you, Daddy. And you look so smart in your chieftain's outfit, you'll create a stir when we walk into the church. But I hope you won't think I'm stupid when I tell you I'm as nervous as a kitten.'

'There's nothing to be nervous about, Laura. The married state is perfectly natural.'

'It's not being married that scares me, Daddy. It's that walk down the aisle with all those people there. We were hoping for a quiet wedding but it's got a bit out of hand and the thought of the long walk from porch to altar gives me the collywobbles. I hope I don't collapse and you have to carry me on your back.'

'Don't you worry your head, Laura. Remember I'll be there to support you – always have been ever since you were a little girl. Lean on me.'

'You're amazing, Daddy. Nothing ever seems to rattle you. You're always so calm and collected.'

Duncan said nothing about his nightmare.

In Gardenia Court, Billy and his family sat waiting for the wedding car.

'This is supposed to be a joyful day,' remarked Les, looking at the anxious faces around him. 'Yet everyone looks as if they're going to a funeral instead of a wedding.'

'I was thinking,' said Billy. 'Brides get dressed up in white, the colour of purity and joy. But men get dressed up in black. Is that a suitable colour for a wedding? We hired these morning suits from Moss Bros and I'm not sure how they'd spell the word "morning". Maybe it's "mourning".'

'You never said a truer word, Billy,' Dad pontificated. 'The suits and the limousine are black. Just the right colour for this occasion.'

'Take no notice of him, our Billy,' Mam said. 'He's a real Jeremiser. Only happy when he's miserable. Weddings are of course happy occasions,' she added, her eyes misting over, 'but for a mother it's always sad as well. In a way, it *is* like a funeral.'

'What makes you say that, Mam?' asked Billy anxiously.

'After today, you'll be gone from here, Billy. Your bedroom will be there empty and we'll miss you. You won't be coming back here no more from school. No more carrying your bike up the stairs. No more asking my advice and sharing your problems.'

'Don't be surprised if he's back in a few weeks for good,' said Dad gloomily.

'It's not as bad as that, Mam. I'll come back to see you regularly.'

'You say that now but you'll soon have your own home and your own family to keep you busy.'

'It's the same for Laura's mother, I suppose,' Billy said.

'No, it's not. You know the old saying, "My son is my son till he has got him a wife; but my daughter's my daughter all the days of her life." There's a lot of truth in that.'

'Don't worry,' Billy reassured her. 'I'll be back all right, when I want to borrow some money. And even though Dad isn't coming to the wedding, I hope he'll still get me those under-the-counter cigarettes.'

Dad nodded sadly.

Billy himself was not feeling as confident as he sounded. Up to this point, he hadn't thought deeply about the ramifications of getting married and of what it really meant. He'd been so busy and so run off his feet what with one thing and another that he hadn't had time to consider the gravity of the step he was about to take. So far it had been exciting fun and games – arranging this and organising that. Now he was all dressed up to the nines, ready to go for a ride in a posh limousine, followed by a church service, a slap-up meal and off for a fortnight's honeymoon in Devon.

He'd been worried and preoccupied about bringing his family into contact with the Mackenzies. The meeting of two social worlds, he'd thought, with himself at the friction point of them both. He'd tried to minimise the possible difficulties by arranging an early nuptial Mass, a quick wedding breakfast, and a train to Exeter for 2 p.m., after which each family would celebrate in its own customary way. Dad might not be at the wedding ceremony but he wouldn't miss the family knees-up for anything.

But now for the first time his mam's words brought home the seriousness of what he was going to do in church that morning. He was quitting home for good and after today he'd be returning to a new life in a furnished flat – a comfortable little apartment but nevertheless strange and unfamiliar. Whilst he wouldn't be sorry to see the back of Gardenia Court and its squalid surroundings, at the same time he felt a pang of regret that he was leaving his old life behind and going on a journey to face whatever fate had in store. Right at this moment, he thought, Laura must be thinking along the same lines. Pre-nuptial blues, the books called it. Today she would be parting from her parents and her family to embark on a risky life adventure with a relative stranger.

'The car's here,' announced Les who'd been looking out of the window. 'Time's up. Time to go.'

'No need to make it sound like the summons to the gallows,' said Billy.

As they emerged from the stairwell, he gazed up at the tenement verandas which reminded him of theatre boxes at the Albert Hall. Every single one of them was occupied by a neighbouring family – women still in their curlers, the men with their braces dangling down. Dad looked down forlornly from their own veranda. A solitary, melancholy figure.

'It's not too late to change your mind, Dad,' Billy called. 'Come on down, we'll wait for you.'

'No, my mind's made up, Billy. You go on without me,' he said sadly.

From one of the stairwells, a mongrel dog appeared, sniffed at the car, and then lifted its hind leg and began peeing on the rear wheel.

'Piss off,' the uniformed driver yelled, giving it a well-aimed kick up its backside.

'Look at the stuck-up 'Opkins lot,' Mrs Pitts screeched. 'They've joined the bleedin' toffs.'

'All the very best to you, son,' Mrs Mulligan called down, 'and don't forget to cook them there Danish omelettes for your good lady.'

Feeling like royalty, Billy waved back to them in acknowledgement.

'Goodbye, everyone,' he shouted, 'and the very best of luck to you all.'

The Daimler engine started up and, accompanied by a pack of mangy, snarling dogs which were bent on devouring the back wheels, the limousine soon left Gardenia Court behind.

St Anselm's Church was already full when the wedding car pulled up outside. Billy and his companions entered the church and surveyed the forest of flowers and outlandish hats. As they made their way to their places, Billy stopped many times to shake hands and exchange greetings with the

486

numerous friends and colleagues who smiled and nodded encouragingly. Towards the front, he spotted the school staff and the whole contingent of ex-pupils from his first class, many of the girls with tears in their eyes, as they sat waiting and whispering impatiently for the ceremony to begin.

Billy stopped to talk to his headmaster.

'Thanks for coming, Frank. You seem to have brought half the school with you.'

'I couldn't keep them away,' Frank said. 'Especially the girls. I think this wedding's going to break a few hearts. All the best to you both, Billy. Don't forget I expect to see you both back at the beginning of the new term. Monday, September the fourth in case you've forgotten.'

'Have no fear, Frank. We'll both be there.'

Billy moved on and had a few words with his old chums from the Damian Smokers' Club who were also much in evidence.

'Thanks for making the effort to support me in my hour of need,' he joked. 'But when I see you all together like this again, I can't help but feel sad that our old friend Robin Gabrielson is not with us here today.'

'I'm sure he *is* here in spirit,' said Titch. 'Well, this is it, old pal. You're the first of the gang to get married.'

'And I shall probably be the last,' added Nobby in his smart lieutenant's uniform complete with Sam Browne belt.

'I doubt it,' smirked Oscar. 'I rather think that honour will be mine.'

'Don't forget,' said Pottsy, 'if you buy your groceries in one of our shops, I can offer you a twenty-five per cent discount.'

'I'll remember that,' laughed Billy. 'Laura and I will probably hold you to it. Maybe we can all meet up some time and go for a drink.'

487

'That's if your new wife gives you permission,' Ollie grinned.

They gave him the thumbs-up – at least, he interpreted it as such though knowing their scurrilous minds, the gesture probably had other significance.

On the right side of the church sat many of the Hopkins family with their children, along with a number of older relatives whom Billy had not seen for years – Aunts Cissie and Hetty, Uncles Matt and Eddie.

When they reached the front bench, Billy and Les sat down and waited for the ceremony to begin. Les kept casting glances back at the extended Mackenzie family gathered on the other side.

'I don't know what kind of rum family you're marrying into, Billy,' he whispered, 'but all those blokes over there are wearing women's skirts.'

'Keep your voice down, Les, they'll hear you. Have you ever noticed how the bridegroom comes into the church unnoticed – no music, no fanfare, no fuss, as if he has only a minor part to play in the marriage?'

'That's about the sum of it,' Les answered. 'You say the marriage. But marriage isn't a word, it's a sentence.'

'Now he tells me. Did you remember the ring?'

'But of course. Were you hoping I'd lost it?'

Their exchange was interrupted by the sound of the congregation scrambling to its feet and the organ playing Handel's 'Arrival of the Queen of Sheba'.

Murmurs of 'Oooh, isn't she lovely' could be heard over the music.

'Into the valley of death rode the six hundred,' recited Les in a feeble attempt at humour.

'Theirs not to reason why, theirs but to do and die,' replied Billy bravely.

Then a radiant Laura was beside him, in her beautiful bridal gown. His fairytale princess come true.

'Laura,' he whispered. 'You look absolutely stunning. How do I look?'

Laura smiled back nervously. 'Be serious,' she said.

Duncan Mackenzie and the two bridesmaids stepped back and old Father O'Flynn came forward.

'Dearly beloved,' he intoned, 'we are gathered here together in the sight of God, and in the face of this congregation, to join together this man and this woman in holy matrimony. Matrimony is an honourable estate and therefore not to be enterprised, nor taken in hand, unadvisedly, lightly, or wantonly, to satisfy men's carnal lusts and appetites, like brute beasts that have no understanding. Hear our prayers for Willibrord and Lorna, through your son Jesus Christ, our Lord, who lives and reigns with you and the Holy Ghost, one God for ever and ever. Amen.'

Billy and Laura walked to the altar with the priest and knelt at the prie-dieux reserved for them.

Father O'Flynn went on: 'Brethren, let women be subject to their husbands as to the Lord, for the husband is head of the wife as Christ is the head of the Church.'

Billy stole a surreptitious glance at Laura, smiled and gave her a big wink. She pulled a face in return.

'For this cause shall a man leave his father and mother, and shall stick to his wife,' Father O'Flynn continued.

There was the sound of subdued sobbing in the body of the church. It sounded like Billy's mam.

'Let every one of you in particular love his wife, and let the wife fear her husband.'

Laura was now definitely frowning. She pursed her lips and adopted a mock frightened expression.

'Thy wife shall be as a fruitful vine on the sides of the

489

house. Thy children as olive plants round about thy table.'

The rest of the nuptial Mass flowed easily and without a hitch. They reached the marriage vows.

'Willibrord and Lorna, I shall now ask if you freely undertake the obligations of marriage. Willibrord—'

'Billy,' whispered Billy.

Father O'Flynn looked perplexed for a moment. 'You'll be given the bill at the end of the ceremony,' he said, frowning. We've got a right one here, the priest thought. 'Repeat after me. "I, Willibrord Hopkins, take thee, Lorna Macmillan . . ."'

Billy repeated his words: 'I, William Hopkins, do take thee, Laura Mackenzie . . .' And went on to vow, 'To have and to hold from this day forward, for better for worse, for richer for poorer, in sickness and in health, to love, to cherish, till death us do part, according to God's holy ordinance; and thereto I give thee my troth.'

The subdued sobbing continued throughout the vow-taking and reached a crescendo in the 'for richer for poorer' bit.

Billy continued, 'With this thing . . . ring, I thee wed, with my body I thee worship, and with all my worldly goods I thee endow.'

'There goes his bike,' Mam said in her inimitable stage whisper – the kind that the whole church could hear.

The ceremony was over when Father O'Flynn said: 'Willibrord and Lorna, I now pronounce you man and wife. Willibrord, you may kiss the bride.'

The wedding bells rang out. Mendelssohn's triumphant march was played *fortissimo*. Confetti and rice were thrown as the newly marrieds ran the gauntlet. The wedding car whisked them away. There followed a mad rush to get back to the house for the free drinks.

For the bridal couple, the ceremony seemed surreal, as if it was happening to two other people, and before they knew where they were, it was all over.

At the house, guests were welcomed in by the sound of several bagpipes played by various visitors of the Mackenzie clan. They might have sounded better had they agreed to play the same tune. For the Hopkins family, however, it was all one. Caterwauling.

'Do you like the sound of bagpipes, Billy?' Steve Keenan asked.

'Let's put it like this, Steve. I prefer to listen to the sound of a chorus of alley cats serenading at two o'clock in the morning.'

'I take that as a no,' Steve said.

The hordes of children were settled at their special banquet in the kitchen and were soon feeding their faces. The adult feast did not go so smoothly. The Hopkins family, lacking familiarity with the concept of 'The Buffet', had seated themselves round the buffet table, napkins tucked into collars, knives and forks at the ready. There was nothing for it but for the other thirty guests to squeeze in and find places at the table.

Meanwhile, Uncle Eddy had been helping himself liberally to the port and sherry which were readily at hand

'You're not in your Greengate boozer now,' remonstrated Aunt Mona. 'You're not supposed to drink sherry from a pint pot.'

The effect of the fortified wine soon became obvious and it wasn't long before he had forgotten where he was.

The meal was proceeding smoothly when Eddy turned to Laura's mother who was sitting opposite him, and said in a voice all could hear, 'You want to get some of this grub into a paper bag to take home. Don't let the waitresses get it all.'

Uh-oh, Billy thought. Here we go.

Later, when Uncle Eddy was looking for the toilets, he addressed Duncan and asked, 'Excuse me, sir, but where's the gents?'

'Sorry,' Duncan replied, perplexed. 'The gents?'

'You know, your back? Your urinal?'

'Oh, you mean the toilet. There's a cloakroom off the hall and one upstairs if that's occupied.'

'Thenk you very much, sir,' he replied. 'Great party – it's a belter.'

At least Mam seemed to be getting on well with Grandma and Aunty. They talked ten to the dozen and even Aunty was running out of anecdotes – almost.

Came the time for the speeches. As was customary, the bride's father was called on first.

'I'm a man of few words,' he said. 'My task today was simply to give away the bride. After paying for this wedding breakfast, the bride is about all I have left to give away. But I'd like to say this.

'Laura and Billy are going to start their married life in a rented furnished flat and with very little money. I hope they know what they're doing. I only wish they'd managed to buy a house but it's no use crying over spilt milk. What's done is done and it's too late now. But when they do finally get round to buying a house of their own, I want them to know that I shall be there to give them my fullest support. I'll simply finish by asking you to join in drinking a toast to the happy couple. We wish them all the luck in the world – they're going to need it.' With that he raised his glass, drank the toast and sat down.

'Miserable old bugger,' Eddy whispered in an aside to

492

Louise. 'He should give them the money now.'

Next to speak was Billy.

'I know I can speak for Laura when I say this is the happiest day we have ever known, for it means the start of a new life together. Today is a day to rejoice and this I do with all my heart. I'm only sorry my dad is not with us on this otherwise perfect day – he has his own reasons and I'll have to respect those though I do not agree with them. And even though he's not here, I want first to thank him and my mam for looking after me up to now. Then thanks to Mr and Mrs Mackenzie for giving me their daughter's hand in marriage. I know that like my own father they're unsure about the wisdom of the step Laura and I have taken but I can promise them that I shall love and cherish their daughter for the rest of my life. Have faith in us. We've only just begun.

'I could fill this speech with jokes and funny lines but I'll leave that to Les who no doubt will tell you my jokes and funny lines anyway. I'm grateful to him for agreeing to act as best man. Blood is thicker than water and Les is thicker than both. I must say, though, that I'm not altogether sure that Laura and I are legally married for Father O'Flynn today seems to have married two other people – Willibrord and Lorna. No matter. I hope they'll both be very happy whoever they are.

'I liked the reference to the Gospel instruction, "Wives, be subject to your husbands", and the part which advised wives to "fear their husbands". Good, sound advice. Did you notice that in the marriage vows, the bride is told that she must obey her husband but no such instruction was given to the bridegroom. No problem 'cos Laura and I have solved the question of who'll be boss and we've come to an amicable understanding. I'll make the major decisions for us, like our attitude to the government's foreign policy, our answers to the economic crisis, and so on. Laura will make the minor decisions such as where we shall live, who our friends will be, where we shall go on holiday, and what I shall wear.

'Those of you who were watching the ceremony closely may have noticed that when the priest asked me, "Do you take Laura to be your lawfully wedded wife?" Laura gave me a nudge and answered for me. "He does!" she said before I could get a word in.

'Thank you to the rest of the company for the wonderful wedding presents you have given us. Especially the toasters. Making toast has long been one of my specialities consisting of the burn-and-scrape method but now the various toasters you have presented us with will raise our culinary standards to new heights. Thank you also for attending this ceremony as I know many of you have travelled great distances to be here. Some from as far away as Stockport and Salford.

'Let me finish by saying that I'm sure Laura and I have made a good marriage and that we shall be happy for the rest of our lives. I know it to be true because Laura just told me to say it. Now, please join me in drinking a toast to our beautiful bridesmaids, Jenny and Katie.' With that, Billy sat down to the applause of both families.

It was the turn of the best man to make his speech and Les stood up to oblige the assembly. He began by reading the many telegrams – one from Hughie serving with the Royal Army Medical Corps in Malaya – offering congratulations and best wishes, though there was one with the strange greeting from the Damian College Smokers' Club: 'Lang may your lum reek.'

'A "lum" is a chimney,' explained Les with a grin at

494

Billy, 'and roughly translated the message is, "Long May Your Chimney Smoke".'

Les cleared his throat and began his speech.

'I'm not used to making speeches so please excuse any mistakes I make. I've not prepared anything and so I can hardly wait to hear what I'm going to say. I congratulate Billy on an absolutely adequate speech. He's never been an easy one to follow. I know personally I can never follow a word he says.

'Laura wanted a simple wedding, and she got what she wanted – you've only to look at the bridegroom. One thing I will say about him, he's always willing to give you half of whatever he's got. And since he's got nothing, it means half of nothing.

'At school though he was always bright – he learned to read at the age of four. Trouble was, he didn't always understand what he was reading. Whenever he saw cautionary notices like "wet cement" or "wet paint", he thought it was an instruction to act. One day Sister Helen, the headmistress of St Wilfred's Infant School, warned the youngsters, "Remember, children, that in the school hall, there is a sign – Wet Floor. So be careful and don't forget." You guessed it. I was called out of class to take Billy home for a change of pants.

'But now, he has left home for good, Billy's career as a bachelor is over! We're going to miss him. He can always come back if he wants to borrow something, like my demob suit for example. I'm not sure but I think he may be wearing it today.

'It's usual at these affairs to warn the bride of the groom's bad habits. In actual fact, he hasn't got that many faults, but he makes full use of those he does have. Take smoking, for instance. He has to have a cigarette first thing in the

495

morning. He gives up smoking every week, usually on a Monday, but by Wednesday he's so bad-tempered he does you a favour and starts again.

'One piece of advice I offer the newly married couple is this: never go to bed after an argument – stay up and finish it off. And for Billy: I hope you learn how to do the washing up, and remember the best time to do it is . . . straight after she digs you in the ribs.

'Ladies and gentlemen, it's now my pleasant duty to thank Billy on behalf of the bridesmaids Jenny and Katie for his generous words. It's a real pleasure to act as spokesman for such a lovely duo. Like everyone here, I wish Laura and Billy long life and happiness. Their long life will be our happiness. Let's drink a toast to the new Mr and Mrs Hopkins – Laura and Billy.'

When Les sat down, Billy looked at him admiringly. 'I never knew you had such hidden talents and powers of oratory,' he said, shaking his hand.

There followed the cutting of the cake, the photographs, the applause, the throwing of the bouquet – deliberately targeted at Jenny – after which it was time for the happy couple to retire to a bedroom to change into their 'going-away' outfits. This they did to the accompaniment of ribald remarks from the assembled company.

'No shenanigans in there.'

'The honeymoon doesn't start till you've reached your hotel, remember.'

'You haven't time for any messing about.'

The taxi to take them to the station arrived honking noisily. The entire wedding party congregated outside the house for the final farewell. More throwing of rice and confetti, more teasing. Billy helped Laura into the limousine but just before he went inside himself, he stepped onto the running board and gazed fondly back at his large family gathered at the gate to wave goodbye. He owed so much to them – for all they'd done for him, and for their unfailing support and encouragement. In his heart, there was a mixture of joy and sadness for he knew that he was leaving the past behind and embarking on a new life with a beautiful bride by his side. A life filled with adventure, promise, and high hopes.

Then he saw him – his dad! Elbowing his way through from the back of the Hopkins crowd. He was waving his wedding-cum-funeral pot hat.

'All the best, Billy lad,' he cried. 'Good luck to you both! I wish you every happiness.'

'Thanks a lot, Dad, for coming,' Billy called, his eyes glistening. 'It means a lot to us. I knew you'd make it in the end.'

'You just make sure you look after that new missus of yours, and come over and see us when you get back.'

'I will, Dad, I will,' Billy shouted. 'I'll have to come over to collect my bike. Half of it now belongs to Laura.'

The tranquil air of Regina Park was abruptly pierced by an agonising moan from sundry bagpipes as they tuned up with 'We're no awa' to bide awa', which the whole Mackenzie clan now sang out with great gusto. Not to be outdone, the Hopkins side struck up with a lusty rendering of Gracie Fields' 'Wish Me Luck As You Wave Me Good-bye'. There was a slamming of car doors, the revving of an engine, the rattling of tin cans tied to the bumper, and to the strains of the polyphonic medley, the cab moved off, turned the corner into Wellington Grove and, quite suddenly, they were gone.

Just for You

Meet . . .
The author

And . . .
Exclusive additional material on
High Hopes

An Interview with the author

You seem to have more than one name. Which is the right one?

On my official birth certificate, I am registered as WILFRED HOPKINS. Only *one* Christian name, you will note, as my Mam and Dad didn't believe in giving kids more than one. Having more was felt to be extravagant and a practice best left to the toffs. Not a single member of my family had more than one name, though when it came to our own kids, we gave them two.

In the family, I had been given the pet name Billy, though I don't really know why. Perhaps it was because I was always acting the goat. Then again, it might have been because it was believed that we were distantly related to Big Bill Cody, Buffalo Bill, as somewhere amongst our long-lost relatives, one of the ladies had gone off to America and married someone called Cody. But it was no more than a shaky legend and I never attached much importance to it. At school, I was given the nickname 'Hoppy', an abbreviation of Hopkins, I hasten to add, and not because of a peculiar gait.

Anyway, Billy was the name I used as a pen name for my book. To add to the confusion, I adopted the name of Tim Lally as a nom de plume for the original version of *Our Kid*; Lally being my mother's maiden name and Tim being the name of some remote ancestor.

So you can well understand my confusion when people ask me my name. An old friend of mine always greets me when he meets me on the street with, 'What exactly *is* your name?' Search me.

I notice on your website that your wife's name is Clare and yet she is called Laura in your books. Why is this?

Laura is her fictitious name but it is not so far removed from Clare – Clara – Lara – Laura.

When and where were you born?

The date and place given in chapter one of *Our Kid* are accurate, namely Sunday July 8th 1928. The place: 6, Collyhurst Buildings, Newtown, Collyhurst, Manchester.

What is your star sign?

My star sign is Cancer, the Crab. But I don't believe in this astrological stuff. As if the sign under which you are born can influence your personality and your future! According to my horoscope – which I check every day – I am sensitive and vulnerable, yet tenacious and attracted to the sea. A load of old rubbish, even though I now live in a seaside town. Cancerians are strongly attached to their homes, families and the past; they are also supposed to possess prodigious memories. When insecure and frightened, they become touchy and crabby. Or hard on the outside and soft on the inside. They also dislike change and cling to the past for reassurance. They are supposed to have an affinity to certain towns, like Mombasa and Manchester. You can tell what codswallop it is. We Cancerians have no time for it and object strongly to anyone telling us about our personalities.

What is your favourite colour?

Blue, especially navy-blue which I associate with the uniform of my hero brother who was in the royal navy and died during the Second World War while serving in the Merchant Navy. Blue was also the colour of Xaverian College, my old school. Perhaps my liking blue explains why I was drawn to the Manchester City Football club since their colour is light blue. But then I also support Manchester United – the Reds – since it has brought honour and international fame to our city. Goes to show what a mixed-up character I am.

How much of your books are fact and how much fiction?

I usually describe my books as fictitious autobiographies. By that, I mean they are based on events that actually took place, though perhaps in a different time sequence. I've also changed names of places and people in case they are still alive and could be identified and I didn't want to cause anybody embarrassment. The characters are all true to life and based on people who lived around the time the stories are set. They are composites of folk I have known and worked with over my seventy-odd years of life. Some readers enjoy playing detective trying to identify people and places. They are usually right in their speculations (but not always!).

As to how much of the stories are true and how much fiction, it's not easy to answer but, if pushed, I'd say around twenty per cent fiction and eighty per cent fact. In my stories my aim has been to portray genuine human truth and that's what really matters. Readers soon sense if a character or an event doesn't ring true.

Did your own or Laura's parents ever get to see any of your books?

Sadly, both my parents died before the books were published. They would have been proud if they had been alive, especially my mother who was a born storyteller herself. Mr and Mrs Mackenzie also died before the books were published. Duncan, especially, would have been pleased to see the influential part he played in my education.

When did you start writing? Have you always wanted to be a writer?

I suppose my writing career started at the elementary school when we were made to write 'compositions'. Mine were the usual kind of school rubbish with *Alice in Wonderland* resolutions like, 'Then I woke up and found it was a dream' or an explosive Hollywood finish, such as: 'Then shots rang out and everyone died.' At about the age of eight I won first prize in a writing competition run by Downing Street. No, not the Westminster one but the Co-op in Manchester. It was for handwriting, not composition, and the prize was a hardback copy of *Flags of the World*. I still have it, though it is hopelessly out of date. I didn't write much after that, except for academic articles in education journals. One of these, about the extent of reading among college of education students, caused a furore and hit the national headlines. As for always wanting to be a writer, I must have been attracted to the idea since my first job was at the *Manchester Guardian*, where I'd hoped I might one day be promoted from copy boy to reporter. Some hope! I found out that you needed an honours degree to write for that illustrious newspaper.

Have you been influenced by any particular writers?

I suppose authors are influenced to varying degrees by all the writers they have ever read. The greatest influence, without doubt, was John Steinbeck and his novels, *Of Mice and Men* and *The Grapes of Wrath*. I have also been particularly impressed by northern writers like Maisie Mosco with her series about Manchester: (*Almonds and Raisins*, *Scattered Seeds* and *Children's Children*). As well as painting a depressing but realistic picture of industrial life and its effects on individuals, she also portrays people trying to escape and overcome their roots, a theme running through my books.

But overall, the writer who has influenced me most in style and storytelling has been the American dramatist Paddy Chayefsky (*Marty, Network* and *The Hospital*), who brought home to me how high drama could reside in seemingly mundane events. He maintained that ordinary lives were filled with dramatic potential; whether it was the man unhappy in his job, the housewife thinking of a lover, the girl hoping to be an actress, or the young man nursing secret ambitions. There are no better subjects for drama than your friends or members of your own family.

Why did you wait till you were almost seventy before you wrote your first book?

The answer to that must be that I was too busy earning a living, paying my mortgage and supporting my family. Writing is not a particularly profitable career – unless you are in the very top bracket.

Have you ever been back to visit the scenes of your Collyhurst childhood?

Yes, several times. I've even taken my grown-up children and grandchildren on a tour of the area. The Forge, the Bone Works and Collyhurst Buildings (the Dwellings) are long gone but the iron bridge connecting the site to Collyhurst Road is still there. Red Bank sidings and the Cut (the latter very much cleaner than I remember it) are there. Even the seventy-seven steps where I used to run to meet my mother struggling with heavy bags of shopping still exist, though in a dilapidated condition. St Michael's Burial Ground (now transformed into a beautiful garden), the Sally Army hostel, Angel Meadow, and the CWS tobacco factory building are there, though the latter has been converted into upmarket apartments. Honeypot Street (Honey Street) is still on the map though all the houses have long been demolished. But oddly enough, my dad's local (The Queen's Arms) is still in existence and I have even been in to drink a pint in his memory.

What do you like best about being an author?

For me, it's the thought that my book might be entertaining someone somewhere, whether it be on a train or on a beach. I particularly enjoy hearing from readers who have been touched or amused by something I have written.

And, like all other authors, I love seeing my books on the shelves in the bookstores; usually between Wendy Holden and Nick Hornby. If my books are not there, I remain optimistic and think it's because they have sold out. When visiting bookshops, my own family always rearrange the books so that mine are on show. The shop assistants must be mystified later when they see that Billy Hopkins has somehow worked its way to the front again!

Did you meet any problems writing High Hopes?

I had a problem with copyright. I wanted to use a poem by Robert Bridges that meant a great deal to Laura and me but unfortunately permission to use the poem (he died on 23rd April 1930, which meant he was in copyright until 31st December 2000) wasn't granted until it was too late for the publishing deadline. The poem I wanted to quote on the occasion of a reconciliation after a temporary estrangement was, 'I Will Not Let Thee Go'. Here is an extract:

> I will not let thee go
> I hold thee by too many bands:
> Thou sayest farewell, and lo!
> I have thee by the hands,
> And will not let thee go.

Was the food at your London college as bad as you have described it?

The so-called Damian Smokers' Club went to school in 1945 just as the Second World War ended. Food was in very short supply and so were competent staff to cook it.

Result: the fare dished up to two hungry adolescents was abysmal. Many resorted to spending their few coppers on a cuppa and a cheese cob at Dirty Dick's café round the corner, near Stamford Bridge football ground.

Mam's cheese and onion pie was something to die for when I got home to Manchester during the holidays.

The Headmaster of St Anselm's School seems particularly easy-going. Was he really as liberal as you have described him?

Yes, he was. Mr Wakefield was an enthusiastic scoutmaster, very keen on the outdoors, and he had a wide concept of what constituted education. For him, it meant equipping students for life and not simply acquiring paper qualifications. As well as the usual academic subjects, he encouraged hiking in the Peak District (under the pretext of map-reading), ballroom dancing (and etiquette), and creative activities like building a model town. He wouldn't be happy with today's educational practices and the modern obsession with examination passing, performance targets and the ticking of boxes.

Did any of the St Anselm's pupils ever come back to see you?

Yes, lots of them. Some of them even brought their children. There was an opportunity to meet them all in later years because ex-pupils formed an Old Pupils' Association which met regularly. The things they all seemed to remember best were the hikes in the Peak District and the bicycle tours. I think these trips helped to give them a genuine love of the countryside. A pity that few schools do them today. As one headmaster recently remarked to me: 'Today, we don't have time for hikes in school time. If it's not in the National Curriculum, we don't do it.'

What books did you read around this time (1945–50)?

Set college texts in French and English kept us so busy that there was little time for private reading. After college I enjoyed the books of A. J. Cronin (*The Citadel* and *Hatter's Castle*), and two Manchester writers; Howard Spring (*Fame is the Spur* and *My Son, My Son!* and *Shabby Tiger* which we thought was very daring since it hinted at sexual love). Howard Spring had been an editor at the *Manchester Guardian* which made his work particularly appealing to me. The other writer was Louis Golding. I especially enjoyed *Magnolia Street*, set in the Hightown area of Manchester and featuring a street divided into Gentile and Jewish sides.

You dedicated High Hopes to your daughter, Catherine. I note that she is also a writer. Is that due to your influence?

Oddly enough, it was the other way round. She began writing long before me under the name Cathy Hopkins. She persuaded (pestered?) me to write after my retirement.

Apart from ballroom dancing, what did you do to keep fit during this period?

I cycled across Manchester (Crumpsall to Longsight and back) every day while teaching at St Anselm's – about ten miles. In addition, I refereed football and cricket (sometimes taking part with the boys!) and from 1949 onwards played centre forward for the Old Boys of my school every Saturday afternoon.

My one regret has always been that I never learned to swim properly, especially since all my brothers were strong swimmers. This omission was due to the fact that my school did all its swimming at the Manchester Victoria Baths after school. This would have meant getting home around 7 o'clock and, with piles of homework to do, it wasn't on. I should add that shining shoes was also on the agenda. There weren't enough hours in the day for all these activities.

Did you support a football team?

In the years immediately after college, along with the male members of my family (ladies were not encouraged to attend as football was felt to be a male preserve), I went to Maine Road football ground every Saturday. The two Manchester teams shared the ground on alternate Saturdays, United's stadium having been bombed during the war; it was 1949 before its own ground was ready.

On the afternoon of April 24th 1948, the streets of Manchester were deserted as practically every Mancunian was glued to a wireless set listening to Manchester United beating Blackpool 4–2 in the FA Cup. The United team comprised: Crompton, Carey, Aston, Anderson, Chilton, Cockburn, Delaney, Morris, Rowley, Pearson, Mitten.

The other Manchester team, Man City, may not have

been in the limelight in 1948 but its glory days were to come later. City won the Second Division championship in 1966, then the First Division title in 1968, FA Cup in 1969 and League Cup and European Cup Winners' Cup in 1970. Colin Bell, Mike Summerbee, Francis Lee and Mike Doyle were among the stars of this side.

What music did you enjoy at this time?

Apart from the Al Jolson songs which half the Marjon students seemed bent on singing in the bathrooms, favourite songs at college were about loneliness, homesickness, and missing girlfriends. Favourite singers were Bing Crosby (*You'll Never Know How Much I love You*); Frank Sinatra (*Saturday Night is the Loneliest Night of the Week*), Dick Haymes (*Love Letters*), Perry Como (*Temptation*), Denny Dennis (*Little on the Lonely Side Tonight*). Many of the songs were popularised on *Family Favourites* on Sunday mornings on the wireless hosted by *With-a-Song-in-Your-Heart* Jean Metcalf. Favourite songs repeated week in and week out were: The Mills Brothers (*Paper Doll; Put Another Chair at the Table*); Harry James (*Craziest Dream*).

When Laura and I began courting, we attended many concerts at the King's Hall, Belle Vue, and came to love much classical music.

What particular films do you remember from this period?

At college, Titch and I ducked out of lectures to go to the Odeon to see *Odd Man Out* starring James Mason. I felt (and still feel) it was a masterpiece.

And, when courting, how could I forget the first film I took Laura to see? It was at the Apollo on Ardwick Green and the film was *Adam's Rib* featuring Spencer Tracy and

Katherine Hepburn. We had to queue in the drizzle to get in but we sat in the best seats (the back row!) at the exorbitant price of 3s.6d each.

In the paperback edition, you talk about Nutty Nibbles baked by Mrs Mackenzie. Could we have the recipe? Or is it a family secret?

Not a secret recipe but I think it may be an old one. For those who want to try baking them, here it is. The grand-children love 'em and so do I!

Nutty Nibbles

An old recipe of the Mackenzie family.

Ingredients

3 cups good-quality oats	3 good tbsp Golden Syrup
1½ cups plain flour	1 tsp bicarbonate of soda
1 cup sugar	2 tbsp water
6oz margarine	

Method

1. Mix together oats, flour and sugar in bowl.
2. Melt margarine in pan with the Golden Syrup.
3. Pour melted margarine and syrup into oats mixture. Mix well.
4. Dissolve bicarbonate of soda in water
5. Add to mixture and mix well. It should be a fairly firm consistency, not runny.
6. Grease baking tray well. Roll mixture into balls and place on tray (well spaced).
7. Cook at 180°C or gas mark 4 until golden brown.
8. Leave on tray until they have become biscuit-hard. Or eat them when they're just out of the oven and soft and warm – that's when I like 'em best!